Possessed

SCOTT CHARLES HOWELL

DREAM MARK
PUBLISHING

DREAM MARK
PUBLISHING

Dream Mark Publishing
POSSESSED by Scott Charles Howell
Copyright © 2022 Scott Charles Howell
All rights reserved.
scottcharleshowell@gmail.com.

All Scripture quotations are taken from the King James Version of the Bible. Public Domain. (Note: Any text effects in Scripture quotations, such as italics or words in all caps, have been added for emphasis by the author.)

Catholic Rite of Exorcism. 1614 De Exorcizandis Obsessis A Daemonio in the Rituale Romanum. Public Domain. (Note: Any text effects in Scripture quotations, such as italics or words in all caps, have been added for emphasis by the author.)

Sid Roth and It's Supernatural used with permission.

2022 Dream Mark Publishing, LLC

ISBN: 979-8-9857604-0-8

DEDICATIONS

To those who dream dreams and overcome all in Christ Jesus.

—

To my wife, Jackie, and my son, Ethan, both
of whom encouraged and supported me
in my dream of becoming a writer.

ACKNOWLEDGEMENTS

A special thanks to J.D. Kudrick for
his excellent editorial work.

—

Cover Art and Formatting: Damonza.com

PART 1
POSSESSION

Be sober, be vigilant; because your adversary the devil, as a roaring lion, walketh about, seeking whom he may devour.

(1 PETER 5:8)

Chapter 1

Adam Matthew

THE LAST REMAINING rays of daylight illuminated the black, billowing clouds blowing in from the east. As the four of us rode our bikes down the concrete street, the tidy two- and three-bedroom ranch homes zipped past us. We made a right turn off Briarwood Avenue onto Oak View Street, and Mr. Redd's German shepherd startled us as it sprang out from behind a tree and started chasing us. We put on the speed to keep him from biting our heels, and soon the dog's barking faded into the background. I looked up and could see the rapidly incoming clouds overtake the royal-blue sky and consume it. Just as quickly, the wind went from nothing to a stiff breeze making it harder to pedal.

Along with the wind came the cold, and the temperature dropped twenty degrees in a matter of a minute. My windbreaker and thin T-shirt offered little protection, and with the breeze blowing through the holes in my faded blue jeans, I was miserable… but there wasn't anything I could do about it. When we reached the edge of the thick copse of pine trees, we ditched our bikes and entered into its inky blackness, with Danny leading the way. He carried our only flashlight, and as he moved it around, long shadows danced off the trees. The pines helped insulate us from the wind, but now that I was no longer pedaling, I grew even colder and started shivering. I zipped my jacket up to my neck and wrapped my arms around me to preserve body heat.

"Hey, D-Danny," I said through chattering teeth. "It's f-freezing out here. Don't you think maybe we should go b-back?"

Danny Pechman, the leader of our group and wearing warmer clothing, turned his head back around and looked at me with mild scorn. "Matthew, don't be such a wuss. Man up and grow a pair."

Rick Kennedy and Hunter Campbell snickered at that and simultaneously mocked me: "Dude, grow a pair already!" Looking at each other in amusement, they said, "Jinx," then bent forward as they grabbed their stomachs, laughing.

Jerks! I groaned inwardly, but I didn't respond to any of them. Instead, I hunched my shoulders forward and lowered my head so that I could keep an eye on the path. We continued walking through the forest on a floor of pine needles that had been accumulating since the trees were saplings. The needles crunched underfoot along with the occasional pine cone. After a hike of several minutes, we cleared the forest and stood on the edge of a haunted place. A dangerous place. At least according to the older kids in the neighborhood. Ted Stone, the preacher's son—already in the ninth grade and knowledgeable about such things—said that if you were stupid enough to come here on Halloween, ghosts would rise up out of their graves and drag you to Hell. A pimply guy named Lenny Bean from the eleventh grade told us another story. He said to stay away from this place because crazy people stole kids right out from under their family's noses. Kids that were never seen again. And that's why no one comes here anymore.

Of course, I'd heard dozens of such stories all my life about this place... the Deadlands... aka Abbott Cemetery. The "Deadlands" is the local name for this place because everything here is, well... dead. While a thriving forest surrounds it, everything contained within this dilapidated graveyard seems to resist life. Bare-thread grasses and barren, skeletal trees and bushes are the only living, or maybe dead, things here, along with its buried residents. No one cares for the graves, and no loved ones ever leave flowers on the headstones. Everyone here was forgotten long ago.

As I stood in the cold and mused about my surroundings, Danny grew more excited by the second to the point of giddiness. My growing trepidation drowned out his enthusiasm, though I kept it to myself. I felt stupid for coming here, but now that I had committed myself to doing so, I wasn't willing to lose face by backing out now. Danny continued walking with purpose, and I realized he was leading us to a large crypt that looked like it had been carved out of a solid block of gray stone. The only feature present on the stone monolith was a massive wooden door with a naked babe and fruit carved into it. As we drew closer, I could see a cool-looking doorknob in the shape of a lion's head. Danny walked up to the door and pushed hard.

As the door silently swung open, with a flourish of his hands, Danny said, "Ta-da!" carrying on as if he were a stage magician. He looked back at us with admiration. "Wait till you guys get a load of this place," he said with an eager tone. "I found the door open earlier today."

We followed him into the silent stone monster and found

the place lit by four black candles, one for each wall. I craned my neck back and forth as my mouth dropped open in awe. I had never seen such a cool-looking place and couldn't believe something like this existed around here. Statues, gems, and paintings were everywhere. Hunter tried to pick up a few things, but nothing budged.

"Hang it up, Campbell," Danny said, while his face took on a glum expression. "I already tried. None of it's going anywhere."

"Bummer," Hunter replied. "This stuff has to be worth a fortune. But if I came back with a crowbar, I bet I could get a new PlayStation."

As Hunter dreamed of illicit gains, I walked over to a black-marble wall with gold lettering all over it. The wall listed names and their associated birth and death dates. Most had the last name *Bianchini* in them.

As I reached out and ran my fingertips over its icy cold surface, a short blue electric arc zapped out of the edifice and burned my hand, and for a single moment, I could see behind the wall—a wall hiding rotting, moldering lumps of flesh and bone. I snatched my throbbing hand back to myself and cradled it with the other.

"Danny," I said uneasily. "This place is full of dead people."

His face twisted into a smirk. "You figured that all out on your own just now, Einstein? The graveyard and crypt weren't clue enough for you?"

I could feel my face turning bright red. "Yeah, um, I guess. Are you ready to leave now?"

"Leave, Matthew? The party hasn't even started." Danny pulled off his pack and removed four beers, a cigar, and an Ouija board. "I snagged these from my old man after he passed out." Smiling with pride, he said, "He was so drunk he'll think he drank them himself. I just committed the perfect crime, so drink up, boys." As we gagged on beer that our thirteen-year-old taste buds were not accustomed to, we sat around the Ouija board, smoking and choking, while prying into the unknown.

After asking the board several questions, Danny grinned and said, "I have a good one." His voice took on a spooky vibe as he whispered, "Spirits from beyond, did Matthew's dad die from cancer, or did he commit suicide to get away from his retard son?"

My mind snapped. I balled up my fist and smashed it into Danny's big mouth without giving it any thought. I split his lower lip, and blood started running down his chin. He wiped it off with his right hand and stared at it as if mesmerized by the sight. After looking at it for five seconds or so, he sprang into action and repaid me the favor. Hunter and Rick joined in, and thirty seconds later, I found myself lying on the floor, beaten up and bleeding. Danny pulled his foot back, readying himself to kick me in the head when all four candles went out.

Rick yelled, "Let's get out of here!"

All three stumbled out the door, the flashlight kicked on, and then its glow rapidly disappeared as they ran out of the graveyard.

That stinks... but what did I expect? Never should've come out here with 'em to begin with. Blood dripped into my mouth and down my chin, and I knew my face was a bloody mess. I reached up and touched my left eye. It was swollen shut. I squeezed my good eye closed too and shook my head as the realization hit me that I was truly screwed. Woods enveloped the Deadlands on all sides, and no roads led into or out of here. The surrounding darkness was so complete that my eyes started creating their own splotches of light, like lively flower blooms or miniature fireworks. I willed my sore body to move and then stumbled about until I found a wall. I sat down and pushed my back up against it.

After sitting there for five minutes, or an hour—I don't really know—an older male voice made me jump. "Boy, what are you doing here?" Whoever he was, his voice had a creepy, distant quality to it—like it was dispossessed of its owner.

My eyes searched the darkness but came up blank. Absolutely nothing could be seen. "I'm sorry, sir," I said in the voice's direction. "I came here with my friends, but they disappeared with the only light we had, so now I'm trapped here till morning."

"Leave now," the voice whispered. "You cannot stay here."

I could feel my face scrunch up in disbelief and my stomach scrunch up in alarm. With more bravado than I felt, I said, "Didn't you just hear me? I said I can't leave because I can't see anything, so I'm not going anywhere unless you have a flashlight for me."

"Get out," the voice said, ethereal and deep. "Grab on to me; follow me."

Do what? If anything, his voice was giving me goosebumps on my goosebumps. Under normal circumstances, I'd never go with a stranger. And Mom would kill me if she ever found out. But this wasn't a normal situation, and I was desperate. The thought of spending the night half frozen with a bunch of corpses got the better of me. I stood and went toward the voice and felt my way around until I'd grabbed on to him. His trench coat felt ice-cold and wet. He started walking, and I followed. Soon, I found myself being pelted by a freezing rain… half-liquid, half-ice. A picture flashed through my mind of strong fingers wrapping themselves around my throat and squeezing. My heart rate went from zero to sixty in, well, a heartbeat. But as we continued on, nothing happened and I could feel the horrible tension loosen its grip on my innards.

"So, do you live around here?" I asked.

I waited, but he didn't answer, and I wasn't sure which was

worse: the creepy voice or the creepy silence. *No, wait… definitely the silence.* So, just to hear the sound of my voice, I asked him how he had found me with no light, but he didn't answer that question either. His refusal to speak to me freaked me out, and I started feeling nauseated… like I might vomit. I would have run away from him as fast as my legs could carry me if I didn't need him so badly. I silently prayed that he wasn't one of those crazy guys Lenny had told us about.

I knew the instant we were off the cemetery grounds because I could feel and hear the pine needles and cones crunching underneath my feet.

As we walked, the continued silence unnerved me, so I broke it again with my own voice. "Thanks for helping me, mister. I know you didn't have to, and I just wanted to let you know I appreciate it."

I had been so sure he'd answer me, but he remained silent. He was so quiet I'd have thought he'd left me if not for the feel of his coat in my hand. The icy rain ended as we continued on, and the moon peeked out from behind the clouds. Now that I'd found my vision restored, my blood froze in my veins, and my breath caught in my throat. As I forced myself to inhale, I looked around me with frantic eyes, and then I ran for all I was worth. As I sprinted hard to my bike, I kept thinking that I was going crazy. I had to be—because I realized I was by myself when the moon came out. There was no one else within miles of me.

CHAPTER 2

ADAM MATTHEW

As I MADE my way home, the moon slipped away again into nothingness, and the ice storm returned with a vengeance. It sheeted the streets in ice, making it too treacherous for my bike. I ended up stashing it between Farmer Blake's rusted tractor—which looked like it belonged in the 1950s—and his brand-new red barn. He was an intense fellow prone to handing out tongue-lashings, and I knew I'd be on the receiving end of his mouth if he found my bike before I returned to claim it... but at least he wouldn't try to steal it from me like others I knew.

Now that I was getting back into civilization, my progress became somewhat faster since I didn't need to wait for the moon's light to see. Still, my progress was slower than it might have been because of the ever-thickening ice. I tried to be careful, but that was offset by the fact that I was wet and freezing to death. I'd already slipped several times on the slick concrete road, so now I had bloody hands and knees to go along with my bloody face.

I finally made it back to the subdivision of homes we'd passed on the way out, and that would have been my journey's end if my father had still been alive. My mom, dad, and I lived here in the Brook Spring subdivision back when we were one big happy family—until May 17, 1996… a day that meant nothing to me for most of my life, but now it was branded forever into my soul.

I pushed the unhappy thoughts of my dad out of my mind and continued on. Me and my mom lived a couple of miles farther up the road in a big, old, spooky mansion with Old Man Crab—as perfect a name as had ever been given to some-body. Like the universe knew what he'd become and named him appropriately.

His wife had died fifteen years earlier, and he never remarried. Instead, he took on a live-in maid named Millie, and she took care of him until she died. Millie and my father passed away at roughly the same time, and my mom had stepped into the vacated role created by Millie's death. She said it was like being married, but without the fun parts. She and I were taken care of in a fashion, but there were no family vacations, no romantic weekends for mom, and no father figure for me. We just sort of existed in a life without spice. Well, except for tonight. There'd be plenty of spice if mom discovered I'd stayed out this late.

I finally made it past the friendly-looking neighborhood with all the lights and was back to darker paths. Here, the homes got a lot larger, and the lighting scarcer. The mansions looked spectacular during the daytime, but haunted at night.

I involuntarily stared at Dr. Samuel Polonsky's house as I approached it. He'd been the only doctor in our township for the longest time. When I was young and stupid, the older kids told us that the good doctor would mark you for death with a lollipop. After examining you, if he took a liking to you, he'd give you a lollipop—and watch out. He'd find you in your bed, drag you back to his house, and chop you up. They said he'd buried hundreds of kids within those walls. I should've asked them how they'd survived Dr. Polonsky to tell the story, but what can I say?… Young and stupid. Even so, childhood fears die hard, and I was happier when his place was no longer in sight.

I passed several more homes and finally came to the largest of them all. It sat like a king atop a large hill—the only hill in the entire neighborhood. The building's round turrets, dark stone and redbrick, tall, narrow windows, black-slate roof, and stone gargoyles gave it a ghoulish appearance. Approaching it was almost always the worst part of my day, as it looked like a hulking predator waiting to devour me.

When I reached the front door, I made the sign of the cross and asked God's angels to watch over me—it was the closest thing I had to any kind of ritual. Though tonight, I added to it. Before stepping into the house, I peeked through several side windows. I spotted my mom's thin frame as she slept on the oversized living room couch. She'd probably fallen asleep waiting for me to come home. If I could sneak past her, I could tell her tomorrow morning that I'd returned much earlier and she'd missed me. I unlocked the door with great care and gently pulled the door outward. I waited and heard nothing. Emboldened to continue, I quietly placed my foot on the brownstone tile of the entryway, and the house's built-in intercom system kicked on… at full volume. Every room in the mansion was treated to "Highway to Hell" by AC/DC. Mom jumped off the massive leather couch like she was being electrocuted, and then she looked around in a confused manner until her gaze locked on to mine. Even from where I stood, I could see the relief in her eyes, and then I watched as they darkened with rage. She rushed to the main control panel on the back wall and shut down the music being piped into the house. She opened her mouth to speak but got cut off by a stream of profanity that issued from the intercom system. Mr. Crab sounded like he was in a mood.

Mom looked at me with laser beam eyes and said, "Don't you go anywhere, mister. After I get him calmed down, you and I are going to have a long talk.

Jeez, and just when I thought the night couldn't get any worse. Will the house explode next for an encore? Feeling dejected, I dragged my tired and cold body to the bathroom and undressed. I had skinned myself up pretty badly. Standing under a heat light to thaw my frozen body, I picked tiny bits of gravel out of my hands and knees. When I finished, I took a super-hot shower, and afterward, I sprayed my wounds with Bactine. Mom said the more it stung, the better it was working. *If that's the case, this stuff better be performing miracles on me right now.* Feeling somewhat better… certainly warmer… I looked at my clear, pale skin covered in purple welts in the mirror and winced at the beating my face had taken. Once mom saw me, she would be even more upset. *Well, nothing I can do about it now.* It was late, so I figured I might as well finish up my nightly routine. Plus, if I didn't, I'd give Mom one more thing to yell about.

I brushed my teeth and then examined them to make sure I had missed nothing. Everyone always told me I was lucky to have such nice, white, straight teeth to go with my pleasant smile. Sometimes, old people would tell me about their friends who had tooth problems. Then they'd lecture me to brush. They'd say that I'd have to brush my teeth every day to keep them nice. That if I missed a day, my teeth would start falling out. Last year, a dentist at our school told us to brush after every meal and floss. Unlike the old people I knew, who mostly had no teeth, it was his job, and he seemed to have all his, so I figured he knew what he was talking about. So I mostly did what he told us to do… mostly.

I finished up by combing my blondish-brown hair and putting on my favorite blue pajamas. Mom always liked them because she said they matched my eyes. Once dressed, my stomach started growling, and I realized I'd eaten nothing since morning. After finishing my nighttime routine, I headed into the dark hallway toward the creaky wooden back staircase originally built for the mansion's servants to use. The steps protested in loud groans as I walked down them, and I could feel a thin layer of cold air as it ran down the stairway like a river—and right over my feet. Normally, I wouldn't have given it a second thought, but I still felt cold tonight after my earlier adventure.

I hurried to the kitchen and approached the cast-iron, pot-bellied stove that sat near its center. The heat from it soaked into my skin, and it felt glorious. I turned in a slow circle so that my whole body could enjoy it.

Mom must have packed it full of wood for me. A covered pot sat on the stove, so I lifted the lid and took a peek. *Stuffed cabbage and rice… no thank you.* I headed to the food pantry that was bigger than the last house I'd lived in, and I looked around the humongous space. My hand touched one of the gray-slate shelves, and my on-again, off-again gift kicked in filling the pantry with a vision from its heyday: exotic foods stacked from floor to ceiling, huge wheels of cheese, tomatoes as big as softballs, and carcasses of boar and deer, along with giant containers full to overflowing with spices, sugar, and flour. The place bustled with kids, important-looking adults, and busy servants running about here and there. It was grand.

Then I blinked, and it all disappeared. Once again, I stood alone among the empty bins, bare meat hooks, and dusty shelves. I closed my eyes and concentrated as I ran my fingertips over a tiled wall. The echoes of my vision remained, so I felt sure that what I had seen was more than just an overactive imagination; I had seen into the past… probably. *Well, whether or not it was real, it was gone now.* That was a certainty as I glanced over at our meager food supply that sat in one small corner. I sighed as I walked over to it. As I searched through our stash, I found one last can of Chef Boyardee spaghetti and meatballs. *Ah, my favorite!* I popped the container top, went back to the kitchen, and placed it in the microwave. My mouth was very happy just a few minutes later! Mom entered as I was finishing up the last few bites. When she saw my swollen face, her look of anger subsided, and worry quickly replaced it.

"Adam, honey," she said as she brushed my face with her fingertips. "I was worried sick about you. What happened to you tonight?"

"Mom… Mom," I sputtered, "I'm sorry if I worried you, but it's not what you think. I wasn't trying to be bad. I promise."

She shook her head and sighed. "So what happened, Adam? Why did you come home so late and looking like a ragamuffin? You know it's after midnight, right?"

I shrugged. "Yeah. I mean, I didn't know before, but then I saw the clock when I came home. So I know now."

"Well?" she said as she crossed her arms over her chest.

"Um, it's kind of embarrassing." I looked down at my feet to avoid Mom's gaze. With eyes still downcast, I said, "I'd rather not talk about it… okay?"

"No, it's not okay," she snapped. "I lost your father, and I thought I lost you tonight. I don't know what I'd do if that ever happened. If you don't talk to me, I can't protect you, so spit it out, mister… now."

I had to admit that she was a master at laying on the guilt—though I suppose I owed her that one. Even if it had been unintentional, it was still pretty crummy of me to come home so late. I spilled my guts about everything, minus the part about the stranger walking me out of the cemetery, and then I sat and watched mom think.

"Honey, you realize Danny Pechman is bad news, right? Why would you risk it?"

I shrugged. "I don't know. I guess I wanted things to be the way they were before Dad died. Danny said he wanted to hang out with me again, and I wanted to believe him. I guess I'm stupid."

Mom's eyes narrowed, and she shook her head. "Don't talk like that. You're not dumb. You just have a good heart and want to see the best in everyone. But you've got to understand, some people aren't good. Some people like hurting others, and Danny is one of them. But you don't have to make it easy for him. You need to be less trusting. You need to toughen up."

Talking to her made my head hurt. I didn't think Danny was bad exactly, but it probably wasn't the time to say that. I wasn't sure how I felt about everything, but I knew I was tired and wanted to go to bed. If I argued with her, that would never happen—at least for quite a while.

So, instead, I threw my arms around her and said, "Thanks for the talk, Mom. I'll try to be smarter next time."

A few hours later, I awoke to scratching sounds. As I listened, I realized the noise came from above my bed—above the ceiling, actually. It sounded like something wanted to claw its way right into my bedroom. I started imagining that one of those corpses from the Deadlands had followed me back home. A clear picture flashed in my head of a big, bloated Bianchini corpse, rotted from head to toe and emaciated. I could see it lying facedown on the attic floor right above my bed, staring at me as if it had X-ray vision. It licked its chops with a sticky pink tongue that looked like a snake, and in anticipation, it clawed at the attic floor with long, chipped fingernails.

A scream burst from my chest as I jumped from my bed and hurried down the hallway to mom's room. I flew through her door and ran to her. The small light on her nightstand was still on, so I could see she'd fallen asleep while sitting up in bed. I jumped on top of her, and her body slid sideways off the head-board and landed on the mattress. As she landed on one arm, the other flopped in the opposite direction, and I heard glass clatter against the wooden floor. Peeking over the edge of the mattress, I saw an empty fifth of Wild Turkey lying there. Feeling scared, I shook my mom to wake her, but she just snorted and continued sleeping. I pushed my body into hers and curled up into a tight ball, lying there and shaking all the while.

Then I lay there praying she'd wake up, but I knew she wouldn't. She'd be out for several hours with all that alcohol in her. I didn't recall ever seeing her drink before Dad passed away, but it had become a common occurrence. I looked up at her pretty face and her blackish hair. She looked like a sad porcelain doll. Even though I knew it was futile, I prayed Dad would return and make her happy again. Then it would be like old times, and everything would be good once more. After a while, I relaxed enough to get up and grab the down blanket that lay folded at the foot of the king-sized bed. I covered her with it and climbed underneath it with her. With the comforting presence of both the blanket and my mom, I slowly drifted off into an uneasy sleep.

CHAPTER 3

ADAM MATTHEW

MY DREAD VANISHED with the light of day, and the sun's golden rays made the previous day's events seem far away. It was Sunday, so at 8:50 a.m. sharp, I found myself walking through the arched doors of Saint Mary's Church, dressed in my Sunday's finest: black slacks, a starched white shirt, and a black clip-on tie. Mom still considered herself in mourning, so she wore a stylish black dress along with all black accessories. Her dress—along with her pulled-back, straight black-brown hair; pale white skin; somber look; and the fact that she hadn't smiled once since my dad's passing—made her look a lot like Wednesday from *The Addams Family* movie. Mom could easily have passed for Wednesday's older, better-looking sister—and not much older either. Even though Mom was really, really old—already in her thirties… people who didn't know her thought she was still in high school. And the people who knew her called her *"lucky."* I think Mom would disagree with them.

As we picked our way through the crowd in the church

entryway, Mom murmured vague pleasantries to the parishioners as we passed them by. Once we made it to our favorite pew, I genuflected and made the sign of the cross just like I'd been taught. Then I took a seat. The church was okay, but I'd have liked it better if they did Mass in English. Once, when Father Ray visited our home, I asked him why he didn't speak like a normal person during service. The Father laughed and said Latin was God's language, and if it was good enough for God, then it was good enough for us. That surprised me because I thought all languages belonged to God. But what did I know?... I was just a kid. Still, I wished I could've understood what he was saying. Going to church would have been more helpful that way. But otherwise, the place was pleasant enough. We had tons of saints watching over us here—or at least their beautiful white-marble statues. Then there was the choir and the humongous pipe organ. I always liked the music in this church and couldn't imagine that the singing in Heaven was any better.

When the priest and his entourage arrived at the back of the church, we all stood as they walked to the front. It took them a while to get to the altar because they were old, like Mom. When the priest finally took the podium, we sat, and then he started speaking. My belly started rumbling, and then I got sicker and sicker as the service went on.

"Mom," I whispered as I grabbed at my stomach, "I think I'm going to throw up." She shushed me and told me to go. Exiting the nave through the main entryway with as much dignity as a sick thirteen-year-old could muster, I rushed toward the bathroom. Surprisingly, I felt better once I got to the lobby, so I turned to go back to the service when I saw a flash of black off to my left. It piqued my curiosity, so I walked to the far side of the lobby and peered down the hallway that led to the classrooms. I saw a black mist stepping into a room. Though I wasn't sure, it looked like a girl to me. My curiosity got the best of me, so I walked down the long hall and peeked into the dark space. Reaching out, I flipped the light switch on, but I didn't see a girl or anybody else. I didn't think I'd imagined it, but it was hard to say with me as I had a tendency to see things other people didn't, so who could know for sure? I certainly didn't. If it had been a girl, she was gone now, so I figured I better get back to Mass before Mom came looking for me.

CHAPTER 4

ADAM MATTHEW

THE FOLLOWING MORNING found me back at school and as I walked toward class, I heard someone behind me say, "Hey, Adam, wait up."

I turned and saw a blond head hurrying toward me through the crowd. As he drew near, I could see his lanky body and boat-sized shoes. John Tillis had two older brothers who were at least ten years older than him, and both stood around six-five. It was a good bet that the rest of John would grow nicely into those feet.

"Adam..." John trailed off. He leaned in and looked closer at my face. "Whoa, dude, were you always this ugly?"

My spine stiffened at his words. "Yeah," I said. "What's it to you four eyes? And what do you want, anyway?"

John used his middle finger to push his wire-rimmed glasses higher onto his nose. "Just wondering if you did anything fun this weekend?"

I shook my head in disbelief. "Does it look like I had a fun weekend?"

"Well… sure." He grinned. "If you're into that sort of thing."

"I'm glad to hear that. Let's try out the look on your face." I balled up my fist and waved it in front of his mug.

"Naw." He laughed. "I wouldn't want to steal your thunder. So dude, did you do anything else this weekend?"

I shrugged. "Not really. How about you?"

"You didn't?" he said with a snicker. "Well, that's not what I heard."

A sick feeling crept over me as the realization hit me. "What did you hear?" I asked with a sense of trepidation.

"I heard you went to the cemetery with Danny, Hunter, and Rick… and you totally chickened out. They said you freaked out about dead people and ran off crying like a little baby. They said they'd never seen anybody run so fast."

"Pfft, that's a total lie!" I said as my pulse quickened. "They're the ones who ran off and left me stranded there without a flashlight."

"Dude, I don't know.… They sounded pretty convincing."

"Really? So you think the three of them kicked the living snot out of me, then let me waltz off with the only flashlight? Give me a break!"

John waved his hands in the air. "Okay, okay, you're right, but nobody else will believe you."

"Well, they're all stupid then!" I said sullenly.

"Hmm, with a personality like yours, I'm surprised they didn't redecorate your face sooner."

"Shut up," I snapped as we walked into class.

Everyone there turned around and looked right at me. *Great.… It seems Danny's been busy this morning.* I didn't want anybody to see my face, so I gazed at my feet as I made my way to the only remaining chair in the classroom: directly in front of Danny and Rick. As I took a seat, Mr. Madigan made his way to the front of the class and preened himself. He was such an unusual little man: about five-three and bald. At least on top.... His haircut would have made Bozo the clown proud. To complete his bizarre appearance, he wore round spectacles and talked in a nasal voice.

As he got ready to teach, I bowed my head just a little and said a silent prayer asking God to make people believe me instead of Danny. Mr. Madigan surprised me when he looked straight at me and said, "Good morning, Adam. Am I interrupting your little conversation with your imaginary friend in the sky?"

"What… what?" I stuttered.

"You know, God almighty, the panacea of the masses," he said and snickered.

I shrugged. "I guess."

"You guess?" he said in a mocking tone. "Well, don't! Not in my class. I reserve this class for logic and reason. If I catch you doing it again, I'll kick you out of here."

I was in no mood for him this morning. A foul blackness swept through me, and I almost told him what I thought of him and his class. Instead, I opened my mouth and said, "Okay, fine, are we done now?"

A sinister clown smile pressed itself upon his pasty face. "Not by any means. I heard through the grapevine that you had a little incident this weekend. Do you want to talk about it and set us straight?"

I heard Danny and Rick snicker behind me, and I couldn't believe this was actually happening to me. I wouldn't have even wanted to discuss it with Mr. Madigan in private. What made him think I'd want to do so in front of the entire class? I felt my cheeks turn red as I shook my head.

"Well, I should think not. Not after the story I heard. But if you'd just pull your head out of your backside and listen to me instead of your imaginary God, life would be much better for you."

What's his problem? And what's he going on about, anyway? These thoughts flashed through my mind, but I said, "Listen to what exactly?" as I slumped a little lower in my chair.

"If you had listened to me and taken up karate, of course. If you had, it would have toughened you up, and you could have stood there like a man." As if to make a point, he karate-chopped his desk. Then he threw his hands up and said, "But no. No one ever listens to me. You all think Mr. Madigan doesn't know what he's talking about." He walked toward my desk and then made a fake lunge at me. He laughed as if he'd done something funny and said, "My body is a honed, lethal weapon. Follow my example, Adam, and you'll never need run again."

The entire class burst out laughing.

I couldn't believe this jerk had just set me up in front of everybody. Instead of saying anything, I crossed my arms over my chest and sat there fuming.

"Don't get mad at me, son. I'm just the messenger. It's a cruel world out there, and without a father to guide you—"

What a creep! I covered my ears and yelled, "Shut up!"

The entire class looked stunned, but I didn't care. I couldn't take it anymore.

"Alright, I can see you're getting all emotional on me. We can continue this discussion after class." He turned his back to me, walked to the board, and started writing. "Today, we will discuss genetics. If you'll turn to the section on DNA…"

After finishing his first instructions to us, the teacher

turned to his desk and sat. He looked around the class and said, "Read." Then he pulled a newspaper out and started thumbing through it.

With the teacher preoccupied, Danny flicked my ear hard with his finger and whispered, "Wuss."

As I turned toward him, Rick reached over, flicked my other ear, then whispered, "Chicken boy."

"Stop it!" I hissed.

The teacher turned up from his paper and narrowed his eyes at me. "Mr. Matthew, is there a problem?"

"Yeah. Danny and Rick won't leave me alone."

"Oh, are the *mean* boys bothering you?" he said, his face smug. "If you'd spend more time in the real world than with your make-believe friend, you'd learn how to treat others. Maybe next time, you'll think twice before you chicken out and run out on your buddies. Taking the only flashlight was cold, son. Real cold."

Unbelievable! Just looking at my busted-up face should've tipped him off that I'm the actual victim here.

He turned back to the board, and Danny snapped my ear with a rubber band. I reached up, and my ear felt wet. When I pulled my hand back, my fingertips were bloody. I grabbed my science book, turned around, and slammed it into Danny's head. The corner of the hardcover book caught the center of his forehead, and it left a red spot that would surely turn into a satisfying lump—satisfying to me, at least.

As I stuck out my tongue at the jerk, a hand wrapped itself around my arm and yanked hard.

My eyes snapped to my teacher's face and were greeted by his flaring nostrils and lips that set themselves in a grim, straight line. He pulled my face to within inches of his own and, with spit flying, said, "Get your butt to the principal's office now!"

After sitting in the waiting area outside Davis's office for a half-hour or so, he finally returned and stormed into his office. The man was of medium height, lean build, and seemed to have an excess of nervous energy. He motioned to me with his hand, so I followed him in. The room itself was plain, but the walls were adorned with pictures of various celebrities. He was an amateur photographer and a part-time paparazzi who went to great lengths and took road trips to snap photos of anyone with a bit of fame. He even had a large framed photo of himself and President Bill Clinton shaking hands at some special fundraiser. It was his pride and joy. I tore my eyes away from the walls and noticed a bunch of books sitting on a shelf off to the side of his desk. The largest was the Holy Bible.

Davis told me to sit, and I sat. He propped his elbows upon his wood desk and rested his chin atop his clasped hands.

He stared at me with intense light brown eyes and sighed. "Okay, let's get this over with. Tell me your side of the story."

When I finished, Davis sat there thinking while he pushed his fingers through his wavy brown hair. "So let me see if I have this right: Danny and friends made up a story… wait… changed the story to make you the villain. Then your science teacher, believing Danny, took it upon himself to chastise you in front of the entire class—unfairly, of course. Does that sum it up for you?"

I shrugged. "I guess so. But it's nobody's business what happened in Abbott Cemetery. I don't even know why we're talking about it."

"Well, Mr. Matthew, you made it my business when you attacked Danny. That's why you're here, and that's why your little escapade over the weekend is my concern now."

Davis hadn't even listened to what I'd said! Clearly, he'd picked sides before he even got here. That didn't stop me, though: "Look, Danny left me behind, and he attacked me first today. You had to have noticed my face. It didn't beat itself up. I—"

He waved a hand to cut me off. "Mr. Matthew, it's obvious that you aren't listening to me. I feel like I'm talking to a wall. Maybe I should get your mother in here instead. Maybe she can talk some sense into you. Speaking of which, how is your mother holding up?"

"My mom?" I frowned. "Okay, I guess."

"Do you know if she's seeing anybody?"

I couldn't believe this pervert was asking about my mom. Dad hadn't even been dead for a year, and he was already sniffing around her. *What a jerk!* I'd shoot myself before letting this doofus become my stepdad. "Yeah, she's seeing this big guy. I think he's a pro wrestler or something."

"Oh… well, good," he said as his smile wavered. "You know I just wanted to make sure your mom is taken care of, right? By the way, let's just keep my concern for her between the two of us."

"Of course," I said as I rolled my eyes.

"Stop that, young man.… I imagine that your mother has enough going on without dealing with your shenanigans. So I'll let you off easy this time." Davis rose from his chair, opened his door, and said, "Now get out of here, and don't cause any more trouble."

I left his office wondering how everything had fallen apart so quickly. When school ended on Friday, everything was fine. Now it seemed everyone was mad at me. As I continued walking, I saw Danny up ahead. At first, I thought about turning around and going the other way, but I wanted answers and felt I didn't deserve any of this. Wanting to know what was going on, I came up behind him and reached out to grab his shoulder—and then I tripped. I fell forward and struck him squarely between the shoulder blades, and he flew forward. His mouth hit a white porcelain water fountain, and blood and teeth went everywhere. Danny started making an escalating high-pitched whining sound, and seconds later, teachers came pouring out of their classrooms. Once everything quieted down, the nurse called an ambulance for Danny, and I got dragged back to the principal's office.

CHAPTER 5

ADAM MATTHEW

THE FOLLOWING WEEK, I found myself suspended from school and grounded at home. The principal said I was lucky that he didn't ship me off to jail, and my mother told me she was seriously considering putting me up for adoption. Meanwhile, I heard Danny was going around school, telling anyone who would listen to him that I'd be getting mine soon. It seemed everybody hated me.

My dad would've known what to do, but he wasn't here for me anymore, and that just didn't seem fair. One afternoon during my confinement, something inside of me snapped. My stomach started roiling, and I ground my teeth together in anger. Then I balled up my fists and started punching the side of my dresser. After five minutes, I was sweating profusely and panting. I fell to the floor in a quivering heap and started yelling at the top of my lungs. The empty room couldn't have cared less. *If someone would just tell me what to do…* But I knew that was stupid thinking. I just hoped that somebody would believe that I hadn't purposefully pushed Danny. The one thing I knew for sure, he was at the center of all my problems, and I didn't know why. Maybe he was just *mean*, like Mom said.

After standing up, I looked at the old antique dresser, and it didn't look like I'd done it any harm, which was good because I'd probably get a whipping for hurting Mr. Crab's precious furniture. I stood there dumbfounded, because I didn't know what to do next. My grounding included no phone, television, or computer, so all of that was out. I thought about opening up my algebra book, but I had the entire week off, so I had plenty of time to get to that. I thought yet again how it was too bad I didn't have a brother or sister to hang out with. When I was younger, I'd asked Mom when she was going to have more kids so I could have a friend. She said something about it not taking, and then she started crying. I didn't know why that upset her so much, but I didn't ask her again after that. Hopefully, the next one would take, and then I'd have a playmate. But I realized it wouldn't help me today, even if it did take. Babies didn't come out that fast.

I tried to think of something else to do and remembered seeing a pillow fight on a television show. It had looked like a lot of fun—but probably more fun if you had somebody else to play with, but my imagination would have to do. I climbed up onto the massive four-post bed and started jumping up and down on the feather mattress while I swung my pillow at my imaginary sister. I pretended she hit me back, and I fell down on the bed, giggling.

Mom entered the room and glared at me with a stern look on her face. "What are you doing, mister?" she said as she brushed her blackish-brown hair out of her eyes.

She only used *mister* when mad at me, so I figured she still wanted to put me up for adoption. It didn't seem I could get a break anywhere, and I started feeling agitated.

"I'm not doing anything wrong," I protested. "I'm just playing pillow fight because I'm bored."

"Bored?" she said as she pushed her fingers through her hair. "Well, I'm thrilled you shared that with me because I could use help around here. Go down to the laundry room and bring the dried clothes up to the kitchen. You can use the laundry basket I left by the dryers."

I felt my scalp tighten and my hair stand up. I looked up at mom as the blood drained from my face. "But, Mom," I groaned, "I don't want to go down there by myself. Can't you come with me?"

She shook a finger at me. "Well, you should have thought of that before you attacked Danny. March, mister… now!"

A vague unease settled upon me as I made my way down to the kitchen. My hand was on the basement door when Crab cleared his throat behind me. I'd been so preoccupied about my current task that I hadn't even noticed he was there. I turned and saw him sitting on a stool at the gray-slate countertop, spooning a watery-looking soup out of a large stone bowl and into his mouth using his old, withered hand, which shook as he brought it up to his mouth. Mom said he was eighty-five, but with his grayish wrinkled skin, liver spots, and tufts of missing gray-white hair, he looked more like a hundred and fifty to me.

He stared straight at me with darkened, rheumy eyes and said in a papery voice, "Where you going, boy?"

Even though I thought Mr. Crab looked ancient and ready to croak, his mind was plenty sharp, so I'd have to answer him appropriately. "Mom said I have to get the laundry downstairs and bring it back up to the kitchen."

"She did?" he said with a look of exaggerated concern. "Oh, that's too bad. I guess she really does want to get rid of you. Well, nice knowing you, kid." With that, he went back to eating his soup.

My chest tightened at his words. "What do you mean *that's too bad*? What's down there?"

"Well, it's just that... wait... Actually, it's not fair to tell you before you go down. I'll tell you if you make it back."

I rushed over to the counter. "Tell me what? It's not going to do me any good if you tell me afterward."

He rubbed his chin as he seemed to think it over. "Alright," he muttered, then nodded. "I suppose you're right, kid. So here's the thing. My last maid had a boy that was... How old are you?"

"I'm thirteen now."

"What a coincidence. Millie's kid was thirteen, too. And just like you, he got himself into trouble, and his mom sent him downstairs to get the laundry. So down he goes like his mama told him, but he doesn't come back up. Nobody thought anything of it for a couple of hours, what with boys being boys, but then we started getting suspicious. We started thinking there's no way it takes two hours to get the laundry, so we go down there to check on him—together, because we know better than to go down there by ourselves. When we got to the laundry room, the only thing left of him was one of his shoes. We never saw the lad again. I reason that whatever snatched him up did it right there in the laundry room... swallowed him whole, me thinks. So, after that, I researched the house, and it turns out this place has a history of snatching up thirteen-year-old boys. There have been twelve disappearances in all. All thirteen years old, all boys. I reckon that if you go down there, you'll be the thirteenth kid snatched. The thirteenth boy of all the snatched thirteen-year-olds. I got to imagine it has something extra special planned for you when you go down there today."

I crossed my arms against my chest. *What an idiot.* "Mr. Crab, stop being stupid. I know you're lying to me."

"Have a care with your tongue, boy. I'm not some fifteen-year-old prankster. It'll cost you if you ignore me."

"If you're telling the truth, why would my mom send me down there? She said she loves me."

Crab wagged a finger at me. "*Why* indeed, boy? She knows the tales. I can only assume she means you harm. She said she wanted to put you up for adoption, but I figure this way is cleaner and cheaper for her. If she gets rid of you legally, there'd be a ton of paperwork to fill out, and she'd have to pay out a lot of money to get somebody to take you off her hands. If the house takes you, there's no paperwork, and she saves a ton of cash."

I'd heard enough from him, and I wasn't going to put up with it anymore. I didn't even care that he was my elder. My mouth opened, and the words poured out. "Mr. Crab, you're just a mean old man, and I'm not going to listen to you anymore. Just eat your stupid soup and leave me alone. I'll tell Mom if you don't."

Old Man Crab started to say something, but I covered my ears tight and hummed loudly while kicking open the basement door with my left foot. I walked down the old wooden-plank stairs, and when I reached the bottom, I pulled on the string dangling in front of me. A weak, anemic looking light illuminated the immediate area.

The enormous laundry room had a damp, stinky smell, and spiderwebs hung everywhere. The occasional thick root from the trees outside had worked their way in here and there in the basement wall and crawled along it in a vein-like fashion, looking for sustenance. If the walls had ever been painted, I figured it must've peeled off fifty years ago. The room would have felt like a tomb were it not for all the junk down here. One side of the room harbored high stacks of paint cans, empty pop bottles, newspapers, old dishes, moldy books, and many other worthless items. The other side of the room contained a series of washers and dryers. The remaining side wasn't a side at all but a large bricked archway that led to the rest of the vast basement underneath the house. It yawned open like an enormous mouth, and it looked like it wanted to swallow me whole.

When I'd been upstairs, I felt sure that Old Man Crab was lying to me. Standing alone in the basement, though, doubts crept into my head: *Would an old man lie about such things to a kid? What if he was telling the truth?* I decided I didn't want to wait around to find out, so I flung open all the dryer doors and started grabbing any clothes I found and throwing them into the laundry basket. It didn't matter if they felt damp or dry; they all got thrown in together. When I'd finished, the basket was full to overflowing, so I grabbed it and staggered to the stairs with it.

When I placed my foot on the bottom step, the door above me slammed shut. It unnerved me so much that I almost dropped the basket. I was tempted to leave it behind and bolt up the stairs just to get out of here. Only the thought of having to come back down here later to get it kept me from doing so. Instead, I forced myself to take a deep breath, and I told myself that Crab had shut the door to scare me. I pictured him on the other side of the entrance having a good laugh about the whole thing while I stood here shaking. *Well, I'll show him.* I went up the stairs, placing the heavy basket on each step ahead of me to help support its weight. I counted the stairs as I went up to keep my mind occupied.

When I reached the thirteenth step, I had made it to the top and could go no farther. I didn't even want to think about what *thirteen stairs* meant. Bracing the laundry basket up against my left leg with a hand, I used my other to reach for the doorknob and turn it—but it didn't budge. It seemed to be locked, but I knew it didn't have one. I started banging on the heavy wooden door with one fist as I yelled, but no one answered back.

As I banged away, I heard a scratching noise… and it sounded like it came from within the door itself. I took a single step down and found myself at eye level with a one-inch knothole in the door. As I looked into it, my terror grew exponentially, and I could feel something warm running down my legs. A baleful yellow eye glared back at me from the knothole, and I had its complete and undivided attention. I retreated two more steps back toward the basement, and the laundry basket I'd left behind tumbled downward and off the side of the stairs, hitting the floor ten feet down.

The basket's impact triggered a cacophony of scratching sounds from the door, and then a ghastly white finger with a long, chipped yellowish nail poked itself through the hole. It felt around the knothole as if discovering it for the first time. Then it inserted another finger into the opening, and the two fingers pulled in opposite directions. The small opening stretched as if malleable or elastic, and as I watched the hole expand, the thing managed to get both hands into it. Pulling the gap wider, the thing pushed its head out of the knothole and locked its eyes on mine. After wriggling violently, it now stuck out of the door from head to waist.

Apparently, my legs had kept themselves moving because I'd made it all the way back down the stairs by the time the thing cleared the knothole and fell onto the stairs with a wet plop. I stopped and watched with sick fascination as the thing stood up as far as it could in the tight space, its wicked eyes still upon me.

The thing was huge. Even though it was hunched over, I figured it stood at least seven or eight feet tall and its large body looked emaciated. Skeletal even. Its skin looked like the pale, whitish rotted flesh of a dead fish, and it looked hungry. I realized I'd seen this thing somewhere before. *Yes… in my head!* But now I stood face to face with the thing I'd been hearing in the attic above my bed… the thing that had been clawing at my bedroom ceiling. *I'm so dead!*

As if reading my mind, it smiled an impossibly huge smile full of shark-like razor-sharp teeth. A long pink tongue slithered out of its mouth and licked its lips in obvious anticipation of me.

My entire body froze in fear for precious seconds as I stared at the predator before me. But as it started down the stairs, I slapped myself mentally and forced myself to back up deeper into the cellar. Looking around my subterranean prison, my mind frantically spun, trying to figure a way out of this predicament. Then something unexpected happened. I heard my dad's voice in my head. Dad always said I had a good throwing arm for a kid, and out of the blue, my mind had hit replay on that one. I didn't know if it would work, but it was the only thing I had. When it reached the basement floor, I bent down and picked up a Coke bottle, then flung it at the thing. The bottle thunked as it hit it in the head, but it didn't seem to bother it in the least. Next, I threw a small chunk of concrete at it, but that worked no better. I saw a tool pouch lying off to my right and as it drew closer to me, I grabbed a hammer out of it and flung it hard.

The steel of the hammer sunk right into the thing's head, and a yellow ichor the same color as its eyes started flowing from the wound. As it raged with an intense howl almost beyond my ability to hear, it hit me that steel came from iron. *So… the old myths are true!* But the thought didn't comfort me because the look on its face became so hideous that, if possible, it made its previous expression seem almost pleasant. With outstretched hands, the thing flowed toward me faster than I would've imagined.

My mind latched onto the idea that if iron affected it, maybe salt would too. I dove to an open bag of rock salt kept for the icy sidewalks, and I grabbed two handfuls. When its yellowed talons were about three feet from me, I thrust my hands upward and released the salt I'd been holding. The salt peppered it all over, and everywhere it touched the thing, its flesh turned black and started smoking. The thing came to a sudden halt, screaming in a high, hideous wail. Banshee-like. Its fury and pain were obvious.

With it momentarily distracted, I fled through the arched dark maw that led into the sprawling basement. I had been down here in the past with Mom and the exterminators, and I remembered the old coal chute built into the western wall. I knew that if I could get there in time, I could climb up and out of it and get to the safety of daylight. Using my sometimes-fallible memory as my only guide, I groped along the walls in the pitch-black, even as I felt it drawing closer to me. But it had gone silent, and I found that more unnerving than its screaming. I could feel the predator's intense desire for me, but I heard and saw nothing. Deprived of my most useful senses, I kept feeling my way along the walls of my prison, sure that I'd never find the chute in such darkness.

An eternity later, but probably less than that, something

tickled my eyes. I wasn't sure at first, but then I knew I could see some light. I headed straight toward it, and when I drew close, I realized that some of the brick had pulled away from the coal chute, letting a bit of light leak into the subterranean room. Much less than a candle's flame, that light saved my life.

Within the dim illumination, a flash of white materialized in the corner of one of my eyes, and I realized the thing was nearly on top of me. There was no way I'd make it to the chute in time, but I spied the open door of the ancient cast iron boiler sitting close by, and I dove through its opening. I crawled deep into its belly and sat, trying to steady my breath. A deathly white face materialized in front of the boiler, hissing in frustration, and it watched me like cats watch mice. I felt around me and found crumbled bits of cast iron and flicked them at its face. It hissed in pain and disappeared. A few minutes later, it reappeared and started smashing the boiler housing with the hammer I'd thrown at its head. The metal rang as a crack appeared in the brittle cast iron of the furnace, and it might have gotten me if the hammer's head hadn't broken off the wooden handle. It watched me again for a short time, then it disappeared again.

I sat in the boiler for at least an hour, but the thing didn't reappear. My intuition was screaming at me to get out of the basement before the sun went down, so I cautiously stuck my head out of the opening and looked around. I didn't see or sense anything. *Here's my chance.* I quietly climbed out of the boiler and crept toward the coal chute. But when I looked into the far corner of the room, I saw the thing standing there, pressed into a depression in the wall as if it had been pressed into a coffin. It flashed its razor-sharp teeth and then flowed toward me. I ran to the chute, reached up, and pulled my body into it. I started climbing up and out when the foul thing wrapped its deathly cold hand around my ankle. Suppressing the fear that threatened to freeze me in place, I turned just enough to reach into my pocket and fling a handful of cast iron pieces into its face. The thing shrieked as it released me and I used those precious seconds to climb out of the basement. I pushed open the ancient chute door, crawled out, and lay on the brownish-green grass in the cold sunshine.

CHAPTER 6

DANNY PECHMAN'S DAD

"Hey, Danny, bring me another beer!" I hollered.

Thirty seconds later, the kid materialized, holding a full can of frosty goodness.

"What took you so long?" I asked. "You go on vacation first or something?"

"No, Pa," he said.

"No, Pa!" I mimicked as I screwed up my face to look like a retard.

Seeing Danny's stupid face with those stupid wires and braces was more than I could stand. I crushed my empty beer can and whipped it at him. It sailed across the room and hit him on that stupid raised purple welt on his forehead. *Bull's-eye! The old man still has it. Once a star, always a star.* As I watched him, his eyes started watering, and it really ticked me off.

"You better not cry, boy!" I bellowed. "If you don't hold it in, I'll use a full beer can next time."

Yeah, it would've been a waste of perfectly good beer, but my kid knew I meant it. He stood there and sucked it up.

There was a knock at the door, so I waved my hand at Danny. He walked over and answered it.

My friend Phil entered the room and sauntered over to his usual spot… the couch. "Hey Bud, what's wrong with your kid's face?"

I shook my head. "That's what happens when you let somebody sucker punch you. The stupid Matthew kid got the jump on him, and the fool didn't even see it coming. Sickens me that my kid is part of my gene pool… though now that I think about it, it probably comes from his mother's side of the family. It's too bad I didn't choose better before I knocked her up. I might've had a real son then."

Phil started laughing at me. "Don't get your brain all tied up in knots over his mama yet. The way I see it, he probably did get it from you. Wasn't it the Matthew kid's father that got the jump on you and got promoted to plant manager instead of you? And didn't he fire you after he got the promotion? Did you see any of that coming?"

I couldn't believe what I was hearing, and I saw red. *Friend or not, how dare he come into my home and disrespect me in front of my kid!*

I got right up in his face and said, "Phil, I swear I'll rip your arms off right now and beat you to death with them if you don't back off. There is nothing remotely similar—let me repeat—*nothing* remotely similar at all between what happened to my retard kid and what happened to me. Heck, even fate knows that. Why else would that idiot Matthew have gotten cancer and died? Kind of like life taking out the trash, if you ask me."

"Calm down, bro. I was just yanking yer chain. Just funning you was all."

I looked over at my kid to make sure he wasn't disrespecting me behind my back. If he had been, he hid it well... which was good for him because life would've gone to hell for him real quick if I'd caught him smirking at me.

I turned back to Phil. "The way I see it, the jerk got off easy when he croaked. If I'd gotten ahold of him first, I would have broken his arms and legs and left him in a ditch to die."

CHAPTER 7

ADAM MATTHEW

THE FOLLOWING SUNDAY morning, I found myself back at Saint Mary's Church. Mom tried talking to me on the way over, but I hadn't said a word to her since the basement incident. I was still mad at her, and I didn't trust her anymore. I hadn't believed Old Man Crab when he'd said she was trying to hurt me, but it was the only conclusion I could come to after what happened.

As we made our way to the pews, Gloria Young—one of my mom's friends, and the town gossip—came up to us and made a pouty face that she directed toward me. "What's wrong, handsome?" she said. "Why the sullen look today?"

I knew better than to talk to her unless I wanted the entire region to know my business, so I spoke up. "Mr. Crab warned me that my mom was trying to get rid of me. You'd look sullen too if your mom just tried killing you."

Mom gasped and followed it up with a small choking sound. She brought a hand to her throat and said, "Gloria, I have no idea what he's going on about. Nobody tried to kill him." Mom bent down low to me and said, "Honey, did some-body try to hurt you?"

I turned my head, looked around, and pretended I didn't hear a word she said.

Mom straightened back up, frowning, and said, "Gloria, I honestly don't know what he's talking about. All I know is I sent him to the basement the other day to get the laundry for me. He returned covered from head to toe in coal dust, and he hasn't said a single word to me since then. As a matter a fact, these are the first words he's uttered since that day."

Gloria licked her lips and smiled. With eager eyes, she said, "Can you tell me what happened?"

I decided I'd already told her enough. By the time Gloria finished gossiping, everyone in town would know that my mom had tried to kill me, making it a lot harder for her to try it again. If she wanted to get rid of me now, she'd have to do it the old-fashioned way, with tons of paperwork and paying people off. At least I'd live to see my fourteenth birthday. I stole a glance at mom, and she looked so distraught she could have won an Oscar for her performance. An unwanted image of the pasty-white thing flashed through my mind, making me shiver. *How could my mother or any mother send their child to something like that?* Disgust for her filled me, causing me to recoil internally. I turned my back to her and stormed off down the main aisle of the church.

My mind and heart burned with anger. So much so that I forgot to genuflect or make the sign of the cross before I sat down in a pew. *Oh, well.* Mom tried to sit by me, but I strate-gically picked a seat that wouldn't allow her to do so without making a big stink about it. I became so lost in my dark feelings that I didn't even notice when the service started. My growing sense of unease gave me the first clue that something was off.

But the anger that saturated me pushed it aside as I continued wallowing in hurtful thoughts. In the end, it was the building nausea in the pit of my stomach that won out and drew me back to reality. The faithful followers around me stared intently at Father Ray as if hanging on his every word, though I knew that wasn't possible because none of them spoke Latin either.

Like last time, I continued to get sicker as the service continued. It got so bad I had to run to the exit before I threw up all over everybody. In fact, I kept running until I made it out the front door and into the parking lot. I let loose, and when I was done, it looked like I had thrown up my last three meals. As I wiped off my mouth with a sleeve, I heard someone call my name. Turning around, I saw a black shadow standing in the shade just inside the church entryway, watching me. The shadow disappeared as I walked toward it, but I knew where to find it.

Soon, I stood in front of the classroom that it had disappeared into the week before. Not knowing what to expect, I gathered up my courage, pushed the door open, and walked in. *Brrr! It's cold in here.* Certainly a good ten or fifteen degrees cooler in here than in the hallway. Someone must've cranked up the air conditioner. *And what's that smell?* A pungent odor assaulted my nose that wasn't unpleasant exactly, but neither pleasant. I'd smelled something like it before but couldn't place it. I reached out and flipped the plastic light switch, but nothing happened. With no lights and the shades drawn, it was dark in the room but not pitch-black. Standing next to the chalkboard was a shadow. It wasn't solid black, though... more like a semi-translucent dark mist that moved around, much like smoke in an enclosed space. The enclosed shape appeared girl-like, and I could even see it was wearing a dress.

"Hello," I said to the mist. "My name's Adam Matthew. What's yours?"

"I'm Bela," the shadow said. "Will you play with me?"

"Sure. What do you want to play?"

The chalkboard eraser levitated in the air and then flew straight at me. It left a big chalk mark on my black pants when it hit me.

Bela giggled and said, "You're it!"

I picked up the eraser from the floor and threw it at Bela, but it passed right through her. Not that it mattered, she was *it* now. We kept at it and had a lot of fun playing the game. In fact, it turned out to be the most entertaining thing I'd done in months.

But after a while, I grew tired and stopped. Breathing heavily, I said, "So… Bela, who are you… and why are you here in the church?"

"Me? I'm your sister… the one that didn't take. Well, that's not true exactly. But that's Mom for you. I took, but I couldn't hold on. After I was born, I lived for ten minutes, and then I lost my grip. I've been stuck here in this church ever since then."

"If you're my sister, why don't you look like a person—like me? You look more like a dirty mist."

"That's just the veil between us that keeps me from coming into your world. Wait one second. Let me try something."

As I watched, the mist slowly transformed into a translucent young girl who looked just like Mom… except she had Dad's brown eyes. When Bela's look of intense concentration left her face, she snapped back to a dark mist.

"There," she said. "I pushed myself deep into the veil so you could see me better. Satisfied?"

I nodded a few times. She looked exactly like I thought my sister would.

I smiled and said, "Sure. So why did you wait so long to introduce yourself? Are you shy or something?"

She put her hands on her hips. "I could ask you the same question. I've been hollering at the top of my lungs for what seems like forever, but everybody ignores me. Till now, of course."

"I don't think people are ignoring you. You're a ghost, that's all. I can see you because I see things that other people don't. By the way, are you real or imaginary? Do you know?"

"Duh! Do you often have conversations with yourself?"

I shrugged. "No, but it's still best to ask. Well, it was nice meeting you, but I better get back now. Church is almost over, and I don't want to get stuck walking home. Do you want to hang out again next Sunday?"

"It's funny you should mention that. Can I go home with you instead? That way, we can still play together."

"How can you do that if you can't leave here?" I said, as I scratched my head.

"Well, I thought if you invited me inside of you, I could just ride you back to your house, and then we could play together all the time."

I pursed my lips as I thought about it. "I don't know. I'd have to ask Mom first, and I'm not talking to her right now."

"Come on… pleeeassse! She's my mom too," Bela said, her voice whiny. "Why would she want you, but not me?"

That kind of logic typically made sense—except I wasn't sure that my mom actually wanted me either. *Mom might really lose it if there were two of us.* I felt it best to proceed cautiously, so I told her no… for now.

CHAPTER 8

ADAM MATTHEW

ON THE RIDE home from church, Mom and I sat next to each other up front in the car, but we might as well have been a thousand miles apart, as neither one of us said a word. I stared out the window and saw the enormous gnarled oak tree standing on Mike Roland's property. I knew from past experience that it sat exactly one mile away from our house. Well, Old Man Crab's house.

As our car passed the road in front of the tree, my mom spoke up. "Adam, honey, why do you think I tried to hurt you?"

I said nothing, so she stole a quick glance at me before returning her eyes to the road. "You know, nothing could be further from the truth. I could never hurt you. And you know I don't lie to you, so you can trust me on this."

My mouth dropped open in surprise. *She lies to me all the time. She might think I'm a stupid kid, but I know when she's being dishonest with me.*

I probably shouldn't have done it, but I called her out on it. I put on my best smile and said, "Mom, I met Bela today."

"Bela who, honey?"

"My sister Bela. The one that didn't take."

Mom's head jerked toward me and her face grew pale. "Who… Who told you… your sister's name?" she stuttered.

"That would be Bela. And she told me she took. She said she lost her grip on life and died shortly after she was born."

What little color Mom had left on her face drained away completely, and she started hyperventilating. "Don't you dare pull this on me!" she yelled. "Tell me now how you found out about Bela!"

"What! I already told you," I said as I crossed my arms over my chest.

Her head swiveled toward me, then she reached out and slapped my face—hard.

I glared at her through slitted eyes, and I felt something toward her I had never felt before. "You bald-faced liar," I said through clenched teeth. "You lied to me about my sister, and you lied to me when you said you'd never hurt me."

She reached out again and hit me even harder and I could feel my left eye swelling shut. Any doubts I had concerning my mother were gone. She was a liar and had no problems hurting me regardless of what she'd said. My father was gone, and I realized I'd lost my mother too. As I sat there, I realized I'd never felt so alone.

Despite her continued questioning, I didn't say another word to her. After she pulled into the driveway, I opened the door and jumped out before she even came to a stop. When she came stomping into the house, she yelled for me to get my butt downstairs, but I didn't listen. She could scream the rest of the day for all I cared. The place was vast and full of hiding places. I could stay away from her all day long, and that's just what I planned on doing. She spent an hour trying to track me down before she gave up and locked herself in her room. Once she was out of commission, I headed down to the kitchen to get something to eat.

As I picked through the meager offerings in the refrigerator, I heard a smacking sound behind me. I turned my head and saw Old Man Crab sitting there, eating his soup again. *How'd he do that?* I thought. *He wasn't there when I walked in.*

"Nice shiner, kid," he said with a grin.

I ignored his jab and said, "You know, I never see you anywhere else in the house. Do you like live here in the kitchen or something?"

Mr. Crab lifted his head from the bowl. "I do. What's it to you?"

I thought about it, then said, "I don't know. It just seems weird is all. Kind of like that soup you eat. Do you ever eat anything else?"

"Nope," he said as he took another spoonful and slurped it loudly. He started cackling as he said, "By the way, kid, your mom wants you to get the laundry from the basement."

I could tell he thought he was funny, but he was just mean, and I wasn't going to put up with it. I stuck my finger in his wrinkly gray face and said, "If you want the laundry so badly, you go get it. There's something down there that's just dying to meet you. Say *hi* for me."

"Me?" Old Man Crab said, then shook his head. "No. I'm old and grisly. I will say, though, it's dying to get its hands on a young buck like you. That's all it dreams about and it shivers with delight when it thinks about devouring you."

"Oh, is that so, you mean old man?" I shook my finger in his face again. "You seem to know an awful lot about this thing.

You said mom sent me down to it but it sounds like you're the one who set me up."

Instead of answering me, Old Man Crab went into a protracted coughing fit and it hit me that he seemed even older and sicker than usual—if that were possible. Mom must have sensed it, too. She'd recently mentioned how she worried he might die.

When he finally finished coughing, he started slurping his soup again. Between bites, he said, "Don't be a fool, boy. She's the one that sent you down there. Though I must say, I'm often mistaken for a sexy young woman, so I can understand your confusion."

I crossed my arms over my chest as I glared at him. "Quit perving on my mom, you dirty old man. You're like a hundred years old. She'll never want you."

He wiped his mouth with a withered, blue-veined hand. "Well, boy, after she feeds you to her pet, she may feel differently about me. She'll probably get so sweet on me we'll have a kid together. I'd say we'd name it after you, but I can assure you that we're both eager to forget all about you."

Mom came flying into the room with fire in her eyes. "What kind of nonsense are you filling my son's head with?"

Old Man Crab looked like he'd been caught red-handed for a second or two, but he recovered quickly. "Like you said, I'm filling his head with nonsense. It's a game we play. Right, kid… just a game."

"Game?" I said. "If you think feeding me to that thing downstairs, then hooking up with my mother is a game, you're an even bigger nut than I thought."

"Bravo, kid," Old Man Crab said, clapping his hands. "That's how you play the game."

"Shut up!" I yelled as I felt the muscles in my neck and shoulders tense up. "You said my mom tried to kill me."

Mom's head snapped sideways as if an invisible hand slapped her. "You told my son I tried to kill him? What the heck is wrong with you?"

"Absolutely nothing, sweet thing," he crooned. "You're the one that sent him to the basement... to his death. Not I. Perhaps you should have a good, long talk with yourself before you point your accusing finger at me."

Mom shook her head and frowned. "What are you rambling on about? Maybe laundry duty is a death sentence for a lazy old man like you, but most people survive it just fine."

Mr. Crab's eyes roved up and down her body as he leered at her. "Deirdre, your ignorance is almost charming. Open your eyes and get your head out of the bottle. Not that it matters for your son's sake, but we can't have you pickling yourself before your time."

Mom's eyes widened, and then her face turned red with anger. "You bastard!" she yelled as she flung a glass at him. "How dare you talk to me like that! Consider this my two-week notice!"

"Tsk-tsk," Old Man Crab said flippantly. "Consider it accepted. Now get your stupid brat of a kid out of my kitchen."

CHAPTER 9

ADAM MATTHEW

WITH THINGS BEING strained at home, I thought I'd be happier back at school. It turned out I was wrong. With not much else going on, my feud with Danny seemed to occupy most people's minds… both teacher and student. But at least I had inspired a little support from some of my classmates. Kids who'd suffered from Danny's wrath started gravitating toward me. They seemed to believe I could protect them. Danny became less overtly aggressive around me, and I might have been happy about it if I hadn't detected something dangerous lurking beneath his contrite features. Danny also did something else I hadn't expected: He started playing the victim. He went around telling people we'd been friends before, so he didn't understand why I had abandoned him at the graveyard or why I'd ambushed him and pushed him into the drinking fountain. When Dad was alive, he told me that Danny and his father were schemers. I didn't believe him at the time, but as always,

Dad was right. Despite Danny's remorseful behavior, I knew I needed to be careful around him.

After lunch, we always had half an hour on the playground to burn off some steam before resuming class. So I made a point of watching my back, and I didn't wander off into any isolated areas. I heard some kid shriek as I stood there next to the baseball diamond talking with Bob and Greg. Looking across the field, I saw—who else?—Danny Pechman picking up apples off the ground and whipping them at some kid stuck up in a tree. The three teachers on duty did not act as if they'd seen or heard anything. Greg and Bob looked at me expectantly, as if it were my job to take care of the situation. Though, deep down in my gut, I knew it was. When I'd been down and out in Abbott Cemetery, someone—don't ask me who or how—had led me out of there before I froze to death. Someone had helped me when I couldn't help myself. Now it was my turn to help somebody else.

I made my way across the uncut field with knee-high grass and weeds pulling at my legs and slowing me down. When I got about ten feet away from Danny, he turned and whipped an apple at me. He missed my head by inches.

"Danny," I sighed. "Leave the kid alone."

"What's it to you, Matthew?" He said as he smirked. "Are you his new mommy now or something?"

"What is it with you? Why are you always hurting other people?"

Danny picked up another apple from the ground, whipped it toward the tree, and grinned. And not in a good sort of way. Somehow, his smile radiated nothing but menace. "Campbell here disrespected me earlier today and I'm administering the punishment."

I looked up at the tree's lower branches and saw Shawn

Campbell, Hunter's younger brother, peeking out sheepishly from behind the thick trunk.

"You know, Danny, you spend all your time in school acting like the innocent victim. Don't you think this is blowing your cover for you?"

He rolled his eyes, then shook his head in disbelief. "My dad always said you and your father were stupid. Look around you, Matthew. Can anyone hear us?" He called out, "Hey, Campbell, we're playing, right? Just having fun?"

"Oh, um… yeah, Danny. Yeah—sure, sure," Shawn said, sounding nervous. "Fun, sure."

"See?" Danny said as he waved a dismissive hand at me. "We're just having fun. Now you better leave if you know what's good for you."

I bent down, picked up an apple, and flung it at the still slightly visible bruise on Danny's forehead. It hit him dead-on, and he yelped. I said, "Pretty fun, huh? Want another?"

With a murderous gleam in his eyes, he rubbed his forehead and said, "You know you'll pay for that." Then he walked off.

Turning around, I saw that everyone on the playground had stopped whatever they'd been doing and stood staring at us. Realization hit me then that Danny had been playacting for the audience. He hadn't actually touched me, but I'd hit him with an apple. Then he looked like the good guy by walking away. Shawn would probably even back Danny's version of events, so I'd come across looking like the bad guy no matter what. Danny had gotten the best of me—again. It ticked me off, but I couldn't do anything about it. At least Danny wasn't attacking Shawn anymore, so I'd accomplished my goal.

I turned back toward the tree and saw that Shawn had made his way down, so I waved him over with my hand and said, "Come on, let's go back to the playground."

That afternoon had everybody taking sides. Some people—again, mostly Danny's previous victims—liked what I had done to him. Others fell for Danny's nonsense and considered me the bully. Unfortunately, the ones who counted were entirely on his side. Toward the end of the day, I stood yet again in the principal's office.

"What is it with you and Danny? I get that the two of you don't get along, but at least he isn't assaulting you. Do you have anything at all to say for yourself?"

I balled up my fists in frustration. I knew nothing I'd say would matter to him, but I had to try anyway: "I was only trying to stop Danny from hurting Shawn. There were three teachers out on the playground today. One of them must've seen something."

Davis shook his head. "I've talked to all three teachers, and the only thing they saw was *your* assault. And before you ask, I've spoken with Shawn too, and he told me he and Danny were just playing a game when you came out of nowhere and, I quote, '*Adam started yelling at Danny and told him he was going to make him pay for ratting him out.*'"

"Well, Mr. Davis, Shawn's scared of Danny, so he'll say anything he tells him to say."

"How about the teachers, Mr. Matthew? Are they afraid of Danny too?"

I shrugged. "I don't know about that, but I know they're lying, if that's what they said. There's no way they missed what happened."

"So, do you see my dilemma?" Davis said as he rubbed his brow. "On the one hand, I have three teachers, both of the other boys involved in the incident, and the entire school playground saying that you attacked Danny. On the other hand, I have you telling me it just isn't so. Do you have anything else to add?"

His words gave me a headache. His mind was already made up, always had been, and he was firmly in Danny's corner and always would be. But it wasn't in my nature to give up, so I decided to go down swinging.

"Really? There's no way that everyone on that playground backed up everything Danny said, including the teachers. Are you sure you talked to everyone?"

Davis turned on me with eyes so intense he looked crazy. "Shut up, Mr. Matthew!" he hissed. "This is how it's going to go down: You are to be suspended for another week. When you return, if you should merit a third suspension, I will expel you from this school, and you'll have to continue your education elsewhere—that is, if another program will accept you. Do you capeesh?"

I nodded as the acid in my stomach burned, but I wisely kept my mouth shut this time. I understood perfectly well, though… I was screwed again.

Davis held me after school while he tried to contact my mom. After an hour or so, he gave up and sent me home. Before I left, he gave me the suspension papers my mother needed to sign. I wadded them up and stuck them in my back pocket. With my head hung low, I walked behind the school building as I began heading home. If Mom had been undecided before, she'd certainly put me up for adoption now—unless she did something even worse. As I walked on, my stomach grew sick with worry; I had no idea how I'd get out of this one. I knew Mom wouldn't believe me any more than anyone else did. As I came around the back of the school, I passed by the bus lot and then reached the dumpster area.

While walking past it, a quiet voice drifted to my ears: "Oh, chicken boy… bock, bock, bock."

As I turned toward the sound, searing pain exploded in my back and froze me in place. I sucked in a sharp breath, then finished turning and saw someone standing inside the nearest dumpster. Even wearing a ski mask, I could tell it was Danny Pechman. As I glared at him, something smashed into the side of my head and a bright light flared in my brain. It felt like I'd been hit by a truck. I staggered as I tried to stay on my feet, but I slipped and fell on my butt. I could feel hot blood dripping down the side of my head and running down my shoulder and back. A coppery scent hung in the air.

"Get him," another voice said—*Rick Kennedy, I think.*

I still had enough of my wits about me to run, but my head was woozy, and my legs didn't work. Then they surrounded me. Three boys in ski masks, previous friends of mine, pelted me with rocks. I fell under the barrage, feeling like I had blood coming out of my body from almost everywhere.

Someone kicked me in the head and, in a faraway voice, said, "I told you that you'd pay for it."

I felt several hands lift me up, and then I crashed into something hard. I think I heard laughter before I passed out.

CHAPTER 10

ADAM MATTHEW

My eyes opened slowly, painfully, and the bright lights around me hurt. I blinked several times before realizing I was lying in a bed… in a hospital. As my eyes continued to adjust, I could make out my mom sitting in a padded chair in the corner of the room. She didn't look right somehow, like I could see two of her. As I glanced around me, I realized Mom wasn't the only thing that appeared to be doubled—everything was. I continued blinking, but it didn't do me any good.

"Mom," I called out, unable to keep the fear out of my voice.

She snapped awake and rushed to me. I could hear her crying and also feel her showering me with kisses at the same time. Even though she had nothing but good intentions, her physical affection toward me made me wince with pain. She backed off and gently rubbed my cheek with her finger when she realized it.

"Mom." I said with a quivering voice, "What am I doing here?"

She tried smiling, but failed miserably. "Oh, honey, you're

getting better," she sobbed. "That's what you're doing. Getting better."

All the talking made me sleepy, and I passed out.

Later in the day, I woke up again, expecting to see my mom, but instead, a police officer stood there at the foot of the bed.

"Can you hear me, son?" asked the officer.

I feebly nodded my head. Anything more hurt too much.

"If you're able, I'd like to get a statement from you." Then he pulled out a pen and a pad of paper. "Can you tell me what happened?"

Why is my mouth so dry? I thought. I swallowed and tried to wet my tongue, but had nothing to moisten it with. "Water," I croaked. I stretched out a trembling hand to the water glass nearby, but I couldn't grasp it. When the officer realized this, he held the glass to my lips so I could drink. After several sips, I told my story in fits and starts while he wrote and asked questions.

At one point, the officer scratched his head and interrupted me. "So, how do you know the identities of your attackers if they had ski masks on?"

My head swam as I tried to pull that information from my memories. I finally said, "Well, they didn't change their clothes before attacking me."

"But, son, clothes are common. People often wear similar outfits."

"True," I responded. "But Danny, Hunter, and Rick were wearing the same outfits earlier today."

The police officer didn't respond to my comment. Instead, he scribbled in his book again.

"Can I ask a question?" I said. Then I paused as the room started spinning. I swallowed a big gulp of air in an effort to hold back my rising nausea. Several seconds later, the motion stopped. "What… what happened to me after they attacked me?"

"Well, son, when you didn't come home from school, your mom called us in a panic. After a mandatory twenty-four-hour wait, a manhunt—"

"Wait, what?" I cut in. Without thinking, my head turned toward the officer in surprise. My neck and back exploded in white-hot agony. Sucking in a short, shallow breath, I closed my eyes and tried to push down my misery and trepidation. "It's… It's the next day?"

He shook his head and said, "Not exactly, but I'll get to that. We initiated a manhunt, and since your last known location was at your school, we started there. We found you unconscious in a dumpster, called an ambulance, and they brought you here. Honestly, it wasn't clear if you'd pull through, but I put my money on you. Young, healthy kids like you can put up with a lot of abuse. Anyway, after forty-eight hours here in the good care of this hospital, you woke up, and the staff contacted us. And that brings us to the present."

After that, he asked me a few more questions, then they left to let me sleep again. Two days later, the doctor discharged me and said I was free to go home.

After riding up in Mr. Crab's creaky, old elevator that had been forbidden to me until now, Mom pushed my wheelchair to my room and then tucked me into bed. Shortly afterward, I woke up and ached all over, so Mom gave me some pills, and soon I felt better. Later that afternoon, a delivery of get-well cards arrived from my classmates. I couldn't read the cards because of my double vision, but it was still nice to get them. Mom said I could go through them when my eyes got better. After another hour or so, I started getting sleepy again. I asked mom about it, and she said I had a *brain contusion*. The rock attack had caused my brain to swell, and that's why the doctors weren't sure at first that I'd make it. That and the blood loss. Mom said I wouldn't die now, but I might have some permanent brain damage. As she said that, her hand flew to her mouth, and she started crying, so I stopped asking questions. However, her response didn't surprise me as mom cries a lot since dad died.

After sleeping for a while, a scratching sound woke me. My eyes snapped open, and I realized that the sound was coming from the attic… directly above my bed. I tried to climb off the mattress but couldn't. My knees were swollen like baseballs, and my arms didn't work well either. I used my imagination to pretend the scratching was nothing more than a raccoon trapped in the roof space trying to get out. That worked until a ghastly white face—all teeth and tongue—wormed itself into my brain. I screamed at the top of my lungs until my mom came running. I begged her to let me sleep with her in her room. Instead, she came and slept in mine. There were no more scratching sounds after that, so I slowly drifted off to sleep.

A few weeks later, another Sunday rolled around, and mom felt I was well enough to go to church again. I both did and didn't want to do so. I'd get out of the house for a few hours and hopefully see my sister if I went. But everyone would see me in my stupid wheelchair, and I wasn't looking forward to that. Throughout most of the previous week, I'd thought I'd be healed up for sure by Sunday, but then Friday came around with a follow-up visit from Dr. Polonsky. He told me it could be months before I ditched the dork mobile. My words, not his exactly. Even worse, he told me my double vision would "probably" clear up, but there was the possibility that it might become permanent too. At least he didn't give me a lollipop.

In the end, I went, hoping to see Bela. That morning, getting ready for church was more work than I could've imagined. Mom had to put me in the bathtub, wash me, take me out, and dress me. It all took time, and it was painful. She ended up borrowing a friend's F-150 pickup truck so that she could get me and my wheelchair around town. By the time we made it to church, Mom looked ready for a nap. But at least she didn't have to push me around. Since my arms didn't work so good, Mom got me one of those electric wheelchairs with the joystick. (I'll never admit it to my dying day, but the wheelchair was kind of fun.)

As we came up to the front door of the church, everyone stopped and stared. Once we'd made it inside, well-wishers and the curious alike surrounded Mom and me.

Right on cue, Gloria Young headed straight for me. "Oh, Adam darling!" she exclaimed as she put a hand over her mouth in shock. "What kind of beast would do this to such a sweet, innocent boy?"

She asked, so I told her everything. Both what happened to me at school and also afterward. By the time I'd finished, I had a large crowd around me, with everyone hanging on my every word. Suddenly, I knew what it felt like to be a movie star, and it was pretty cool.

When I'd finished talking, Gloria asked, "What happened to those three hoodlums? Are they in jail?"

"I don't know," I said as I tried bunching up my semi-responsive hands into fists. "After the police officers took my story down, they left, and I haven't heard from them since."

Gloria patted my right cheek and said, "Well, don't you

worry, honey. Gloria will get to the bottom of it for you. As soon as I know anything… you'll know it too."

And I had no doubt about that. Gloria's connections included a network of gossips who worked overtime to dig down, and root up the dainty morsels. Like pigs grubbing for truffles.

Charlie Reid stuck his head out of the entrance to the nave and looked at the crowd surrounding me. He was a senior in high school, and he'd tell anyone that would listen to him he'd was going to seminary. That one day, he'd be a priest just like Father Ray. While it might come true someday, Charlie was just one of several ushers here today. Not that this deterred him in the least.

"Hey, folks!" Charlie shouted, his chest puffed out in apparent pride. "Mass is about to begin, so we need all of you to get to your seats so the procession can begin."

Pipe organ music started drifting to my ears as the crowd filtered into the nave. The pretty melody gave me a vague sense of unease, so I looked up and asked Mom if I could listen from the lobby today. I told her I didn't think I could make it to the bathroom in time if I got sick during the service like the last few times.

She thought about it and frowned, but then she said, "Alright, honey, I'll make an exception for you this time, but don't get used to it."

I flashed her a small smile. "I won't, Mom… thanks."

She left, and I made myself as comfortable as I could in my wheelchair. Sitting there listening to the service in Latin, my mind wandered, and I glanced down the darkened hallway from time to time. I saw a black flash at about the halfway mark—like a Polaroid flashcube going off. But instead of flashing white, it flashed black. *Bela?* I hightailed it down to the classroom, and sure enough, I found my sister standing there.

"Hi, Bela," I said. "Are you ready to play?"

"Sure," she said, and then she threw the blackboard eraser at me.

My hands came up, but my fingers couldn't close enough, so the eraser flew through them and then bounced off my chest, creating a puff of white chalk dust. Then it hit the floor, making another puff of white.

I smiled meekly. "Sorry, sis. Guess we'll have to play something else today."

"You know I could've protected you if you'd let me come home with you last time, but you didn't say yes."

"Don't be upset. I wanted to, but Mom's been off lately, and I didn't want to make her cry. And also… oh… never mind. I don't want to talk about it."

"I can protect you from Mom and all the rest of them if you let me."

"But you're just a ghost," I said as I looked straight through her transparent form. "How can you possibly protect me from anything?"

"I'll do it for you because you're my brother. You just have to let me in."

I shrugged, then winced from that action. "Well… maybe. But if you come home with me, you need to know there's something bad in the house."

"I can protect you from the ghoul, too. And then we can play. Don't you want to play with me, Adam? I'm lonely. Aren't you, too?"

I had to admit she seemed alone and abandoned, and I certainly was sensitive to that. I'd felt much the same way over the past year, and I didn't like it one bit. So… if I let her come home, we could hang out together, and then neither one of us would be sad anymore. *Problem solved.* "Well, now that you mention it, it would be nice to have a sister around. All right, you can come home with me."

"You're inviting me to enter you?"

"Yes, already. At least for the ride home. Now come on before Mom comes looking for us."

Bela flowed toward me—and then *into* me. I felt super sick for a few seconds, but thankfully, it passed.

"Bela? Where are you?" I said. "Bela? Hello?… Hmm, where did you go?"

Sitting in my wheelchair, looking all around me, I glanced at the wall clock and saw that Mass would be over shortly. As I made my way back to the lobby, I realized everything looked normal again. My double vision was gone.

I yelled out, "Thanks, sis! I owe you one!"

CHAPTER 11

ADAM MATTHEW

THAT EVENING, I called out to Bela when neither mom nor Old Man Crab was around. I rolled my wheelchair through several rooms as I searched for her, but I didn't get any response. *So much for playing together,* I thought. *Oh, well… It's probably better that way.* Mom had reminded me that school started up again for me tomorrow and I'd been putting off my assigned homework. Sighing as I went over to the large ancient dresser that contained all my worldly belongings, I pulled on the big copper handle attached to the bottom drawer, and it slid open with a creak. I secretly hoped that the resident ghoul had a hankering for math. If my book disappeared—or, better yet, got ripped to shreds—no one could blame me for not studying. I shook my head in mock disbelief and horror when my eyes settled upon my intact math book. I guess I wouldn't be using "*The ghoul ate my homework*" excuse.

Speaking of which, now that I had a name for the thing, I needed to do a little internet research. And I would once I got my computer privileges back. Hopefully, I'd find something useful. Something to keep the ghoul away for good—like garlic and crosses kept vampires at bay. Maybe sis knew of something, and I'd ask her when she showed herself.

I reluctantly pulled out my math book along with a pad of paper and pencil and sat down on the cold wood floor. After my sister had entered me, not only had my double vision gone away, but I could walk again too. I didn't tell anyone at church about my sister, so they all thought it was a miracle when I got out of my wheelchair after Mass ended. But to me, it didn't feel like one. My pain wasn't agonizing now, but it still hurt a lot on the inside when I moved, so I continued to use the wheelchair. Whatever Bela did to me, it seemed to work like the OxyContin mom gave me… only way better. I could still feel the pain, but I didn't care or think about it nearly as much. Nevertheless, my rate of healing was miraculous, so I'd probably be pain and wheelchair free soon. Maybe within days.

I opened my algebra book to the chapter on the distribution of two binomials with the FOIL method… first, inside, outside, and last. I skimmed through it before it could put me to sleep. Not that the material was too hard for me, but just the opposite. Like most of my schoolwork, this stuff proved ridiculously easy. It bored me to where it barely kept my attention. I'd heard calculus was harder, so I had high hopes that I'd like it better. I figured I'd find out in three or four years.

As I worked on the assigned problems, I heard a scratching sound coming from the floor beneath me and then felt its vibration on my butt. I jumped up as if I'd been sitting on a snake. It was the fastest I'd moved since my incident with Danny and the gang. Somehow, this thing had tracked me down again. *Well, good for it… and me.* After getting home from church, I'd lifted a salt shaker from the kitchen, and I was dying to try an experiment. I pulled the warm glass-and-chrome object out of my pocket, and I sprinkled some salt on the floor right where I had been sitting. I sensed the briefest flash of hunger and frustration, and then the feelings disappeared… and so did the scratching. This salt shaker was so going to become my new best friend. I knew the salt might not stop the ghoul during a full assault (no pun intended), but if it bought me some peace, quiet, and sleep in the meantime, that was still worth a lot to me. I sat back down right on top of the salt and continued studying. Later that night, before I went to bed, I sprinkled salt under and around my bed, and the following morning, I found I'd enjoyed a good night's sleep.

The next day, after Mom took me and my wheelchair to school, I sat in algebra class, feeling thankful that I'd studied the night before, because Mrs. Holmes sprang a surprise quiz on us. I made it about three-fourths of the way through when the overhead speaker came to life. It started squawking, and then announced, "Mrs. Holmes, please send Adam Matthew to Principal Davis's office." My math teacher told me I could finish the quiz when I got back, so I rolled myself out of the classroom and made my way down the hall.

Nothing more had happened since I'd been attacked, so I didn't know why Davis wanted me to come see him. *What did I do now?* Maybe I was overthinking things. He probably just wanted to see how I was doing. They had banged me up pretty bad after all.

When I made it to his door, I could hear two men arguing behind it. I turned the wheelchair to move away, but his receptionist said I was expected and to go on in. She opened the door, and it startled me when I saw Danny Pechman's dad, Bud, sitting there glaring at me. I painfully extricated myself from my wheelchair and limped into the principal's office. Once inside the door, Davis went around me and shut it. That made me a little nervous. *Why close it? Are they going to beat me to death in here?* As I stood there looking at Davis, he motioned with his hand, and I took the seat he had pointed to.

Davis started by saying, "Mr. Pechman came to see me today because he's upset by certain accusations that—"

Danny's dad interrupted him. "You can shove your *accusations* talk. This kid is straight up lying. My son had nothing to do with this, and if he doesn't stop disparaging my kid… he and I are going to have a big problem."

"But… But, Mr. Pechman," I said. "I—"

He cut me off. He screwed his face up and said, "*But… but, Mr. Pechman,* what? Did I give you permission to speak to me, you lying brat? Don't you dare open your mouth again unless I give you permission to talk. Got it?"

"Fine, I won't speak to you." Then I turned my head to Davis instead. "He wasn't even there. How would he know what happened?"

Danny's dad shook with barely concealed rage. I thought Davis would say something to him, but he looked plenty afraid of the man himself. As I sat there staring at the nervous looking principal, a dark figure stepped out from behind him. It was my sister Bela, and seeing her made my heart happy. She walked up to me and put her hand on my shoulder. I don't know how to describe it exactly, but understanding flooded me. Richard Davis—also known as Dick to his close friends—had gone to school with Bud Pechman. I also knew that Dick was scared to death of Bud because childhood fears die hard. Bud had been the school bully, and Dick had been a frequent recipient of his special attentions.

Bela leaned toward me and whispered, "If you give me permission to take control of your body, I can take care of this mess for you. Do you give me permission?"

I shook my head *no.*

I looked up and saw Danny's dad glaring at me again. "What's wrong with you, boy?" he said. "Are you queer in the head or something?"

My sister Bela whispered to me, "Okay, fine. I can help you in other ways, so if you want me to, don't talk unless I tell you to say something."

I looked at her and nodded my head, yes, but I didn't speak.

Danny's father looked at me with suspicion, and then he continued, "So, how do I know my son didn't do it? I know because he was with me. In fact, Danny, Rick, and Hunter were all with me. We watched the ball game on TV, and my friend Phil will back me up on that. So if you continue to spread your lies at church and here at school, I'll make you regret that you ever saw my face."

My mouth opened to say I already regretted it, but my sister touched my shoulder again and shook her head no, then she whispered in my ear.

I looked at Davis and said, "Can I use the bathroom? I really have to go."

The principal flicked his hand at the door and said, "I expect you back here in five minutes."

As I left the office, Bud Pechman said behind my back, "See... the little turd's going to wet himself. That's how you handle a snot-nose brat. You've got to use a firm hand and—"

I was soon out of earshot, so I couldn't hear the rest of his little speech. When I reached the bathroom, I turned to my sister and said, "Okay, I'm here. What is it?"

She looked up at me—or at least I think she did, since she

doesn't actually have eyes. "Bud Pechman is a man of violence," she said. "I had you leave before you ended up saying something that would get you killed before your accorded time."

Her words made me nervous, so I started biting on my lips. I knew Danny's dad was mad at me, but I didn't think he was that angry. "What am I going to do, sis?" I said in a panic. "I don't want to die."

"First, stay here for exactly eight more minutes, then return to Davis's office. When you go back, tell him this." She whispered her final instructions in my ear.

When I returned, Davis sat alone in his office. He motioned to the chair Bud Pechman had been sitting in and said, "Please sit, Mr. Matthew."

I complied and sat down. I could feel Pechman's lingering warmth heat my backside.

"So, Mr. Matthew, I've listened to Bud and find that he makes a compelling case. As of this moment, you are to quit making unproven accusations against Danny and friends. If it were me, I'd sue you. But fortunately for you, it's not. You're lucky that Bud is a gracious man. All he asks is that you respect his alibi and apologize to all involved for your false statement. But if you refuse, he's requested that I expel you from school."

I shook my head in disbelief. There were several things I wanted to say, but I didn't. Instead, I repeated Bela's words verbatim: "I'll make you a counteroffer… Expel Danny Pechman instead, then apologize to the students and parents for the twenty thousand dollars you stole from the school funds, and I'll forget we ever had this conversation. Turn down my offer, and earthly gain will be the least of your worries."

I could tell that whatever Davis had thought I might say, that wasn't it. His eyes opened wide like circles and then his face blanched. Bela whispered in my ear to keep my mouth shut and leave, so I did just that.

After my crazy encounter with Pechman and Davis, several uneventful days went by and everything seemed peaceful and back to normal again. Even Danny and the gang had backed off. While I sat in geography class listening to the teacher discuss the breakup of the Soviet Union, the overhead speaker started squawking. A female voice said, "Adam Matthew, can you come to Mr. Davis's office, please?"

I groaned internally. *What could he possibly want now?* I was no longer wheelchair bound, so I rose and excused myself. I walked down the hall and all alone—until I wasn't. Bela appeared out of nowhere and started walking beside me.

"Hey, sis! There you are. I thought maybe you'd gone back to the church. Decided to come walk with me instead?"

"I came to warn you. Davis has decided to expel you from school. He's going to do it now."

My heart sank into my stomach. *Why won't people just leave me alone?*

"Oh, Bela, what am I going to do? Mom is going to be so upset with me."

The black mist constituting her form swirled faster as she said, "I told you I'd protect you—that is, if you'll let me?"

"How can you do that if you're a ghost?" To prove my point, I poked my hand into and through her. To my surprise, my hand and arm tingled as if full of pins and needles, so I quickly snatched my arm back to myself.

"Like I said before, I don't have my own body, but if you let me use yours, I can take care of everything for you."

My stomach fluttered. She was my sister, but it still seemed weird to let someone else use your body… even family. "I don't know," I said uneasily. "Do you promise to give me my body back?"

"Of course. What makes you think I'd want to stay in a yucky boy's body, anyway?"

I struggled within myself, and then I shrugged. *It's that or get expelled.*

"Okay, I guess it's all right. Go ahead."

"So you give me permission to use your body as my own?"

"Yes, just as long as you give it back later today."

Bela flowed into me. The hallway grew darker, and the sound of my footsteps grew faint. My remaining pain disappeared, too. I realized I wasn't even moving my own feet anymore. I seemed more like a passenger in my own body—it was kind of cool and scary at the same time. As I watched my body walk to the front exit, I took a quarter out of my pocket. Then my body walked to the payphone attached to the outside wall of the redbrick building. My hand placed the quarter into the coin slot and dialed a number. I could hear my voice pleading with someone, but couldn't quite make out the words. My hand hung up the phone a few minutes later, and my feet carried me back into the building. Someone was whistling a tune. I think the sound came from me.

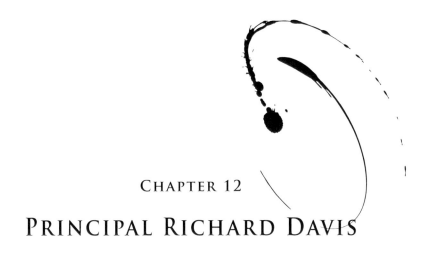

Chapter 12

Principal Richard Davis

Where is that Matthew kid? I wanted to get this over with already and move on with my day. Bud Pechman was insufferable, but being threatened by a thirteen-year-old was even worse. I couldn't risk the kid talking, so I had to put back all the money I'd taken. It drained me of every last penny and then some, and I sure resented it. I don't know how the kid found out about it, but I was tired of being in the middle of their feud and it ended today. If I had to choose a side, I'd rather be in Bud's good graces. Even so, I could think of a way for Adam to find himself back in my favor if I played my cards right. I'd seen Adam's mom several times, and she was a total hottie. I was sure we could work something out if she really wanted her kid back in school bad enough. That something put a smile on my face.

Standing there, lost in my own little fantasy world, I looked over and saw the Matthew kid staring at me. He had a knowing, penetrating gaze that seemed out of place with his youthful appearance, and it caused me to flinch. I had the creepiest feeling that he was reading my mind, as if he were a giant leech sucking on my brain. Of course, I knew that was silly, and I shook the idea from my head. *Well, showtime,* I thought.

"Mr. Matthew, please come in and take a seat."

The kid entered and closed the door behind him. *How strange is that?* In my experience, most people detested being in a closed space with an authority figure. I suppose it was the whole fight-or-flight thing.

Well, if nothing else, the kid has balls—and the thought of busting them put a smile on my face. "What took you so long to get here?" I asked. "You know, I expect an immediate response when I place a call over the intercom. What did you do, walk around the building three times first?"

"Yes."

Okay, that didn't seem to rattle him.

"Yes, *what*, young man?"

"Yes, as in yes."

Defiant to the end. Certain kids just never seemed to learn. Well, let the fun begin. Maybe one day he'd get it through his thick skull that power has its privileges.

In my sternest voice, I said, "So, do you know why I've called you here today?"

The kid looked at me with a deadpan face. "I suppose you want to apologize to me for all of your lying and deceit and for being a jerk."

As if. This kid was insufferable.

I shook my head in disbelief. "Mr. Matthew, I can see you've been spending way too much time in fantasy land."

"No, Richard, that honor belongs to you."

My mouth fell open, but I quickly caught the mistake and closed it. My eyes narrowed to slits. "Did you just call me by my first name, Mr. Matthew?"

"No, sir. I would have said, *Dick,* if I had."

Unbelievable… he even said it with an emphasis on "Dick." The little snot just insulted me again, and a vein started throbbing in my temple. This wasn't working out like I planned, and I wasn't going to spend all afternoon getting into a verbal sparring match with this smart-mouthed kid.

I realized I'd made a good decision when I expedited his expulsion. The kid was nothing but trouble. *Time for the chopping block!*

"So, Mr. Matthew," I said with concealed glee. "Your enrollment in this school ends today. I've drawn up your expulsion papers, and you're no longer my problem. Go spread your mayhem elsewhere."

I waited for him to cry or beg or something, but he didn't say a word. He didn't even give me any indication he'd heard me. My face dropped with disappointment. "Do you even care to know why you're being expelled?"

"Why would I care about that?" he said with a dark grin that seemed too wide for his face… like it belonged to a devil. "I'm being expelled because you're a loser, *Dick.*"

"What did you just call me?" Then I shook my head. "Never mind…. I demand you apologize to me right now, or I'll bring the police into this!"

"Loser, loser, loser," he said in a creepy, singsong voice. "Amy Bergman knew you were a loser. She dumped you at the prom. All the pretties dumped you once they knew you—each and every one."

All the hairs on my body stood up on end. *How could this freak know that?*

"*Adam's mom is a total hottie,*" he continued in that creepy voice that was giving me the chills. "*A little expulsion for ole*

Adam boy, and she'll be on her knees, naked, of course. And I'll think of all sorts of interesting ways for her to earn my forgiveness."

My face blanched, and I tried to move my mouth, but nothing came out.

"So, *Dick*," he continued. "My dad was a real man who earned my mom's love. You're just a little creep that extorts women for sex. Perhaps if you pray earnestly to your god, you'll find forgiveness for your sins."

I'd had enough of this punk. *Does he think he's my priest now?* I grabbed him by his shirt collar to drag him out of my office, and he screamed like a banshee.

"Shut Up!" I yelled just as my office door got kicked in, and Adam simultaneously wailed, "Please, Mr. Davis, don't make me touch you there again!"

Two cops stood on the other side of my doorway, one just behind the other. The shorter officer, who was built like a barrel, and closest to me, placed his hand on his gun.

"Oh, no no no no no! Officers, please wait," I said. "Hear me out. It's not what it looks like."

The officer unsnapped the leather strap over his holstered gun. "Step away from the boy."

I released the kid's collar and backed up.

"Son, are you okay?" the same officer asked.

He shook his head. "No, sir, I'm not."

"Can you tell me, son, what happened?"

"Certainly, Officer," I chimed in.

"You shut up," he said as he pointed his gun at me. "I'm talking to the boy."

The faker kid started crying as he said, "Sometimes he makes… he makes me come in here and touch him. I told him I didn't want to do it anymore, so he said he'd expel me from school. He said right now was my last chance to make amends."

I stood there, stunned. The little punk was setting me up, and I wasn't going to stand for it. I flung my arm up in the air to make a point, and both officers tackled me and put me in handcuffs. I tried to talk, but they read me my Miranda rights instead. *Perhaps shutting up is the best thing I can do. I'll just dig myself in deeper otherwise. Besides, they'll have to drop everything once they realize it's my word against the kids.*

As if reading my mind, Adam walked over to the front of my desk and said to the officers, "I need to show you something, sirs."

My heart started pounding in my chest as he opened my second desk drawer. He pulled the manilla folders out of it and felt around. I thanked my lucky stars that I had taken precautions… or so I had thought. I saw him reach way back in the drawer, and then I heard a snick. Hot vomit started rising in my throat. The kid pulled up the false bottom that held some of my private photos and then handed them to the officers.

A tremor swept through my frame as Adam said, "That's Stacy Clineman and Connie Jones. One is in ninth grade, and the other is in tenth now. If you look at the pictures, you'll see he made them do things for him. Mr. Davis said he'd add me to his picture collection once I learned how to behave."

After flipping through the pictures, the officers swore under their breaths, then called me a few choice names. They became rough with me, dragging me forward and out of my office. Then they ushered me down the main hallway in front of the entire school. Once we were outside, they shoved me toward the back seat of their police cruiser, with the door still closed. As I bounced off the door, both officers laughed and said, "Oops!" After opening the door, they shoved me inside the vehicle, clipping my head on the door frame. Blood started trickling into my eyes, but I couldn't do anything about it with my hands cuffed behind me.

While the officers were busy conversing on their walkie-talkies, the little twerp walked out of the school building and over to the half rolled-down vehicle window next to me.

He leaned in and whispered, "It would have been far better for you if you had chosen to be in my good graces." Then Adam did something I will never forget, even if I live long enough to have that opportunity. His eyes turned solid black, and he said, "Don't worry, Dick. I'll come visit you in the penitentiary for Halloween, and we'll do things together. Things that I'll enjoy. Now don't forget to mark down the date. I promise you I'll be there." Then he stuck a hand through the open window and pushed his forefinger against my bleeding forehead. He drew the bloody finger back and licked it. "Yum," he said. "Consider it a dinner date." Then he flashed me an unnaturally large smile... full of pointy, fang-like teeth.

As I stared at him with wide eyes, my jaw fell open, and I felt something warm on the car seat.

CHAPTER 13

ADAM MATTHEW

FEELING AGITATED THAT night, I exited my bedroom and paced up and down the upstairs hallway. I'd never heard exactly what Bela and Davis talked about, but something just didn't seem right. I asked my sister about it, but she told me to drop it because she took care of everything and I didn't have to worry about expulsion or Davis anymore. When I pushed her for details, she got huffy and stopped talking. I tried smoothing things over with her, but she wouldn't budge. After a while, she left, and I was back to walking alone.

As I continued pacing back and forth, I remembered Father Ray saying to pray to God whenever you needed anything. I tried that when dad died, but he still hadn't come back. Once I realized that prayer didn't work, I gave up on it and didn't try it again. Though, for some reason, I felt an urgent need to pray. I went to my bedroom, got down on my knees, and prayed the Hail Mary. I only got a few words in when I felt like throwing up. After I stopped, I started feeling better again. Hmm, that prayer didn't work, so I thought I'd try the Our Father next. But I started getting sick again as soon as the words came out of my mouth. I tried to push through it, and ten words in, I vomited on my bedroom floor. Mom would get mad at me if she found out, so I went to the bathroom and grabbed a bunch of toilet paper. I was on my knees cleaning up the last bit when she walked in behind me. Mom looked at the vomit and then me with great concern. In fact, her face was puffy, and she looked like she'd been crying.

"Honey," she said. "Is there anything you wanted to tell me?"

I shook my head.

"Really?" she said with a trembling voice. "A police officer just left and told me that Richard Davis was arrested today for being abusive toward you and a few other students. They want you to see a child psychologist. Can you tell me what happened?"

I shrugged.

Mom became emotional. "I know you've gotten it into your head that I don't want you anymore, but nothing could be further from the truth. You're the only thing that truly matters to me, and I would give my very life to protect you. So much has been going on in your world lately, and I want to help you, but you won't let me in. Please tell me what Davis did to you."

I didn't want to make mom sad, but I had nothing to talk about. The problem was, I didn't know what happened earlier today. Also, when I tried telling her the truth before, she'd slapped me for it. I looked up at her and said, "You'll just get mad at me if I tell you what happened."

She came to me, knelt down, and hugged me. "Oh, Adam, you can tell me anything. No matter what you say, I promise you I won't get mad at you."

"You promise?" I asked sheepishly.

She smiled. "Yes."

"Okay, Mom… if you say so. So several days ago, Danny Pechman's dad showed up at school and said Danny didn't throw any rocks at me. He told Mr. Davis that I was lying, and if I didn't apologize, he wanted me thrown out of school."

She frowned and looked directly into my eyes. "Wait… I want you to be crystal clear on this because I've heard none of it. Are you sure you're telling me the truth?"

Maybe talking was a mistake. I could feel myself shutting down on the inside. "Mom," I said with hesitation. "You promised you wouldn't get mad at me."

She grabbed my hand and said, "Honey, I'm not mad. You caught me off guard is all. Please keep going."

"Okay, Mom. So after Bud Pechman left, Bela told me that Mr. Davis was stealing money from the school, so I told him that if he expelled me, I'd tell everybody what he'd done."

Mom's right eye started twitching, and she looked like she might be getting upset again, so I stopped.

After about twenty seconds, she said, "I was just thinking about what you said. Go on. I want to hear the entire story."

"Well, I thought everything was okay after that, but I got called back today to the principal's office. While walking there, Bela appeared and told me Mr. Davis was kicking me out of school. I got scared because I didn't want you to be mad at me. I didn't know what to do, but Bela said she could help me. She told me that if I let her use my body, she would take care of everything for me, and she did. I could kind of tell what was going on, but I couldn't make out the words exactly, and that's everything I know… honest."

Mom was shaking from head to toe by the time I'd finished. When she finally spoke, she said, "Is Bela inside you now?"

"No. Bela said she didn't want to be stuck in a yucky boy's body. I talked to her earlier tonight, but she's gone now."

Mom gave a slow nod. "Do you think you can call her for me?"

"I can try, but Bela's not real good about coming when I call her. She mostly shows up when she feels like it." I put my hand to my mouth and started hollering, "Bela, can you hear me? Bela, Mom wants to meet you. Can you come out?"

We waited, but nothing happened.

I shrugged. "I don't think she's going to show up tonight."

When Mom didn't answer me, I glanced over at her, and she looked confused. Well, not confused exactly, but more like a combination of disbelief and hopefulness at the same time. I guess I was the confused one. I'm pretty sure I couldn't make a face like that.

She started to say something, but stopped. She shook her head *no*, but then she seemed to change her mind again. "Adam, honey, does your… does your dad ever come and visit you?"

Her question caught me off guard, and thinking about it made me a little sad. "Oh… uh, no. I mean, if he does, I've never seen him—though it would be nice if he did. The next time I see Bela, I'll ask her about it. Mom, can I ask you something else?"

"Of course."

"Can I sleep in your room tonight?"

She looked me up and down. "I suppose that would be okay, but make sure you take a shower first. And don't forget to wash behind your ears."

"Okay, Mom," I said. It thrilled me she'd said yes. I'd figured out that the nights she told me no were the nights she drank herself to sleep, and I was pretty sure all that drinking couldn't be good for her.

CHAPTER 14

ADAM MATTHEW

THE ENTIRE SCHOOL revolved around me the next day like a crazy circus. It seemed the only thing on everyone's mind was the confrontation between Davis and me. Before I even got to homeroom, different classmates kept approaching me about the stories floating around. There were rumors out there that he'd tried to kill me or expel me... that he'd hit me, pushed me, spit on me... and even one where he wanted to sell me to a kiddie trafficking ring. But Bela still hadn't talked, so I knew little more than anyone else.

Lucas and Leslie walked up to me as I stood before my locker, thinking about everything. They wanted to know what really happened. I felt it would have been more productive if I just got on the intercom system and spoke to the whole school at once. At least I had my spiel down after repeating it fifty times.

"I'm sorry, guys," I said to their eager looking faces. "Everything went down so fast, I'm not sure what happened. Davis was bellyaching at me about something when two police officers busted down his office door and dragged him off. I don't even think it had anything to do with me. I just happened to be there when they arrested him."

Behind me, I heard Danny Pechman snicker. "My dad told me they caught you touching each other's pee-pees."

Without turning around, I said, "Well, Danny, I guess he'd know. I heard he loves grabbing yours."

Danny came around from behind me and poked me in the chest with his finger. "You know, Matthew, you better watch your mouth or else."

"Or else what?" I said as I shoved his hand away from me. "You gonna stand in a dumpster and throw rocks at me? You gonna get your buddies to help you?"

Danny glared at me, then said, "My dad made it clear to you, you stupid pea brain, that I didn't do that and you're in big trouble when I tell him you're still flapping your mouth."

I laughed in his face. "What's he going to do? Get his buddy Davis to expel me from his jail cell. Good luck with that."

"Don't you worry," he said as his face bunched up into a scowl. "My dad will think of something, and then you'll be sorry."

A tall, serious-looking woman dressed in a dark brown wool jacket and skirt walked up and interrupted us.

"Hello," she said, "My name is Mrs. Johnson and I'm the interim principal filling in for Mr. Davis."

Danny butted in, "If you're the new principal, I'd like to report him for threatening me." He pointed at me. "He said he was going to break my arms and legs and dump me in a ditch."

Before I could defend myself, Leslie said, "Shut up, Danny. You're such a liar. I've been here the whole time, and you're the one doing all the threatening." She put her hands on her hips. "Don't listen to him, Mrs. Johnson."

Mrs. Johnson looked Danny over with stern eyes and said, "I'll talk to you later." Then she looked at me. "I need to borrow you for a second, Adam. If you could come with me, please."

I followed her while listening to her heeled shoes click against the tiled floor.

When we reached the conference room, she stopped outside the door and said, "There's someone here I'd like you to meet. She's a psychologist who helps out here sometimes, and we brought her here to speak with you. It's okay if you talk to her. She's safe, and you can trust her. Whatever you tell her will be between the two of you only."

She pushed open the door and introduced me to Dr. Charlotte Brown.

After the new principal left, Dr. Brown stood and smiled a friendly smile at me and told me she was a psychologist. Then she asked me to sit. "Please call me Dr. Charlotte. So… do you like dogs, Adam?"

"Um… yeah," I said, nodding.

"I like dogs too," she said as she pulled out her wallet and handed me a picture. "That's my dog. His name is Bernie. Do you know what kind of dog he is?"

"A beagle…"

She smiled. "Very good, Adam. I guess you do like dogs. Do you have a dog too?"

I shook my head. "No, my mom's allergic to them, so I can't have one."

"Well, that's too bad. How about brothers or sisters?"

I shook my head again. "No, I don't have any of those either. I had a sister once, but she died a few minutes after being born."

"Does that make you sad?"

"Not really. I was too little to remember her, but Mom cries if I mention it."

"I can imagine. It's hard to lose someone you love. Have you lost anybody like that?"

"Yeah, my dad," I said as I felt my throat tighten. "Both me and mom are sad about that."

"How has it been for you?" she asked gently.

"I dunno. We ended up moving in with Old Man—I mean, Mr. Crab. He's a grouchy old guy, but Mom said he puts a roof over our heads, so we put up with him."

She rubbed her chin. "Is that your mother's boyfriend?"

"Ha, he wishes!" I blurted out. "He's like a hundred years old. We live with him, and Mom takes care of us."

"Can you tell me more about him?"

"Not really. He sits in the kitchen eating soup, and that's about the only time I see him. I never go to his bedroom on the third floor. He said little snots can't go to the third floor, so I don't."

Her eyebrows bunched up in concern. "He did, did he? So he's not much of a father figure for you?"

A laugh escaped from my lips. "Mr. Crab? No, he's more like a mean older brother."

"Is it hard not having a father around?"

Now I felt tears welling up in my eyes. I nodded.

"How has the principal—Mr. Richard Davis—been through all of this? Has he been there for you?"

Frowning, I said, "I'm sorry. I don't understand your question."

"Oh, let's see," she said as she tapped her chin with her pen. "Has he been like a father figure for you?"

"Mr. Davis? Maybe in his dreams. I think he has the hots for my mom."

"Really? How does he feel about you?"

"I think he hates me. He's always yelling at me and tells me he's only letting me off because of my mom."

"That's interesting. Does he punish you by making you touch him?"

I shook my head.

Dr. Charlotte pulled a male rag doll out of her bag. "Can you show me on this doll where he makes you touch him?"

"No."

"Why not?"

Even though I hadn't heard what had gone on between Bela and Davis, I could still sort of see and feel what was happening, and I didn't remember him touching me anywhere he wasn't supposed to. Maybe I missed it, but I didn't see how. I said, "Because I can't remember."

She leaned in toward me and looked at me with sympathetic eyes. "Can't remember, or don't want to remember?"

"I wasn't there, so I don't know."

Dr. Charlotte scratched her. She looked confused. "Well, if you weren't there with him, who was?"

"My sister."

Her eyes narrowed. "I thought you said your sister died."

"She did, but she visits me sometimes."

"How long has she been visiting you?"

"I don't know. Maybe a few months."

"What do you do when she visits?"

"We play."

"Do you have any close friends? Living ones, that is?"

"Not anymore."

"Can you tell me about it?"

Thinking about it made my stomach hurt. "No, I don't want to."

A sad smile crossed her face. "You know, Adam, I'm here specifically for you, so you can trust me. Anything you say to me is just between the two of us. Okay?"

"Like cross your heart? Like that?"

"Cross my heart. Mum's the word," she said as she traced out an imaginary X over her chest. "So, what happened between you and your friends, Adam?"

"I still don't want to talk about it."

"Okay, that's fine," she said. "Perhaps you could tell me a little something about your sister?"

"Sis? Well, her name's Bela, and she died when she was only ten minutes old. She said she couldn't hang on."

"Hang on to what?"

"Life."

"What does she look like?"

I rubbed my lower jaw as I thought about it. "Well, she mostly looks like a black swirling mist, but she said that's the veil between us. She pushed herself into it once, and she looked like my mom, but with my dad's eyes."

"Were you happy when she visited you?"

"Yes."

"Where did you meet?"

"At church."

She nodded to herself as if deep in thought. "Okay, Adam, well, she seems nice. So there's something you said that I don't understand. You said your sister was there with Mr. Davis instead of you. What did you mean by that?"

I opened my mouth to answer Dr. Charlotte, but stopped when a hand touched my shoulder. I turned a bit and saw

Bela standing there, shaking her head. She said, "Don't talk to Dr. Charlotte anymore."

"Why not?" I asked Bela.

"Because she's a liar, that's why."

"Who are you talking to?" Dr. Charlotte asked.

"My sister."

"Your sister's here? Can I talk to her too?"

"No."

"Why not?"

"Because she said you're a liar."

"And why does she think that?"

I leaned into Bela, and she whispered in my ear.

"She told me that Bernie's not your dog. It's your sister's dog, and it's not even alive anymore. It got hit by a car and died. She said only a bad person would lie about a dog."

Dr. Charlotte looked shaken. "Bela told you all that?"

I nodded.

"If Bela's here, can she tell me how she knew Mr. Davis was abusing young girls?"

I shook my head. "She's not going to tell you. She won't even talk to me about it. I'd tell you if I knew anything, but I don't. Can I go now? I'm tired of answering your questions."

"Of course you can go, Adam. Can I ask if it's okay to talk to you again in the future?"

I shrugged. "I don't know. Bela doesn't want me talking to you anymore. If she changes her mind, I will."

When I left the second-floor conference room, the hallways were empty because classes were in session. To get back to the art room, I could take the long way around or take the shortcut through the service area hallway. The area was restricted to staff only, but I didn't see anyone else around and I was already late for class. *Why not,* I thought.

With my decision made, I hung a right and started walking. As I came up to the service elevator, I glanced into the empty shaft through the padlocked gate. Looking up, the old box elevator hung above me on the third floor. Struck by curiosity, I stuck my head between the rungs of the gate and swept my gaze around. Much like Old Man Crab's elevator, it was old. The metal had rust spots, the wood planks of the box elevator floor appeared bowed and cracked, and the whole thing looked like it could use several coats of fresh paint. Looking down, the shaft disappeared into a deep darkness as if it were bottomless.

A searing pain exploded in my back and something clattered at my feet. I whipped my head around and saw Rick Kennedy standing there, smirking. At my feet laid a glass soda pop bottle.

"What the heck is wrong with you?!" I yelled while trying to ignore my throbbing back. "Did your mom drop you on your head or something?"

"You're the one that got dropped on your head," Rick retorted. "Apparently, you're too stupid to understand that Danny's dad has an alibi for us, so you can't accuse us of anything. So we're going to do this the hard way now. I'm going to beat some understanding into you."

A black shadow appeared right beside me, and then Bela stepped into me without even asking. My body shook with rage, and I could sense strength and energy flowing through my limbs. Rick came at me with a double-punch combo that I easily dodged. I grabbed him by the crotch and the hair on his head, causing him to squeal in pain and surprise. I twirled like a discus thrower and flung him up and over the six-foot-high metal gate. He flew through the opening into the elevator shaft, then grunted once as his head bounced off a sidewall with a loud crack. With his forward momentum stopped, his body tumbled down the elevator shaft like a rag doll. I heard him land hard, and then he made a pained groaning sound. Then silence.

Righteous anger welled up in me, and I yelled down the shaft, "Say hi to Bud Pechman for me!"

It caught me by surprise as I walked away because I couldn't remember what had gotten me so worked up just a moment ago. No matter how hard I tried, I just couldn't remember what I'd been doing. It seemed like it had been important, but nothing came to mind. I walked back down the service area hallway, but I saw nothing. I noticed a bottle lying on the floor by the elevator, so I picked it up and tossed it in the trash. *Maybe it'll come to me if I stop thinking about it so much.*

CHAPTER 15

ADAM MATTHEW

AT HOME THAT evening, my heart skipped with excitement when I heard the front doorbell ring. Company was rare since we moved in with Old Man Crab and I enjoyed getting visitors. Mom always told me to look first before opening the door, but I forgot. I flung it wide open, and Dr. Charlotte, the psychologist, was standing there.

As I stood there staring at her, she said, "Hello, Adam. How are you doing tonight?"

"I'm okay."

"I'm glad to hear that," she said, then smiled. "Is your mother home by any chance?"

"Yes."

"Can I talk to her?"

"Mom!" I turned and yelled. "Someone's at the door for you!"

Mom came around the corner with a dishrag in her hands. "Hello, can I help you?" Then her eyes seemed to widen in recognition. "Charlotte Brown, right? We met several years ago at that New Year's Eve bash. Remember? Your husband and mine were friends."

Dr. Charlotte touched her hand to her chest. "Wow, you certainly have an impressive memory. I'm surprised you remember that."

"Well," mom said as her cheeks flushed. "You and your husband made a very striking couple. Some people are just harder to forget than others."

"Thank you, Deirdre, that's so sweet."

"So, what brings you here tonight?" Mom laughed nervously as she rubbed the back of her neck. "Is it Girl Scout Cookie time already?"

Dr. Charlotte shook her head. "Actually, I'm here on business."

Mom's eyebrows bunched together in confusion. "But aren't you a psychologist or psychiatrist or something? And you're making a house call? Here?"

Dr. Charlotte stole a quick glance at me and then asked my mom if they could speak in private.

As mom led her deeper into our house, I started following them. Dr. Charlotte whispered something in mom's ear, and then Mom told me I had to go to my room. I turned around and started heading up the stairs, but then I snuck back down and hid behind an ornate walnut sideboard in the formal dining area next to the sitting room.

"Thanks for meeting with me, Deirdre. The school board assigned me to your son's case, and I wanted to talk with you personally."

"What?" Mom said as she bit her lip and looked down at the floor. "Why were you assigned to my son?"

"I'm a child psychologist who works with sexually abused

children. After your son's encounter with the principal yesterday, the board brought me in to talk to him. As a general rule, I don't divulge the explicit contents of my sessions with the child's parents, but some of the things your son said were troubling."

Wait a second? What happened to the *"She's safe, and you can trust her"* spiel Mrs. Johnson had given me? Dr. Charlotte had even crossed her heart. *Bela was right; She's a liar.* She even had Mrs. Johnson fooled. Thankfully, Bela knew and stopped me before I told the big, fat fibber anything else.

Mom's forehead furrowed up. She looked sick. "Why would the school call in a sexual abuse expert?"

"Well, because of the sexual accusation your son made against the principal, Mr. Richard Davis."

"My son did what?" Mom blurted out.

"Yesterday, at 1:14 p.m., he called the local police office from a school pay phone. The dispatcher said Adam sounded distraught and stated that the principal had been forcing him to touch him inappropriately."

Mom looked like someone had just slapped her.

"Two police officers responded to the call, and upon entering Davis's office, they found him threatening your son both verbally and physically."

Mom's face twisted in rage. "He did what?!" She started shaking as she said, "I swear I'll kill him!"

"Please calm down, Deirdre. Your son provided proof concerning his activities, and I can guarantee that Davis will spend a long time in jail. However, there seems to be an inconsistency and I'm hoping we can clear it up."

Mom took a deep breath, then nodded. "Okay, what do you want to know?"

"Late yesterday afternoon, the police raided Davis's home, and it turns out that he's been sexually abusing students in the school for several years. The problem from our perspective is that all of his victims have been female. Targeting your son doesn't seem to fit with his MO. We were hoping you could help us better understand the situation."

Mom appeared panicked as she tilted her head downward and made quick, jerky attempts to tuck several loose strands of hair behind her left ear. "I swear, Charlotte… Dr. Brown, I didn't know any of this was going on. My husband passed away recently, and it's been really hard on me. I know I haven't been the best mother lately, but I promise I've been doing the best that I can. I swear I knew none of this."

Dr. Charlotte touched Mom's right forearm. "Deirdre, relax. You're not under investigation. We just need additional information."

Mom just nodded nervously.

Dr. Charlotte flipped through her notes, then her finger landed on a page. "Are you aware that Adam believes Davis has an interest in you? He said the principal has '*the hots*' for you, to use Adam's words."

Mom looked stunned. "I… I had no idea. Nothing has ever happened between us. I don't think we've even talked for more than a minute or two."

"Once again, I'm not accusing you of anything, but I had to ask." Dr. Charlotte pulled out another folder in her briefcase and thumbed through it. As she skimmed through her papers, she said, "While we weren't able to confirm your son's specific sexual assault allegations, we were able to confirm one of his peripheral ones. It appears Davis had drawn up an order of expulsion for your son's removal." She paused and looked at Mom. "Were you aware of its existence, Deirdre?"

"No… I mean, maybe. I heard nothing about it from the school, but I think my son may have mentioned it to me. I thought little of his story, though, because I never heard anything about it officially, or even unofficially. Is it even legal to expel him without informing me first?"

Dr. Charlotte cocked her head. "I don't know the answer to that, but I wouldn't think so."

Mom's face looked a little green. "Is he going to be expelled?"

"Not that I know of. Davis hadn't submitted the signed order to the school board, and I doubt that they will follow up on it now that the sexual assault allegations have come to light."

After another pause, Dr. Charlotte said, "I'd like to shift gears a little. Are you aware that your son claims his deceased sister visits him?"

Mom nodded. "Yes, he's mentioned it to me."

"He also said something else I found unusual. When I asked him what occurred in Davis's office, he said he wasn't there. He said his sister went in his place. Do you have any idea what he meant by that?"

"I think I might. Adam mentioned his sister stepped into his body and took care of everything for him."

"You mean like a possession?"

Mom shrugged her shoulders. "Those were his words, not mine. I have no idea what he meant."

"Okay, that could be important." She set the folder aside and looked at Mom. "I have two divergent observations concerning this, Deirdre. The first one comes from my role as a psychologist. Sometimes when a child is confronted with something they just can't wrap their mind around, they will invent an imaginary friend or protector and use it as a defense mechanism. They stand behind the persona and use it as a shield.

"My second observation is as a Catholic and someone who has seen things no one should ever have to. Contrary to current cultural beliefs, nothing in the Bible supports human souls wandering the Earth. Unfortunately, the Bible gives numerous accounts of demons doing so. Demons often portray themselves as young females to gain their victim's trust. The only reason I'm even considering this option is that your son told me things about my sister's dog that he had no way of knowing. He said that Bela told him… though it's possible he may have unrealized latent psychic abilities. Our job is to figure out what Bela represents: a manifestation of his psyche or a possible possession. I can help you on the psychological end, but I recommend you get in touch with your priest or minister for the spiritual side of things. Perhaps you could start by doing a house blessing."

Mom's face fell. She looked disappointed. "Have… Have you considered that maybe his sister really is visiting him?"

Dr. Charlotte's features softened. "Deirdre, my heart goes out to you. I know you want to believe your little girl is coming around, but don't succumb to your emotions on this. You'll only end up heartbroken. Trust me when I say it's not her. Guard your heart in this."

CHAPTER 16

DR. CHARLOTTE BROWN

ADAM AND DEIRDRE had been on my mind for days. They seemed like such a sweet little family, and it was a shame they were experiencing so much hardship in their lives. I didn't mention it to them, but I also had some psychic-like abilities. Like Adam, as a child, sometimes I saw dark shadows too. Though my talent didn't seem as strong as his, on occasion, I also knew things I couldn't possibly know. In fact, my angst over possible but improbable psychic abilities was one of the main factors that drove me to become a psychologist in the first place. Trying to figure out if I was insane or supernaturally gifted. In the end, I chose neither, settling on a highly sensitive and intuitive psyche instead.

And my psyche knew two things for sure after meeting with Adam and his mom: First, something was wrong with their house. Second, something was wrong with Adam. Both gave off a sickening negative energy that I couldn't possibly ignore. I hoped a simple cleansing and house blessing would take care of their dwelling. However, figuring out the proper course of action for Adam would be more complex.

I pored over my case notes again to see if I'd missed anything and decided to take a break. I went to the refrigerator to grab a soda, but we were out. Rummaging around to see if anything tasty remained, the pickings appeared pretty slim. Either I could go grocery shopping or go on a diet, and I liked food way too much for the second option. It was probably a good idea to step away from my work since I wasn't making any progress anyway. But that might change if I looked at everything with fresh eyes. I would have liked some company, but my husband was stuck at the office working late to finish up some big project. I grabbed my keys and purse, hopped into my old gray Suburban, and left my modest two-story saltbox home behind.

Upon leaving my immediate neighborhood, I drove down some cracked concrete side streets that ran between nondescript forested areas and isolated homes. Accessing the larger county road that tied together several nearby communities, I stayed the course until I exited and merged onto the expressway. Pushing down on the gas with my foot, the car surged and its rapid acceleration filled me with a pleasant sensation. As I was getting the vehicle up to speed, I saw what appeared to be a young boy walking along the guardrail and a surge of fiery anger coursed through me. Maybe it was judgmental, but I didn't care. Abuse comes in many forms and his parents should be shot for letting this happen.

As I drew closer, he stopped and turned his face toward me. I did a double-take. "Oh my!" I whispered.

I decelerated and pulled to a stop in front of the boy. I cautiously exited my vehicle and approached him. "Adam, what are you doing out here on this road? Don't you know this is dangerous?"

"I'm sorry, Dr. Charlotte. It's just that it's my mom's birthday tomorrow, and I wanted to get her a card. There's nobody to take me to the store, so I have to walk there."

"Well, Adam," I said, frowning, "it's an honest desire, but walking alone on an expressway can be dangerous. If you promise me not to do it again, I'll drive you to the store."

Adam's face seemed to light up. "Really? You'd do that for me?"

I raised an eyebrow. "And why wouldn't I do that for you?"

Adam shrugged. "I don't know. I guess it's just that nobody ever offers to help me with anything. Mom helps me a little on her better days, but that's about it. I've gotten used to doing everything on my own."

My heart went out to the poor kid. I'd come from a large family and always had someone to help me when I was growing up. I couldn't imagine what it was like to be so young and isolated.

"Well," I said, smiling, "I don't know about anyone else, but I would be happy to help you." I held out my hand to him. "So, do we have a deal?"

Adam shuffled his feet back and forth on the ground, and then he kicked a small pebble. "Well, thanks for the offer, Dr. Charlotte. I better get going now before it gets too late."

My mouth fell open in stunned surprise. "Wait, Adam, what am I missing here?"

He shrugged again. "It's just that I can't promise you that, and I don't want to lie. Like I said, I have to do most things myself."

It broke my heart. The boy was being abused at school and apparently at home, too. I figured it might be time to get social services involved. However, I didn't say any of this to him. Instead, I kept a neutral look on my face and said, "Never mind about the promise. Get in the car, and we'll go get your mother a nice birthday card."

As I drove, I waited to see if Adam would initiate any conversation, but instead, we sat in silence the whole time. I glanced over at him and had to admire his looks. He was handsome for someone so young, and he radiated a calm, intelligent, contemplative look. I felt confident that he'd receive lots of female attention when he was older. However, his looks reminded me not to judge a book by its cover. This was a kid who looked like he had it all, but in reality had very little. It seemed like life was conspiring to cheat him out of what he could be. I was so deep in thought that I hadn't even noticed that I'd exited the expressway. I was driving on autopilot.

My reverie ended when Adam said, "Mr. Davis told me he'd take me there when I'm a little older." He pointed ahead off to the right.

I followed his finger, and to my surprise, the first thing I noticed was my husband's Ford pickup ahead of me just a little further up the road. The second thing I noticed was his truck turning into the area's only gentlemen's club… the same club Adam had been pointing to. My heart sank as my mouth opened and I let out an involuntary groan. I pulled in after Mark, but stayed back a bit. I was sure he hadn't seen me. My so-called spouse pulled around to the rear parking lot on the other side of the building, away from the street. *What a little sneak!* Mark knew I dealt with sexual perversion and its repercussions for a living. He knew how many lives and marriages this sort of thing ruined. He even knew that a family friend had raped me on my fifteenth birthday. A white-hot fury descended upon me. *How could he?!*

After he parked, I pulled up behind his car, blocking him in. *I should have waited and run him over.*

As I stormed out of my car, I looked over at Adam and said, "Stay here in the car. I have to take care of something, then I'll be right back."

As Mark climbed out of his truck, I clenched my fists at my sides and yelled, "How could you?! What's wrong with you?!"

He turned around, and his face fell.

We stood right there and had it out for the next ten to fifteen minutes. I wasn't even paying attention to the time until I saw flashing lights behind me. Turning around, I saw a police cruiser blocking my car in. The hair on my skin bristled at the thought that someone in this den of sin had actually called the police on us. Two officers stepped out of the vehicle and approached us. I opened my mouth to speak, but they walked right past Mark and me and into the building. *What the…?*

I stood there, confused. I glanced back at my vehicle, and I didn't see Adam sitting in it. *Oh no… it can't be?*

I ran into the building, and the place was dead quiet. The eyes of the strippers and the numerous clientele were fixed on a young boy and the two police officers talking to him. I heard Adam say, "Dr. Charlotte brought me here." He turned and looked at me with that calm, intelligent face. Then he raised an arm and pointed at me. "That's her right there."

CHAPTER 17

ADAM MATTHEW

THE NEXT DAY found me back at school—and grounded at home yet again. Mom had been furious with me when the police brought me home the night before and told her they'd picked me up at a nightclub for "gentlemen" and that Dr. Charlotte had taken me there. I had little memory of it, so I shrugged when Mom demanded an explanation. She grounded me until I answered her, and that was that. Dr. Charlotte was removed from my case, so I had to meet with a new psychologist and she brought up the same exact subject my mother had. I just shrugged my shoulders again. She didn't seem any happier with me than Mom had, but at least she couldn't ground me.

After my session, as I headed for my locker, I heard and then saw a big ruckus forming down the hall. My classmate, John Tillis, came running past me, so I grabbed his arm and said, "What's going on?"

He whirled in my direction and said, "Dude, they found Rick Kennedy and he's alive!" Then he continued running.

Even though Rick was a creep, a sense of relief washed over me. He'd vanished about a week ago from school, and no one seemed to know anything. Some people thought Rick had run away; others thought he'd met a bad end.

I arrived at the freight elevator service area, and through tiny breaks in the crowd of kids and teachers gathered there, I saw Rick being brought out of the elevator shaft by a couple of firefighters. They had strapped his body to a thin, flat board and lifted it up and out to the floor. A trio of EMTs moved the board and his supine body to a waiting stretcher. As I pushed deeper into the crowd, I caught my first real glimpse of him, and it pulled at my stomach. Rick looked horrible. He had dried blood, grease, and dirt all over him, and he looked super skinny. His skin hung loose, like a bag. I couldn't tell if he was alive or not, but he looked kind of dead to me. Emma Brooks stood in a corner fidgeting, so I walked over to her and asked her what was happening.

She told me that an elevator repairman had found Rick alive at the bottom of the elevator shaft, but he couldn't talk because he was in a comma or coma or something like that. Then she told me the teachers were surprised that he hadn't died… something about kids being super tough. She added the ambulance people were taking him to the hospital to experiment on him.

Emma could be a little slow, so I doubted that, but I kept it to myself because I didn't want to hurt her feelings.

As she continued chattering away, Mrs. Johnson showed up with several police officers, and they started shooing people away so that the EMTs had space to work. She told us we didn't need to be watching it and instructed us to go back to our classrooms. They started hooking up an IV to Rick's left arm as I walked away.

After using the restroom and then backtracking to my

locker, I headed to my next class. I happened upon Danny and saw him staring into his locker. He didn't see me, and I was happy to keep it that way. As I walked behind him, I heard my name, turned back to look, and my feet got tangled up. Something soft broke my impending fall—Danny's back. He pitched forward, and his face hit the edge of his locker, then he groaned in pain. He got up off his knees and turned around. His eyes widened when he saw me, and then he started cursing while his hand reached up and touched his bloody face. His nose looked misshapen, like someone had pushed it off to one side, and I realized it was broken. I stood there in disbelief. When I'd tripped and busted his teeth out, no one believed it had been an accident. And if they didn't believe me the first time, they definitely weren't going to believe it a second time. I didn't know what to do, so I started walking. I barely heard Danny when he yelled I would pay for this. As I kept going, the whole world just faded away.

That night, I was fast asleep in bed when I awoke to a licking sensation on my face. *Ghoul!* My heart pounded in my chest and my ears boomed to its beat as my eyes flew open, looking violently about. My expectations in relation to what I saw caused a wave of disorientation to hit me, and I forced myself to swallow the hot vomit that tried escaping from my throat. I found myself staring into the face of a curious black lab mix, and to my surprise, my bedroom walls didn't surround me, but cornstalks. I jumped up, looking around. Nothing but corn greeted me in every direction—that, and a bright full moon overhead, unobstructed thanks to the cloudless night. I tried to get my bearings straight, but it was impossible in the endless sea of corn.

"Bela!" I called out into the night.

No answer came.

It seemed to me that my house should be to the moon's right, so I started following a row of corn in that direction. The dog kept pace with me for a while, but it seemed to lose interest and disappeared.

Black shadows and faces flitted in and out of the surrounding corn as I walked. I felt sure that it wasn't just my imagination, but it was all out of the corners of my eyes, so I couldn't be certain. After what seemed like an eternity, I finally came to a road and walked along it. Coming to an intersection, my heart fell as I stood at the intersection of County Line South and Orchard Road. I was at least ten miles away from home in the middle of the night. I tried calling out to Bela again, but still no answer. The world felt like it had been fading away earlier today, but it was in extreme focus now as I stood alone in the silvery moonlight. As I continued toward home, every sound made by a frog, bug, or leaf etched itself into my mind. The light breeze seemed to howl, and every shadow contained hidden menace. At one point, I even thought I heard footsteps behind me and the face of Malachai from 'Children of the Corn' flashed through my head. The vision of the crazed murderer sent a small shudder through my frame. I was absolutely miserable, and it hit me hard that no one even cared. Though Mom might a little if she wasn't passed out drunk right now.

As I walked alone, I started thinking about my life. Before Dad died, things had been good. He was my friend, we hung out together, and we had lots of food to eat. Mom was happy then too, and she acted like moms were supposed to act. But now, sometimes it seemed like I was the parent and she was the kid. Some days were okay, but she'd get drunk and fall apart on others. At first, she only drank at night, but now it was becoming a daytime thing too.

A spark of anger arose in me, and I realized who was to blame for everything: my father. Things were fine before he died, but he didn't stick around for us. Like my sister, he wasn't strong enough to hang on to life. But unlike her, he didn't even bother to come around to see how me and Mom were doing. And we weren't doing good at all. We could have used his help. I felt a new emotion toward him then: hatred. *What kind of father leaves his kid anyway?* I figured he could have found a way to stick around if he'd loved us enough.

As I fumed and walked onward, I realized the hate and anger I felt had driven out my fear and loneliness. I'd always heard these two emotions were bad things, but they seemed pretty good to me at the moment. They empowered me and made me strong.

When I'd made it about halfway home, I started getting back into civilization. More and more farmhouses appeared, which was good because I had my eye out for something specific. My gaze finally landed on my desire. By the moon's light, I could see a water pump sitting in a yard unguarded by any household pets and not surrounded by a fence. I was so thirsty I felt like I could drink an ocean. Tiptoeing toward the pump because I knew someone could get shot in these parts for trespassing on private property, I started working the handle, and soon, clear, cool water flowed out of the water spout and splashed into a tin bucket below. I lifted it to my lips when it was half full and drank. Nothing ever tasted so good to me. I took several large gulps before lights came on in the house and someone started fumbling with the door locks.

Hurling the bucket aside, I ran for all I was worth. I made it back to the safety of the street and then slowed to a walk once I'd gotten far enough away from the house. My running had triggered barking from several nearby dogs, but I didn't see anybody around, so I figured I was in the clear for sure.

As I drew closer to Old Man Crab's house, I made a slight course correction and walked past my old home first. When I saw it, disgust bloomed in my chest and I didn't know what I'd ever seen in the stupid place.

My feet continued to eat up the distance until I found myself in front of Mr. Crab's ancient mansion. I only hesitated a moment before stepping into the entryway, but I knew I had worried about nothing. I wasn't in trouble. No one even knew I'd been out. The clock showed it was four in the morning, but no one was waiting up for me. In fact, no one was even around, which made me sad. I'm sure Old Man Crab was sleeping soundly in his bed with a belly full of warm soup, and mom was sleeping soundly in hers with a belly full of Jim Beam.

As I dragged my tired, aching body over to the couch, I knew I was well and truly alone and no one really cared whether I lived or died. Mom's actions made it clear that she didn't care about me, despite all her words to the contrary. All she really wanted was my dad and Bela, but she'd gotten stuck with me instead. I felt anger at first, and then a cold indifference settled over me.

Screw it all, I thought as I collapsed onto the big leather sofa and instantly fell asleep.

CHAPTER 18

ADAM MATTHEW

Morning arrived, and I was fast asleep when the front doorbell rang. I ignored it, but the doorbell rang again, and then someone started beating on the door with their fist. I half sat up and saw my mom stumbling down the stairs in her nightgown with her hands over her ears. She looked hungover to me.

Mom didn't even notice me as she went by, then she fumbled with the door lock. When she got the door open, two men in blue uniforms pushed their way into the foyer. Over Mom's protests, I could hear them demanding to know my whereabouts. One of the policemen glanced over and saw me, and he smacked the other on the shoulder. They powered past my mother and approached me. One officer spun me around and cuffed my hands behind my back while the other officer read me my Miranda rights. They hauled me out of the house over my mom's objections, and then they put me in the back seat of their squad car. At least they didn't shove me into the side door first like they had with Davis.

We rode to the police station, where they took my fingerprints and photographed me. Then they stuck me in a small room with a desk and one mirror and left. I called out to Bela several times under my breath, but she didn't answer. Finally, the door opened, and a different police officer sat down in front of me.

"Good morning," he said. "My name is Officer Wilkes. Do you know why we've brought you here today, Adam?"

I shook my head.

He took a picture out of the manila folder he was carrying and laid it on the desk.

Whoa, that's messed up.

Before he could say anything, I said, "What happened to Danny's nose? It looks like somebody smooshed it."

The officer looked me directly in the eyes for several seconds, and I swear he didn't blink once. "That's what we're hoping to find out, son. Can you tell me what happened?"

"Well, like I said, it looks like his nose got smooshed… like it met up with a sledgehammer. Did Danny tell you who did it?"

The officer pulled at his chin and said, "Yes, son, he said it was you."

"Well, that's not true," I said as I shook my head.

"Why not?"

"Why?" I said with an incredulous look on my face. "Because I'd remember it if I'd done something like that."

The officer raised his eyebrows in mock surprise, and I knew he didn't believe a word I'd said. "So if you didn't do it, why is he blaming you for it?"

I shrugged. "I don't know. Maybe his brains got smooshed too."

He placed his face within several inches of mine. "Are you being funny, son? Is this funny to you?"

"No."

"So if you didn't do it, why did you leave school without permission early yesterday afternoon, and why didn't you show up at school this morning?" Then Officer Wilkes steepled his fingers together and looked directly into my eyes… like he was waiting for my confession.

As if.

"Well, I got all freaked out after seeing what happened to Rick Kennedy, so I started walking. And then I didn't get home until late last night, so I overslept."

"Why would that upset you? If I thought someone had tried stoning me, I might feel vindicated. But certainly not 'freaked out,' as you say."

I swallowed hard, then licked my dry lips. "Well, yeah, I was mad about that until I saw Rick come out of the elevator shaft. He looked dead to me, but Emma said he was still alive, but I still felt bad for him."

Officer Wilkes reached into his folder again and pulled out a picture of Rick lying on a stretcher. "Is this what you're referring to?"

I nodded.

"You know," he said as he rubbed his chin. "I find it interesting that you had an altercation with both boys, and a short time later, they both got assaulted. And Danny more than once—"

"Does 'altercation' mean like when they hit me with the rocks?"

He looked down at his folder and flipped through several pictures, then he looked back up at me. "Yes. Do you feel they deserved what happened to them?"

I shook my head. "Not really. Especially not Rick."

"Why not Rick?"

A slight shudder went through me as I pictured him lying

there all dead looking. "Because he was hurt bad. He could have died. "

"So, do you have an alibi? You know, someone to vouch for you?"

I shook my head again. "I don't think so."

"So why should I believe you?" With that, he sat there doing his staring, non-blinking thing again.

"Well, Officer Wilkes, do you have anybody that saw me smoosh Danny's nose or push Rick into the elevator shaft?"

"No."

"Then couldn't I ask you the same question?"

"Alright, kid, that's a fair point." Then a thin smile stretched across his stony face. It looked like it hurt. "Why don't you just tell me what happened and I'm sure I'll understand and be able to help you out."

"Help me out with what?" I protested. "I did nothing wrong."

"Okay, fine, kid. But if I find out you're lying to me, I'll come down extra hard on you."

"Okay."

"Do you have anything else you'd like to add, Adam, before we let you go?"

I was about to tell him I didn't, but before the words made it to my mouth, something flashed through my head like a movie—almost like I was there. That had never happened to me before without touching something first, but maybe it was Bela's doing. I'd have to ask her if she ever showed up. I still planned on keeping my mouth shut, but then I started feeling angry and mean again, like I'd felt last night. My dad was already dead, so I couldn't get back at him. But maybe getting back at Danny Pechman's dad would be the next best thing. After all, he was a dad, and he certainly was a jerk. He'd lied about the whole alibi thing, and he even tried to get me expelled from school.

"So, Officer Wilkes," I said as I fidgeted with my hands, "if I told you something bad about Danny's dad, would that be tattling?"

He placed both hands out, palms up. "It depends. Tell me what you know, and I'll let you know either way."

"Do you remember that robbery at Mr. Jones's hardware store a few weeks ago?"

That got his interest. His eyes perked up as he rolled his right hand in the air and said, "Yes. Go on."

"Bud Pechman did that. He hid the tools he stole in three barrels in his garage. He put old auto parts over them to make it look like he's collecting scrap metal in the barrels."

"And how, pray tell, would you know that?"

"Easy. I heard Danny bragging about it to Rick before Rick disappeared."

Well, I thought, *I didn't really hear it in real life, but I saw and heard it in my head just now, so that's probably close enough.*

His eyes widened in disbelief. "And why would he tell him that?"

"Because they're friends. All I know is if you check the barrels, you'll find Mr. Jones's stuff. So is that tattling, Officer Wilkes?"

He finally flashed me a genuine smile. "No, kid. If it's true, you've done well."

CHAPTER 19

ADAM MATTHEW

SEVERAL DAYS PASSED, and nothing worth mentioning happened to me. It felt like a minor miracle. Late one evening, Old Man Crab was sitting in the kitchen eating his soup while I sat in the living room with Mom, watching TV. As the movie neared its end, someone banged hard on the front door.

Mom gazed at the entryway and asked, "Were you expecting somebody, Adam?"

I shook my head. "Nope. Nobody."

She looked at me out of the corner of her eye. "You're not in trouble with the police again, are you?"

"No!" I said as I crossed my arms against my chest. "And I wasn't in trouble with the police in the first place, so there can't be an *again*. I can't help it if Danny accused me of something I didn't do."

She gazed at me and rolled her eyes, smirking the whole time. She looked amused.

As we continued watching TV, the pounding started again. Three times now.

I looked at Mom and said, "Are you going to get that?"

"Nope," she said. "How about you? You going to get that?"

"Nope!" I laughed.

And that would have been the end of it except for the cement flowerpot that came crashing through the side window. The flowerpot hadn't even come to a complete stop when I saw a foot kick out the remaining jagged glass at the bottom of the windowsill, and then I saw a man's body squeeze through the narrow opening. As he rushed us, Mom and I jumped up from the couch—and I recognized him immediately. It was Danny's dad, Bud Pechman. His face looked crazed, like someone else had just drunk his last beer. He came right at me and punched me in the forehead. The blow was so fast I never saw it coming. Then he did it again. Once in the mouth... then he popped me in the nose... and I could feel blood trickling from both.

He gloated as he said, "That's for my stupid kid." Then he grabbed me by my hair and pulled me close. "Who ratted me out, boy?"

Mom looked furious as her outstretched fingers reached toward his face like claws. He flung me at her, and we both tumbled backward.

He leered at my mom and said, "Don't you worry, sweet-cheeks. You'll get your chance. You and I are going to have a real good time after I get done with this trash."

Mom snarled and rushed him again, but he flung his arm around and hit her in the face with a pistol. She collapsed, and I saw red on her face and on the floor by her head.

Something powerful swept through me, and I rushed Bud and knocked his legs out from underneath him. He tumbled forward and cracked his head on the floor.

He grabbed at his head with one hand and started cursing while raising his gun toward me. As I ran through the closest doorway, I heard a bullet make a wisp-like sound through the air inches from my head, and then I heard it thunk into the far wall. I scurried into the kitchen and ran right past Old Man Crab, who was still sitting there eating his soup. I made it to the back door, but Mr. Crab had padlocked it. That was a first, and I didn't know what kind of game he was playing.

He looked at me with his rheumy eyes and said, "What you gonna do now, boy?"

Then Old Man Crab looked over at the basement door with anticipation. The creep was actually setting me up for round two. My heart dropped when I realized my choices were to stay in the kitchen and get shot or head into the basement and get eaten. Me and the old man were going to have a good long talk if I made it out of this alive.

I exited through the basement door and started down just as Bud Pechman entered the main kitchen area. Halfway down the basement steps, I heard Old Man Crab cackle and say, "He went that way." I'd just cleared the bottom step when Bud appeared at the top of the stairwell and fired off another shot at me. It ricocheted off the concrete floor next to my feet. I fled into the darkness as his feet clomped down the old wooden stairs. As I ran, my mind came up with a plan to run back to the coal room and hide in the old cast iron boiler until Bud tired of looking for me and left… or got eaten by the ghoul. Somehow, though, I got turned around in the dark, so my plan never materialized. Without my vision, I realized I had no idea where I was in the basement. As I felt along the stone wall, I put my hand into something sticky and wet. I thought it was the ghoul, so I jerked back and fell on my butt.

Bud chuckled and said, "I hear you, boy. Come on out, and I'll make it quick-like. You tell me what I want to know, and all your worldly problems will be over with. You'll never know what hit you."

He sounded much closer to me than I would have liked. I estimated thirty feet or so. I heard a click-click, and then a small flame came to life. Bud was standing there holding a cigarette lighter, and we could easily see each other. Fortunately, I found myself right next to a doorway, so I ducked behind it as he squeezed off another round. Before the flame went out, I saw another opening in the dim light, and I made it through that one too without having to feel my way around.

As I tried to find my way out of my predicament, Bud continued his running commentary: "Yeah, boy, me and your mama go way back. Me and your daddy both courted her, but it turned out she had a thing for weasels. Just think, boy, you could have been a real man if your mama had been born with any sense. But she went and stuck you with weasel genes instead. Well, don't you worry none, son; after I get done with your fine-looking mama tonight, your baby brother will get the real man genes you so desperately needed."

My chest tightened with fear at the realization that Danny's dad was genuinely crazy—and that he wasn't kidding when he said he'd kill me and rape my mother. He'd do it and feel completely justified about it.

"Bela," I hissed under my breath. "Where are you?"

Her voice wafted up to me: "I'm right here next to you. Right where I've always been."

"If you've been with me the whole time," I whispered, "Then why haven't you answered me?"

"Oh, that. I'm mad at you… that's why."

"Mad about what?" I said, rubbing my forehead in confusion. "I thought we were friends—brother and sister! You said you were lonely and wanted to play together."

"It just doesn't seem fair to me," she pouted. "You have a nice body to live in, and I don't. But if you shared your body with me, then I could have one too."

I shook my head. "But you said you didn't want to live in a yucky boy's body."

"I've changed my mind. I'm tired of being a ghost."

"Well, what if I say no?"

"That's okay with me, Adam. You're about five minutes away from being a ghost too, and then we can be together forever."

"But what about Mom?"

"Don't worry about her. She'll be with us soon enough. Later tonight, by my estimation."

"Okay, well, what if I say yes?"

"If you say yes, I'll protect you from Bud Pechman, and then we'll both share this body together, and Mom will continue to live and take care of both of us."

I heard exaggerated sniffing sounds, and then Bud said, "Oh, Adam boy, I smell weasel."

Bela said, "So what's it going to be, brother? Either we both have your body, or neither one of us has it.… Choose."

I groaned in frustration and fear. "Alright, Bela, you can come live in my body."

"I can come live in it, and I *never* have to leave, right?"

"Yes yes yes! You can live in it and you never have to leave. Now help Mom and me!"

I felt Bela flow into my body, but unlike before, her presence felt much stronger now—overwhelming even.

"Bela, stop it!" I hissed. "You're scaring me."

Her laugh echoed in my head. Then, using my own vocal cords, she said, "Stupid fool. Pathetic and weak. Now shut up."

I tried to respond, but my mouth wouldn't move. My body started walking, and I realized I could see perfectly well in the complete darkness thanks to a silvery light that came from everywhere and nowhere. Whatever its source, it illuminated everything. But that wasn't the only difference I noted. Now that I could see with Bela's eyes, blood liberally decorated the walls and floor around me and foul things scurried about. The very walls of this place seeped with corruption—almost as if the basement itself were alive and evil. I finally understood why me and mom had fared so poorly after my dad's death. It was this place and we were its victims. But whatever I had inside me now was something else; it wasn't part of this place. Suddenly, I knew I had carried it with me from the graveyard that night. I'd been its ticket out of there—and it wasn't my sister. It had never been human. Dr. Charlotte was right when she called it a "*demon.*"

I felt something else, too. It hated me passionately, and I sensed that we'd never been friends. The demon could barely stand to be in my presence, and it had used me just as much as it had used those around me. Like it said, I was so stupid.

I tried to fight against it, but its will proved too strong for me.

"Ohhh, Buddy boy," I heard the demon say in my voice. "Come out, come out wherever you are."

An explosion of muttering and swearing drifted to my ears and then Bud Pechman came into view, holding his lighter above his head. I stepped behind another stone wall as he lifted his pistol toward me, and then he started swearing again. My body started walking deeper into the basement as the demon in me whistled a casual tune. Bud followed the sound for a few minutes, and then he stopped. Maybe his common sense was starting to kick in. The lighter went out, and after three attempts, he managed to flick it on again. Then the maniac did a double-take because the walls looked much older in this part of the basement. They appeared more like someone had carved them right out of the limestone or, maybe more accurately, looked like something had clawed its way through the stone.

Bud rubbed a hand against one wall just as my voice sang out, "Olly Olly oxen free."

His head snapped toward me, and all his hesitation was forgotten. He rushed at me as I stepped into a side tunnel.

My voice rang out again. "Come on, Buddy boy. Snap to it. Your time is almost up, and then you'll be it. Then I'll go play with your bastard son, and Buddy boy's line will be dead. Father and son, together."

Bud's voice dripped with venom: "So the little weasel thinks he's grown a pair? Welcome to the chopping block, son."

He rushed into the large cavern-like room like a rhinoceros as he held his flickering lighter above his head.

I crept up behind him as he looked at the skeletal remains scattered around the room… human remains. I could feel a sense of anxiety rising in Bud as my voice said, "Boo!"

He whirled around, and when his eyes locked on to my face… he blanched. Grasping his pistol tight, he spun and tried to land a roundhouse. While his punches had seemed lightning fast to me before, this one seemed slow and my body easily side-stepped the incoming blow. Realizing his sucker punch missed, he decided to shoot me this time. I could see his pistol coming up to my eye level in slow motion even as my hands pushed him in the chest… hard. He flew backward several feet, and his body made a splatting sound as it hit a wall of mud and dirt.

Bud shook his head and was getting ready to disengage from the muck when ghastly white arms reached out from the mud wall and enveloped him. A massive head materialized above him, and a pink snake-like tongue slithered out of its mouth and licked Bud's face. Bud looked up and screamed. The ghoul smiled that impossibly large smile, and then he clamped his pointy teeth down around Bud's shoulder. Bud's arm and fingers spasmed, and the lighter fell from his grasp, plunging the room back into silvery darkness. His free arm swung back and forth in a crazed circular motion as he took a few potshots and hit nothing.

As the ghoul dragged him back into the muddy wall, Bud's screaming intensified as he was drawn beneath its surface. Once fully submerged, I heard muffled sounds and then saw frantic movement under the mud for about thirty seconds, and then nothing.

As I stared through my eyes in disbelief, Bud emerged from his final resting place. Or at least his soul had. He'd left his body behind in the wall. Looking around wildly, Bud approached me… eyes pleading and lips moving. He appeared to be talking frantically, but nothing but silence greeted my ears.

My muscles relaxed as the demon inside me released its control, and my body collapsed to the ground. The blackness that had been inside of me coiled around Bud's soul, and a giant, snake-like mouth swallowed him whole. As his soul went down in the unnatural silence, I felt a primal scream issue from Bud, unlike anything I'd ever experienced in person or seen portrayed at the movies. It shook me to my very core, and I picked myself up off the floor and ran into the pitch-black maw of my dark surroundings.

PART 2
EXORCISM

ONE YEAR LATER

And the man in whom the evil spirit was leaped on them, and overcame them, and prevailed against them, so that they fled out of that house naked and wounded.

(ACTS 19:16)

CHAPTER 20

DEIRDRE MATTHEW

SITTING ALONE IN the hospital cafeteria, I looked around as I waited. Long Formica tables and cheap plastic and chrome chairs dominated the décor. The subtle smells of cafeteria food hung in the air and it made my stomach grumble. With pens in their front pockets and stethoscopes hanging around their necks, doctors sat in small groups talking animatedly to each other. Other groupings of nurses, patients, and business types also sat around chatting as they ate. I seemed to be the only one sitting alone. Of course, that felt entirely natural to me. At least for the current me. In high school, I was a cheerleader and homecoming queen. I was smart, popular, and had lots of friends.

When I'd left for college, my future looked bright. Then, in my last semester in school, I made the mistake of getting pregnant. I ended up dropping out and getting married, and it seemed like a good idea... for a while. My husband was a good man—along with being smart and motivated... and he had a skyrocketing career. When he became the youngest plant manager ever at any of the company's numerous locations, I knew we were on our way to Robin Leach's champagne wishes and caviar dreams. Then the unthinkable happened. Just mere months into my husband's new position, his doctor diagnosed him with pancreatic cancer. At the time, I knew very little about it. Not long after that, though, I knew all too well that the disease has a five percent survival rate.

After his passing, I crawled into a bottle and left my son behind. Not physically, of course, but emotionally and mentally. He tried to get my attention, but I had little to do with him. Then the day came when he went into the basement and never came back to me—the slap in the face that finally woke me up. Since then, I started working hard to make me right again.

Seeing my lunch companion approaching me brought me out of my reverie. Dressed in smart-looking business attire that complimented her dark brown hair and brown eyes, she looked as professional as I'd remembered her.

I stood and shook her hand, then said, "Thank you for seeing me on such short notice, Dr. Brown."

"Please, Deirdre, this is an informal get-together. Call me Charlotte."

I nodded. "Okay… Charlotte. Well, thanks for seeing me."

"My pleasure. So how have you been? Are things going well for you?"

"I suppose?" I shrugged. "I finally got a job—here, as a matter of fact—and moved into my own place. I also met someone here a few months ago, and things seem to be going well between us. I don't know if anything will come of it, but we'll see."

She gave me a warm smile. "That's wonderful. So what can I do for you?"

Well, here goes nothing. I took a steadying breath and pushed my hair out of my face before proceeding. "So, Charlotte, I was hoping you could tell me what happened to Danny Pechman. Did they ever find him? Is he still alive?"

"Deirdre," she said, "why would you call me here to ask me that?"

I folded my arms across my chest and frowned. "I have my reasons. Please indulge me in this. Is he still alive?"

"Honestly, I don't know," she said with a certain impatience as the well-manicured, lacquered fingernails of her right hand tapped on the table's hard surface. "After his father Bud disappeared, he went into social services because none of his relatives would take him. A few weeks after that, Danny disappeared too. It's thought that his father snatched him out of the place because that makes the most sense, but no one knows for certain."

A chill shot through my body. "Oh, Charlotte," I said as deep remorse settled into my bones, "Danny's dead."

She shook her head. "That's not a factual statement." Then she cocked her head and appeared to be thinking. A few seconds later, she said, "He's missing… and almost certainly alive. His father will mess up at some point, and he and Danny will be found. I'd stake my career on it. Now… is there anything else I can help you with?"

"Well, I notice you didn't ask about Adam. May I ask why?"

Charlotte's smile faded and her face betrayed a certain sense of unease. "I wanted to, but with our history together and Adam's—well, um, his current condition—I know he's still recovering here and I guess, well, I didn't want to hurt you by stepping on such a sensitive subject. I decided on the way over that I wouldn't bring him up unless you did first. Would you like to talk about it?"

"Maybe. Probably. Please forgive me for my bluntness, but there is something that I need to know. Can you tell me what possessed you to take my son to a strip club? I asked Adam about that night several times, but he never answered me. Even grounding him didn't loosen his tongue. "

Charlotte's face flushed with embarrassment. She adjusted her seat and said, "You know, I lost my job over that incident, and I almost lost my license to practice psychology. The thing is, I never intended to take him there. I was driving him to the store to get a birthday card for you."

"Why would you do that? My birthday was four months away when that happened."

"Really?" Her eyebrows raised in surprise. "He told me then that it was the next day."

"Charlotte, please tell me everything you can think of concerning that night. And leave nothing out, no matter how small the detail may seem to you."

I leaned in toward her and listened intently as she repeated the entire story for me. When Charlotte finished, I said, "I visited Richard Davis in prison, and he swears my son set him up. He said he had no interest in boys, and the evidence they found in his possession seems to back him up. Do you think maybe Adam set you up too?"

She shook her head. "I don't see how Deirdre. He was just thirteen, so I'm sure it was nothing more than a series of unfortunate events. Besides, there's no way he could have known my husband would show up there."

"Really?" I said in a snippier tone than I had intended. "You told me he knew things about your sister's dog that he couldn't possibly know."

"Yes, that's true." She sighed. "But, Deirdre, knowing something and setting me up in a situation that complex are two different things. It would've taken a mastermind to pull off a stunt like that."

"Well, honestly, I blamed you at the time, not Adam. I wanted to wrap my fingers around your throat and squeeze whenever I thought about it. Please forgive me for saying it, but I thought you were a cougar. Like you had a thing for young teenage boys. But now that I've cut back on my drinking, my mind is clearer, and I've noticed some things. Then a couple nights ago, something happened, and I find I need to talk to you about it."

Charlotte seemed to stiffen at these words. She looked aghast. "Why would you contact me then?" she said as her hand fluttered to her throat. "Given your feelings toward me, there are plenty of other professionals out there that you could speak with."

"Well, as I said, I *felt* that way, but I don't any longer. In fact, I think you may have been the victim that night. Besides, I'm not looking for your insights as a psychologist. It's your openness to certain other things that I need and I didn't know who else to turn to."

Charlotte looked intrigued and a little relieved. "Okay, I'll bite. Talk to me."

I tucked my hair behind my ears as I gathered my thoughts together. "Life definitely became harder for us after my husband died, but things didn't get weird until Adam and some of his friends went to Abbott Cemetery and played Ouija in one of the crypts. He came home late that night cold and shaking. He said he was just freezing, but I know my son. Something freaked him out, but I couldn't get him to talk about it. All I could get out of him was three boys had ditched him there, and he had to find his way home alone after dark. I wouldn't have thought anything more of it, but after that, my son claimed he tripped and accidentally knocked out Danny's front teeth, and later on, the same boy claimed Adam broke his nose."

"I'm aware of those incidences, Deirdre, but I'm not sure what you're getting at."

"Like I said, I know my son, and I know he wasn't lying when he said he did nothing, but somehow it all seems a little too coincidental. Then Rick Kennedy, another boy involved in the cemetery incident with my son, fell down a locked and gated elevator shaft and almost died. When they questioned Rick, he didn't remember how he ended up at the bottom of that shaft. The investigators assigned to the case believe he received an intentional, well-placed blow to the head separate from his other injuries and it was this blow that caused his amnesia and motor issues. I asked Adam about the incident, and he swore up and down that he had nothing to do with it. In fact, he said he felt sorry for Rick—and I believed him."

Charlotte frowned. "I remember reading about that case in the newspaper, but I saw nothing that tied your son to it. Though, I'll admit it does seem extremely coincidental. But if I remember correctly, nothing ever happened to the third boy, right?"

My pulse quickened as the following words tumbled from my lips. "Two nights ago, I went out on a date with Jeremy, and afterward, I returned to check up on Adam before heading home. When I got to his room here in the long-term care wing, he wasn't in his bed, and we couldn't find him anywhere."

Charlotte grimaced. "But Deirdre, what does that prove? He's a teenager. Adam probably felt cooped up and slipped out of his room when no one was looking. I'd do the same thing in his situation."

Trying to keep the irritation out of my voice, I said, "Did you know that two days ago was one year to the day that Bud Pechman broke into our house and tried to kill my son?"

"I'm sorry, but I didn't."

"Well, that incident left my son in a coma and he's been in one ever since. So he didn't just slip out of bed for a stroll."

Charlotte looked mortified. "I'm so sorry. I didn't realize—"

I slashed my hand through the air and cut her off. "Then, to worsen matters, Hunter Campbell—the third boy in the Abbott Cemetery posse—also disappeared two nights ago. The police officer in charge said the boy probably just got a wild hair in him, but I know in my heart he's dead. Then the next morning, Adam's back in bed like he never left, but he's different now."

That caught her attention. Under her breath, she muttered, "Hunter's missing?" In a strained voice, she said, "Deirdre, how is Adam different?"

"Honestly, Charlotte, it would be easier if you saw for yourself. He's upstairs if you'd like to do so."

"I would. So do you actually believe your son killed Hunter?"

"No, I don't!" I said. "I think whatever resides inside his body killed Hunter… and Danny… and maimed Rick."

"Come again?" she said incredulously.

Unable to look her in the eyes, I bent my head and looked at my lap instead. "I think he's possessed by something evil. He kept telling me his deceased sister visited him and would step into his body, but I ignored your warning because I wanted it to be true. I wanted it to be my daughter. I wanted to believe that my husband might come back to us too. You warned me, but I wouldn't listen."

Charlotte's cheeks reddened. "Oh, Deirdre honey, it was just a thought. One of many. Your son seemed like he might be exhibiting certain limited signs of possession, but I didn't mean to imply that your son was actually possessed, and I apologize if my thoughtlessness caused you so much grief."

"Well, even if it was subconscious on your part, I think… I think you had it right. Why don't you hold off on your apology until you've seen Adam? Then you can decide if an apology is in order."

I paid close attention to Charlotte's face when we walked into Adam's room. Maybe she was expecting him to have horns or something, but I felt confident she wasn't expecting this.

She looked him over and said, "I thought you said he's been in a coma. I've seen long-term coma patients, and this isn't what they look like."

I went over to Adam's side and gently touched his face with my fingertips. "Over the past year, I've watched his physical body deteriorate. Three days ago, he had the sallow skin, flaccid muscles, and bedsores associated with this condition. Two nights ago, like I said, both he and Hunter Campbell disappeared. Then yesterday morning, my son was back in bed and he's still in a coma. But now he looks like this. You're welcome to check with the hospital staff if you don't believe me."

"It's not that; it's just that he looks so, so—"

"Healthy? I know. Look at him. Creamy, clear white skin. Rosy red cheeks and lips. Perfect skin and muscle tone. He literally glows with vitality. You could put him on the cover of a health magazine; he looks so good. So tell me, Charlotte, is your apology warranted?"

She placed her right hand on her chin. "Honestly, I don't know what to make of it, but you have my attention now. I'll do a little research into this and let you know what I come up with. Would you mind if I stayed up here alone with him for a little while today?" she asked hesitantly.

"That depends," I said as I looked at Adam's supine form

with an ache in my heart. "What are you hoping to accomplish by that?"

Charlotte looked a little embarrassed. "This isn't something I tell most people, so I'd appreciate it if you keep it between us. I come from a psychic family, and I've inherited a bit of talent myself. It's not much, but sometimes I can discern things."

"Discern what kind of things?" I asked.

"Oh… I don't know. Little things like I can feel when a room is empty or not. It made me real good at hide-and-seek when I was little. Sometimes I just get a sense of things. I don't know if it will do any good in this situation, but I figure it's a start. So is it okay if I stay with him for a bit?"

I rubbed the back of my neck as I thought. Then I opened my mouth and said, "I guess so. I'm getting desperate to figure out what's going on with my son, so go ahead if you think it might help."

CHAPTER 21

DR. CHARLOTTE BROWN

I WATCHED AS Deirdre left the room, then I closed the door behind her. Looking through its glass inset, I turned back to Adam's bed after she disappeared from my view. I'd been truthful when I told her I could sense the presence of others, though I'd failed to mention that I couldn't sense Adams. And the bed was obviously occupied by him, but I felt nothing... like nobody was there. That meant either my ability failed me, which hadn't ever happened—at least not this close to somebody—or that my ability was working just fine, but something had thrown it off. That might happen if he was just an empty shell of a body. Or maybe he was actively blocking me somehow, as his abilities seemed to be greater than mine. I hoped to use my time here to figure that question out.

Sitting down on the floor in the lotus position, I relaxed and extended my consciousness outward from me. Pushing hard, I could feel a glimmer of multiple presences in the surrounding rooms, but I felt nothing here in Adam's room.

I stood, then walked over to Adam's bed, looking at his handsome face. It oozed with unbridled vitality. It was hard to believe I couldn't sense something from someone with that much life within. I placed my hand on his forehead and tried to push my senses into him, and a moment later, I found myself sitting on my butt on the floor. A shock had flown through me and pushed me over. The hand I'd used to touch him felt numb and unresponsive. Then, as sensation returned, my hand felt full of pins and needles.

A thought came to mind, so I hurried downstairs to the small store next to the hospital chapel. I was in luck, as they had just what I was looking for. I made my purchase and hurried back to the room. Once I had closed the door behind me, I pulled out my new bottle of holy water. While making the sign of the cross, I flung sparkling droplets of the water at the room entrance as I said, "In the name of the Father, Son, and Holy Spirit." I could feel a slight tension rise in the room's atmosphere, but nothing more. I went over to the window and did the same thing, and I felt another tiny increase in tension. Looking at the plastic bottle I held in my right hand, I thought—*Why not?*—and went over to Adam's bed.

I lifted my hand to make a sign of the cross with the water over Adam, but then he spoke in a voice that wasn't quite right somehow. "You'll regret it if you get any of that water on me."

It so startled me that my fingers fumbled the water bottle, and it dropped on the bed behind his head. I backed up and looked at his face. He still appeared to be sleeping.

"And… uh, why… why is that, Adam?" I asked, my heart racing. "Do you, um, have a problem with holy water?"

I watched as his lips moved and said, "No, I just have a problem with crazy old ladies flinging water on me while I'm sleeping."

I stared at him, feeling a little calmer. "You should amend that to *pretending* to be sleeping. Why are you pretending, Adam?"

His face morphed into a sneer. "It spares me the tedium of inane chitchat with morons."

He opened his eyes, and I drew back even as my heart started thumping again. Those did not look at all like the eyes of a teen. They looked bluer than I remembered, and they seemed piercingly intelligent... and cruel. I also noted a hint of insanity in them.

While I rubbed at the goosebumps that suddenly appeared on my arms, Adam blinked, and his usual eyes gazed back at me. I heard a shriek in the hallway, and then the door burst open.

Deirdre flew through the entrance and rushed up to the bed. Her eyes glittered with hope as she said, "Adam, is that you in there?"

"Hi, Mom," he said in his normal voice. He pursed his lips and furrowed his brow as he looked around the room, then back at Deirdre. "Mom... uh, where am I? Is this a hospital?"

Tears started running down his mom's pretty face as she said, "What's the last thing you remember, honey?"

He concentrated, then said, "We were sitting on the couch watching TV. Someone started knocking on the door, but we decided not to answer it. Then I woke up just now, and I don't know how I got here."

Deirdre leaned into him, and then she started showering his face with kisses. She turned and looked at me. "I don't know what you did, Charlotte, but you have my thanks. I was so worried about him, but now that he's awake, he seems to be his normal self. Maybe it was all coincidence after all."

"Yeah, maybe," I said under my breath. But I could only

think how quickly we had switched places. A moment ago, she'd believed Adam possessed, and I'd been skeptical. Now she was the skeptic and I knew that something was seriously wrong with him. I needed to get out of here to think, so I said, "I'm going to leave now so you two can get caught up."

Deirdre came over and hugged me. "Thank you again for helping us."

Adam said from the bed in a pleasant voice, "Don't forget your holy water, Dr. Charlotte."

I took hesitant steps toward the bed and leaned over him to grab the bottle, and as I did, the golden cross that I'd received for my Holy Communion slipped out from underneath my blouse and dangled mere inches from Adam's face on its golden chain. He flinched as if I'd struck him physically, but Deirdre missed it because my body had been blocking her view. I left the bottle where it lay and hurriedly exited the room. Before I left the hospital, though, I ran back to the chapel store and bought several crosses and their remaining bottles of holy water. After leaving the building, I still needed a few more items, so I drove around town to visit other Catholic shops. After I exited the second store, I blessed my car with the purchased holy water right there in the parking lot, and then I headed home to cleanse my place.

I walked around the house, jiggling all the outside windows and doors to ensure they were secure. Then I proceeded to my bedroom and groped around in the top dresser drawer for my rosary. I kneeled next to my bed and made the sign of the cross as I prayed the Apostles' Creed. Then I went through the rosary beads, one by one, praying the appropriate Our Father or Hail Mary. I finished the rosary by beseeching the Father, Son, and

Holy Spirit to protect me, my husband, and our home. I also prayed for Adam and Deirdre. My last request was for wisdom.

When I was done, I made the sign of the cross over my body, then I stood and went into the kitchen. I took my purchases out of their bags and placed each item on the kitchen table for inspection. After I was satisfied, I poured several bottles of holy water into a clear glass spray bottle and then added a teaspoon of blessed salt. From room to room, I went around my house, reciting prayers and spraying holy water. I cleansed, blessed, and sealed my doors, windows, walls, floors, and ceilings. After that, I sprinkled blessed salt crystals around the outside of my home and then used blessed olive oil to make the sign of the cross on all of my window and door frames. Still not satisfied, I strategically placed several crucifixes around the house. When I finished all of that, I sat down, exhausted. I could only think, *If this doesn't work, nothing will.*

Later that evening, my husband and I were lying on the couch together watching TV. Our favorite late-night routine. He'd just fallen asleep and was snoring lightly next to me—yet another part of our nightly ritual. I looked at his handsome face, and once again, I felt lucky to be with him… well, mostly. Working through his little stint at the nightclub had been trying, but we were through it and our relationship was stronger than ever.

A commercial appeared claiming it would take care of all my incontinence needs, which would have been awesome if I'd had any. I picked up the remote and started flipping through the channels. I kept my fingers crossed that maybe I'd get lucky and find a product that would take care of my husband's snoring. It'd be like my Christmas present coming early for me. I'd even pay for that present out of my own money and then fork over extra cash for overnight shipping and handling. As I fantasized about finding the perfect present, my husband stirred from the loud sounds coming from the TV. I decided to be nice to him and turn down the volume, and that's when I heard it. A faint tapping sound coming from my window. It sounded similar to a small tree branch hitting a windowpane. I thought nothing of it until the tapping sound moved to another window. But even then, it wasn't until the sound shifted to a third window that it truly caught my attention. I flew up off the couch, pulled open the window shade, and saw... nothing. I also looked out the other two windows in the living room but saw nothing unusual. Even so, a small chill shot down my spine, and I hurried back to the couch and my husband. I pushed myself up against his warm snoring body and pulled the soft, brown cashmere blanket over me, and I started feeling better immediately. Being next to him felt like home. It was just right somehow.

As my nerves slowly unwound, I picked up the remote and started surfing again. While in the throes of a critical decision—continue my search for the perfect Christmas present or tune in to the latest *Friends* episode—the tapping started again. At first, it came so quietly that I thought I'd imagined it. But then the intensity picked up, and I knew it wasn't my imagination at all. Another chill shot down my spine when I realized it was coming from the back door. Then rationality flitted through my mind. *Neighborhood kids just pranking us.* I hopped off the couch again and listened to the wood floorboards creak underneath my feet as I headed toward the noise. Entering the kitchen, my hand instinctively reached out to the light switch on the wall and flicked it on. As soon as the room lit up, the tapping morphed into a regular knocking sound. I cautiously approached the back door and opened the wood shutters covering the windowpane.

As my eyes adjusted, I realized someone was standing outside in the velvety darkness. I turned on the porch light, and in its yellowish glow, I could see Adam standing there in his hospital gown. He oozed with the same vitality I'd seen earlier today, but his countenance appeared heartbreakingly sad. My maternal instincts kicked in, and I threw open the door. An unseasonably chilly wind for this time of year blew in and hit me. My arms automatically wrapped around my midsection to preserve body heat. Adam's moist eyes locked onto mine, and I could see a single tear running down his cheek.

"What happened, Adam?" I blurted out. "Why are you here?"

He wiped the bottom of his nose against his sleeve. "I didn't know who else to go to. Can I come in, Dr. Charlotte?"

My mouth opened to say yes, but a little voice inside me told me it would be the last thing I ever did. I clamped my mouth shut mid-word and then said, "You know, Adam, you can tell me from there what you came here for. How can I help you?"

His face twisted in distress as he said, "It's Hunter Campbell, ma'am. I heard he'd disappeared, so I went looking for him. I found him, but he's hurt real bad."

"Adam, how is he hurt exactly?"

"I already told you, ma'am… real bad. Can you come outside and help me, Dr. Charlotte?"

I shook my head, and as I did, I saw the spray bottle with the holy water in it just off to my left. I leaned sideways, snatched it off the countertop, and then pointed it at Adam.

He cocked his head sideways. "I told you you'd regret it if you got any of that water on me."

His words caused me to hesitate for a second or two, then I pressed the nozzle anyway. As the holy water rushed at his face, a stiff, cold breeze with the faintest hint of sulfur in it caught the puff of water and blew it back into my face.

Adam took a single step backward and cocked his head again. "That was totally uncalled for, Dr. Charlotte. Now invite me in so we can talk about it. It's the civilized thing to do."

Civilized? What kid his age talks like that? And his insistence that I invite him in or come out to him... *How strange is that?* Most would ask to come in and the rest would just do it. But no kid I knew of would offer me the choice of coming outside, especially in the middle of the night. Whatever stood in front of me, I knew it wasn't Adam. It was the proverbial wolf in sheep's clothing. My lips frowned, and my nostrils flared involuntarily with that realization. The whole thing creeped me out, and my inner voice screamed that I was in grave danger.

I took my internal trepidation to heart and yelled, "Get off my property, now! You are not welcome here!"

Then I slammed the door shut in his face. After engaging the locks, I shooed him away with my hand as we stared at each other through the door's windowpane. His eyes seemed to flash black before he turned and walked off of my deck, but I wasn't entirely sure. There, alone, in the dark of night, Deirdre's initial intuition concerning Adam rang true, and my heart started hammering in my chest.

By the time I made it back to the couch, I shook uncontrollably from head to toe. My rational side tried to tell me I simply had a big imagination. It also suggested that Adam's appearance here at my home was innocent and I was reading way too much into it. My intuitive side reminded me I saw what I saw and that my phone number was unlisted. I'd never told Adam or his mother where I lived, so it seemed near impossible that he'd find my doorstep, especially in the middle of the night. From what I'd heard of such things, if a demon or spirit followed you home, it meant the situation was escalating. And I was in big trouble if this thing was as crafty as Deirdre portrayed it. *But that's crazy thinking… right?* There had to be a rational psychological reason for Adam's condition. A guilty realization hit me that it might be my fault. What if his mom had told him I thought he was possessed? His mind might have latched on to the idea and run with it. Still, I saw what I saw. The internal war of ideas raging inside me made me feel like my mind would rip apart.

I grabbed the standup cross off the TV console and clutched it firmly against my breasts as I climbed back under the cashmere blanket with my husband. I thought about waking him, but he'd just think me crazy so I chose to just lay there instead. Even though the cross and the closeness of my husband brought me a certain amount of comfort, my ears still strained to hear every little noise while my mind raced through a variety of options. I finally reached the inescapable conclusion that I was in over my head and needed to involve the Catholic Church. As a large international organization with an occasional history with possessions and exorcisms, I thought I should hear what the church had to say about these subjects.

CHAPTER 22

DR. CHARLOTTE BROWN

THE NEXT DAY, I headed to the Basilica of the Holy Heart, located in the next town over. Somehow I managed to hit every red light between my home and there, and to my irritation, I estimated I would be about ten minutes late for my scheduled meeting with Father Stephen Casey. As I drew closer to the massive edifice, I could see the glittering spires of the basilica peeking up over the treetops. I pulled up to the impressive cathedral and admired the limestone handiwork adorned with gold leaf, marble tracery, and large stained-glass windows. Driving to the north side of the property, I parked next to the only other cars in the lot. I knew it was irrational, but it still felt safer that way. I grabbed my leather tote out of the back seat, locked my car, and made my way into the building. As soon as I walked through the doors, I felt cocooned in peace. It was glorious, and I let it soak into me.

I made my way to the parish office suite and snuck a peek into the Father's office. He was attractive for an older man, and he wore his gray hair well. While all black clothing could make some look austere, it didn't have that effect on him. His face gave off a sense of warmth and wisdom, and he seemed comfortable with himself. Unfortunately, as a trained psychologist, I saw very few people who actually accepted themselves for who they were. It was because of such qualities that I'd sought out Father Casey. From what I knew of him, he was thoughtful and even-handed in his dealings.

He looked up from behind a large mahogany desk and locked his eyes on mine. He waved a hand at the wooden seat directly in front of the desk and said in a pleasant baritone voice, "Dr. Brown, please come in." As I sat, he said, "So what can I do for you today?"

I placed my brown tote on the travertine floor beside me as I considered certain pleasantries. But realistically, it was nothing but fluff and I was already late for the meeting. Father Casey's time was valuable, so I decided to get straight to the matter. "Well, Father, I've come across something in the course of my job that has me at a loss, and I'm not sure what to do about it. I'm hoping for some guidance."

"Don't let my wise looks fool you," he said and chuckled. "Unless you're looking for spiritual advice, my advice is no better or worse than anything anyone else will give you."

I smiled. "Well, I guess I'm in luck, then."

I proceeded to tell him about my observations and thoughts. He sat there and listened intently, not interrupting me once.

When I finally finished, Father Casey looked me in the eye and asked, "Do you have any proof of possession?"

Proof? My hands fidgeted as my mouth frowned. "What do you mean by *proof?*"

"You mentioned that he knew about your sister's dog. Did you record this conversation by any chance?"

I shook my head. "No, but I couldn't legally share it with you even if I had."

"And that, Dr. Brown, is the crux of our problem… or maybe your problem. While the Catholic Church accepts the possibility of possession, we still consider it a rare thing, and we will not act upon it unless there is proof. We've been burned, so to speak, in the past in this area, and it has made the church reluctant to pursue such cases."

My shoulders sagged a bit. "But what about the boy? He needs help, and I'm not sure how to give it to him. Before proceeding, I need to know if he needs intense psychiatric therapy, an exorcism, or both."

Father Casey steepled his fingers together. "Are you familiar with the Anneliese Michel case?"

I wasn't, so I shook my head.

As I watched, the good father stood and made his way over to a black-stained wood bookcase that lined an entire wall. After a quick browse, he removed one of the tomes and placed it in front of me. "I think you'll find this instructive, but let me give you the CliffsNotes version for now."

I nodded.

He cleared his throat and then proceeded. "This was a possession case that started in Germany in 1975. Anneliese had been diagnosed with temporal lobe epilepsy at sixteen years old and spent several years after that receiving psychiatric care, all to no avail. When she became averse to religious objects and started hearing voices, her parents became convinced that a demon possessed her and persuaded two local priests to exorcise her. Anneliese eventually died of malnutrition at the age of twenty-three in connection with the sixty-seven exorcisms performed on her. The priests and her parents were convicted of negligent homicide, and churches worldwide became more hesitant to pursue possession cases."

My lips pressed together as a deep, black agitation crept over me. With more bile than I had intended, I said, "So if I understand you properly, you're telling me that because of something that happened decades ago in another country, you're not willing to help a boy that desperately needs your help; here and now."

Father Casey didn't answer me right away. Instead, he sat there in silence behind a desk covered in religious trinkets. He picked up a small pewter statue of Moses and appeared to be studying it, though, in reality, I knew he was appraising me. He looked stressed as he rubbed the back of his neck, and as I watched, he seemed to come to some internal conclusion.

Father Casey opened his mouth and said, "I'm a fairly good judge of character, Dr. Brown, and my instincts tell me you're legitimate, so I'm going to level with you. I've always known that this sort of thing might end up in my lap as a parish priest, so I'd looked into it. I have studied Anneliese's case and other published and unpublished possession incidents, and I've concluded that there is some truth to these claims of demonic possession. Unfortunately, we live in an unbelieving world full of fierce critics and—"

"Wait a second," I interrupted. "You're worried about what someone may say about you?"

He held up a hand. "Please let me finish, Dr. Brown. To answer your question, yes, I am worried about the critics, and so should you. Some can't accept anything more than themselves and what they can see, and they will go to great lengths to make sure that nobody else accepts it either. If anything happens to this boy, they will discredit you, ridicule you, and destroy you. They will come after you with such ferocity that

I have come to believe that they are unknowingly possessed themselves and represent the useful idiots of the demonic world. Regardless, pursuing this could cost you your career, husband, home, freedom, and even your life. This is because you are not asking me to pursue the mundane. If this boy is indeed possessed, we will be pursuing a thinking creature… a creature likely as old as time itself… a creature that doesn't sleep, doesn't forget, doesn't forgive, and is always watchful. Are you ready for such an enemy?"

Exasperation replaced my agitation, and I felt he didn't read people as well as he thought he did. "What do you expect me to say? I became a child psychologist to help children—*all* children, not just the easy cases. I don't think I could live with myself if I walked away from Adam and did nothing."

Father Casey smiled. "Good. I thought I read you properly. You came to me for advice and direction, so here it is. Based on what you've told me, in my mind, Adam's case meets the minimum criteria for a bona fide demonic possession. If he's suffering from an actual possession, my intuition tells me this demon likes to destroy, so its endgame will always be the destruction of whatever it moves against. In fact, the name *Bela* means 'to destroy' in ancient Hebrew."

"Is there anything more I can do to protect myself than I'm already doing?"

The good father appeared thoughtful. "First, you need to realize that you're not protecting anything. It's the mercy and grace of God in the cross and holy water that protects you, and as you get closer to this thing, you're going to need much more of each. I suggest you start by going to Holy Confession because any unconfessed sin can be used against you. Demons are legalistic, and sin gives them rights over you in the spiritual realm, so get rid of your unconfessed sin. You also need to spend much time in prayer—and don't neglect Holy Communion. And never ever try to confront this thing alone. If the Catholic Church takes this case on, it will only be confronted as a team under the full authority of the church."

I blinked rapidly. "So… wait, I'm confused. Are you or are you not helping me?"

"I'm already helping you because I believe you believe it, and I don't believe you're given over to vain superstitions. But it's not my help you need. You need the help of the corporate Catholic Church, and to get that, you'll need to convince the bishop that help is justified."

I closed my eyes and said, "And how do I convince the bishop to help me?"

"To do that, you'll need proof, and it won't be easy to get. Demons are intelligent, and they will not sit there and let you dissect them. Their greatest strength is in secrecy and unbelief. These creatures thrive there, as they can destroy unimpeded, as no one will even bother them if people don't believe in them.

So, first, I will need a mental health assessment of the boy by a qualified professional other than yourself. "I also need you to write down everything you've told me, and then I need you to find evidence. The church will consider supernatural strength, knowledge of the unknowable, speaking in languages not known to the subject, blasphemous rage, and an aversion to holy things as proof of possession. If you can get them, photographic and audio recordings are definitely helpful. Reliable people willing to testify to such evidence are also beneficial. Have you talked to this principal you mentioned—Mr. Richard Davis—by any chance?"

I shook my head. "I haven't, Father, but he's being held in the state penitentiary, so it shouldn't be too hard to arrange."

"Great. I'd also like to meet the boy and the mother myself. Do you think you could arrange a meeting for us?"

"Absolutely, Father. Thank you for listening to me and not just dismissing everything I had to say. I really appreciate it, and I'll get started right away."

After I rose and headed for the door, Father Casey said, "Be careful, Charlotte. I will pray for you."

After leaving, I decided my first order of business would be to talk to Richard Davis at the state penitentiary. But instead of heading straight there, I wanted to drive home first to grab my case notes on him and then get something to eat. As a child psychologist specializing in sexual abuse, I'd had several past cases requiring me to interview the abusers at the state pen. I planned on using my good working relationship with the staff to schedule a late-afternoon meeting with the disgraced principal. After making it home, I started putting my key in the front door lock, but as I did so, the pressure I applied caused the door to swing in on its hinges a couple of inches. I hadn't known the door was ajar, and it startled me, causing me to take a step back. Looking closer at the door and then the side windows, I didn't see any signs of forced entry. I plucked up my courage and pushed. The front door swung open, and I found myself staring at a Frankenstein monster hunched over in the hallway.

My shoulders relaxed, and I said, "Oh, honey, you scared me. I thought maybe... Oh, never mind what I thought. I forgot today is Halloween."

My husband looked up from the spider webbing and orange Halloween lighting he was stringing up in our hallway. "How could you possibly forget that?" He grimaced. "I reminded you yesterday evening to come home early today so we could get everything set up before the kids start arriving."

Mark was and still is a longtime Halloween aficionado who loves to put on a good show every year when it rolls around. For several years, trick-or-treaters have come from three neighborhoods over to see the setup and get the full-sized candy bars he freely hands out.

"I'm sorry, honey," I said as I pushed the side of my head up against the cool wood of the door frame. "It's just that this case has been weighing on my mind, and I'm currently pursuing a lead. Would you mind if I bowed out of tonight's festivities?"

"Come on, Charlotte," he said, then looked at me with pleading puppy dog eyes. "You know how much this means to me. You might as well ask me if it's okay to have an affair with one of your coworkers. Your lead can certainly wait until tomorrow, can't it?"

I groaned internally and then, against my better judgment, said, "Oh… all right, but you owe me."

His amazing smile lit up his face. "Sure thing, darling! Now go dig that boom box out of the attic for me. And see if you can find the Halloween CD for it too."

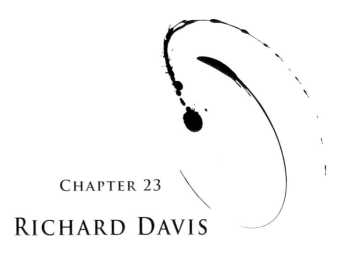

CHAPTER 23

RICHARD DAVIS

I'D FELT AWFUL ever since dinner the night before. I sat on my bed with a sick feeling in my stomach and looked at the calendar hanging on the wall, staring at today's date. It wasn't that I didn't know it. I'd been waiting for and fearing this day since I'd arrived here. I'd experienced the same debilitating fear last Halloween too. Still, after I'd survived it, I realized demon boy had told me he'd come for me on Halloween in the *penitentiary*. I hadn't been in the pen last October 31st, only local lockup.

I stood and shook the bars with all my might, but of course, they didn't budge. After that, I started pacing my cell like a caged animal. I had to get out of here, but I didn't know how. I asked myself for the millionth time how I'd been so unlucky to end up at the same school with demon boy. There were tens of thousands of schools out there that he could have gone to. *Why did he have to show up at mine?* And it wasn't like the girls I played with didn't want it. Despite their protests, I knew they wanted it bad. They all did. I just provided a service. *And look where that service got me.* I realized the problem was I'd been born too late. No one would have thought anything of my activities if I'd been born twenty or thirty years earlier. People saw nothing wrong with female students dating their older male teachers back then. It was considered natural. I'd come to realize I was just a victim of the times.

Nevertheless, I had more important things to think about at the moment. I needed to figure out a way to thwart demon boy when he showed up today. Since I'd arrived at the pen, I spent nearly every free moment of my time in the weight yard, and I'd grown buff. Still, my instincts told me it wasn't going to be enough. Fortunately for me, my cellmate was a giant beast of a man. Nico had been an enforcer for a mob boss before getting put away. We had completely different backgrounds personally and professionally but got along great together as fate would have it. We bonded instantly and became the best of friends. He appreciated my ability to corral the young ladies into bed, and he would sit and listen for hours as I recounted my escapades. In addition, he thought it was a hoot that I kept a Bible in my office to get my young, impressionable charges to trust me enough so that I could do my thing. My friendship with my cellmate paid dividends because it shielded me from some of the more unsavory prisoners here. In fact, I hoped I could prevail upon him to protect me when demon boy showed up tonight.

"Hey, Nico," I said as I waved a hand. "I have a proposition for you. Do you care to hear it?"

He turned his bull-like head toward me and said, "Sure, just as long as it's got nothing to do with that demon kid you keep going on about."

"Hmm, well, it does, but listen. If you take him out tonight when he shows up, I'll get you five packs of smokes."

Cigarettes were like gold in the pen, and I thought Nico would quickly jump at the offer, but he just stood there silent like.

What if he says no? What then? I could feel my mouth go dry at the thought.

"Camels?" he said.

"Sure," I nodded, "if that's what you want."

He looked me up and down. "And how is a skinny little white boy like you going to come up with such a kingly gift?"

"Don't you worry about it, Nico. I have my connections." Then I flourished my hands in front of his face like a magician.

His mouth twisted into a half-smile. "Fine, if that little sucker is stupid enough to show up tonight, I'll shiv him good. But when he doesn't, I'm still gonna make you give me those smokes for making me listen to your stupid, delusional stories about some wacko demon kid. I thought my boss man was paranoid, but you take the cake."

"You laugh now, but wait. He'll be here soon enough, and you'll have to be fast because he's sneaky."

"Don't you worry about me," Nico said as he flexed his arms, then rolled his massive shoulders. "You just worry about getting your hands on those smokes."

I let out a huge sigh of relief while enjoying the giddy feeling that started seeping through my body like warm honey. Demon boy might be able to take me on, but Nico was a walking mountain of muscle—like a force of nature unto himself. I imagine that Nico had been very, very good at his job of enforcing on the outside.

Our cell lock clicked and I stepped back from the bars as they automatically slid open. The morning work detail started now and unfortunately, I was part of "team toilet bowl" today. I walked down the nondescript gray concrete corridor and joined up with the rest of the work crew. As a prison guard escorted us to our first work detail of the day, I told my teammates to keep a lookout for a kid with solid black eyes and a mouth full of snake fangs.

"Davis," one of my workmates groaned. "I'm going to kill you myself if you don't shut up about that kid. Just stop already."

I flashed him the evil eye. "Don't be giving me no lip, Kirby. You'll see him soon enough, and then you'll believe."

Happy Halloween to me! I thought glumly. We'd been cleaning together over the last few hours as a team, but the next job was so bad we drew for it. Only one unlucky sucker would get stuck with it—and guess what? As if my life could get any worse, I'd just drawn the worst duty of all. My workmates clapped me on the back as they walked by, smirking at me.

Kirby, laughing his butt off, yelled back at me, "Hah, you doofus, I see God has a sense of humor after all!"

Jerk!

Minutes later, I found myself standing in a hellhole. *Dear God, it smells horrible in here. And the sight…* I thought it'd be okay if I avoided breathing through my nose, but then I could taste it and it made me want to vomit. Several inmates had fought in here and flung whatever they had on hand. Needless to say, it was everywhere, and it was disgusting. I started scrubbing down the floors, walls, and toilets, and after I was about halfway through the cleanup, I heard a faint, high-pitched giggling sound—much like a young teenage boy would make. I went back to the cart, picked up a plunger, and tested its weight by swinging it back and forth like a sword. It was hardly my first weapon of choice, but you work with what you got. I held the plunger in front of me as I went down the row of toilets separated by walls but with no stall doors. I saw… nothing. *Maybe my nerves were getting the best of me.* I went back to scrubbing, and when I was almost finished, I heard another laugh that was high and clear… creepy, even. I went down the row of toilets again but still found myself alone.

Violently swinging the plunger back and forth around me, I yelled out, "Come on, you little turd! Bring it on!"

A prison guard poked his head through the door. "What the heck are you yelling about in here, Davis?"

I cocked my head toward him. "Nothing, nothing. Just thought I heard something is all."

"Lemme guess." He smirked. "Was it demon boy?"

"Maybe."

"Well, just keep it down, Davis. You and demon boy can play together all you want, but don't make me come in here again."

I watched the smug jerk walk back out. *One day, he'd get his. Just not today…* I went back to scrubbing, and after I'd finished, I started on my final chore: the urinals. As I cleaned, I clearly felt a hand touch my back. I whipped my head around, but no one was there. That turd-faced demon boy was playing with me again. I didn't know how I knew that… I just did. I got about halfway done with the urinals when I felt a hand touch my shoulder again. Grabbing the plunger that I had purposely kept by my side as I worked, I swung it with all of my might. It connected with the prison guard's head, and he stumbled back a step. *Oops… my bad!* With smoldering rage coming out of his ears, he drew out his baton and beat the living snot out of me.

After the guard finished his tap dance on me, he tossed me back into my cell, which was a win-win situation as far as I was concerned. I didn't have to clean any more toilets today. And if he had thrown me into solitary, Nico wouldn't have been there to protect me.

As I nursed my bruises, I started pacing again. The waiting was driving me nuts, and I wished that demon boy would get it over with already. Well, not exactly already—*already* as in when Nico was back in the cell with me. After waiting for what seemed like forever, Nico finally returned sporting a full belly. I had been a bad boy, so there'd be no supper for me tonight.

Nico laughed at me as he poked me in the chest. "You are one crazy dude. I can't believe you actually plungered the guard. It's too bad you picked today to do it too. They served filet mignon, pheasant under glass, and beluga caviar for dinner. And to think, soon I'll have some fine smokes to follow up that delicious meal."

I flipped him off. "Bite me, Nico. They served rancid food tonight just like they served it last night and will serve it tomorrow night."

"Well, a fella can dream, can't he? Try sprinkling a little imagination on it next time, and then sit down and enjoy a fine meal with me." He made an exaggerated show of rubbing his belly as he said, "Mmm-mm!"

I narrowed my eyes. "You know, Nico, I'd kick your butt for that if it weren't... well, you know... so unkickable."

"Yeah, buddy, stand in line," he said and grinned. "It's good to be me."

"Amen to that!" I smiled back. "And if I can't be you, at least it's good to be your cellmate. All joking aside, though... thanks, man. I know you all think I'm crazy, but thanks for watching out for me anyway."

"Oh, don't go getting all weepy on me, Davis.... And I still want my smokes."

That night, Nico climbed up into his bunk and passed out almost immediately. Soon, his loud snoring echoed down the corridor. I continued pacing because, frankly, there wasn't anything else I could do. As I walked in a tight circle, I considered smacking Nico in the head to shut off the infernal racket he was making. I knew demon boy well, and I needed all my senses to keep him from sneaking up on me. It was hard to concentrate with all the clamor. However, I needed him and I didn't want to tick him off, so I let him sleep.

At 10:39 p.m., the lights malfunctioned, and the cell plunged into total darkness. The emergency lighting system kicked on about ten seconds later, and a thin red glow trickled between the bars, giving minimal illumination to our space. Simultaneously, Nico's snoring stopped, and besides the near darkness, I was thrust into complete silence. Having my senses cut off so abruptly was eerie. I pushed my face between the cold steel bars as far as it would go, and I moved my eyes from side to side and up and down, but I saw nothing unusual.

Several minutes later, I walked over to my bunk and sat down again. I had never been a praying man, and much to my mother's disappointment, I'd never had a use for religion. *Well, except for the Holy Bible… heh-heh. But that's another story.* My views were imminently reasonable because I wasn't given over to delusions, superstitions, or magic sky daddies. I'd always been a practical man and levelheaded in my dealings. Unfortunately for me, these were not practical times, so with my back up against the wall, I needed to consider more nefarious means to get myself out of this mess. At the very least, I figured it couldn't hurt. Putting my hands together like I'd seen Catholics and Protestants do, I tried to cut a deal with the Big Guy. I reminded God that all in all, I was a pretty good fellow that had fallen on bad times. I told him that if he could see me out of this mess, he could ask me for a solid favor when I got out of the pen—within reason, of course—but I kept this last part to myself. Anyhow, it seemed like an all-around win-win to me. I tried to pray more, but I think I dozed off instead.

"Hey, Dick…"

My eyes snapped open, and I looked around. According to the wall clock, the time was now 11:19 p.m., so I knew I'd definitely fallen asleep. I could've sworn I'd just heard that turd-faced Adam Matthew calling out my name. I looked around, but I didn't see him anywhere. Probably just jumpy nerves causing me to hallucinate, or maybe I'd just dreamed it. That had to be it. Whatever the case, I didn't see him, and that's all that really mattered. At this point, I knew I wasn't going to fall back asleep, and I felt prayed out. I'd gotten tired of pacing around too. So, instead, I sat on my bed and focused on the clock on the far wall. As I waited for the stroke of midnight, I got scared and didn't want to be alone anymore. I shook Nico a few times and then a few times more to wake him, but he was sleeping like the dead. If he thought I'd give him a single smoke for sleeping through the whole thing—or for letting me get murdered, God forbid—he had another thing coming.

"Wake up, you bonehead!" I yelled at the top of my lungs.

Nico shifted to his side and smacked his lips a few times. And that was that. However, several inmates from the surrounding cells yelled at me to shut up and called me a few choice names. *Just great!*

At 11:55 p.m., my heart started beating like a drum until my chest felt like it would explode. As I stared at the clock, each second ticked by slower than the last, and at some point, a dizziness overcame me and I realized I was hyperventilating. I forced myself to slow my breathing. At 11:59 p.m., I started seeing a glimmer of hope. Halloween would be officially over in less than one minute, and I could move on with my life. With five seconds left until midnight, Nico startled me by jumping off his cot and facing me. I looked back at the clock. It was now November 1st.

With great relief and feeling kind of stupid, I stood and punched Nico on the shoulder. "Thanks for looking out for me, buddy. If it makes you feel better, I'll admit that you were right all along. And for having to listen to me go on and on about it, I'll get you those smokes as soon as I can. I—"

Nico's massive fist smashed into my throat, and I felt an explosion of pain even as I heard something crack. I tried to scream, but nothing came out except for a painful wheeze.

Nico leaned in close, then his head whipped forward snake-like, and he bit one of my ears clean off my head.

I started shrieking, but nothing came out other than a quiet hiss. Confused and shaking hard, I forced myself to look at Nico's face. *Oh God no!* Blood dribbled down his chin, and a silent terror arose from within me. Nico stared back at me with solid jet-black eyes like deep, dark voids and his enormous smile revealed a mouthful of pointy, fang-like teeth. My face contorted in horror as he spit my severed ear out of his mouth and into his hand, then gently, almost lovingly, placed it on the floor.

CHAPTER 24

DR. CHARLOTTE BROWN

SINCE I ENDED up staying home and helping my husband pull off another highly successful Halloween for the neighborhood children, I had called the state penitentiary and arranged to speak with Richard Davis the following morning. I figured that getting it out of the way early would free up valuable time later in the day.

The sun came up as I drove to the state pen and everything it touched seemed to be an absolute blah. The sky seemed gray, the buildings seemed gray, even my soul felt gray. It didn't help that it was drizzling outside too. I would have preferred all-out sunshine or an honest-to-God storm full of fury and lightning. The weather felt maddening—like a harbinger of doom. A little voice inside me told me to turn around and go back home, and I felt so rotten on the inside that I almost listened. But that's not the person I am. When I decide to pursue something, I do it with my whole heart.

I pushed on despite my inner trepidation and didn't stop

until I arrived at the first security checkpoint. The guard in the booth took my identification information and wrote down my plate number. After opening the gate, he waved me through a tall metal fence with loops and loops of barbed wire sitting on top of it, and I drove until I found parking near the front door. I stared at my destination and marveled at the sense of violence and misery that emanated from the building, as if they were living things. I shook the feeling from me and shoved my case notes into my tote. After a short walk, I stood in front of the barred door leading to the administration building. A thin layer of precipitation had already gathered on my forehead and cheekbones, and I wiped it off with the sleeve of my black raincoat. I pressed the buzzer that said *Push* next to it, and I heard a click. The door unlocked, and I walked through it.

After going through a metal detector and a pat-down by a female guard, I signed in. Spotting a row of empty plastic seats pushed up against a white cinder block wall, I walked over to them and chose one. As soon as my butt touched the plastic chair, a klaxon started wailing, and then I heard a loud click come from the front doors. The guard at the desk told me something had happened, and the building had to go on full lockdown. I asked if I should come back, but the guard told me I couldn't go anywhere until the warden lifted it. *Well, so much for that extra hour I carved out for myself.*

I pulled out my case notes and reviewed them more than once. After that, I scribbled down some of my thoughts. If I planned to see this all the way through, I needed to document everything, reminding myself of what Father Casey had told me. After that, I thought through every likely response Davis might have to my questions. I felt supremely prepared, and I didn't think he'd be able to throw any curveballs.

I got antsy after finishing all the work I'd brought along

in my tote bag. The building remained on lockdown, so I thumbed through some of the magazines in the waiting area. My boredom grew, and I was about to complain to anyone who would listen when the locks on the front doors suddenly clicked and the distant klaxon quit wailing. I walked to the front desk to talk to the guard on duty when, much to my surprise, the prison warden appeared and said he wanted to speak with me. I'd never met the man before. He seemed a little young for a warden, appearing to be in his mid-thirties at most. He looked tall and fit, and he carried himself well in his navy-blue pinstriped suit. His looks were average except for his striking eyes—large, intelligent eyes that might have been pleasant if not for the calculated look behind them. It gave him a shifty appearance, and I distrusted him immediately.

"Dr. Charlotte Brown," he said with a plastered-on smile that never wavered. "I'm Warden Owen Smith. May I ask what brings a noted psychologist like yourself to my prison today?"

It seemed odd that the head honcho would care what I was up to. He definitely hadn't shown an interest in my presence before.

"Nothing much really," I responded as nonchalantly as possible. "A patient of mine—a teen—claims one of your inmates sexually assaulted him. I'm trying to work through the details, so I came here to get your inmate's take on the accusations."

He raised his brow. "Would your patient be named Adam Matthew, perchance?"

"Uh… yes," I answered hesitantly. "But how could you know that? Did you memorize all of the prisoner case files?"

"As a matter of fact, I have," the warden said as he gave me a dismissive glance. "I don't believe in leaving anything to chance. But in this case, I have a personal interest in this individual, even to the point of recompense."

I could feel my spine stiffen at his insinuation and then shook my head in disbelief. "Are you threatening my client?"

A hard smile slowly spread across his face—a predatory smile. "*Threatening* is such a tepid term—a watered-down word for the weak. I never threaten."

What the heck is this guy's problem?

"Warden, Adam Matthew is a boy who woke from a coma only days ago. I am a state-employed psychologist that specializes in child abuse cases." I gave him a cold stare as I slowly enunciated my words and underlaid them with a hint of threat. "Consider your next words carefully."

The warden's face twisted with disdain, then he turned and said, "Follow me."

I walked behind him, but with his long legs, I found it challenging to keep up. I sensed it was an intimidation tactic, so I slowed down and walked at my normal pace. He'd said to follow him, so he could just wait for me if he wanted to play this game. As I approached the security checkpoint between the admin building and the main prison, I could see the warden standing there, staring at his wristwatch and tapping his foot.

As I came up to him, I smiled and said, "Are you ready to continue, Warden?"

He muttered something under his breath, which I'm sure was in no way complementary to me, and then he said in a sarcastic tone, "Indeed. I wouldn't want to waste your time by making you needlessly wait on my inconsiderate behavior."

"Apology accepted," I said with cheer. "Lead the way."

His eyes flashed with barely contained hostility while keeping his fake smile in place. *Good... I'm not one of his lackeys or an inmate, so I certainly don't have to put up with his theatrics.* As I continued to walk behind him, at my own pace, of course, I marveled at the sameness of everything in the place: floors of

gray concrete, walls of gray concrete blocks—*And the ceilings?…
Yup. Gray concrete.* Just like outside this morning, the place felt
visually depressing. I wondered if the color scheme was pur-
poseful or just a casualty of being built by the lowest bidder.
I thought a little color would go a long way toward helping
the inmates maintain their mental stability. And I would have
mentioned it to the warden if I'd thought he cared, which I
knew he didn't.

As we entered cell block B, I immediately noticed the
absence of catcalls. Being separated from females 24/7, the
men always went nuts when they saw me. Looking around, I
realized all the surrounding cells had been vacated. The next
thing I noticed was the warden had stopped up ahead in front
of a cell. As I neared where he stood, the coppery scent of blood
assaulted my nose… likely from the splattered brilliant red substance that decorated the cell walls, floor, and even the ceiling.
The color stuck out like a beacon in a sea of gray.

When I looked down, what I noticed next was… horrible.
A gasp escaped from my lips as my right hand flew to my
mouth. My brain had trouble registering what my eyes insisted
lay before them. The *thing* in front of me looked like some kind
of… Play-Doh man, for lack of a better metaphor. Something
had turned someone into a Play-Doh man like kids would do
on top of a piece of construction paper to create a scene. Except,
in this case, instead of paper, the floor had been used. A male
prison uniform lay stretched out on the floor sans person. Its
owner's naked, bloody, broken corpse lay curled up in the far
corner. I felt my stomach churning as I moved my gaze back
to the prison uniform.

Outlines for the hands, feet, and head had been artistically
drawn in blood and placed in proper position in relation to the
clothing. In fact, whoever had drawn it showed genuine talent.

But that's where the art ended. Someone sullied it by turning it into a collage of body parts. The entire scalp (with hair), along with the eyes, ears, nose, lips, tongue, genitals, fingers, and toes had been removed from the victim and placed in anatomically correct positions within the blood-painted outlines.

I looked away, only to find an equally bloody painting on the wall depicting a hideous-looking demon tormenting and dismembering a terrified man. Above the art piece, I saw a single word handwritten in blood: *PEDOPHILE*.

I turned my surely ashen face toward Warden Smith, and in between quick sips of air to keep myself from vomiting, I said, "Who is this?"

"Do tell, Doctor," he said with a wave of his hand toward the dismembered corpse. "You don't recognize the man you had an appointment with this morning?"

"That's Richard Davis?" I gasped.

"The one and only... what's left of him anyhow."

"Who would... Who would do such a thing?"

"That's the million-dollar question, Doctor," he said as he cocked his head. "I've been hoping you might shed some light on the perpetrator's identity."

"What—me?" I said. "Warden, what... what I mean is, why do you think I would know who did this?"

"Well, you're the expert." He said, his smile smug. "Perhaps one of his victims? Perhaps one of their loved ones? His killer made a point of writing Davis's proclivity on the wall. Has the motive of revenge crossed your mind, hmm?"

"But... But Davis was in lockup. Do you think one of my clients pulled an invisible man stunt and did this?"

"Don't be obsequious, Dr. Brown. Of course I don't think any of your clients personally did this, but perhaps one of them took out a contracted hit on the man."

I could only shake my head in disbelief as I forced myself to even my breathing back out. "There are several problems with that hypothesis. First, the client in question is just a teenage boy, and his single mom is not a woman of means. Second, none of his other victims come from wealthy families either. Third, it would imply an inside job. Are you suggesting one of your employees either committed the murder or helped the perpetrator commit the murder?"

The warden shrugged. "Dr. Brown, are you suggesting that money is the only possible means of payment? An attractive woman could pay using… oh, you know… other equally tantalizing assets."

An ember of anger wormed its way through my brain and straight out of my mouth. "Warden, that comment makes you sound like a pig. Is that what you are: a pig?"

He frowned at me. "Name-calling and getting all emotional isn't going to help me solve this crime. I'm a *pragmatist* if you feel the need to pin a label on me. Nothing about the murder adds up, and I'm willing to consider any and all options."

A short, annoyed laugh escaped from my lips. "Well, good luck proving your 'sex for a hit' theory. And it still doesn't relieve you of the fact that it had to be an inside job. But have you considered the most obvious suspect: his cellmate?"

The warden clasped his hands together. "Ohhh, goody, Dr. Brown. How could I have let that slip my mind? It's fortuitous for me that I have you around to remind me of such things."

My eyes narrowed to slits. "You know, instead of being a condescending jerk, you could try working with me. Why isn't his cellmate a serious contender for the crime?"

His eyes bored into me with great intensity, and then he seemed to come to some internal decision. His smile returned, and he said, "It's simple, really. Davis wasn't relieved of his body parts with a knife. Somebody used a set of very sharp teeth on him instead. He was bitten to death, and his cellmate's dentition doesn't match the bite marks."

"And fingerprints?"

"Only his and Davis's prints were found in the cell."

"Did his cellmate see anything?"

He shook his head. "He claims he fell asleep and didn't hear any of it. And while that would normally be a red flag, the perpetrator apparently paralyzed Davis's vocal cords first with a rather heavy blow to the throat. It was quite professionally done. In fact, no one in the surrounding cells heard or saw anything either."

I turned my head and looked back at the two drawings painted in the cell. "What about the bloody artwork on the floor and on the wall? It exhibits talent, even if it is macabre. Is his cellmate artistic?"

"We've already considered that angle," he said with a dark and brooding look. "No, his cellmate doesn't have an artistic bone in his body."

"Well, where does that leave us now?"

He pointed a finger at me. "Well, Dr. Brown, that's where you come in. I'll be needing the files you brought with you today along with anything else in your possession that may be relevant to the case."

My face dropped. "My files? This is privileged communication between doctor and client, and I will not hand it over to you."

"Well, fortunately for me," he said as he thrust out his chest and looked down his nose at me, "I thought we might hit this roadblock, so I took the added precaution of getting a court order. You will not be allowed to leave the premises without turning over your files to our legal representative."

"Look," I said, flabbergasted, "I just came here to interview the guy… not murder him. Why are you doing this to me, and why are you so fixated on my patients?"

"Why?" He said, then glared. "I'll let you in on a little secret. I'm doing this because Davis's cellmate, along with several other inmates and guards, have been clear on one thing. They all claimed that Davis had been going on and on for days that some Adam Matthew character was coming to get him on Halloween. Davis said he looked like a boy but was really a demon. Everyone here thought Davis was a nutcase, but he didn't care. The more they laughed at him, the more emphatic he became. He even tried to arrange protection for himself."

I rubbed a hand against my forehead. "But that makes little sense. Isn't it more likely that Adam is just a normal teenager and Davis was just crazy?"

"That may all be true, Dr. Brown, but Davis is most certainly dead, and he was convinced that the boy was going to kill him on Halloween. And after looking at all of this… who knows… maybe it was a demon."

"Do you really believe that, Warden?"

That hard, predatory smile reappeared on his face. "Frankly, it doesn't matter what I believe. Nobody does something like this in my prison and gets away with it, so I'll follow the leads to Satan himself if that's where it takes me. Now please, hand over your case notes so I don't have to get extra security involved."

CHAPTER 25

DR. CHARLOTTE BROWN

FATHER CASEY AND I met with Deirdre Matthew in her apartment kitchen that evening. I'd asked for the get-together to discuss Richard Davis's murder. Her kitchen turned out to be a little too cozy for the three of us, but with Adam out of the hospital and living at home again, I didn't want to take a chance on him overhearing our conversation. I especially didn't want him to know that Davis thought he was an actual demon. Such a thing could be traumatic on a tender young psyche.

As Father Casey and I took a seat at the kitchen table, Deirdre smiled and asked, "So can I get either of you a coffee?"

Its aroma hung in the air, and it had a pleasant quality to it, so I said, "Yes, please."

Father Casey shook his head no.

"Do you take cream or sugar?" Deirdre asked.

"Both." I grinned. "I have a real sweet tooth and like it best when it tastes like dessert."

I watched as she went into the cheap wood cabinet with a

slightly askew door and then to a small refrigerator not even as tall as she was. Even though the cabinet and the fridge had little in the way of space, I could see both were mostly empty. It dawned on me that she had little money, and I felt guilty for not being more considerate of that.

"On second thought," I said as I waved a hand at her, "I think I'll drink mine black."

Deirdre's eyes narrowed with suspicion, so I added, "I forgot, I'm on a diet."

She turned back and returned the cream to the fridge and the sugar to the cupboard, and then she set the steaming-hot black cup of coffee in front of me before taking a seat at the table with us.

As I slowly sipped the hot beverage, I told them what happened at the prison, and they listened without saying a word. When I came to the part about Richard Davis, Deirdre became visibly distressed. Her eyes became watery as I continued, and then silent tears ran down her cheeks.

"What's wrong, honey?" I asked.

"I'm sorry," she said as she swiped at her eyes with a hand. "I just thought Richard Davis was trying to get back at me with his crazy story, so I said nothing to you about it."

That caught Father Casey's attention. "About what, Deirdre?"

"His story sounded crazy at the time," she said, then frowned. "But after listening to you, I think my son may have done that to him."

Deirdre's accusation against Adam caused my hackles to rise. "How could you say that about him… your own child? My story concerning Davis is horrible, but in reality, my words don't begin to describe what I saw with my own eyes. To think Adam could do something that evil is beyond anything I'm ready to accept."

My words shut Deirdre down. Her mouth moved a few times as if she might respond, but then her lips pressed tightly together. She bent her head down toward the table and stared at it with sad eyes.

Father Casey clasped Deirdre's pale white hands in his own as he gently said, "Deirdre, seeing an active murder scene firsthand—especially a gruesome one—can be very hard on a person. Charlotte is not in a good place right now mentally, but that doesn't mean she meant to insinuate that you're a bad mother. None of us think that. But you must talk to us. Please tell us why you think your son might be behind his murder."

She sat there unmoving as if she hadn't heard his words until I said, "I'm sorry, Deirdre. Father Casey is right. I'm not in a good place right now. Please forgive me for taking it out on you. To be honest, I'm kind of freaked out by everything going on around me, and I desperately want to believe in the innocence of youth. I don't want to think that evil could make your boy or any boy do that to someone. But that's my issue, not yours. Please continue."

Deirdre reached out with a trembling hand and started picking at a tiny sliver of wood peeling off the kitchen table. Her eyes took on a faraway look. "Richard Davis said that on the day he was arrested, Adam came up to him in the police car and told him he would visit him in jail on Halloween and that he would do things to him… things that Adam would enjoy. Then he said Adam's eyes went completely black as his mouth morphed into a huge smile full of fangs. It sounded like crazy talk to me, but now I'm not so sure. Since Adam woke from his coma and came home, several butchered animals have been found in the surrounding area. Two homes in the adjacent neighborhood have burned to the ground, and a few cars have been decimated. And now you're telling me that Richard Davis was brutally murdered in prison on Halloween. The thing is, I was so excited when Adam first came back home, but now that he's here, I find he scares me. Before he went into a coma, he was just a normal boy. In a way, he's still the same boy, except he seems both better and worse than before. At times, he seems angelic, almost holy. Then there are the other times. Times when I feel like I'm inches away from death. Times when I can almost feel unbridled rage beneath his placid features. As if his control was hanging by a thread." She covered her face with her hands as the tears started flowing.

"Oh, Deirdre," I said. "I'm sure—"

Father Casey looked at me and put a finger to his lips.

My jaw dropped. I couldn't believe he was shushing me.

"Charlotte," Father Casey said, "I need to speak to Deirdre in private. Can you give us a few minutes alone?"

I felt like I was being sent away so the grownups could talk, but I complied. Excusing myself, I walked to the living room down at the end of the hall. I found Adam lying on a tattered but clean tan fabric sofa. He was dressed in jeans and a Black Sabbath T-shirt and had headphones on. The volume was so loud I could clearly hear the music. He stared up at the ceiling as if there was nothing there. It worked well with the look on his face, which looked like nobody was home. I stood there and mused that his vacant face made him look like a mannequin, and even though he was listening to music with a heavy beat, he just lay there like the dead. His person seemed banal at first glance, and in the waning light of day, I could almost convince myself that I had misconstrued his intent when he'd stood outside my door the other night asking to be let in. But as I continued looking at him, I noted something indefinably eerie about him. I had the strangest feeling that he was intensely aware of my presence even though he gave no indication that he had even noticed me. I turned away from him and walked over to the picture window.

Two gray-and-tan saltbox buildings, identical to the one I stood in, greeted my sight. The architecture was blasé and the small apartment complex held nothing appealing to me. It obviously sat on the poor side of town, and I could only imagine how hard it had to be on Deirdre. A few years ago, she'd been happily married and well on her way to upper-class living. Now she found herself a struggling single mother. I couldn't imagine what it would be like to lose my husband.

As I stood there thinking, I noticed movement out of the corner of my eye. I turned back toward Adam, and his face no longer looked mask like. Instead, he appeared to be panicked, even fearful, and he stared up at me with pleading eyes. Then, just as quickly, he slipped back into his mannequin routine.

I shook my head and said under my breath, "Adam, you're definitely a riddle waiting to be solved."

In a low voice, not much above a whisper, he said, "Yes, I know… and if you look closer, you can see I'm wrapped in a mystery. Some might even go so far as to say I'm an enigma. What do you think, Charlotte? Would you say I'm a riddle wrapped in a mystery inside an enigma? Do you think you could say that about me?"

His words startled me. "You heard me call you a riddle with your headphones going full blast? How is that possible?"

Adam smirked as his eyes gleamed with… *Malice… or something else, maybe?* I couldn't tell for sure.

Then he turned those eyes on me as if he were pinning an insect to a board. "I thought we just established what I am. Talking to you is like talking to a shrub. Do you find it soothing to ask yourself self-evident questions? Does it keep your brains from flopping out of your skull and splatting on the ground?"

"You know," I said as I crossed my arms across my chest, "I'm your greatest advocate. And you might actually see that if you weren't so antagonistic toward me."

"Well, I'm glad you cleared that up for me, Charlotte. I especially enjoyed that bit of advocacy you did for me after you promised that our conversation would be completely confidential. Mum's the word, pinkie promise, cross your heart, amigos to the end. Of course, as a woman of your word, you ran straight to my drunk, grieving mother and told her everything. Then there's your dear, dear husband. But that's just pillow talk, so that doesn't count. Next, you handed over my entire case file to that turd-faced warden. Oh, and let's not forget dear old Father Casey. If you think about it, you're giving the town gossip a run for her money."

"Adam, that wasn't gossip," I protested. "I talked because I'm trying to figure out how to help you. I handed over your case file because the law required it of me. But how could you possibly know this?"

"Helloooo," he said as he rolled his eyes. "Earth to shrub! Riddle, mystery, enigma. Try to keep up." Then he waved his hands out and upward with a magnanimous air as if he were an emperor bequeathing a tidbit to the town idiot. "I'd like to say I'm appreciative of your so-called advocacy, but I am a fast learner. While I can't say thank you, I can assure you that I will return the favor and do some advocacy for you on your behalf. Just thinking about it gives me the shivers."

"What happened to you, Adam? What's your endgame here?"

"My endgame?" A lewd expression broke out on his face as he eyed my body, then his eyes snapped up to mine. "Well, I don't know that I like you enough to tell you that. It's not like we've been out on a date or anything. But I will tell you this. Because you've decided to pursue me, it will cost you your career, husband, home, freedom, and even your life. This is because you are not pursuing the mundane. You are pursuing a thinking creature… a creature as old as time itself. A creature that doesn't sleep, doesn't forget, doesn't forgive, and is always watchful. You are now my enemy, and these things will come to pass for you. In the end, you will take your life by your own hand, and all the demons in Hell will celebrate." Then he shrugged. "Of course, forewarned is forearmed. Stop me if you can… or don't…. I couldn't care less either way."

Feeling all the blood in my face drain away, I wanted to vomit. I found my courage and weakly said, "But… But how could you know that? Father Casey said those words to me in a church."

"But but but," Adam sputtered in a mocking tone. "You know, shrub, I want to amend my earlier statement to you in the hospital about wanting to be spared 'the tedium of inane chitchat with morons' to 'inane chitchat with morons *like you.*'"

My mouth dropped open, but nothing came out. As I stood there speechless, Adam's face started showing undertones of fierce intelligence, hatred, rage, pain, and insanity as he hissed, "From now until the burning pit, I'll never know what he sees in you freaks."

Father Casey and Deirdre walked into the room right then and stood near me.

Adam pulled off his headphones and said in a pleasant voice, "Hi, Mom."

I turned my startled face to Adam, and he smiled back at me like a radiant cherub. *Dear Lord, Davis and Deirdre weren't losing it after all.* Even after everything I'd seen, I had been in denial and didn't want to believe it, though I knew that wasn't exactly true even as I thought it.

I understood quite well that it was one thing to believe in something intellectually and another to drown in the reality of it. With the dangerous waters of my situation threatening to cover my head, my belief moved beyond uncertainty, moved beyond the intellectual. It hit me hard that I was dealing with an honest-to-God demon. An enemy of all that was holy and good. An actual enemy of God. It also meant that Hell wasn't an abstraction but a real place. The realization hit me like a ton of bricks, and my body started trembling from head to toe.

I turned and stumbled to the door without saying a word. After three attempts, I got the door handle to work and I ran out the door. I don't even remember if I closed it behind me.

CHAPTER 26

ADAM MATTHEW

I GRABBED MY groggy head in both hands and groaned. I had just awakened from a bad dream. In fact, I realized that I'd had horrible dreams all night long. That would teach me for sharing my body with my sister. If she didn't stop it, she'd need to leave because I didn't want to go through another night like that. The dream that just woke me up was terrifying. In it, I grew large claws and ripped Dr. Charlotte apart. She was nothing more than a bloody pulp by the time I'd finished with her. It felt real, like I was really doing it, but thankfully…

I sat up in bed and forced myself to slow my breathing, and then I willed my heart to slow down. Once I'd gotten myself under control, I attended to the next issue. I had to pee… bad, so I staggered out of bed, but everything seemed off somehow. I realized my full bladder would not give me the time to figure it out as I rushed for the toilet. Once there, I was surprised to find a wall where the bathroom was supposed to be. I turned my head back and forth until I spotted the bathroom several feet down the hall and on the opposite wall. I ran to it and think it was about five minutes before I got done.

Feeling much better, I went to the sink and washed my face. Looking up into the mirror, I would've peed my pants if I hadn't just taken care of that. Somebody's face stared back at me, and I froze. A few seconds later, I looked behind me and in the shower, but no one was there. I looked back in the mirror and realized the face was mine. But it looked different now… like I was really, really old. Maybe fifteen or sixteen instead of my actual age, which scared me.

"Mom!" I screamed.

She came running in with a panicked look and said, "What's wrong, honey?"

"Mom, what happened to my face?" I blubbered. "Why do I look so old?"

"What?… What are you going on about? There's nothing wrong with your face. In fact, it's a very handsome face. You should consider yourself lucky."

I started shaking. "But… I don't understand, Mom. What did you do to my face?"

She grabbed my hand and said, "Let's go to the living room and you can explain to me what's going on in that head of yours."

My head jerked up in surprise when we walked into a sparsely decorated living room that I'd never seen before. "Mom, where are we?"

"What do you mean? We're home."

"Well, I know the house is big, but I don't remember seeing these rooms before." *Oh, probably the third floor.* "Mom, Mr. Crab told me little snots can't come up here, so we better leave before he finds me. You know how grouchy he gets about everything."

Mom gasped, then her eyes got all bulgy. In a weird squeaky voice and sounding like she could hardly breathe, she said, "What… What's the last thing you remember, Adam?"

"That's easy. We were sitting on the big brown leather sofa in the downstairs living room watching TV when someone started knocking on the front door, but we didn't answer it. Then I woke up just now because I had a bad dream, and here we are."

Tears started running down mom's pretty face as she pulled at her clothing with her hands. Something boomed outside, probably a car backfiring, but it made mom jump a mile high off the couch. She wrapped her arms around herself and hugged tight. Then she said, "You don't remember waking up in the hospital? You don't remember being in a coma and then coming home?"

"Huh?" I shook my head. "No."

"So… so, all this time, it really wasn't you in there?" Then her face fell and she started sobbing. "Nooooo!" she cried out.

Mom backed away from me, and she looked really sad and scared, so I went to give her a hug. Her eyes got wide, and she held her hands out in front of her. As I drew near, she pushed me hard and I fell on my butt. She yelled, "Stay away from me!"

She turned and ran into another room, then she slammed the door shut. After that, I heard the door lock click into place, so I went and sat on the couch with my head swimming in confusion.

I waited for hours for Mom to come out so I could apologize to her, but she never did. I knocked and called out to her several times, but she never answered me. Not once. I must have decided to leave the house at some point because I found myself walking down an unfamiliar road. The strange thing was I didn't even remember leaving Old Man Crab's place. I had my jacket and shoes on too, but I didn't remember putting them on either. I concentrated, but my mind was blank on the subject. It all felt so weird.

My heart flickered with a twinge of panic because I had no idea where I was, so I just kept walking. I figured I'd run into something I knew eventually. The surrounding homes were old and run-down and packed together at first. But as I kept going, the housing thinned out, and then I started passing farms. After a while, they disappeared too, and I walked down completely wooded roads. It reached a point where the trees on both sides of the road were so tall and overhung that I could only catch glimpses of the wispy clouds in the whitish-blue sky above. As I considered turning back around and retracing my steps, I finally saw something I recognized up the road. Farmer Blake's red barn came into view… the one I'd stashed my bike behind after being ditched at the cemetery, and it brought back memories.

In my mind's eye, I could see the forest I'd walked through with my so-called friends to get to the Deadlands. I watched in my head as we entered the Bianchini crypt together, and then I watched as they ran off and left me stranded there without a flashlight. If it hadn't been for that strange man leading me out of the graveyard, I don't know what would have happened to me. Still, it had been pretty cold that night, so it was a good bet that I would have frozen to death.

Fortunately, that wouldn't be my fate today, as it was only cool outside. The bad news was I still had several miles to go, so I had a long walk ahead of me. I concentrated again, but nothing came to mind. I didn't know how I'd made it so far away from home.

The gravel crunched underneath my feet as I walked. From

time to time, I stooped down and scooped up gravel pieces for target practice. I'd gotten pretty good at hitting what I aimed for, and I realized I really did have a decent throwing arm. As I thought that, I saw movement up ahead off to the left in the high grass, so I cocked my arm and let the rock fly. It hit something that made a loud whistling squeak, and then a big, fat groundhog came tumbling out of the tall grass and ran across the street. Stopping midway and looking at me, it stood on its hind legs and started chittering at me as if scolding me. Ten seconds later, it finished its lecture and continued on its way and disappeared into the tall grass on the other side of the road. I felt kind of bad for hitting the fat little fella, so I dropped the remaining rocks I held and continued on.

After walking for a while, I must have zoned out because I found myself standing in front of my old home in the Brook Spring neighborhood. It was just there. As I stared at the tidy white house with its dark brown wood shutters, I desperately wanted to believe that my current life was just a bad nightmare, and if I went and opened the front door, my mom and dad would be inside, and I would be happy again. As if in a dream, I felt my feet carry me toward my real home as hope rose in my chest. I felt my hand reach for the doorknob, but it was locked. I knocked on the front door, and through a fog, I saw a cranky old woman with iron-gray hair wearing a black-and-white muumuu and fuzzy pink slippers. She told me that my parents weren't there and to get off her front porch. I also heard her say something about the police. As she shut the door in my face, cruel laughter rang out in my head. It sounded like my sister. I looked all around me, but I didn't see her anywhere.

"Bela?" I called out. I called again… nothing.

I looked behind some of the bigger bushes, but she was nowhere to be found. If possible, I felt even more depressed.

It was getting dark outside, so I gave up on her and hurried the rest of the way home—though I use home loosely. Once I got there, I realized I didn't have my house key, so I walked over to the large black-granite rock and took the spare key out from underneath it. I stepped onto the brown tile stone of the entryway and looked around, but I didn't see Old Man Crab or mom, which was fine with me. I didn't want to talk to either of them anyway. When I walked into the kitchen, it hit me how hungry and thirsty I was. After eating two peanut-butter-and-jelly sandwiches and drinking about a gallon of water, I went up the back stairway to my room and passed out on my bed without even bothering to take my clothes off.

CHAPTER 27

ADAM MATTHEW

SOMETIME LATER, I opened my eyes and realized it was light outside. More often than not, I had trouble sleeping through the night in Old Man Crab's house, so I figured that I must have been exhausted—probably due to all the walking I'd done the day before. I stood up, stretched, touched my fingers to my toes, and headed off to my bathroom. After taking care of business, I stripped out of my clothes and stepped into the oversized shower. As the water stream heated up, I stepped off to the side of the old chrome shower head and waited. Looking around, the whole thing looked dingier than I'd remembered. The shower curtains were streaked and dusty, while mold or something like it grew in the grout between the tiles. Once the temperature was to my liking, I grabbed the washcloth off the sidebar, and it felt hard and stiff like it hadn't been used in ages. *Oh well*, I thought. *Once it's wet, it'll loosen right up.* I stepped under the hot water, and it felt great as it washed away the dirt and my sore muscles. After drying off, I went to my drawer for my toothbrush and comb, but it was empty. I ran my fingers through my hair to straighten it up and thought, *Hmm... Well, Mom can't get mad about anything if she took all my stuff.* I walked back to my bedroom and opened my underwear drawer, but it was empty too. Then I discovered the entire dresser was empty. I scratched my head in confusion, then returned to the bathroom and put my dirty clothes back on.

I stepped back into the empty hallway and yelled, "Mommmm!" When she didn't respond, I hollered even louder.

After standing there for twenty seconds or so, I turned and headed for the stairs. But before I got there, I heard the running of feet, and I expected to see her materialize in front of me.

And then she came around the corner... except... it wasn't my mom.

A pretty blonde lady and I stood there in shock, staring at each other.

She backed up two steps and placed a hand on her throat. "Who are you?"

"Adam," I answered. "And you are?"

Her face scrunched up in fear and anger. "I live here, young man. What are you doing in my house?"

"What? *Your* house?" *This lady must be crazy in the head.* "Listen, ma'am, this is *my* house. Where's my mom?"

She stood there looking a little freaked out, and instead of answering me, she yelled, "Tim!"

Moments later, a boy about my age came tearing around the corner. Well, he would have been my age if I didn't look so old. He looked around the age I was supposed to be. He reached out, grabbed the woman's hand and stared at me too.

She nudged him toward the stairs and said, "Go tell Mr. Crab someone broke into the house." She pointed a long finger at me as he left and said, "I already called the police. You'd better leave before they get here."

Unbelievable. "Look, lady, I have no idea why you think this is your house!" With an ache forming in the back of my throat, I yelled, "Where's my mom?!"

The pretty lady just stood there with her mouth agape, so I left her and took off for the back stairs. Old Man Crab could clear things up for me if he wasn't being too ornery today. Entering the kitchen, I saw the boy talking animatedly to a man. When Tim saw me, he turned and ran. When the man saw me, his eyes widened in surprise, and then they narrowed. I think my eyes did the same exact thing. The man standing in front of me looked familiar. He kind of looked like Old Man Crab, but where Crab had always been old as dirt, this man was just old. He couldn't have been over fifty or fifty-five tops.

I strode up to him and got into his face. "Where's my mom and Mr. Crab? And what are you and that lady doing here in my house?"

The man looked down at me in an arrogant, condescending way. Then he poked me in the chest. "And who exactly is your mom, young man?"

"Deirdre Matthew."

He chuckled. "Oh, the maid. Yes. I can see how you'd be confused. Let me introduce myself. I'm William Crab… Mr. Crab's son. And the lady you met upstairs is my fiancée."

"Your fiancée?" I said, as I considered his words. "Nah, I don't think so. Who are you really?"

He seemed nervous as he rubbed the back of his neck. "As I said, I'm William Crab. Do you doubt me?"

I shrugged. "She's got to be in her twenties. Aren't you kind of old for her?"

His stiff posture seemed to relax somewhat. "Well, you

have me there. She's my soon-to-be fiancée. She just doesn't know it yet."

I put my hands on my hips and shook my head. "You know, mister, I don't care about you or your girlfriend. Just tell me where my mom and Mr. Crab are, and I'll get the answers from them."

"Well, kid…" He snickered. "You're two days late for my old man, but he's right here if you'd like to say hello to him." He reached over and patted a sealed black-marble urn sitting on the countertop. "As you can see, he's dead, and I'm here to ship his cremated remains back to our ancestral homeland and claim this mansion as its rightful heir. As for your mom, she's down in the basement doing maid things."

A chill shot through my body. I couldn't imagine Hell being any worse than that place, and just thinking about going into the basement tied my stomach up in knots. With a trembling voice, I said, "Why… Why would you let my mom go down there?… It's dangerous."

William Crab smirked at me. "Dangerous? Ha, do you think the boogeyman lives down there?" Then he grew thoughtful and said, "You know, though, now that you mention it, I thought she would only be down there for a minute or two, but I think it's been more than an hour now." A look of concern lit upon his face. "Do you think she's lost her way down there… or worse?"

My stomach fluttered in fear. Mom was the only person I had left in the whole world, and if I lost her, I'd have nobody. I'd sworn I'd never go down into that basement again, but I also couldn't lose my mom. An internal battle raged inside me, even though my final decision was never in doubt. I went to the ornately carved and gilded wood cabinet and grabbed a salt shaker from it. Then I grabbed a butcher's knife from a drawer underneath the slate countertop. Last, I snatched the flashlight we always kept next to the stairs.

The heavy bronze handle on the basement door groaned in protest as I twisted it. Then hard eyes bored into my back as I pulled open the solid wood door.

Turning, I saw William Crab raise an eyebrow. "You sure are an unusual lad. Maybe you should grab the black pepper and a fork too, just in case you're attacked by a turkey-and-mashed-potato dinner down there." With that, a peal of laughter emanated from his mouth.

Hmm, like father, like son.

William Crab was definitely hiding something from me behind his sarcastic demeanor. But whatever it might have been, it wasn't his family heritage. He gave off the same vibe as Old Man Crab, and they had the same mannerisms too. Even though the old man had never mentioned having a son when he'd been alive, they were too much alike not to be related. They even had the same eye color. While the thought of losing my mother was devastating to me, Crab's passing didn't bother me. He'd been way too sarcastic, condescending, and just plain mean to me to feel any sense of loss at his death. Hopefully, William Crab would treat me and my mother better than his father had. That was, of course, if I still had one.

I plucked up my courage and slowly headed down the creaking wooden steps. When I reached the bottom, I hurried to pull the light string that hung down, and the bulb above came on, giving off a wan light that somehow didn't cast enough illumination into the room. The weak, watery light seemed to heighten rather than lessen the spooky quality of the place. Regardless, there really wasn't enough light to see by, so I clicked on my flashlight and stood completely still as I extended all of my senses.

Neither my mother's nor the thing's presence pressed in upon my psyche, so I forced myself to walk to the center of the room, and I tried again—but still nothing.

"Mom," I hissed in a voice just above a whisper as my eyes darted to and fro. My voice sounded like a bullhorn to me in the dead silence surrounding me.

Something seemed off down here, but the answer eluded me because of the fear clouding my brain.

Salt had been effective against the fiend the last time here, though I realized the salt shaker in my pocket wouldn't be nearly enough. My eyes quickly scanned through the assortment of junk lying about, and much to my relief, the open bag of rock salt remained. My pockets were overflowing with the stuff by the time I finished since you could never have enough salt down here. I even rubbed down my hair, exposed skin, and clothing with some of the salt that had degraded to a dust-like consistency. Hopefully, it would give the thing a burn to remember if it snuck up behind me and tried to grab me.

With my flashlight and knife in hand, I walked under the large brick archway into a blackness that threatened to overwhelm me. After crossing its threshold, my heartbeat and breathing picked up noticeably, so I stopped and waited as I willed them to calm down. Leaning against the cold basement wall for support, a strong sense of corruption bloomed in my soul, courtesy of my special gift. I violently jerked away from the wall and moved into the center of the room. It sorely tempted me to turn and run, but I reminded myself that this time I had a flashlight and had come armed with weapons and knowledge—also, I wasn't alone either. My mom was down here in the basement with me. All I had to do was find her, and then we could get out of here.

I realized that if I hoped to accomplish anything in the

basement, I was going about it all wrong. James Bond wouldn't have been afraid of anything. He was the greatest secret agent in the entire world, and nothing scared him. He would've come down here and kicked the fiend's butt and rescued his mom, and that would have been that. If I was gonna succeed, I needed to be just like him.

I cupped my hand to my mouth and yelled out, "Hey, demon, my name is James Bond—007, to be exact. And I'm coming for you."

Then I put a swagger in my step. Standing tall, I walked into the next room, and still… nothing. I walked into the next two rooms exactly the same way, and then my courage failed me.

It was really, really dark down here. And really, really quiet. It was so quiet that my breathing and heartbeat sounded loud to me. Even my pant legs rustled loudly against each other as I walked. I stood still again so that I could listen, and that's when I first sensed it—not the thing precisely, but it felt like it… just deeper. I don't know how I knew it, but I knew what I was feeling: death—like many lives had passed away down here in this basement. The sensation pressed in upon me until I literally felt cocooned in the misery of hard deaths. I knew if I died down here, I would be away from my mother and everyone else forever. I'd end up like a pebble lying alone in a deep, cold river. That thought should have scared me, but instead, I felt a seductive urge to lie down on the hard stone floor and give in to it. To give in to death. It simply seemed better that way. No more struggles. No more heartbreak. I would be dead, alone and forever, and that would be enough for me.

As my butt touched the cold stone floor, a wave of anger arose in me, and it cut through my melancholy. *Mom wouldn't give up on me, and I wasn't going to give up on her.* I picked myself up off the floor and forced myself onward before my anger could subside. Rooms stuffed full with junk suddenly gave way to a series of empty brick-and-stone rooms filled with varying degrees of earthy smells, mold, and rot. The scent of lime and water started creeping into the mix too. It surprised me when the manufactured walls gave way to natural ones. At first, it looked like someone had cut into the solid rock, but as I continued, my surroundings looked more natural and cave-like, as if the walls had been cut from the flow of an underground river.

I walked into a large natural chamber and froze. My flashlight played low across the floor, creating a pattern of light and shadows against the skeletal remains strewn about... human remains. A gasp caught in my throat as my mind fully registered the slaughter surrounding me. My panic and despair became palpable as I involuntarily stared at the mishmash of skulls, rib cages, and other bones—bones that had once been the property of others who had loved their bodies no less than I loved mine. With a sick feeling rising in my stomach, I tore my eyes away from the spectacle and ducked under a low archway to get away from the sight.

Unfortunately, the scenery was no better as I found myself standing among several desecrated tombstones. Amidst the spoiled graveyard, I saw several holes and broken coffins, along with more human remains scattered about. Something had dug up the graves in the past and tossed the human remains here and there—and I had a pretty good idea of what that *something* was.

The muscles in my throat and jaw spasmed as a horrifying thought flitted through my mind—the thing that had bothered me about the basement when I first came downstairs... the detail that had eluded me. It was the light... or the light bulb, to be exact. I'd had to pull on the light string to turn it on when I'd reached the bottom step in the basement. *And come to think of it, Mom didn't take the flashlight with her either.* She wasn't a bat, so she wouldn't have gone into the basement without light. All at once, I realized my mother wasn't down here. Like his father before him, William Crab had lied to me. If I managed to survive today, it would be the last time I ever made that mistake.

Finding myself *alone* in the creature's den… or maybe dining room… the shadows grew longer and the dark places scarier. I hurried back under the low archway and into the large chamber that contained the first human bones I had come across. As I headed for the chamber exit, a small, sharp rock slipped into my shoe and sliced my foot. I placed the flashlight in my mouth and laid my knife on the cavern floor. Then I balanced myself against a wall with one hand as I dug the stone out of my shoe with the other. Without warning, my hand sank into the muddy wall and hit something solid. I pulled back hard, but I remained stuck for just a second, and then I heard a snick, and my hand came free. I started shaking the crud off of my dirty appendage even as the vertical mud wall in front of me began to sag. Suddenly, a whole human skeleton oozed out of it and collapsed at my feet. As I stared in disbelief, all my skin tightened, and every hair on my body seemed to stand on end.

Before I could start moving again, two long arms ending in ghastly white fingers and long, yellowish talons burst from the muddy wall and grasped my shirt. The hands smoked and burned when they came into contact with the salt dust on my clothes, and its fingers reflexively let go of me, which caused me to stumble and hit the ground. The fiend emerged from the wall as I got back up, lunging at me, but I reached into my front pockets and flung two large handfuls of rock salt at it. It screeched hideously as I turned around and ran. I continued running until I came to a complete stop in the kitchen, staring at a clearly disappointed William Crab. Hunched over with my hands on my knees, I dragged deep breaths of air into my burning lungs.

"My mom wasn't down there, you liar!" I yelled. "Why did you lie to me, you liar?!"

"Why?" He sneered. "Because I could, that's why. You and your mom haven't lived here for more than an entire year. You deserve what you get if your stupid pea brain can't even remember something that basic." He paused and laughed. "In fact, that might be the very definition of a retard."

My body shook with rage. "You bastard, you tried to kill me! You wanted that thing to murder me. I'll… I'll… "

"Oh yeah? Prove it, kid. All I know is you broke into my house and rummaged through my basement for things to steal. And you sure look all alive and healthy for someone I tried killing. At least, that's what I'll tell the police if you care to involve them."

I wanted to transfer my anger to Crab's smirking face via my fist. Balling up my hands into weapons, I had every intention of doing just that as I swung. But I pulled back at the last second… I just couldn't. I'd been taught to respect my elders, and I couldn't overcome my upbringing. Instead, I turned away and walked out the front door as he flung insults at my back.

I shut the door behind me and took several deep breaths. *Well, at least I'm still alive.* I dusted the salt off my body, and then I turned out all my pockets to empty the remaining rock salt from them. As I did, two small bones fell out of one of them and hit the ground. I picked them up, examined them, and thought they might be human finger bones. Not that I was an osteologist, so I might be wrong. I didn't know how they'd ended up in my pocket, but there was no way I was going back into the mansion with William Crab and that monster, and it seemed sacrilegious to leave them lying on his front lawn, so I pocketed them. I figured I could decide what to do with them later.

Crab's words flattened me. *Not lived here for over a year?* My confusion fogged my brain and made my head hurt. I put my hands in my front pockets and started walking, but there was no place for me to go… I no longer had a home. And I'd lost my mom. With hunched shoulders and a bowed head, I walked to the only other home I had ever known: my real home in Brook Spring. Since my mom and dad didn't live there any-more, after returning, I curled up in a ball in the middle of the front lawn and covered my ears and closed my eyes.… *Maybe if I wish hard enough, the world will all go away.*

Unfortunately, the world remained, but the old woman in the muumuu called the police on me as promised. In the end, the nice police officers got me back home to my mom and our apartment.

CHAPTER 28

DR. CHARLOTTE BROWN

I TURNED OFF the mini recorder and said, "So what do you think, Father Casey?"

He leaned back in his chair and pushed a hand through his nicely trimmed salt-and-pepper hair. "I think it was an exceptionally risky thing for you to do, but I wouldn't have believed it if you hadn't."

"So you approve?" I asked hopefully.

"Maybe. I'll let you know when it's all over with. But I will tell you you've made a believer out of me."

"Do you think Bishop Arroyo will accept this as proof of possession?"

"Maybe." He shrugged. "It depends on how much stock the bishop puts in my personal witness. In retrospect, we should have recorded our earlier conversations."

His answer surprised me, and a short, snorting laugh escaped from my lips before I could catch myself. "Really?" I blurted out. "You're a priest. You don't think he'll believe you? Does he know something about you I don't?"

Thankfully, Father Casey seemed amused by that. "Well," he said. "You have to understand that the bishop has people he answers to as well and the church can be very touchy about this subject. They'll demand a high level of proof before giving their blessing for an exorcism."

"Well, get on with it then," I said as I swatted a hand in the air from right to left. "It's not like Adam has all the time in the world. And if we don't get this demon, it will get him, and I don't think I can live with that."

His eyes and face laughed with merriment. It enhanced the deep smile lines etched into his features from a lifetime of use. "You would've made a good nun. You could have smacked my knuckles if you'd brought a ruler with you."

The father's friendly manner and humor loosened me up, and I giggled. "Jeez, I've been waiting my whole life to be compared to a nun. Such a sweet-talker. Thanks."

"Well, I guess you can cross that off your bucket list. But, seriously now, have you been protecting yourself? Have you been praying diligently?"

"Sure," I said cheerfully. "I pray almost every day. I also cleaned, blessed, and sealed my house, so both soul and property are safe now." *As safe as a bug in a rug.*

"Charlotte," Father Casey said with a look of concern. "I watched you the day you stumbled out of Deirdre's apartment. You were deathly afraid, and rightly so. But the Charlotte sitting before me today has discussed this with her rational mind, and her rational mind won. The world will tell you 'Bravo,' but I'm telling you that you're being a fool. That thing wasn't making idle threats; you need to be careful."

"Okay." I sighed. "I'll admit that I've calmed down a lot

since that day. But that's because I realized that it's only a demon, and demons lie. They're not all-powerful, so instead, they try to get under your skin and unnerve you. That's what they do. It tried scaring me away, and I've decided I'm not falling for it. And don't you worry… I've bought every bottle of holy water in town."

Father Casey shook his head. "You need to listen to me or you're going to get yourself killed. While it's known that demons lie, what's less well known is that they usually tell the truth."

My lips turned down in a frown as I considered his words. "And why would the father of lies and his cronies do that?"

"Remember, Charlotte, their ultimate goal isn't lying but deception. If everything they said was a lie, you wouldn't believe them. Instead, they'll load you down with tons of brutal truth and then intermingle it with just enough untruth to get you to make very incorrect conclusions. It's subtle and deadly. Don't let your guard down and don't fall for it."

My face twisted in disbelief. "But, Father, the Bible says that only God is omniscient. Are you claiming that this demon is too? That it knows my future?"

He folded his arms against his chest. "No, I'm not, though demons may seem like they do." Father Casey pinched the bridge of his nose before continuing, "You have to remember that these creatures operate in the supernatural world. They're not omniscient, but somehow their realm allows them to see further than we can in ours."

"Okay, if you say so, but I still don't see why that's so important."

He shook his head. "You're thinking about this the wrong way. Why do people consult Ouija boards?"

My head tilted to the side as I thought about it. Finally,

I spoke. "There are many reasons, I suppose: for fun, to find things, know things, fortune-telling. But truthfully, I've never played it myself, but I have friends that swear by it. What do you think, Father? Do you think it works?"

"Well, Charlotte, I know this boy who lost his dog, and the Ouija board told him he would find her in three days, and he did. Later on, it told him about his future career choice. Even though that boy had no intentions of doing something like that, that's exactly the profession he chose later in life."

"But, Father," I protested, "that's not evidence. These things could have happened anyway, and did you ever think this person may have been lying to you… or at least exaggerating his experience?"

"Not really." He shrugged. "That boy was me, and I guarantee you that rebellious lad had no intentions of becoming a priest when he grew up. But my point is that the only reason the Ouija board works at all is that some things out there can see future events better than we can."

"Okay, fine," I said in exasperation. "So you're telling me there's no hope and that I should just throw my hands up and walk away from this case?"

"Not at all. I'm telling you to be careful."

I nodded. "Like I said, I *am*."

"The problem is your idea of being cautious differs from mine, and it will get you killed. A good example of what I'm talking about is the holy water you like using. You think of it as some kind of bug killer in the spiritual world, and when you use it, you imagine your actions are killing the bugs. On the other hand, I think of the holy water as a vessel that contains God's blessings. When I use the holy water, I understand I am doing nothing myself and that it is God's grace contained within the water that protects me. You see, you're leaning on yourself while I'm leaning on God. It's a subtle but deadly mistake on your part."

My hands flew up defensively. "Fine, I'll concede that I look at it that way, but what difference does it make? You use the holy water… I use the holy water… we both get the same results. And it's not that I don't believe in God; I'm just practical and don't like getting bogged down in semantics."

The Father shifted in his seat uncomfortably. "But, Charlotte… look… what happens when the demon comes at you in a way that you didn't expect? You can't put holy water on a situation, and you can't put it on your heart. You can't put it on future or past events, and you certainly can't put it on anything when you're not around and the demon works fervently behind the scenes to bring about your downfall. And that is why you need to spend more time in prayer, as God knows what you do not and he can go where you cannot."

Tiny fingers of doubt started crawling around on my skin… like evil ants. "I… I guess I didn't look at it that way. So where do you and I go from here?"

"We turn to the church. That's what the church is for, and that's why we need the church's blessing. The Catholic Church is God's representative on Earth, and with the power of the church behind us, this thing can be defeated. You need to pray to God fervently, and you need to submit to the church's protection, and that is how you will defeat the enemy."

I grimaced. "But, Father, there must be something more I can do. Something—"

"There is: Help me gather more proof. We can have too little of it, but we can never have enough."

I shrugged. "All right, I guess I can do that, but I still have another question for you. The demon in Adam took the words you spoke to me right here in your office and flung them back in my face. I've always thought the church was a protected place. How were they able to get in here and listen to us?"

"That's easy," he said as he waved his hand at the entrance. "They walked through the front door just like you did. This building is nothing more than a physical gathering place, and all are invited to enter it, but it is not *the* church. The church is God's chosen people—a living body."

I shook my head. "But that's crazy. How is it possible that God would allow demons in a church building?"

"Well, Charlotte, the books of Job and Revelation state the devil stands before God in Heaven so that he can accuse the brethren, and he does so day and night. According to the Bible, the devil will continue to do so until he is cast out of Heaven in the end times. So it's reasonable to assume that if the devil can stand in Heaven in the presence of a holy God, he can certainly stand in our presence too—though I can't imagine that standing in the presence of God or standing in a worship service for God is a positive experience for demons."

"But why does God allow it?" I complained.

"Because life is all about choice and people get to choose their path. Good or bad. Not everybody that comes to this building for Mass belongs to God. Some are God's people, but some belong to Satan. Some are holy, while some are possessed. Most are neither. But if God only allowed his children to come to church, then the church would be empty because you have to hear about God's mercy and grace before accepting his sacraments, before becoming part of the church. Some of our best parishioners today used to be some of our biggest sinners, but where would they be if we hadn't taken them in when they were lost?"

"Well, that makes sense for people, but why would a demon want to come to church?"

"Well, the Bible says that our adversary, the devil, prowls around like a hungry lion seeking whom he may devour. I imagine his demons are looking for prey among those gathered here just as the lion watches the gathered antelope: They're trying to poach the weak and vulnerable."

My stomach tightened. "So you're saying I'm not safe even in church?"

Father Casey clasped his hands together and shook them. "Yes, that's exactly what I'm saying. Quit putting your faith in things. It's not the vessel that protects you. The church building doesn't protect you. The water in holy water doesn't protect you. The cross you hold in your hand doesn't protect you. It is the power of God inside of these things, in conjunction with your faith, that protects you. Of course, all of those things are important vessels of God's power, and they have their uses in the fight against the enemy, but they cannot protect you from all the devil's schemes. Pray to God and draw close to the body of believers in Christ, and then the church as God's representative on Earth will protect you."

CHAPTER 29

ADAM MATTHEW

AFTER THE POLICE returned me to my frantic mother, she said she forgave me, which was weird considering I had done nothing wrong. Certainly nothing to be yelled at and pushed to the ground over. Then she had a heart-to-heart talk with me so there'd be no more unfortunate misunderstandings. Apparently, Danny Pechman's dad had followed me into the basement at Mr. Crab's mansion and disappeared, and as unbelievable as it sounded, I had fallen into a coma. After that, I slept for a whole year and that's why I looked older in the mirror now. She told me she'd moved us out of Mr. Crab's place shortly after the incident because it didn't seem like a safe place to live anymore. Then Mom told me she was kind of seeing somebody named Jeremy, but she wanted me to know that she still loved Dad and me, and that would never change.

Mom said she needed to tell me something crazy, and that I was old enough and mature enough to deal with it, so she wanted to level with me. She said sometimes I forgot things and sometimes I acted weird. My doctors said that I had sustained permanent brain damage from getting pelted with the rocks and then again by whatever had put me in a coma. She said some other people had another theory concerning my behavior, and sometimes she believed that one and didn't think I had sustained any brain damage at all.

"Adam," she said. Mom paused and took a deep breath. "Sometimes… I believe you might have gotten possessed by a demon or evil spirit. Would you be honest with me and tell me about anything in your life that seems strange or kind of crazy to you?"

I told her I didn't think I was possessed, but I didn't know for sure. I swore Bela hadn't talked to me once since I woke from my coma, though I had a few bad dreams with her in them. Then I told her I had no idea why I forgot things.

Fortunately, she didn't ask me any specifics about my trip to Mr. Crab's mansion, and I didn't tell her anything because we no longer lived there, so it didn't matter anymore, anyway.

After my experience in William Crab's basement, things quieted down significantly for me. In the three months since that incident, I didn't have any lapses in my memory, saw nothing weird, and I hadn't freaked Mom out once. Or so I thought. All seemed to be going along smoothly.

"Adam, honey… Adam, wake up," Mom said as she shook my shoulder. "Today's Sunday, and I'd really like you to start going to church with me again."

I half opened one sleepy eye and gazed at her. "But, Mommm," I whined. "I don't want to go to church today. You didn't make me go last week or even before that, so why do I have to go now?"

She went to my window, pulled open the shade, and then turned on the overhead light. The glare soaked through my closed eyelids and into my reluctant eyes, so I pulled my bed cover over my head. I felt the mattress sink as mom came over and sat next to me. Then she pulled the blanket off my face and gave me the 'mom' look.

"After everything that happened to you, I wanted to cut you some slack. It's been more than a year and a half since your last church visit, and it's time you started participating again. I'm not raising you to be a heathen."

I sat up and crossed my arms. "But I don't like church."

Her mouth dropped open. "And why, pray tell, don't you like church? Don't you love God?" Her voice sounded strained.

"Come on," I said as I rolled my eyes. "All Father Ray does is talk in stupid Latin, and I don't understand any of it. Besides, I've never met God, so how would I know if I love him?"

Her face reddened with anger. "Watch your mouth. I'll not have that kind of talk in my house, and after listening to you, it is high time you go back to church."

"Jeez, Mom! It's so boring there. Don't make me go."

"Adam, I don't want to hear another word." She pointed and said, "Go to the bathroom now and get ready. We're leaving in fifteen minutes."

"Fine," I mumbled. My teeth clenched together so hard my jaw hurt.

I fumed as I reluctantly put on my new church clothes and started fantasizing that we would get in a car accident on the way there, or maybe the church roof would fall in on me and I would be horribly maimed. *Boy, would Mom feel bad about making me go then!* She'd cry and cry and tell me how sorry she was for making me go to that stupid place. Then I sighed and realized I wasn't going to get that lucky. We'd end up sitting in that boring church service—and next week too, then we'd do it all over again… and again. *Life really sucks sometimes.* Though, when I thought about it, I couldn't remember when I'd grown to dislike church so much. I never enjoyed going exactly, but I'd never disliked it either. *I figured I just outgrew it since I wasn't a little kid anymore.*

As we walked into Saint Mary's Church, all heads turned toward me, and I realized I had gained minor celebrity status as the boy who lived. A boy surrounded by several suspicious circumstances and death. The same boy who'd been followed into a basement by a madman and somehow survived. Rumors abounded about Bud Pechman's ultimate fate. They ranged from me being a stone-cold killer to Bud being sucked into the afterlife through an interdimensional rift to Bud laughing his butt off in the Bahamas with all his ill-gotten gains. Everyone seemed to have a theory, yet they presented everything to me as "He said," "She said," and "So and so heard." Not a single person took any direct responsibility for their tales. As person after person spoke their gossip, they'd hang on to my every word as if I'd spill all of my secrets and confirm their pet hypothesis. Although I could tell that everyone wanted to ask me what actually happened to Danny's dad, only two people had the guts to ask me directly. In both cases, they left disappointed. I told them I didn't know what had happened to him, and that was an honest answer.

When I walked out of the lobby and onto the main church floor, I felt agitated. I meant to dip my finger in the basin of holy water, but I just couldn't do it. Instead, I pulled back my fingertip just before it touched the water's surface, and I made a halfhearted, partial sign of the cross with my dry finger. I'm pretty sure Mom didn't notice.

When Mass started, my mood went from agitated to foul. I felt so, so dead on the inside, and the only thing that gave me a modicum of relief was thinking about punching the stupid priest in his stupid face. Sitting there in agony as I listened to a Latin service that I was sure would never end, I could only hope the church roof would cave in on me and put me out of my misery.

CHAPTER 30

DR. CHARLOTTE BROWN

"So, DO YOU think this will work, Father?"

"It should as long as Deirdre follows through and brings him to church today."

I watched as Father Casey walked over to a small pile of plastic water bottles. He grabbed one and blessed it. He set it off to the side and then picked up another bottle and did it again. I watched him do it several more times, and my curiosity got the best of me.

"Father?" I asked quizzically. "What are you doing?"

"Oh, this." He smiled. "I want to make sure that I have blessed water with me, and the best way to do that is to do it myself."

"Okay," I said, but I thought it would've been a whole lot easier to bless one large bottle of water and then pour it into the smaller bottles.

When he'd blessed about half of them, he stopped and went over to a side cabinet. He pulled out a digital camera, a digital recorder, and what appeared to be a present wrapped in colorful paper. He put the wrapped package into a black duffel bag and blessed the camera and the recorder, and put them in too. Next, he picked it up and walked over to the water bottles.

That's curious. I pointed at the bag and said, "Why did you bless the camera and recorder just now?"

He turned toward me, and as he did, the duffel bag swept over the water bottles and knocked them to the floor.

Oops! My bad. I scrunched up my face as I looked at the small mess. "I'm sorry," I said. "I didn't mean to distract you. Did the bottles get mixed up?"

"Don't worry about it," the Father said as he placed the duffel on the floor. "It's my fault for being so clumsy. And I know which is which." He bent over, picked up several of the fallen bottles, and put them in his bag. "I blessed the equipment because I don't want any demonic interference mucking them up today."

I tilted my head to the side. "Um, so why didn't you bless the package too?"

Father Casey chuckled. "It's my nephew's birthday today. It's one of those new super-soaker squirt guns that all the kids are crazy about. It's going to drive his mother nuts. By the way, would you mind dropping me off there afterward? It's in town."

I rubbed my belly. "Only if I can get some cake."

"Done! Now, before we go, let's pray for success today."

We arrived at Deirdre's church a little early and sat toward the back. Father Casey wore casual dress clothes minus the priest collar in the hope that we would blend in better. I had never been to Saint Mary's Church before, which was too bad. It was definitely the most beautiful place of worship I'd ever visited. I gazed one after the other, at twelve beautifully detailed stained-glass windows depicting the twelve stations of the cross, each accompanied by a larger-than-life carved white-marble statue of an apostle. The nave and crossing sections gleamed with highly polished gold-and-silver Calcutta marble floors offset by the dark mahogany wood pews. The dome in the sanctuary was a magnificent stained-glass construct that depicted the Father, Son, and angels in Heaven. The massive altar in front stood several feet above the congregation and was a massive, carved, gold-gilded beauty. Behind it hung an enormous white alabaster cross decorated in gold filigree. Everything in the place screamed affluence.

As I sat there marveling at my surroundings, the church's steeple bell rang three times, and then music started flowing from the large pipe organ. That must have been the cue because the parishioners began pouring in and taking their seats. Father Casey nudged my side with his elbow, and I looked up and saw Adam and his mom entering the sanctuary.

As I watched, Father Casey whispered in my ear, "I don't think Adam actually dipped his finger in the holy water font… and did you see him make that vague circle with his hand instead of making the sign of the cross? He did it well, though. If you weren't paying attention to him, you wouldn't have noticed it."

"I'm not surprised," I whispered back. "He's shown an aversion to both holy water and the cross in my dealings with him. And see?… If you look at his face, he seems tense… agitated even."

Father Casey nodded. "He does indeed, but it's probably the demon inside him. When I spoke to Deirdre, she told me that Adam had liked church before his sister Bela showed up, then became resistant to it after she came into the picture."

As planned, Deirdre chose seats several rows in front of us, giving us an unobstructed view of Adam from where we sat. That way, we could keep an eye on him as the service progressed. A noticeable change occurred in him right when the service started, almost like the flip of a switch. His body stiffened akin to what I'd seen in chronic pain patients, as his neck cocked at an unnatural angle… slightly back and to the side. He literally seethed with tension.

A moment later, much to my surprise, Latin started coming from the priest's mouth… and then it continued. As the service proceeded, Adam's uneasiness seemed to affect those around him, as if something palpable were causing them to shift away from him. As I looked on, a faint black mist seemed to form and swirl around him. My eyes narrowed, and I leaned forward as I tried to get a better look. Focusing so much, though, proved a mistake. He became hyperaware and still, like cats do when they detect prey, and I realized he could sense me staring at him.

I quickly bowed my head as if in deep prayer, and about twenty seconds later, I whispered out of the corner of my mouth, "Is he still looking at me?"

Father Casey whispered back, "No… but it doesn't matter. I'm pretty sure he spotted us anyway."

Toward the end of the service, Adam turned around and locked eyes with me. He gave me a smile that seemed to stretch from ear to ear, causing my skin to crawl. He could be so creepy for such a handsome young man.

Father Casey and I waited around for Deirdre and Adam in the parking lot after Mass ended. They were among the last parishioners to come out, so the parking lot had mostly emptied when they finally appeared.

As they exited the church, I waved at them, and they headed our way.

I put my hand over my eyes to block out the bright sunlight and said, "Hi, Deirdre! What a beautiful church you go to! I can see why you like it so much."

Before she could answer, Adam butted in, "Oh, so you're a Latin aficionado, Dr. Charlotte? And you, Father Casey—your own services at the basilica aren't doing it for you anymore? Had to get your religious fix somewhere else?"

Deirdre's face reddened at his words. She opened her mouth and then closed it again. She looked directly at Adam but appeared conflicted and unsure of herself.

"Let's drop the sophistry," Father Casey said as he placed his duffel bag on the ground. "We're here because we are worried about you; your mom is worried about you. We're here because we're trying to figure out how to help you."

Adam's smile twisted with mockery. "How touching. A man of the cloth and his shrink are worried about me. Well… what's stopping you? Help me already."

"Adam!" Deirdre snapped. "I've had enough of your mouth already! I raised you to be respectful of others. Apologize to them right now or else!"

Adam rolled his eyes. "Or what—you'll drink yourself to death?"

His crudeness toward his own mother caused me to gasp, and she reacted by slapping him hard across his face.

As Adam glared at Deirdre, Father Casey said, "Drop the melodrama, Adam, and answer my question: What are you?"

Adam rubbed his rapidly reddening jaw and grinned. "You mean whether I'm nuts or possessed? Well, what if I'm both, Father… or neither? Did you ever think of that? What will you do then?"

"It's not as hard as you think," Father Casey said with a challenging gleam in his eyes. "I already know that I'm speaking to a demon. I'm just trying to figure out if the boy you reside in is mentally ill too."

Adam seemed amused by the statement and broke out into a peal of laughter. "Well, you can speculate all you want, but good luck proving it. It's a shame you'll never know for certain."

Father Casey bent down, picked up his duffel bag, and unzipped it. "I don't have to speculate at all." He reached into his bag and grabbed a small plastic bottle. He tossed it to Adam and said, "Pour some holy water on your hand."

"And why would I do that?" Adam said as he held the bottle up to the sun looking through it.

Father Casey shrugged. "Why wouldn't you?"

Adam smirked. "Oh, I don't know… because you want me to?"

"That's fine. Your refusal to do so is an answer in and of itself, and I still have what I need."

Adam smiled, unscrewed the cap, and said, "Bottoms up." With that, he chugged the entire bottle.

My eyes flew open in shock. I'd thought for sure that he was possessed. But maybe he was just mentally ill after all. As I looked at the three of them, Father Casey pulled his nephew's birthday present out of his bag and, with a single swipe, ripped the wrapping paper right off of it.

"Surprise!" He pointed the super-soaker straight at Adam's head, then pulled the trigger.

A fat stream of water hit the young man dead center in the forehead, and he screeched hideously.

As his head smoked and the skin started blackening, he growled in a deep guttural voice, "You'll pay for that, priest!"

Father Casey responded by pulling out the digital camera and snapping several pictures.

That enraged the demon in Adam even more, and he came at the Father with outstretched hands.

Reaching into his duffel bag again, he snatched out a large wooden cross and held it up in front of him like a shield.

Adam came to a complete stop inches from the cross, then he slowly backed up while he snarled and gnashed his teeth at it. In that same deep voice, much deeper than Adam's normal voice, he said, *"Rotundum adibit tangeret sacerdotem,"* and then he ran off.

My legs suddenly felt like rubber, and I thought I would collapse. I looked over at Deirdre, and she didn't look like she fared any better.

"Father Casey," I said as my eyes frantically took in everything around me, "what did I miss? What just happened?"

"Well, Charlotte," he said with a certain giddiness and looking pleased with himself. "The demon fell for my subterfuge, forcing it to reveal itself."

"What subterfuge?" I asked in an uncertain voice.

"I knew the demon in Adam was keeping an eye on us, so I needed a way to trick it. I purposely knocked over and mixed the small bottles of blessed and unblessed water in my office and then placed some of the unblessed bottles in my bag while leading our observer to believe I thought they were all blessed. Did you see how Adam held up the plastic bottle and looked through it? The demon knew the water in that bottle wasn't blessed, so he drank it. But he didn't know that I knew it too. Gloating, and with its guard down, I was able to hit it with actual holy water."

I stared at him incredulously. "So you lied about it being your nephew's birthday?"

He shook his head. "No, and that's the beauty of it. It is his birthday today, and that is indeed his birthday present. The demon knew it too, and that's why my subterfuge worked. Now I have pictures, an audio-recording, and proof that Adam spoke in a language he doesn't know."

My mind was racing. "But, Father, how do you know the demon spoke in an actual language instead of making up some gibberish?"

"Because I've studied Latin, that's why. And if my translation skills are still good, I believe the demon said, 'Touché, round one goes to you, priest.'"

Deirdre's face, meanwhile, was a pained mix of concern and relief. She wrung her hands together as she said, "I'm glad you got your proof and all, but what are you going to do about my son? You hurt him—bad—and he's still possessed. But now he's gone."

Father Casey walked over to Deirdre and put a hand on each of her shoulders. "Deirdre, look at me. The holy water hurt the demon… not your son. Adam's possessed, but he's still your child, and he will come back to you. But right now, I have a greater concern, and that's protecting you when he does."

CHAPTER 31

FATHER STEPHEN CASEY

BISHOP JOSÉ FRANCISCO Ramírez Garcia de Arroyo—aka Padre Pepe—had a foreboding presence: a big, heavyset, muscular man with no neck, topping out somewhere around six-foot-five or maybe even six-six. His build, along with his black eyes and black crew cut, made him look more like he belonged in the military or, even better, on some professional wrestling circuit than in the Catholic Church as the head of a diocese. Fortunately, the heart that belonged to this beast of a man was gentler and more even-keeled than his looks might have suggested.

Padre Pepe had two vices in life, and he was enjoying both as he thumbed through my photographs. With a sweep of his massive hand, he spread the pictures out like a deck of cards. He picked one up, held it close to his face, and squinted at it. Taking another puff off his fat Cuban cigar, he swirled it around in his mouth as if enjoying a fine wine. He blew the smoke out and said, "So you actually managed to get photographic evidence?... Impressive. And audio too... complete with a deep, male voice threatening and growling and even speaking in Latin." The padre looked thoughtful as he spoke next. "I know how hard it can be to pin a demon down, so it makes me wonder if you obtained this evidence too easily?"

I sat across from him and waited as he picked up his crystal tumbler filled with Irish whiskey and ice and took a sip. He placed the sweating glass back down on his desk and asked, "What do you think, Stephen?"

I shrugged my shoulders. "Well, Padre, the thought crossed my mind too. It's possible I'm being outplayed by a master-mind, but it's also possible we're giving this demon too much credit. I realize I may never know, but either way, evidence is evidence regardless of how it was obtained."

The padre gave me an appraising glance, and I could sense a sharp mind operating behind those dark, intelligent eyes. "Perhaps or perhaps not. In my experience, it is best not to underestimate demons. While there are exceptions, I find them to be desperately tricky creatures. If it was given too easily, you're probably walking into a trap."

My agitation increased along with my blood pressure, and I forced myself to calm down. I took a few deep breaths and said, "All I can say is I went to great lengths to hide my true intentions from the demon."

I told him about all my preparatory prayers and my sleight of hand with the holy water. He nodded his massive head as I talked—at least as much as one can without a neck.

When I finished, Padre Pepe steepled his hands together and said, "So what is it you want from me?"

"Me? I think it's obvious: I want permission to perform an exorcism on Adam."

The bishop took another sip of whiskey and another drag on his cigar as he sat there, deep in thought. Finally, he opened his mouth and said, "If it's a setup, I could be sending you and the boy to your deaths and opening up the church to bad publicity and legal trouble."

I made my appeal to him as I lifted my hands, palms up. "But, my dear Padre, if we do nothing, we'll be leaving this young man and his future victims to this wolf. And if his future crimes turn out to be sensational—and I suspect they will, based on what I've seen from the Davis case—then it will also look bad for the Catholic Church if it comes out that we knew about the boy and did nothing."

The bishop scratched his beefy head. "I need to discuss this case with my superiors. I'll let you know in a day or so if your exorcism request has been granted."

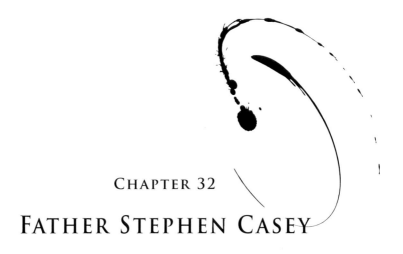

CHAPTER 32

FATHER STEPHEN CASEY

"DEIRDRE, NO," I said. "You're not safe here in your apartment. I insist that you and your son stay on the church grounds under my protection for the time being. We currently have a vacant guest house used for visiting priests, and I'd like you to take advantage of it until we resolve this matter."

We'd only been talking for a few minutes since my unexpected arrival, but I was already tired of standing, so I asked if I could sit with her for a bit. She led me to the kitchen, and we sat on rickety chairs on either side of the wood table.

She gave me a weak smile. "Can I make you a cup of coffee, Father?"

I waved my hand. "No, thanks. I'm already wired and want to sleep tonight."

I continued talking and assured her that Charlotte was arranging for a mental health professional to evaluate Adam and that an exorcism would only be undertaken if a clean bill of mental health was obtained—though my gut told me he would be cleared. Then I gave her a quick update about my meeting with the bishop. I kept it short because I wanted to return to my primary purpose for being here: her safety and Adams.

After I spoke, Deirdre sat silent for a moment, then she shrugged and said, "But, Father, I don't want to be a burden, and besides, despite my fears, Adam has never hurt me. In fact, he's never even threatened to hurt me. I'm touched that you're so worried about my well-being, but I think staying on the church grounds may be going a little overboard."

I shook my head. "Please trust me on this, Deirdre. I've looked into this matter extensively, and you're in danger, not from your son, of course, but from the demon that inhabits him. Just because it hasn't chosen to hurt you so far doesn't mean it can't or won't. Besides, if it's needed, performing an exorcism can get very noisy and weird. After one or two sessions, I can almost guarantee that your neighbors will become hostile toward you."

She touched the base of her neck and, with a shaky voice, said, "So the padre approved the exorcism then?"

I shook my head. "Not yet, but I'd be surprised if he didn't, as the evidence I've compiled is pretty damning."

"Well, I have to be honest with you, Father," she said as her ears and cheeks reddened. "I can barely afford to pay for this place. I'd never be able to swing payment for two places at once."

Smiling generously at her to help ease her tension, I said, "Deirdre, please, you'll be staying as my guest. Food and housing will be provided free of charge for the duration of your stay."

"I guess that's okay, then… but aren't you forgetting something?"

"What's that?"

"Adam," she breathed. She looked down, then looked up

at me with moisture-laden eyes and voiced her fear: "What if he doesn't come back?"

A mother's love. I leaned in toward her and tried to speak in a comforting voice. "Don't worry. Adam's still in there, so he'll come back. Of course, I don't want you here when he does. I want you to pack a bag right now and come back with me."

With a pained expression, she started chewing her lower lip. "But how will Adam find me?"

I pointed at the door. "Leave a note. Tell him where you are and that you're waiting for him."

CHAPTER 33

DEIRDRE MATTHEW

THE GUEST HOME for visiting priests turned out to be well-furnished and nice—much nicer than my apartment anyhow. All the furniture appeared to be transitional by design and meticulously cared for. The general décor felt comforting, and it gave the home that 'sit down, kick back, and put your feet up' kind of feel to it. I went to the kitchen, opened the refrigerator, and to my pleasant surprise, it was fully stocked. My husband had still been alive the last time I'd had a refrigerator this full. Next, I opened the food pantry and found it fully stocked too. I giggled. *A girl could get used to this.*

After I finished in the kitchen, I picked a bedroom for myself and unpacked my belongings. Then I chose a bedroom for Adam and did the same for him. As I continued puttering around the house, familiarizing myself with everything, I heard a knock at the door, and my heart fluttered.

"Adam, is that you?" I called out.

"Deirdre, it's me—Charlotte!" said a feminine voice through the door.

I opened it a few moments later and saw her smiling face. "Hey there. What brings you here? Is everything okay?"

She nodded. "Father Casey let me know you were here, so I came by to see how you were getting settled in and to help you clean the place. See," she said, twirling around, "I even dressed the part."

She did indeed look ready to clean. Instead of her usual business ensemble, she wore faded blue jeans, a clearly worn but clean designer navy-blue T-shirt, and floppy sandals.

Charlotte stepped inside and said, "Oh, this place is lovely—wow… and clean too. Is there anything else I can do for you?"

I smiled and followed it up with a wink. "Well, there is a delicious-looking box of donuts in the kitchen. Care to take some calories off my hands?"

Charlotte grinned. "I'm here to serve—and I guess to *be served*. Lead the way."

We made idle chitchat as we sat in the living room eating donuts and drinking coffee. At some point, the conversation turned serious.

Charlotte looked at me with eyes and a smile that radiated warmth and caring. "Deirdre, I know these last few years have been really hard on you, and if you ever care to talk about it or need anything at all, please call me."

Her statement caught me off guard, and I found myself holding my breath. I sighed and said, "Thanks. And maybe… I think I do need to talk. I'll take you up on your offer right now… if you don't mind?"

Charlotte smiled in a kind fashion and I knew she wanted me to continue.

"You're right when you say these last few years have been tough. It seems that everything I've ever loved is being stripped away from me. After my husband passed away, I wanted to die myself. Here I'd gone and dedicated most of my adult years to building a life with this man, and it was gone in an instant. My comfortable life. My great husband. My beautiful home. All gone, just like that. When he died, I felt like a leaf blowing in the wind. And it's not just the time we spent together. He really was my soul mate. Don't get me wrong—like everyone else, we had trying times together, and we almost split up once. But the thing is, we didn't, and we grew stronger together."

I stopped talking and sighed. Then I compulsively pulled at the loose strands of my dangling hair as I continued, "Watching my husband war with cancer and the chemo as it slowly took him apart felt so… so heartbreaking, yet it made me love him even more. I thought I'd be ready when the inevitable came, but I realize now that I'd been strong for him and not for me, so I fell apart when he was no longer around. I thought his passing would be like a cleaving, like separating two pages in a novel. You know, turn the page and move on. But it wasn't like that at all. In reality, it's like somebody took the pages and ripped them out of a book, then ripped up the pages and burned the whole mess. His death tore at my mind, heart, and soul… it has even affected me physically. It's left me… *damaged.*"

"Oh, honey," Charlotte said. "You should have gotten this off your chest much sooner. This is the sort of thing that eats people alive. But are you healing now? Today? I know you said you were dating somebody. Are you still seeing him?"

I shook my head. "I'm certainly better today with his passing than I was a few years ago, but I don't know if I'll ever be better. And, no, I broke things off with Jeremy."

"I thought things were going well with him. What happened?"

Shrugging, I said, "Adam, is what happened. With my husband and daughter gone, he's the only thing I have left from my previous life, and now he's slipping through my fingers too. I have to fix this. I have to fix him. I can't lose him… I can't."

Bursting into tears, Charlotte came over and hugged me, and as she did, I said, "I have to save my son, Charlotte. Please help me save Adam."

Charlotte whispered, "I promise you, Deirdre, Father Casey and I are doing everything in our power to save him."

Then Charlotte became silent and let me cry.

CHAPTER 34

FATHER STEPHEN CASEY

THE DIOCESE OFFICE summoned me back to meet with Padre Pepe two days later. His secretary ushered me into his office, and I sat there in hopeful anticipation. While I waited, I looked around the room to take my mind off the impending meeting. The space was tastefully done with dark, rich cherry wood walls, along with a gleaming well-veined marble floor that was partially covered with exquisite Persian rugs. Beautiful leather-bound books rested in mahogany bookshelves inlaid with gold-gilded filagree, along with what appeared to be several expensive religious artifacts. His office was a discreet reminder of the difference between his station and mine in the church.

I heard Padre Pepe dismiss one of his attendants for the day through the open office door, and then the mountain of a man came bursting through it.

"Father Casey," the bishop said. "Thank you for coming on such short notice."

I hadn't actually had a choice in the matter, but I thought

it nice that the bishop kept up the fiction that we were equals. Shaking the hand he'd extended toward me, I rose and said, "You're welcome, Padre. So were you able to secure the approval for the exorcism?"

"Ah, straight to business, I see." He waved a hand and said, "Please, take a seat."

After sitting, he said, "So, as you well know, the rite of exorcism is a sensitive issue in the Catholic Church. I have discussed the situation with my superiors, and they are of the mind to deny your request."

My brow furrowed and my stomach muscles clenched in frustration. "But, Padre, a boy's life is at stake here."

A brief look of irritation flashed across the padre's face. "Stephen, please let me finish without interruption. Even though my superiors are of this mind, they have left the final decision to me since it is occurring in my diocese. I've looked over your past performance evaluations, talked to several of your present and past coworkers, and have concluded that you are thoughtful, stable, and not prone to flights of fancy."

"Thank you, Padre. I—"

He looked me directly in the eyes and said, "Stephen, please don't make me reconsider my assessment. Right now, your silence is required."

I nodded. *Fine. Consider my mouth shut. You obviously don't want or need my input.*

The padre leaned back in his chair, intertwined his fingers, and balanced his hands on top of his gut. "So, on the one hand, I have a stable, thoughtful man who has brought me compelling evidence of a bona fide possession. On the other hand, the Catholic Church's handling of possession cases is less than stellar, and this particular one smells like a setup. I've put considerable thought into this and find I'm divided on how to proceed. My mind tells me to walk away from this case while my heart tells me to protect the boy. It's not well known, but the Catholic Church actually has the services of a competent full-time exorcist in this country. He has proven himself to be discreet, and he gets results. The problem is, he's only one man, and he's currently backlogged for two years. Assure me you will not let things spin out of control if I let you proceed with this case. Assure me that your faith is sufficient to the task." With that, he gave me a nod.

Oh boy, permission to speak. But I carefully kept the irritation off of my face. "Padre, first let me state that my heart is in the right place. I'm not doing this to write a book or a screenplay. I'm not doing this to make a name for myself in the church either. And I certainly have no desire to be an exorcist. Adam's soul is in eternal danger, and I'll never forgive myself if I don't act. It's central to who I am as a priest. Second, I'd like to tell you my faith is sufficient for the task, but I've never performed an exorcism before, so I just don't know. I suspect I will be leaning heavily on the church and Jesus Christ before it's all over. And last, because of that, I'm not going into this arrogantly, and if I sense I'm losing control, I'll shut it down immediately."

Padre Pepe stared at me with an intense gaze. He had his poker face on, and I couldn't tell what he was thinking. He continued eyeing me to the point that it became uncomfortable.

"Alright," he finally said. "If you can provide me with a clean bill of mental health for the boy, you'll have my approval. Stephen, I'm trusting you, so don't mess it up."

CHAPTER 35

DEIRDRE MATTHEW

ADAM SHOWED UP late Sunday evening at the church guest house as if nothing had ever happened. He remembered nothing, and he didn't carry any of the burns that the holy water seemed to inflict on him earlier that day. In fact, he seemed his old self again, but I still walked on pins and needles around him. After a couple of days had passed, things seemed like they'd gone back to normal.

Toward the end of the week, Charlotte came by with a mental health questionnaire and asked Adam all sorts of crazy questions. As I listened, I remembered something Father Casey had said to me after his meeting with the bishop.

When Adam left the room to use the bathroom, I asked her, "Charlotte, didn't Father Casey say the mental health evaluation had to come from someone other than you?"

She grimaced, and as her lower jaw worked back and forth, I could hear the faint clicking and popping sound of grinding teeth. "Yes, but that could take weeks or even months, and your son doesn't have that much time."

"But… isn't… isn't… that breaking the law?" I sputtered out.

She rolled her eyes. "No, Deirdre, it's not a court order. It's Padre Pepe's request, and… well, what he doesn't know won't hurt him."

"But isn't it best to do it the way he wants it done?" I asked, feeling unease in the pit of my stomach.

"No, it's a silly request actually," she said as she shook her head. "I'm a fully trained and licensed child psychologist, and I also happen to be familiar with your son's case. In my mind, that's a positive and not a negative. On the other hand, Padre Pepe is neither a psychologist nor very familiar with this case. His request is designed to make him feel better about… about God knows what really. Now shush and let me get this finished up."

The next afternoon, I sent Adam out to play while Father Casey, Charlotte, and I met with another priest, Father Delroy Raines.

After Father Casey made introductions and some opening remarks, he continued on, "So the reason I brought Father Raines into this is for a rather unique talent he possesses. He has the gift of discernment, and it is a gift that has proven useful when dealing with demons."

I shook my head. "I'm not familiar with that gift, Father Casey. What is it exactly?"

"Deirdre, I'll let Father Raines explain that himself," Father Casey said, motioning to his fellow priest.

Father Raines placed his clasped hands under his chin, and he appeared thoughtful. But, his reddish-silver hair—which stuck out all over the place like Albert Einstein's—kind of counterbalanced his studious looks and brought him to the edge of appearing like a silly, albeit mad, professor.

The father rubbed his chin and said, "The gift of discernment is like empathy on steroids. People with empathy can read others well and often perceive their emotions, even if they try to hide their true feelings. My gift takes things a step further and allows me to sense the goodness or truthfulness of a person. My gift also allows me to detect angels, demons or other spirits attached to a person, place or thing. This ability has proven useful during exorcisms because demons sometimes try to hide and pretend they've left the person when, in fact, they haven't."

Feeling a small surge of fear well up in me, I gave a half-hearted nod and looked at Father Casey.

"Thank you for that explanation," Father Casey said. "Now, the next thing I want to talk about is vitally important. Demons will try to derail an exorcism by bringing up sins from our past. Pornography and substance addictions, previous crimes, and deceptions, moral shortcomings, anger issues, gossip and malice… these are all things that demons love to bring up to embarrass the individual members of the exorcism team. The only protection against this is the confession of sin. Once you've confessed and been absolved of your past iniquities by a priest, demons no longer have access to these past wrongs. It's almost as if they'd never existed, at least as far as the demon is concerned. So, each of you needs to confess your sins to me, or if you are not comfortable with that, go to confession this evening and confess to the priest in the confessional. However, be prepared for a certain amount of embarrassment during the exorcism. The demon will still have access to your unconfessed sins, as you will not remember to confess them all." He looked from me to Charlotte, then asked, "Are there any questions so far?"

"Yes, Father Casey," Charlotte said. "Are we required to fast during this process?"

"That is an excellent question," the father replied. "The Bible is clear that fasting is not required for casting out demons, except for a certain type. However, I believe it never hurts and is likely helpful, so I would recommend fasting and prayer if you can do so. But it's better to eat than to pass out from hunger in the middle of an exorcism. If you choose to fast, balance the need for fasting against your need for food. It goes without saying that you need to remain in prayer throughout all of this."

Father Raines nodded in response, as did Charlotte, so I gave a single nod, keeping my gaze toward the floor to hide the emotional turmoil that surely showed in my eyes.

"So," Father Casey asked, "any more questions?... Anybody? No. Okay then. Eat or fast as you see fit, get a good night's sleep, and I'll see you all at 9:00 a.m. sharp. And don't forget to go to confession tonight and to pray."

I pushed aside my warring feelings. "I think we're, um, all good, Father Casey. And I just want to thank all of you again for helping Adam."

After seeing them out, I dropped the façade I'd been wearing on my face as anxiety continued to gnaw away at my stomach. I just couldn't shake the feeling that this whole exorcism thing was wrong. I tried reasoning through my fear but couldn't come up with anything specific. Could I just be overreacting to the fear of the unknown?

CHAPTER 36

EXORCISM: DAY 1
FATHER STEPHEN CASEY

JUST AFTER 9:00 am the following day, I stood with Deirdre, Adam, Dr. Brown, and Father Raines in the living room of the church's guest house.

"Okay, Adam… are you ready?" I asked, while watching him for any unusual behavior.

"I think so, Father Casey," was his only reply.

"Good. As mentioned before, we need to tie you down for your safety and ours. Do you understand?"

Adam fidgeted with his hands, then nodded. "Yes, Father."

I pointed to the solid oak chair we'd brought here for the exorcism and asked Adam to sit. We bound his wrists and ankles to the chair with plastic zip ties—tighter than I would have liked, but I needed to ensure he wouldn't slip out of them.

Standing in front of him, I asked, "Is Bela here right now, Adam?"

A look of concentration descended upon his face, and then he replied, "I don't know for sure, but I don't think so."

I turned to my left and waved Father Raines over. "Is Bela here?"

He concentrated similarly, then nodded. "Yes, she is."

"All right, let's get started." Going over to the living room closet, I retrieved my surplice and purple stole. After putting them on, I had Deirdre and Charlotte stand behind Adam and off to each side while Father Raines and I stood in front of him, facing him. We each opened a copy of the 1614 Rite of Exorcism to the Litany of Saints, and I started reading:

"Lord, have mercy on us."

"Lord, have mercy on us," repeated my team.

"Christ, have mercy on us," I said.

"Christ, have mercy on us," they echoed.

After finishing the litany, I read several psalms aloud, then moved on to the three readings of exorcism. We ended with an imploration to God for mercy, and then we gave him thanks.

Adam sat there as if he'd been watching mildly boring TV, then he farted. He looked up at me and said, "Well, that stinks."

Humor? I chuckled in amusement. Of all the things I'd been expecting, it certainly wasn't a fart joke.

We watched him for another twenty minutes, but nothing more happened. In disappointment, I cut Adam's bonds and dismissed him.

CHAPTER 37

EXORCISM: DAY 2
FATHER STEPHEN CASEY

DAY TWO WENT pretty much the same as day one—the only difference being that Adam laughed at us instead of passing gas.

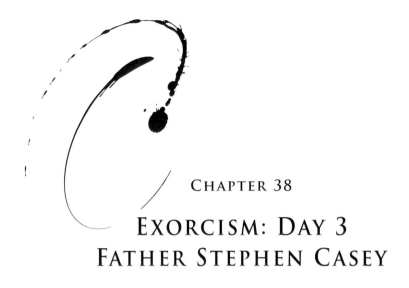

CHAPTER 38

EXORCISM: DAY 3
FATHER STEPHEN CASEY

DAY THREE YIELDED essentially the same results, and I found myself questioning my faith. I fancied myself a strong man of the cloth and thought I was up to the task, but now I didn't know.

The demon seemed to shrug off the exorcism with grave indifference. I spent the rest of the day in prayer and fasting, and I asked my team to do the same.

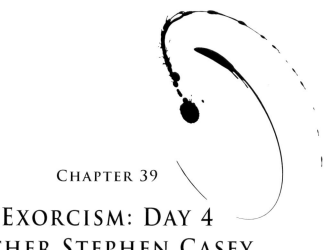

CHAPTER 39

EXORCISM: DAY 4
FATHER STEPHEN CASEY

DAY FOUR PROCEEDED the same as the first three... until I reached the first reading of the main body of the exorcism. At that point, Adam started sweating profusely, and he looked like he might throw up at any second. He regained his composure, but it slipped again during the third reading.

I made the sign of the cross over the boy and then read aloud a passage from the Rite of Exorcism. "I cast thee out, every unclean spirit, every phantom, every encroachment of Satan, in the name of Jesus Christ of Nazareth."

Adam's frown stretched unnaturally wide, and the demon in him growled. Then the satanic entity yelled out in a deeper voice than Adam's, "Leave me alone, you f***ing priest!"

Afterward, Adam collapsed in the chair, appearing to be unconscious. After waiting several minutes, we untied him and placed him in bed, and he slept for close to a day after that.

I know that I should have been elated that we'd finally made a dent in the demon's defenses, but instead, it just added to my growing sense of unease.

CHAPTER 40

EXORCISM: DAY 5
FATHER STEPHEN CASEY

ADAM APPEARED AGITATED before the exorcism even began. It was no small feat to tie him down, and it took all four of us to do so. After securing him, he became catatonic and didn't move until I started reading from psalms.

He started thrashing fiercely against his bonds as he yelled, "Stop it! Stop it! Stop it! Stop it!" Then he giggled uncontrollably.

I instructed Deirdre and Charlotte to continue reciting the Our Father in the background while Father Raines and I pressed the main attack.

Adam continued to strain against his bonds, and then he slumped in the chair. A moment later, he lifted his head, looking around as if he had no idea what was happening. "Mom!" he cried out. "Why are you hurting me? Please stop. It burns. Mom, please make it stop!"

Deirdre's eyes went wide, and I could tell she was ready to rush to her son's side.

Thankfully, Father Raines yelled out, "No, Deirdre! That's the demon talking." He rushed forward and held her back before she could embrace the boy.

I looked at the demon through the lenses of Adam's eyes and said, "In the name of the Father, the Son, and the Holy Ghost, I command you, foul spirit, to tell me your name!"

Using the boy's vocal cords, the demon let loose with a volley of cursing, snarling, and growling that I wouldn't have thought possible if I hadn't heard it myself. I commanded it to tell me its name several more times during the session, but it just yielded more of the same gibberish. When we finally finished, I thought the four of us might collapse from the strain.

CHAPTER 41

EXORCISM: DAY 6
FATHER STEPHEN CASEY

ADAM'S SKIN WAS pasty white, his eyes had dark circles around them, and his hair was disheveled. Even though the boy looked tired and worn down, I had to call in extra help when it came time to bind him to the chair, as he exhibited enormous physical strength. It took me a moment to catch my breath after all the exertion I had put into it. Once my breathing slowed, I instructed the freaked-out groundskeeper and janitor to leave us, which they hurried to do.

Before I even started the exorcism, the demon in Adam spoke. "Priest, let's make a deal, you and I."

I knew well enough not to engage in extraneous conversation with the deceptive creature, so I kept my mouth shut as I donned my surplice and purple stole.

"Priest," it repeated as it giggled. "Would you like to be a bishop? 'Cause I know a secret… a dirty little *Pepe* secret. You heard how the *Grand Pepe*—the arrogant Bishop José Francisco Ramírez Garcia de Arroyo—talked to you. Ordering you to shut up like you were a barking dog. As if all his names make him more important than you. Release me, and I will lay the bishop's position at your feet. Think of all the good you could do as a bishop.... Bishop Stephen Casey: Don't you think it has a nice ring to it?"

I considered what it had to say, then found myself appalled on a few fronts. It sickened me to think the foul thing had access to a private conversation in the bishop's office. Even though I knew it had the legal right to do so, I still didn't have to like it. I felt even more appalled that the demon knew my greatest desire: to be a bishop. I had never shared it with anyone, including my own mother. *How could this thing know that?* I knew it wasn't omniscient, but it sure seemed like it. Last, what appalled me more than anything else was that I had actually considered its offer for the briefest of moments. It shamed me to think I'd entertained a deal with the devil to gain position in the church. Even though my mind raced in a fervent manner, my mouth stayed closed. I didn't say a single word to it.

"No?" the demon said with a sigh of disappointment. "Pity.... So, Father Raines, I happen to know that Father Casey's position will be opening up shortly. How would you like to head your own church?"

"Shut up!" I yelled. Turning to Father Raines, I said, "Don't listen to this thing.... No one is going anywhere. The demon is deceptive and a liar. It's trying to use our desires against us to divide us."

That sent the demon into a litany of "Shut up, shut up, shut up, shut up," like a human metronome, and didn't stop for the rest of the exorcism session. It completely unnerved me, and I don't think the others fared any better.

Chapter 42

Exorcism: Day 7
Father Stephen Casey

We made our first major breakthrough on the seventh day, though we had to endure the demon's usual shenanigans as it alternated between curses, pleadings, threatening, and bribes. This time, it focused its attack on Deirdre and Charlotte instead of Father Raines and me. It tried using Deirdre's maternal instincts against her and Charlotte's professional instincts as a child psychologist against her. I thought one or both might break, but they held firm. In the end, the demon itself ended up breaking.

"In the name of the Father, Son, and Holy Spirit," I said with authority, "I command you, demon, to tell me your name."

Adam's face and arms turned bright red, and then, entirely against his will, he said, "A... Abad... Abaddon."

My pulse quickened, and I stifled the shock I felt at hearing the name. I stepped forward and got right up in Adam's face. I made the sign of the cross over him and said, "You're the destroyer from the Bible?"

Adam acted as if he didn't hear me.

"You're the demon that torments mankind?"

Adam's face went catatonic.

"You're the king who controls the locusts from the bottomless pit?"

The faintest of smiles appeared on Adam's face.

"You're that Abaddon?"

"Maybe," Adam smiled. "What will you give me for such valuable information, priest?"

"I command you, Abaddon, in the name of all that is holy to answer my question."

Adam's eyeballs looked like they might pop out of his head. He strained hard against the restraints, and then "Yes" came out of his mouth.

"Yes *what*, Abaddon?" I said as I pushed my crucifix against Adam's sweaty forehead. "Are you the king of the locusts of the bottomless pit? I command you to tell me in Jesus Christ's name."

"N... N... No... ahh... it burns...Yes... Yes, I am that Abaddon. Now leave me alone!"

Adam's whole body tensed up and shuddered, and then he seemed to relax. He looked up, with all traces of the demon's vestige gone. "Father Casey," Adam said. "It's me—Adam. You... You did it. The demon left. It didn't want to reveal any more information to you, so it left me. I'm free!"

Deirdre put her hands together, pulled them to her chest, and mouthed a silent *"Thank you."*

Charlotte, in turn, hugged Deirdre and said, "It's finally over."

I motioned to Father Raines, and he laid his hands on the

boy. After closing his eyes, he concentrated for about thirty seconds. Suddenly, he jerked his hands back from Adam as if he had laid them on a hot stove. "It's lying. It's still in there."

Adam's face twisted back into a parody of evil. "Stupid priest. Now I'll have to plan something special for you too."

As I looked around, I could see that the demon's little stunt had demoralized the entire group, which I realized was the point of the demon's ruse in the first place. It knew we were close to accomplishing our goal, and it had tried to stop us from doing so. The thing was smart and strong, and I wanted to make sure everyone was at full strength before attempting to send Abaddon back to hell.

I ended the session early as the team had been through enough for the day. Even though I had felt a little uneasy about performing an exorcism, things seemed to be coming along, and I realized tomorrow would probably bring the big breakthrough we sought. I hoped so, at least, because I looked forward to getting back to my normal routine. I couldn't imagine why anyone would want to do exorcisms for a living.

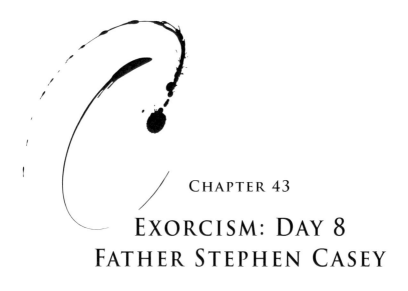

Chapter 43

Exorcism: Day 8
Father Stephen Casey

The following morning, I came to a sudden halt upon entering the guest house. Adam was standing in the middle of the living room, and he looked positively ill with skin that appeared bluish and slack. He started falling in slow motion, but I rushed over and caught him before he hit the floor. Holding on to him, I could feel Adam trembling violently as if freezing, and I could also feel that he was burning up with fever. My face twisted at the smell of rotten eggs emanating from his body. I marveled that it took several people to manhandle him to the chair yesterday, but today he was so weak I easily sat him down.

"Oh, Father Casey, you're here. Good!" came Charlotte's worried voice from behind me.

A moment later, both Charlotte and Deirdre appeared at my side.

"I took his temperature," Deirdre said as concern flashed

in her eyes, "and it's one hundred and three point nine. Don't you think maybe we should hold off on the exorcism until he's feeling a little better?"

I rubbed the back of my neck with indecision. Honestly, I didn't know what to do. He might be sick, but it could also be a trick. I didn't see how the demon could fake a human fever, but that didn't mean it wasn't possible. Of course, that didn't make it possible either. My ignorance on the matter didn't influence it one way or the other. However, I knew the demon would grow strong fast if we gave it time. The exorcism could end up being drawn out for months if this devil could manipulate events in its favor.

I told Deirdre and Charlotte that I felt it best to proceed as planned and that we would start as soon as Father Raines arrived.

Deirdre's hands fluttered as she tugged at and adjusted her blouse.

I eyed her and asked, "What is it you want to say, Deirdre?"

She reached up and twisted the hair on her head with one hand while pain flooded into her eyes. "It's just that... he's so sick. Look at him; he's shivering. If we have to do this today, is it against the rules to put a blanket on him?"

I could see the worry in her beautiful, but sad eyes. In fact, she had the most beautiful eyes I'd ever seen on anybody anywhere. Her bluish-green, silver-flecked eyes reminded me of the color of arctic water and were offset attractively by her luxuriant dark hair and pale, flawless skin. Her beauty, along with her apparent vulnerability, pulled mightily on my heartstrings. As these thoughts swirled in my head, I found myself admitting that she had a fine figure too. Her whole look was powerfully attractive to me, and it brought out my protective side. I felt a strong urge to want to please her, to make her happy again.

I mused that maybe she and I could have been husband and wife in another life.

Amidst these intoxicating thoughts, I heard myself say, "Of course not. Cover Adam up nice and snug."

Listening to my own words shook me out of my daydream. I forced the lustful feelings down and wondered where they were coming from. As a dedicated man of the cloth, I wasn't prone to fantasizing about women.

Regaining control of my emotions, I said, "Give him a blanket. But when we bind him, make sure his hands and feet are visible at all times."

Deirdre nodded, then she and Charlotte wrapped Adam in a warm-looking wool blanket of black, brown, and gold. We had just finished tying his ankles to the chair when we heard a thunderous crash upstairs, making us all jump.

I asked both ladies, "Did Father Raines sneak past us while we talked?"

Charlotte's face looked pensive as she glanced at the stairs. "I don't think so, Father. I wouldn't have missed something like that." She crossed her arms over her chest and said, "Deirdre and I will go check it out while you finish tying down Adam."

I had just finished securing his right hand to the chair when Deirdre called out in a panicked voice, "Father, you need to see this—now!"

I left the sleeping boy, rushed up the stairs into the back bedroom, and my mouth dropped open. The entire room looked ransacked. The bed frame and mattress were upside down, the dressers were lying on their sides, and their drawers were strewn about. In addition, someone had ripped the light fixture from the ceiling, and wall pictures lay shattered on the floor.

Shaking my head in disbelief, I looked at Deirdre. "You didn't do this, right?"

She swallowed hard as her eyes traveled around the room. "No, Father, of course not."

A suspicion lit upon my mind, so I rushed back down the stairs, but I could only muse; *hmm, maybe not.* Adam remained precisely as I'd left him.

Father Raines entered as I tied Adam's left hand to the chair.

"Sorry I'm a few minutes late," he said while looking at his watch. "I know you like punctuality, but I couldn't break away from Mrs. Wallace without being rude. You know how much she likes to talk."

I nodded, then hurriedly explained the situation to him and sent Father Raines upstairs to see for himself. When the three of them returned, I spent a few minutes calming everyone down. After that, we proceeded with what would hopefully be the last exorcism I ever performed. As I read through the rite, Adam emitted a weak moan from time to time, but none of the demon's usual shenanigans manifested.

I'd made it about a third of the way through when Sister Agnes came rushing through the front door. She said Padre Pepe had arrived in my office and needed to see me immediately. I asked her to inform the padre that I was in the middle of an exorcism and I would see him as soon as I finished. Sister Agnes returned several minutes later, out of breath, and said Padre Pepe told her that if I wasn't in front of him in five minutes, I should consider myself excommunicated from the church.

"Argh," I cried out. "I don't need this right now. Father Raines, just hold down the fort for a few minutes while I'm gone. We'll proceed with the exorcism when I return. I'd like the three of you to pray the Our Father to keep the pressure on. I promise I'll be back as soon as I deal with the padre."

Perhaps the bishop isn't as even keeled as I'd thought. Exiting through the entryway, I slammed the door shut behind me.

I stormed into my office to find an unhappy looking Padre Pepe sitting in my chair behind my desk. With thinly veiled agitation on my face, I said, "Pardon me, Padre, for being disrespectful, but what the heck could be so important that I had to attend to you in the middle of a formal exorcism?"

The frown on his face deepened. "Oh, is that what we're going to call it? A formal exorcism? Okay, well, how is your *formal exorcism* going?

"Fine. We've discovered the demon's name, and I think it's about to break. But can't our little chitchat wait until later today?" Though I tried to hide my impatience from the padre, the emotion seeped down my right leg and into my renegade foot. The appendage was tapping out a furious beat on the floor.

The padre's face grew dark. "No, I don't think it can," he said with fire in his eyes. "Now, what is the only thing I made you promise me in all of this?"

"Padre, you were there," I said in exasperation. "Why are you asking me this?"

"Just humor me, Stephen."

"Okay, I promised not to let things spin out of control."

He pursed his lips together. "Yes, you promised me you wouldn't let things spin out of control. Yet I find myself sitting here right now. Why is that, Father Casey?"

I crossed my arms against my chest. "Padre Pepe, just spit it out if you know something."

"That's an apt way to describe it," he said as he narrowed

his eyes. "Can you tell me how the police received a call in the middle of your *formal exorcism* from the guest of honor?"

"They what?" I blurted out.

"Yes, it seems, and I quote, 'My name is Adam Matthew, and I'm being held hostage at the Basilica of the Holy Heart by a cult. They keep me tied down most of the time, and they torture me. They want me for their bone collection. Please… Please help me. Oh, God! They're coming…'"

He paused and stared at me. "So… do you have anything you'd like to share with me, Father Casey?"

"Oh my God, no!" I exclaimed as understanding hit me.

I rushed out the door as fast as my legs could carry me.

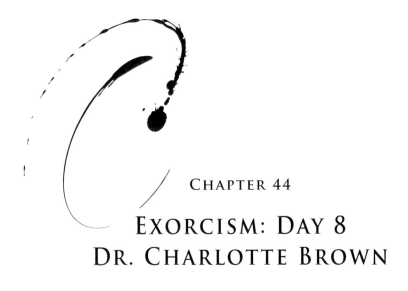

CHAPTER 44

EXORCISM: DAY 8
DR. CHARLOTTE BROWN

As soon as Father Casey shut the front door, Adam's eyes snapped open, and he said, "I didn't think that old boar would ever leave."

"You were awake the whole time?" I asked, my tone uncertain.

"Oh, Charlotte... my dear, dear shrub." Adam sighed. "How tedious it must be to be you."

Deirdre snapped, "I will not tolerate your disrespectfulness, young man!... Apologize now."

"Mother!" Adam exclaimed, smiling from ear to ear. "Just the person I wanted to talk to. You have no idea how much I've been looking forward to this, and now the time is upon us."

Deirdre shook her head. "What are you going on about, Adam? We see each other every day. You can talk to me any-time you want."

Adam grinned. "Yes, but today is a special day, you little minx."

Deirdre's mouth dropped open, and she said, "What did you just call me?"

"Oh, Mom, don't get your feathers ruffled. It's just a word. Minx, hussy, tramp, strumpet… they all work for me."

I grabbed her by the shoulders and shook. "Deirdre, that's not your son. Don't talk to it!… Shut up and pray."

"Oh, shrub, don't be such a killjoy. I want to talk to my mom about her affair—the one meant to fill up her empty, meaningless life. So did it work, Mom? Did it fill you up?"

Deirdre's eyes became watery. "Adam… honey, you have to understand, it wasn't anything your father did. It hit me hard after your sister Bela died, and it left me feeling angry and depressed. Your father and I hit a rough patch, and I felt… hollow… empty on the inside. And I just… I needed something exciting… something to make me feel young again… like I still had my whole life ahead of me."

"Deirdre!" Father Raines snapped as his eyes refocused and he came out of his apparent stupor. "Father Casey warned you. Why didn't you confess this sin? Wait, don't answer that, it's too late now. But don't be a fool! It's not your son! You need to stop talking to it—now!"

Deirdre whirled around and shouted, "Father, don't you dare talk down to me like I'm stupid! I know I'm talking to the demon, but my son is in there listening." She faced Adam again and said, "Adam, believe me when I say I didn't do it to hurt or replace him. Even then, it was your father that I loved, and it made me good for him again. I know what I did was wrong, but the affair was brief, and your father never knew. No one was hurt by it."

Father Raines' lips turned down into a frown, and then he ran out the front door.

My eyes went wide with shock. I couldn't believe the father had just abandoned us, leaving Deirdre and me alone with this thing.

On the other hand, Adam seemed delighted, and quivered with barely concealed excitement. "Mom, really, no one was hurt by it? This is just too delicious. I guess you didn't know then that Dad came home early for your birthday to surprise you and walked in on you and your lover doing it in Dad's very own bed—well, your bed too. You remember, right? The time he went out of town and made that big business deal that secured him the project manager position... the night you found the front door wide open after your tryst and it freaked you out so much.... Ringing any bells for you?

Dierdre looked mortified as she buried her face in her hands, but remained silent.

"Anyhow, I digress. The important part is he returned early from that business trip to surprise you—'Happy birthday, babe!'—and instead, he got the big surprise! He stood there shaking as he heard you tell your lover, 'Oh baby. Oh baby, do me good. Do me again, and again, and again.' Dad wanted to kill the two of you as he listened to your moaning and all your naughty exclamations. Oh, and listening to your lover groaning on top of you added to the flavor. As he stood outside the bed-room door, the blood drained from his face and his heart went pitter-pat as he pictured slitting your throats... and he almost did it too. But, boo-hoo, he loved you so much, he just couldn't bring himself to do it. Instead, he bent his head and cried. Then he walked back out the front door... and hated himself for it.

"But that's not even the good part!" Adam exclaimed with joy. "Your moaning and your lusty pleas to your well-endowed lover rang in his ears and pierced his heart every single day for the rest of his remaining miserable life. It ate away at him until he killed himself instead of you. Swallowed a bunch of pain pills. No one even thought to check for that seeing he had pancreatic cancer and all. But look at the bright side, Mom, at least *nobody* was hurt by your fling."

Deirdre stood there, looking lost and trembling hard. I realized the thing in Adam could be mesmerizing, and somehow I'd been sucked into listening to a story that was none of my business. I rushed to Deirdre's side and shook her hard, then yelled in her ear to get her attention: "Deirdre, we need to get out of here now!"

"Shrub!" Adam said, grinning like the Cheshire cat. "If you leave now, you'll miss the encore. So, Mom, do you want to tell Charlotte the very bestest part of it all? No? Are you sure? Well, let me…. No, really… I insist. Charlotte, my mom's lover… wait for it… her lover was your *oh so precious* husband. That's right. But don't go putting all the blame on Mom. Your husband's specialty is vulnerable women, after all. And it's delectable when you think about it. The expert on sexual predators is married to a sexual predator, and she doesn't even know it. Now that's something that can get a demon's juices flowing."

All of a sudden, there wasn't enough air in the room, and I found it difficult to breathe. *My husband? Deirdre?* It couldn't be true… could it? After all, it was coming from a demon, and demons lie.

"You… You slept with my husband?" I heard myself say in a hurt tone.

Deirdre's shoulders slumped, and she started crying.

Oh dear God, no!… It can't be true.

"I'm so sorry," she whispered. "If it… if it helps, it only happened once or twice."

"Once or twice?" Adam said as he rolled his eyes. "Please, Mother, don't be so modest on my account. You were a machine. He hit your thang for six months straight. You and your lover rutted like dogs in heat… in every spare moment the two of you could find."

Deirdre started hyperventilating and looked like she was ready to vomit. "Please forgive me, Charlotte," she pleaded. "It was a long time ago, and we did end it."

All I could see was red. I tried to fight my feelings, but I couldn't help myself. Pulling back my right arm, I swung with all my might and connected with Deirdre's right eye. A vicious glee shot through me as she went down.

As she sat there on the floor sobbing with her head in her hands, I screamed, "I trusted you! I helped you! And you slept with my husband? You stupid, lying whore… I hate you!!!"

Through the red blur and through my tears, I watched as Adam's smile stretched impossibly wide. To my utter dismay, Richard Davis had been right: Adam's mouth was full of fangs.

Adam turned his attention back to Deirdre and said, "You know, Mom, when you think about it, Dad loved you dearly, and in return for that love, you pleasured Charlotte's husband daily. Your infidelity drove Dad to commit suicide, and it damned his soul in the process… being an unforgivable sin and all. It seems to me he'd have been far better off if he had never met you. But, hey, at least no one was hurt by your silly little love affair, and I'm sure dear old dad would come to that same exact conclusion if he were here right now. Of course, he has an eternity in Hell to contemplate it, so ask him about it when you run into him down there."

I watched as Deirdre picked herself up off the floor and stumbled to the entryway bathroom. She looked… shattered. I can think of no other way to describe it.

Then I looked at Adam, and even through that cruel, maniacal grin, I could tell he was immensely pleased with himself. As I watched, Adam pulled up hard on his left arm, and the zip tie holding it to the chair snapped. He reached under the blanket and tossed me a cell phone. I looked at it and then felt around in my side pocket and realized it was mine.

Tearing my eyes from the phone in my hand, I looked up at Adam's gloating face, and when I did, he said, "Checkmate."

I realized in that moment that Adam was pure evil and he needed to die.

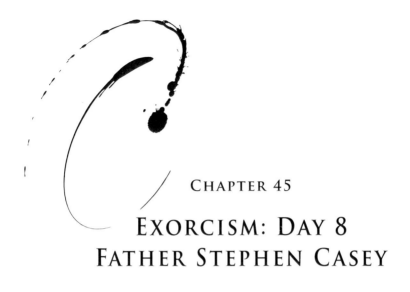

CHAPTER 45

EXORCISM: DAY 8
FATHER STEPHEN CASEY

As I RUSHED out of my office door, I collided with Father Raines, who was running in. I looked at him in disbelief and said, "What!… What are you doing here? What part of '*hold down the fort*' didn't you understand?"

He looked at me with wide, rounded eyes. "Father, forgiveness, please, but you need to come back right now. The demon was faking sickness the whole time, and as soon as you left, everything started falling apart. Something is very wrong with the demon. I could sense giddiness or maybe even excitement coming from it. It almost felt happy… if such a thing can be said about one of these creatures."

Behind me, I heard the bishop shout, "Father Raines! Get in here now and tell me what's going on!"

"No disrespect, Padre, but there isn't time!" Father Raines

yelled back, then yanked on my sleeve and said, "You must come now."

With that, we rushed out to the parking lot. Of course, the guest house would have to be on the opposite side of the extensive property. We ran hard and when we reached it, we flew through the front door and came to a complete stop. Charlotte had her hands around Adam's throat, throttling him. I heard a crash and a tinkling of broken glass in the bathroom off to my left, then I heard a body hit the floor. Adam's face was beet red as he struggled with little effect against Charlotte with a freed left hand.

I motioned to Father Raines to help Adam while I turned and kicked in the bathroom door. I stepped in and struggled to process the sight. As I kneeled to attend to Deirdre, in the background, I heard, "This is the police! Put your hands up!"

Moments later, a set of hands reached into the bathroom and dragged me out backward.

PART 3
SALVATION

"For God so loved the world, that he gave his only begotten Son, that whosoever believeth in him should not perish, but have everlasting life."

(JOHN 3:16)

CHAPTER 46

THE DAILY BEE

IN A STORY worthy of the front pages of New York City's finest newspapers, a scandal is sweeping through our sleepy little town. Yesterday, at 9:53 a.m., police received a tip that a young man was being held hostage and tortured at the Basilica of the Holy Heart. Officers arriving at the scene found Adam Matthew, age fifteen, tied to a chair in the living room as child psychologist Dr. Charlotte Brown, age thirty-six, was attempting to strangle him.

In the entryway bathroom, police discovered Deirdre Matthew, age thirty-six and mother of Adam Matthew, lying in a large pool of blood with her throat slit. Kneeling over her body was Father Stephen Casey, age fifty-eight and head priest of the Basilica of the Holy Heart. Deirdre Matthew remains unconscious as of this writing but is expected to survive. Both she and her son are in a local hospital under guard for their own safety.

At the time of this writing, it is unclear if Deirdre Matthew attempted to take her own life or if it represented attempted murder on Casey's part. Police are leaning toward the latter, as they discovered two human finger bones in Casey's pocket when arrested and searched. Police cataloged the bones and sent them for DNA analysis, the results of which are still pending.

Another priest at the scene, Father Delroy Raines, age thirty, was also taken into custody, though it is not thought he played a direct role in the events. While he was part of the exorcism team, it is speculated that he may have been trying to rescue Adam Matthew.

According to the police, Adam Matthew said that Father Casey and his "posse" made it clear to him that he was possessed. He further stated that they'd been trying to "torture the demon" out of his body. The boy said they'd kept him tied to a chair for most of eight days but managed to free a hand from one restraint and sneak Brown's cell phone away from her before calling 911 when the opportunity presented itself.

Initial questioning of Brown and the two priests confirmed Adam Matthew's basic assertions that an exorcism was being performed to remove what they deemed to be "a powerful spirit or demon." However, all three participants vehemently denied the hostage and torture allegations.

Pending further investigation, both priests and Brown have been suspended from their positions, and Casey and Brown are being held without bail in the local county jail.

CHAPTER 47

ADAM MATTHEW

MY STORY RAN like wildfire throughout our entire community and then worldwide. The area surrounding the hospital turned into a circus, with reporters camped out everywhere. The media, critics, believers, the holy, the satanic, experts, and even the average joe or jane were present. Everyone wanted to talk to me, even when they weren't supposed to do so. People were pushing and yelling, cameras were flashing, and it started freaking me out. The police put an entire hospital floor on lockdown and placed me and mom together in a suite there. I had access to anything I wanted, and even the mayor stopped by to see if I was comfortable. All I really wanted was for mom to be okay. Something had happened to her, and she'd been hurt real bad.

A nurse told me Mom had almost died, but no one I talked to ever told me how. I could remember bits and flashes of things, but I couldn't recall enough to create a complete picture. One of the "experts" who had been allowed to talk with me said that sometimes when bad things happen to a person, their mind forgets the details to prevent them from becoming overwhelmed. With me, it was either that or due to my preexisting brain injury. The one I got when Danny Pechman and crew threw rocks at me. Apparently, Dr. Charlotte's strangulation attempt didn't help matters in the brain department either. Nor did the coma that lasted for a year. My head was screwed up in a million which ways but he couldn't say how exactly. He also didn't know if I'd ever get all of my memories back. For an expert, it didn't seem like he knew a whole lot. But none of it mattered. If I could just get mom to tell me everything, then I could pretend I remembered it all. But first, she needed to wake up.

Another week went by in the hospital, but Mom still slept. More experts visited me during that time, and they always asked me lots of questions, but they never seemed to answer mine. I managed to remember a few more details in the meantime, and my dreams also provided some too—like my brain wanted to talk to me, but I was too slow to get it when awake.

Three days later, something terrible happened. I was sitting in a lumpy, brown fabric chair, reading through my collection of Superman comic books, when I glanced to my right. I'd looked over in that direction a thousand times, and each time, I was greeted by the sight of my mother's comatose form lying under the hospital bed's crisp white sheets. I had expected the same, but now she was sitting up.

"Mom?" I shouted, leaping up from the chair.

She looked at me with lifeless eyes, then turned her head in the other direction.

I ran to her bed and touched her arm, but she pulled away from me. "Mom, are you okay?… Mom?"

She said nothing and wouldn't look at me.

I ran over to the call button and pushed it. A few minutes

later, the duty nurse showed up. When she saw my mom sitting up, she hurried out and returned with a doctor. Even though Mom was awake, she still acted comatose, even while the doctor examined her. But she became agitated when he started questioning her, and after she took a swing at his head, he turned around and left.

Twenty minutes later, another expert came in—a detective expert. He was big, bald, and heavyset, and he stalked into the room like a rhinoceros.

He nodded at me, and then he walked straight to my mother's bed and said, "Deirdre Matthew?"

Nothing.

"Deirdre Matthew… is that your name?"

Nothing.

"Do you know why you're in the hospital?"

Nothing.

"Can you hear me?"

Nothing.

He turned toward me, and even though he was trying his best to convey a friendly look, he looked more like a pit bull dog that just had its food stolen. "How long has she been like this, son?"

"Awake?… A little less than an hour, I think." Then I scratched my head. "I tried to get her to talk to me, but she won't say anything. She won't even look at me."

"Huh. Is that so?" The detective seemed to take that as a challenge. He turned to Mom and said, "Why won't you respond to your son, ma'am?"

Nothing.

"Are you ashamed of what you did to your son, or are you sorry that you weren't able to finish what you started? Which is it?"

Nothing.

"Are you trying to make an enemy of me, ma'am?"

Nothing.

The detective grabbed my mother's pale-white arm in a vise-like grip. She shrieked and then looked at him as if she'd just noticed him for the first time. She struggled to pull away from him, and when that didn't work, tears ran down her cheeks. The detective tried several more tactics with her, but she never spoke a single word. Not to him. And not to me.

The next day, a doctor and some nurses moved me to another hospital room, and despite my repeated requests over the coming weeks to see Mom again, they wouldn't allow me to do so.

CHAPTER 48

THE DAILY BEE

STILL IN THE process of revealing all of its secrets, the ongoing saga of the Adam Matthew exorcism continues.

The case of participant Dr. Charlotte Brown is particularly perplexing. She was a well-respected child psychologist and sexual abuse expert with a clean record in her personal and professional lives. That is until her encounters with Adam Matthew. Brown was first introduced to him as a consultant after he made sexual abuse accusations against the former principal of his school, Richard Davis (deceased). After Brown started counseling Matthew, age thirteen at the time, she took him to a gentlemen's club, where police arrived to discover him inside the premises watching the dancers perform. Officers arrested Brown, and subsequently, her professional license was called into question. However, The State Board of Psychology accepted her argument that it had been a series of misfortunate events. The board reprimanded her but allowed her to continue to practice. From her case notes, Brown thought of Matthew as nothing more than a regular but traumatized boy during this incident.

However, another series of events would change all that. Less well-known are how these events brought out Brown's demonic delusions. To recap the story: One evening, Bud Pechman, a man with an ax to grind, broke into the home where Matthew lived. Bent on vengeance against the young man, Pechman chased him into the basement with intent to kill. Pechman disappeared while they found Matthew in the basement's laundry room in a coma.

Matthew awoke from this state a year later, and Brown evaluated him at his mother's request. Brown first became convinced he had an aversion to holy things during this post coma interview. Brown's husband recounted that her obsession with the boy became so fervent that she "spiritually cleansed" their house daily and always kept a bottle of holy water on her person. He also stated his wife believed the boy had tried to get into their home to kill them. According to her husband, he never saw Adam Matthew once and further stated he worried his wife might have been suffering from mental illness herself.

Brown's fallacy of demonic possession grew so passionate she convinced Father Stephen Casey, head priest of the Basilica of the Holy Heart, to perform an exorcism. Some evidence exists that she also attempted to recruit the late Richard Davis to her cause, as the former principal shared her demonic delusions. When reporters spoke to Warden Owen Smith at the Preston state penitentiary, he felt that something nefarious had been going on between Brown and Davis: "Some type of scheme that fell apart," he stated and found it suspicious that Brown showed up within hours of Davis's brutal murder. As if she had become impatient and tried to confirm the hit firsthand. While that may or may not be accurate, it is not likely that anyone will ever know the truth.

The next twist in the case came when Father Casey sought approval for the exorcism from his bishop, José Francisco Ramírez Garcia de Arroyo, known to parishioners and clergy as "Padre Pepe." Arroyo reluctantly agreed to the request after receiving a clean bill of mental health for Matthew from a qualified psychologist. However, Arroyo should have looked deeper into the matter, as Brown had falsified the record. While Arroyo requested that the report come from an uninvolved mental health provider, Brown did, in fact, write the assessment and then forged the signature of a colleague. She stated she didn't intend any deceit in doing so; she was just trying to speed up the process. We should note that her colleague disagrees with Brown's methods and has sued her.

Regarding the exorcism itself, it seems at some point, Brown became convinced that Adam Matthew was evil incarnate. She stated unequivocally that he had shown every sign of possession by a malevolent spirit. Interestingly, none of the other participants corroborate her story. Casey appears to be non-committal concerning what happened, while Deirdre Matthew isn't talking—literally. Adam Matthew was so traumatized by the horrific events he cannot recall the details. Delroy Raines, the final participant and priest, said he was "pretty confused the entire time and was just following orders from his superiors."

All the notes and recordings made during the eight exorcism attempts have disappeared, so it has become Brown's word against everybody else's. When asked why Adam Matthew needed to die, Brown said she became angry because the boy revealed a previous affair between her husband and Deirdre Matthew, and then he 'viciously' taunted her. She stated, "I hadn't planned on hurting him. My mind just snapped, and I started squeezing." Her accusations could not be confirmed. When questioned, Brown's husband vehemently denied ever having a relationship with Deirdre Matthew.

Upon review, The State Board of Psychology has revoked Brown's professional license to practice psychology. The District Attorney (DA) has charged her with falsifying a medical health report, child endangerment, assault causing bodily harm, and second-degree attempted murder. If found guilty on all counts, she may face a twenty-year jail sentence.

The DA has charged Casey, the priest who requested and oversaw the exorcism, with child endangerment and false imprisonment. Police anticipate further charges against him in connection to two finger bones found on his person during the arrest. DNA analysis has linked one phalange to Bud Pechman (deceased), while the other belongs to Chad Bowman (deceased). Both men were on the regional missing persons report. A report containing a long list of individuals who have mysteriously disappeared over the years. Police believe this may be the break that has been eluding them. Casey has denied any knowledge concerning the bones and maintains he doesn't know how they ended up in his pocket. It has not been determined to date whether Deirdre Matthew's near-death resulted from attempted murder on Casey's part or attempted suicide on hers. The Archdiocese has stripped Casey of all titles and responsibilities in a separate ruling. He is to be excommunicated next week.

Despite his standing in the Catholic Church, Bishop José Francisco Ramírez Garcia de Arroyo remains one of the lesser-known and least-involved participants in this case. While authorizing the exorcism, authorities do not believe he had any direct role in the events that transpired. However, further investigation into his activities revealed an ongoing embezzlement scheme. He reportedly siphoned off tens of thousands of dollars over the last three years from parish bingo funds for his personal use. Funds earmarked for various charitable activities throughout the diocese. Pending a complete investigation, the Archdiocese has suspended Arroyo from all duties. Law enforcement authorities expect charges are forthcoming.

No charges have been brought against the other clerical participant, Father Delroy Raines, and we speculate that his role and possible criminality are still being determined.

Of all the participants in the exorcism, Deirdre Matthew has fared the worst. Though awake, she is nonresponsive to questioning and appears to vacillate between agitation and profound grief. After a thorough examination, medical professionals have determined she suffered a psychotic break. She is not mentally fit to be questioned or charged at this time.

In an ironic turn of events, Adam Matthew appears to have fared the best. Other than dealing with gaps in his memory, he appears normal. As one psychologist stated, "It is precisely those gaps that allow him to be healthy in a mental and emotional capacity. With his terrible memories carefully shut away, Adam can live life like any other teenager."

CHAPTER 49

ADAM MATTHEW

THE PAST YEAR has been hard on my mother and me. Mom drinks the days away, and it is a rare, unpleasant thing to see her sober. She is at her best mentally when she climbs into the bottle and stays there. Physically, her new lifestyle has left her emaciated, and she looks like hell. Though they have lessened, we still receive phone calls or in-person visits from eager reporters or book publishers. One and the same, they always wave around the prospect of big money. But Mom remains oblivious to it. She has never talked about what happened during the exorcism, though the memory of it is still etched into her neck.

From what I understand, a huge lawsuit is weaving its way through the courts, one that will make us rich if we ever win it. The lawyers say the Catholic Church needs to pay big for what it did to us, and they want to make sure the church thinks long and hard before it ever considers doing another exorcism.

As for the rest of my merry band of exorcists, they live in various states of disgrace for their sins. Padre Pepe got off the easiest with just the loss of his position. Now he is just plain old Pepe, and he does janitorial work for the church.

Father Raines fared about the same. After being defrocked and serving six months of probation, he now sells car tires for a department store's auto center.

Father Casey received three years in prison for his part in the exorcism, but I've heard that the bones they found in his pocket are still making his existence hell. The FBI has turned over every square inch of his life and investigated everybody he knows. His life has been dissected and placed under a microscope for all the world to see. The media have dubbed him "The Bone Collector," and parents scare their unruly children with threats of visits from the mad priest.

And then there's Charlotte. Poor old Dr. Charlotte Brown. Father Casey got off easy compared to her. I guess the public, and the courts, just don't like the idea of a child psychologist strangling her own adolescent client and then claiming the devil made her do it. She got twenty-five years in the slammer for her sins.

Then, of course, there's me. In a way, I'm doing the best of them all, but I'm still not well. I see things, and hear things, and I seem to be angry a lot. I have lots of freedom now that my mom is… well, you know. I claim I like it, but I secretly long for the days when I had boundaries, and mom cared what I was up to. Deep down inside, I think she blames me for everything and would be happy to see me get hit by a bus, but she doesn't talk much, so who knows? I wish I could go back in time and kick my butt for even thinking of going with Danny Pechman and his friends to that accursed cemetery. It's not like I had a lot to begin with, but what little I had went flying out the window after that.

Evening came, and I'd tired of sitting at home—and even more tired of being hungry. For the past several days, the only food in the house had been a ten-pound bag of Idaho potatoes, and I'd polished off the remainder of that the night before. Food... gone. Water and whiskey in abundance... check.

After changing clothes, I yelled, "Mom, I'm going out! Don't wait up for me!"

Using my imagination, I pretended she grunted a response to me, but I could tell from her whitewashed eyes that she had achieved nirvana with her special friend Jim Beam and had gone incognito in plain sight.

I wanted to get mad at her, but instead, I went over to her inert form, kissed the top of her head, and said, "Bye, Mom."

I shut the door behind me and walked five blocks to the local grocery store. Once inside, I went over to the return bin for pop bottles and counted the number of eight packs there. I came up with twenty-one, so I figured I could get away with claiming five of them as my own. I walked to the customer service center and smiled at the older white-haired woman behind it.

"Hello, Mrs. Kenney. Can you give me cash for five eight-packs, please?"

She glanced over at the return bin, and then she looked back at me. "You must be in a hurry tonight. You were so quick I didn't even see you come in."

"Yeah, I'm like that," I said nonchalantly, but I could feel sweat beading on my forehead. If she busted me, I'd go hungry tonight... and then I wouldn't be able to pull the trick again. I had no idea what I'd do for food then.

I smiled at her once more as she looked at me over the top of her horn-rimmed glasses, and then she opened the cash register drawer and handed me four dollars.

"Thanks, Mrs. Kenney. I'll be back with more in a few days."

With that, I took off to the produce aisle and picked up a bag of red potatoes and a bag of green apples. I had a little money left, so I splurged on a can of soda pop. I hadn't had one in a whole month, so it would be a real treat. Someday when I got rich, I would drink pop all day long. The only thing I'd use water for then would be to bathe in it... or maybe not. Maybe I'd bathe in pop too.

I took my precious cargo up front to Carla, the checkout girl who couldn't have been much more than two or three years older than me. She pointedly looked down at my purchases and said, "Potatoes again? Are you like a potato connoisseur or something?"

I shrugged. "It's all I can afford. They're cheap and filling."

"Really?" she said. "I heard you had a big book deal."

"Nope. My mom couldn't care less, and I just turned seventeen. I'm too young to get a book deal right now." I didn't bother mentioning to Carla that my mind was a year younger than my outer looks, courtesy of my coma.

As I gazed at her, I could see quick thoughts sliding around behind her blue eyes. She laid a hand on my forearm and said, "Remember me when you come into your millions."

"Sure thing, Carla," I chuckled.

After paying, I took my purchases, headed outside, and sat on the curb while consuming my dinner of an apple, a potato, and a can of pop.

After eating, I walked home like a wraith down the dark streets. I found Mom exactly as I'd left her: drunk and staring off into space. I waved an apple in front of her face, but it didn't elicit a response. About five minutes later, I saw her arm move, and then the bottle went to her lips. *Another kiss from her lover,* I mused. I put the apple by her side and went to bed.

The following morning, I awoke to the sound of retching. I walked into the bathroom and found Mom draped across the toilet with yet another case of the dry heaves. Leaving her there, I headed down the hall and found an empty bottle of whiskey on the living room floor, with the untouched apple sitting next to it. I continued walking to the kitchen, and I opened all the cabinets and the refrigerator just to make sure some food fairy hadn't visited us last night—but… still nothing. I walked back to my bedroom, grabbed a potato, and munched on it. When I walked back out, Mom was sitting on the couch staring at me with dead eyes framed by sallow skin and stringy unwashed hair.

She grabbed at her stomach. "I don't feel so good," she mumbled.

Mom didn't look so good either… and she looked like she'd be throwing up any second again now.

"Well, maybe you should cut back on your drinking and eat something instead."

Her eyes narrowed to slits. "What, you a doctor now or something?"

"Mom, it was just a suggestion."

She lifted her head and looked at me with a sour expression. "You want a suggestion? Next time I do myself, don't save me."

"They tied me to a chair, Mom, so I didn't do anything." I wrapped my arms around myself and said, "The paramedics saved you."

"Well… you should've stopped them."

"Yeah, sure… whatever. But if you're so upset about it, why not just do it again?"

She looked away from me as she wrung her hands together. "Because I'm a coward, that's why. You happy now?"

I frowned deeply. "Mom, just stop it already."

"Stop it?" she said with a slur to her voice. "It's too late for that. Don't you know… I'm on my way to Hell… same place I put your father."

What is wrong with you? I thought. Putting my hands on my hips, I said, "I don't like it when you talk like that, so stop it. You're not going anywhere… especially Hell."

"Whatever," she grunted.

She stood on shaky feet, and with a slow gait, she headed for the freezer. She pulled out an ice-cold bottle of vodka and took a big swig.

That would be the end of our conversation for the day… any conversation. Once she started drinking, the talking always stopped, which was just as well. Our conversations were nothing but depressing anyway.

CHAPTER 50

ADAM MATTHEW

A FEW NIGHTS later, I stood in our living room in front of the picture window, watching the outdoor shadows grow long and blend into the surrounding darkness. Standing there, the fingers of my right hand started opening and closing. I brought my hand to my face and watched as my fingers began wiggling… on their own. I willed them to stop, but my hand didn't belong to me anymore. Pushing my hand against the windowpane, my individual fingers started tapping on the glass as if playing a drum. The tapping stopped as my hand curled up into a fist and smashed into the window. It hit so hard I thought for sure I'd cracked it, but I hadn't.

As I peered at the clear substance of the window glass, something subtle and beyond its surface drew my attention to it. Amidst the black shadow of one tree, I saw something there, up in the limbs—something much blacker than the tree itself. I stared until I pegged it as some kind of man *thing* in a hunched, squatting position. Somehow, I knew it was watching me even though I couldn't make out any of its features. I stepped away from the window, and with the hand that still belonged to me, I grabbed at the old, off-white wool drape and pulled it shut.

"Mom!" I yelled out reflexively, but no answer came. *No surprise there.*

At a loss as to what to do, I started pacing circles around the living room. I tried to wrap my mind around what I'd just seen, and as I did, I became more paranoid by the second. I convinced myself that my impending doom was at hand and in a matter of seconds, the man-thing would come crashing through the door and get me. Breathing in short, shallow breaths, my head turned back and forth scanning all the windows and doors. I realized I needed to get out now before the thing trapped me in here.

Rushing to the front door, I grabbed a pair of tennis shoes from the small pile there and hastily put them on. As I stood to flee, a thought occurred to me, and I went back to the window. I put a hand on the curtain and hesitated. Then I pulled my hand back. *Oh, chicken boy... bock, bock, bock* flitted through my brain and the thought made my face flush with embarrassment. I gathered up my courage, reached out, and flung back the curtain. The thing still squatted up in the tree, watching. *No, no, no... I'm so stupid! It wants me to leave the apartment. As soon as I venture outside, it'll swoop down and spirit me away, never to be seen again.* I closed the curtain.

Leaving my shoes on, I went back to pacing circles in the living room. My innards did a flip-flop as a picture bloomed in my head of the thing bursting through the door and snatching me up. I ran to my bedroom with fear plastered on my face and locked the door behind me.

As I sat on my bed rocking back and forth, my right hand broke out into a flurry of activity, and it seemed to be writing in the air. *Hmm.* I grabbed the box of black charcoals and paper I'd received in the hospital as a form of art therapy, and I put a charcoal stick into my wayward hand and laid a piece of paper in front of me on my desk. I gave myself over to it, and I watched in horror as I drew the tree with the black thing sitting in it… in great detail. When my rebel hand finished, the charcoal dropped from its fingertips and I felt my body slump. I flexed my fingers, realizing that control of my right hand had passed back over to me. Relieved, I climbed into bed and pulled the cover over my head. I must have fallen asleep because it was five in the morning when I looked at the clock again.

I'd left the bedroom light on when I'd gone under the covers last night, and it was still on as I sat up in my bed—with my mouth hanging wide open. Apparently, my body had been quite busy during the night. An entire wall contained a detailed and artistic charcoal depiction of an underground church and graveyard, complete with hideous demons hiding among ancient graves. Ghost-like children with pleading eyes also hid among the same graves as they stared back out at me. My skin tightened when I noted a full rendition of the basement creature from my past, captured down to the finest of sickening details as it watched me hungrily through one of the arched church windows.

It was a nightmare brought to gruesome life on my bedroom wall. I ran out of my redecorated room and into the living room, but it felt creepy there too, so I locked myself in the bathroom until the sun came up.

My dread dissipated in inverse measure to the incoming dawn. When the first golden ray of sunlight burst over the horizon, a palpable wave of relief washed over me, and I marveled at the sun's power to dispel the darkness within me. With my courage returning, I unlocked the bathroom door and headed to the kitchen. I grabbed an apple out of the fridge, filled a glass with tap water, and sat on the floor.

After finishing breakfast, I headed back to my bedroom and stopped at its closed door. *What the heck?* I thought. *What now?* I knew I hadn't shut the door behind me. I stood there staring at the doorknob, and then I slowly reached out and grabbed it. If it had still been dark, I would have made a completely different decision, but it wasn't, so I turned the knob and pushed. I stepped into the room, and my mouth dropped open again for the second time in two hours.

My previously redecorated wall was completely untouched: no graveyard... no demons or children... no basement creature. I looked to my desk and saw the charcoals sitting out... and a blank sheet of paper where I'd left the drawing of the tree.

I know the paper and my wall had been marked up, just like I knew I had left my bedroom door open, but... was I going insane?

A laugh escaped from my throat as the point was rhetorical at best. I'd lost my sanity long ago based on most people's standards.

Mom snored loudly in her room, and I knew it would be hours before she woke. I decided that today was as good a day as any, and I made up my mind to just do it. I'd often thought about that night in the graveyard, and it seemed like all of my spooky problems started then. After listening to my story, others had gone there looking for the crypt, and all claimed no such thing existed. Newspapers reported it as a case of "childhood imaginations run amok," or worse, just a made-up story by children to get attention. Whatever the case, everyone knew my account of events had been thoroughly debunked. But it hadn't been debunked in my mind, and I realized I needed to see it for myself and that I needed to do so in the sunshine.

The graveyard would be too far a walk from our apartment, so I took my one and only bike... a bike that I had outgrown long ago, and rode off into the beautiful morning. I ended up parking it on the edge of the same pine forest that I had years earlier. As I walked among the trees, I smelled the pleasant aroma of pine and listened to the pine needles crunch underfoot, and it reminded me of that night so long ago. After a several-minute stroll, I cleared the forest and stood on the edge of the Deadlands... aka Abbott Cemetery.

It had been dark the only other time I'd visited here, so I hadn't realized how quickly the living forest gave way to death. In a span of about ten feet, life around the dilapidated cemetery dwindled until only its husk remained. It seemed clear to my eyes that the Deadlands actively resisted the thriving forest that surrounded it. Only some bare-thread grasses and barren, skeletal trees and bushes dotted its landscape. Not only that, but in the light of day, I noticed that animals and insects avoided the place too. While the forest surrounding the cemetery teemed with birds, squirrels, spiders, beetles, ants, and various other critters... the Deadlands appeared to be as devoid of them as if I were standing on the moon. Nothing living flew over the land either.

When I stepped over the visual border from life to death, the light breeze died along with the forest smells. While the sun still shone overhead, it felt diminished, like salt that had lost its saltiness—as if the place resisted the very sun in the sky. Spotting the square monolith in the distance—my destination—I headed toward it. As I drew closer to the block of stone, the reality surrounding me shifted with my every footstep until the day became night under the cold, shining sun… until even the sound of my own footsteps died away in my ears. An inner trepidation assaulted me as I looked down at the now dusty, bone-dry ground beneath my feet. Apparently, moisture avoided this place too, and that unsettled me further. *How could so much life surround such a desolate place?* An inner voice yelled at me to turn around and leave, and I almost obeyed its silent command. Yet, I had to know, so I forced my reluctant legs to press forward.

Like I had years earlier, I stopped and stood before the only feature present on the stone monolith: a massive wooden door whose surface displayed an intricately carved, naked woman holding fruit. *Mother Nature?*

I grabbed the brass lion's head on the door and pulled hard. Once again, I found myself standing inside a strikingly beautiful place. Golden flickering light emanated from gold torches, illuminating crowns, scepters, and vases filled with large gemstones of every type. I saw framed mosaics made of millions of sparkling gems, massive gleaming statues carved from single gemstones, and still others cut from solid blocks of gold and marble. Splendor dominated every inch of the place, but a particularly magnificent statue of a beautiful angel appeared to be the centerpiece. It grabbed my attention and drew me to it. I hadn't a clue how I'd missed it the last time I was here.

I stood before the angel in awe as I drank in its details. The statue looked so expertly cut that it seemed alive. The giant cut gemstone reflected light in such a way that it gave the angel's eyes a fiery intelligence and the face a look of thoughtful contemplation. Light seemed to be concentrated at the tips and edges of the wings and along the folds of the robe, giving the angel a majestic look… like some kind of mighty, benevolent philosopher-king.

I looked down and saw a gold plaque next to the statue. It read: *"Lucifer, son of the morning, by Michelangelo."*

I scratched my head. *Could this be Satan?* It didn't seem likely, but who could know for sure?

Regardless, now that I knew who it might represent, it gave me the chills, so I turned away from it. As before, only one wall didn't host any artwork: the black-marble wall that contained the tombs of the Bianchini family. Unlike before, though, I could read the lettering carved into the graves. The various writings comprised dedications and praises to Lucifer and his works. I ran my fingertips over the beautiful gold lettering on the wall, and my perception shifted again.

Now it seemed I was looking at a different set of names with similar dedications. Reaching out with my special sense, an explosion of information flowed through my fingertips. I detected tens of thousands of such tomb-containing walls existing throughout worlds, galaxies, and dimensions, yet somehow all resting right here underneath my fingertips.

I turned my head and saw shadows of men, angels, demon hordes, and other fantastical beings that I had no name for, and they appeared to be walking in and out of the crypt. It felt utterly spellbinding—in an academic sort of way—until one shadow took notice of me. As we stared at each other across an immeasurable gulf, the shadow became more substantial, and its vast bulk gained detail. The thing looked huge… bulbous… and spider-like, though it was none of those things. Somehow it defied explanation, and I couldn't wrap my mind around it. Even though we remained about ten feet apart visually, the unfathomable chasm that separated us decreased somehow. A keening sound drifted to my ears that made me mad with fear as the sound rippled through my mind and body. It was the single worst sensation that I'd ever experienced, and hot vomit started rising in my throat. Somehow, I knew that if the nightmare creature made it to my world, it would devour me and many others and usher in a time of great misery.

I jerked my hand away from the marble wall, and the apparition evaporated immediately. Shaking from head to toe, I ran back out the door into the cold, dark sunshine, and I didn't stop until I crossed back into the land of the living. As I crossed the invisible, undetectable barrier, warmth, sounds, scents, and light came rushing back to me. I looked back into the Deadlands and realized that was the coolest thing I'd ever experienced in my entire life.

It made no sense to me that I'd found the crypt, but nobody else had done so. I decided it represented a true mystery—one that I knew I would never solve since I had no intention of ever going back there again… even if I lived to be a hundred years old. I decided one other thing too: I was most definitely insane.

CHAPTER 51

ADAM MATTHEW

As THE WEEKS dragged by on leaded feet, weird little things started happening. My best experience occurred in Spanish class. Something clicked in my head one day, and suddenly I understood all the words coming from my teacher's mouth. I was as fluent in the language as I was in my native English, and everyone there, including the teacher, thought I had to be some kind of language genius.

On the opposite end of the spectrum, my worst experience came during physical education. My head filled with fuzz in the middle of a dodgeball game, and I blacked out. When I came to, I was kneeling in front of the coach and gripping his hands. To my great embarrassment, I found out that I hadn't blacked out at all. I'd just stopped playing dodgeball and dropped to my knees, announcing that my name was Arato and that I came from the Land of Heart. I'd crossed both arms against my chest and then made a circle in the air with my left hand, and after that, I placed both palms up in a supplicating manner and said, "Remember this." When I started humming like a monk, the coach walked up to me and said, "What are you on, boy?" I heard that's when my hands struck out as fast as snakes and latched onto his. I pulled them to me and spit on them as I thanked him for his service.

That incident earned me the "King Dork of the Year Award" as far as my classmates were concerned, but they left me alone anyway since they also feared me. The disappearances of Danny and Hunter, and the maiming of Rick, had seen to that. It turned out my instructors were afraid of me, too, because even though they thought I was weird in the head, not a single one of them said anything to me concerning my strange behavior. I'm sure the sagas of Dr. Brown and Mr. Davis remained fresh in their minds even though a bit of time had passed.

Since my last visit to the graveyard, another problem kept cropping up. I'd slipped into the habit of revealing others' secrets in a public sort of way. Well, not me... but Arato. But as far as everyone else knew, it was me.

One day, as I was walking down the hallway, I accidentally brushed up against someone hard. I turned, looked, and blushed as I found myself pushed up against Susie Clark. And she looked perfect in her mid-thigh skirt and tight sweater. She was extremely popular and the best-looking girl in the entire school. I backed away from her and tried to apologize, but nothing came out.

Susie glared at me as if I were a sub-dweeb and said in a disgusted tone, "Don't touch me."

Before I even knew it was happening again, my mouth opened. "Tell me, is it me? Cause that's not what you said when Tommy put his hand underneath your top. Nope, not at all. You were all happy and moaning then."

Her face turned bright red and just before she stormed off, I felt the sting of her hand against my cheek.

The next day, I was sitting in science class when Ms. Buell asked me if I was paying attention to her.

My mouth opened and said, "More than you can possibly imagine. And I have to say the black nightie you wore for coach last night looked fabulous on you. You should let his wife know so she can get one too."

Ms. Buell placed her hand over her mouth as tears formed in her startled, guilty eyes. Then she ran out of the room.

After a few more incidents like that, everyone avoided me like I had the black plague, and in a sense, I did. But instead of killing with germs, I killed with words. And so it was that nobody talked to me at school or at home.

CHAPTER 52

ADAM MATTHEW

As LIFE WENT on and on, my isolation, depression, and anger continued to grow. No one at school talked to me... ever... and Mom barely spoke to me, and when she did, I wished she hadn't. I could have lost myself in TV or radio if we still had those. But, hey, I had a blank wall and my imagination to keep me occupied. I felt so trapped and bound, lonely and alone. I wondered how I could escape from a cage with no bars and then how I'd even gotten trapped in one in the first place. Other than the completely oblivious social worker that came by twice a month and rubber-stamped our living conditions as acceptable, no one else even acknowledged my presence. I engaged in no real conversations, and I had nothing to do. It seemed like I had my own invisible *"Keep Away"* sign that followed me around like a vigilant guard dog. I walked down modestly crowded streets as if I were alone in the wilderness.

One night, I had a nightmare in which I jumped off a high bridge and died. Surprisingly, upon waking the following morning,

I felt at peace with the dream. Suicide seemed like a sweet release to me, and I understood mom's attraction to death for the first time in my life. It didn't seem like killing myself could be any worse than my current life. I was seriously over it already, and the thought of living another twenty years made me sick to my stomach. I started contemplating suicide that morning and then for several more weeks until, one day, the inevitable happened.

Mrs. Kenney from the grocery store's customer service department finally busted me for claiming money for pop bottles I hadn't actually returned. She said she'd call the police on me if I ever tried it again. With my only source of food gone, slow starvation was the only thing I had to look forward to in the coming days, and it gave me the incentive to do what I needed to do… what I wanted to do. If all went according to plan, I got dressed and ate the last potato I would ever eat.

Before I left, I kissed Mom on the top of her comatose head, told her I loved her, and apologized for ruining her life. Not that she would ever know it, but it was something I needed to do for myself. I'd been wandering around town a lot in my free time, and I knew just the bridge I wanted to use. It was perfect, really: about a hundred feet up in the air, with a shallow river running beneath it. Plus, being an old, unused railroad bridge, nobody would be there to stop me. I thought about it again and realized I actually looked forward to the jump because, for a hundred feet, I would fly like a bird and be free.

As I drew closer to my intended destination, I saw a footpath I hadn't noticed before and took it on a whim. The side trip turned out to be an excellent decision because it went through the prettiest little park I'd ever seen. I knew I wouldn't be back again, so I sat on a park bench and soaked up my surroundings. I fell asleep as the sense of peace surrounding me infused my soul.

After taking a decent nap, my eyes snapped open. *Huh? What? Where am I?*

Startled and confused, I found myself sitting on an old folding chair surrounded by overgrown brush and weeds. *Had I been dreaming?* Empty food packages lay scattered round about me too. I figured I'd ended up sitting in some homeless guy's chair. Standing, I looked around and saw something shiny and golden lying at my feet.

I bent over and picked up what seemed to be a small folded piece of paper, soon seeing *One Ticket to Heaven* printed on it. *A ticket?* I stuffed it in my pocket and started walking. Considering I was standing on the edge of the last day of the rest of my life, it made me happy to have the ticket. I took it as a good sign from God. I'd already assumed I was good enough to get into Heaven in the first place; otherwise, I wouldn't have considered jumping. But it still felt strangely comforting to know where I'd be going before I died. I mused it was too bad everybody didn't get a Heaven ticket before they died. I knew people wouldn't mind dying nearly as much if they did.

As I walked and let my thoughts meander, the railroad bridge came into sight. It stretched in a broken line between a pair of long, towering hills that had separated the two largest metropolitan areas back in the day. With the coming of the automobile, the bridge slowly dropped into disuse until even its knowledge disappeared from the memories of most of the region's residents. I stepped out onto the bridge and put my full weight on it. It protested loudly with creaks, groans, and clicks, so I stopped for a moment to evaluate the situation. Though dilapidated, it still seemed sturdy enough to hold me, so I walked out about fifty feet on the old bridge, careful to avoid the rotting sections I encountered. I came to a halt because I could go no farther, as the next fifty-foot section had collapsed and fallen into the valley below.

I sat on the edge of the bridge with my feet dangling off the end, taking in the view. The view wasn't new to me, but somehow I appreciated it more, knowing that life would all be over for me in about five minutes. I'd read somewhere that the land below me still represented the original virgin forest that had once blanketed most of the state. It survived because of the severe flooding that sometimes occurred between the two ridges, which kept the builders out. As I sat there thinking, a dark pressure started building in my mind. It reminded me that I wasn't on a sightseeing trip and that it was time to jump… to fly… to be free. I sighed and stood.

As I tensed my muscles to launch myself into the open air, I heard a small, still voice in my head say, *"Do you still have your ticket?"*

My ticket? I wondered.

Honestly, I didn't know. I reached into my pocket, and to my relief, it was still there. Pulling it out and looking at it, I realized it wasn't a ticket at all, but a pamphlet. I opened it up and started reading:

+++

KNOW THAT GOD LOVES YOU AND HAS A PLAN FOR YOUR LIFE!

If Jesus Christ returned today,

do you know for sure that you would go to Heaven with him?

You can have Heaven if you desire. All you have to do is ask!

+++

THE BIBLE TEACHES ABOUT A PLACE CALLED HELL WHERE THOSE WHO HAVE SINNED WILL PERISH FOR ALL ETERNITY

Hebrews 9:27—"It is appointed unto men once to die, but after this the judgment."

Romans 6:23—"For the wages of sin is death…"

Revelation 20:15—"And whosoever was not found written in the book of life was cast into the lake of fire.

+++

ALL ARE SINNERS

Romans 3:10—"There is none righteous, not even one; there is none who understands; there is none that seeks for God. All have turned aside; together they have become useless; there is none who does good; there is not even one."

Roman 3:23—"For ALL have sinned, and come short of the glory of God."

1 John 1:8—"If we say we have no sin we deceive ourselves, and the truth is not in us."

+++

WE CANNOT SAVE OURSELVES BY BEING GOOD ENOUGH

Titus 3:5—"Not by works of righteousness which we have done, but according to his His mercy He saved us."

Galations 2:16—"By the works of the law shall no flesh be justified."

Romans 3:20—"Therefore by the deeds of the law there shall no flesh be justified in his sight."

+++

GOD HAS MADE A WAY FOR US

John 3:16—"For God so loved the world, that he gave his only begotten Son, that whosoever believeth in him should not perish, but have everlasting life."

John 3:3—"Except a man be born again, he cannot see the kingdom of God."

Romans 6:23 (continued)—"… but the gift of God is eternal life through Jesus Christ our Lord."

+++

ETERNAL SALVATION IS A GIFT FROM GOD TO YOU

Romans 5:8—"God commendeth his love toward us, in that, while we were yet sinners, Christ died for us."

Ephesians 2:8-9—"For by grace are ye saved through faith; and that not of yourselves: it is the gift of God: not of works, lest any man should boast."

Romans 10:13—"For whosoever shall call upon the name of the Lord shall be saved."

+++

GOD'S PROMISE TO YOU

Romans 10:9-10—"That if thou shalt confess with thy mouth the Lord Jesus, and shalt believe in thine heart that God hath raised him from the dead, thou shalt be saved. For with the heart man believeth unto righteousness; and with the mouth confession is made unto salvation."

Jesus came to seek

and to save those who are lost.

Jesus died on the cross to take away the sins of the world.
He rose again after three days and ascended into Heaven to
be with his Father and he is waiting for us to join him.

Heaven is not earned. It is a gift of God,
so you do not have to wait until you think
you are good enough to ask God to save you.

All you must do is believe in Him and accept
the free gift of life he has extended to you.

If God is knocking on your heart,
ask him to come in.

If you would like to accept Jesus Christ as your personal
savior, please pray this prayer:

*Dear Lord, please forgive me, for I know I'm a sinner. I
believe that your son, Jesus Christ, died for my sins, was resurrected from the dead, is alive, and is coming again. I ask
you now, Jesus Christ, to come into my heart and life and be
my savior. Amen.*

+++

Well, that came as news to me. I'd gone to church most of my
life, and I had never heard anything like that. I'd always thought
that if I went to church regularly, did some sacraments, and
did more good things than bad, God would notice me and let
me into Heaven. But according to the pamphlet, all I had to

do was ask. It seemed that the only catch was I had to really mean it when I said it. I realized that I did want Jesus in my life… desperately.

I opened my mouth and repeated the words of the prayer aloud: "Dear Lord, please forgive me, for I know that I am a sinner. I believe that your son, Jesus Christ, died for my sins, was resurrected from the dead, is alive, and is coming again. I ask you now, Jesus Christ, to come into my heart and life and be my savior. Amen."

I stood there waiting for something to happen, but nothing did. I looked at the pamphlet and saw that I'd read it exactly as it said, so I thought something should have happened, but it didn't.

I opened my mouth again and yelled out, "Come on in already, Jesus! I'm waiting!"

A beautiful, cool breeze picked up and blew through my hair, and it felt great, but nothing else happened. I started wondering what I'd been expecting to happen in the first place as I unconsciously made my way back off the bridge. I was about halfway home when it dawned on me that I was about halfway home. I guess I'd decided not to jump after all. As I continued on, I started humming some of my favorite tunes. As my throat vibrated pleasantly, it hit me that I hadn't hummed anything in a long, long time.

PART 4
FREEDOM

Put on the whole armour of God, that ye may be able to stand against the wiles of the devil. For we wrestle not against flesh and blood, but against principalities, against powers, against the rulers of darkness of this world, against spiritual wickedness in high places. Wherefore take unto you the whole armour of God, that ye may be able to withstand in the evil day, and having done all, to stand.

(EPHESIANS 6:11-13)

Chapter 53

Adam Matthew

When I returned home that afternoon, I found three bags of groceries and an envelope sitting outside our front door. I took the bags inside and dumped their contents on the countertop, and my heart started thumping hard at what I saw: bread, cheese, lunch meat, Kool-Aid, cookies, peanut butter, fruit, nuts, and many other mouthwatering items. I'd been hungry for so long that I actually cried as I ate some of the food. Now that my biting hunger had abated, I picked up the envelope, opened it, and read the letter it contained:

Dear Adam,

After you left the store yesterday, I was pretty upset about your thievery. However, once I calmed down, I realized that you've been using the money to buy meager bits of food. God started working on my heart, and he reminded me that not everyone is blessed with an abundance, and so he put it on my heart to bring you these groceries today. No one was home when I arrived, so I left them here for you to enjoy. Please forgive my harsh words to you, and if you ever need anything, please ask.

God Bless,

Mrs. Harriet Kenney

I stared at the letter, barely able to breathe. *God talked to Mrs. Kenney for me? God asked her to bring me food?*

Tears ran down my face. Who was I that God himself would speak to her for me? I'd always thought that things like this might happen for other people, but not for me—at least not till this second.

I got down on my knees, and I thanked God with all my heart. As I did so, a peace washed over me, and I knew somehow that asking Jesus into my life had been the best thing I'd ever done.

CHAPTER 54

ADAM MATTHEW

ABOUT SIX MONTHS went by—good months. Not great necessarily… but good. About a week after Mrs. Kinney had brought me the groceries, I'd almost gone through all of them. I prayed, and another mini-miracle happened. The next day, I went to the mailbox and found two envelopes from the food assistance program instead of the usual one. My mom had received duplicate food stamps. I gave one packet to her, which she quickly converted into alcohol, but I kept the other one for myself, which meant I no longer had to steal to eat. With the addition of regular food to my diet, my weight and muscle mass increased and I started looking like a normal teenager again.

Yet another mini-miracle concerned Mom herself. I prayed for her often, and she seemed to get a little better. She still drank way too much, but not quite as bad, and her periods of sobriety seemed to last a little longer than before. In addition, she didn't seem as fatalistic, and she actually started eating little bits of food here and there.

I also worked on improving my school situation. I had seriously damaged my relationships with others and totally trashed my reputation, so it wasn't a simple thing to do. Of course, my classmates weren't instant buds with me, but at least they didn't flee from my presence anymore. I was also back to getting A's in my coursework, so there was hope for me yet on that front too.

My life had found a new equilibrium that wasn't ideal, but at least it seemed stable and sustainable. I also knew that I knew I had Jesus, which brought me peace. Sometimes, I even found that I missed church and considered going back. I used to go because of my mother, but when she stopped, I stopped.

But from my point of view, the important things that had been happening to me were internal…. I still felt black as night on the inside, but somehow it didn't have the same effect on me as before. My mood had improved a great deal, and my episodes of depression and rage just didn't have the teeth they'd had previously. And my attitude had gone from doom and gloom to cautious optimism. In that whole time, neither Abaddon nor Arato rained down any misery upon me, and I hoped they were long gone.

One day at school, as I walked from math to science, I saw Susie Clark and her friend Abby heading straight toward me. Susie's friend nudged her in the side with her elbow, and then they both started giggling.

"Hi, Adam," Susie said in a singsong voice, "I was hoping I'd run into you today." Then both girls giggled again.

"Why's that?" I asked suspiciously.

Susie made a pouty face. "Do I have to have a reason? Maybe I just wanted to see you."

"Um… okay," I said, a little confused. "Why did you want to see me?"

"Well, it turns out I have a reason." She flashed me a smile that lit up the hallway. "Abby and I are having a party at my house tonight, and I was hoping you could come by."

"What?... Me?" I said in surprise. "Aren't you still dating Tommy?"

Susie smiled and rolled her eyes, then exclaimed, "I'm not asking you out on a date if that's what you're thinking. I've invited lots of people to come over."

"Oh," I said, then looked down at my feet. "Aren't you still mad at me about what I said about... um... Tommy's hand?"

She shrugged. "I guess not, seeing I'm inviting you to my party tonight. So can you come?"

"Uh... yeah, I'd like that. And thanks for understanding.... I wasn't myself then. So where do you live?"

She grabbed my hand and wrote on my palm with a pen. My hand and arm started tingling all the way up to my elbow, and then I felt my heart pounding so hard I figured both girls could hear it.

I think Susie knew the effect she was having on me, and I think she liked it because she held on to my hand a little longer than necessary as she said, "Now make sure that you're there at eight p.m. because that's when all the fun begins."

We talked for another minute or two, and then they turned and left. As Susie and Abby walked off, I looked at the address written on my hand, and I felt a sudden surge of hope. *All of my hard work was starting to pay off!... It'd be really nice to have friends again.* Even though I tried to put it out of my mind as I headed to class, I could still feel Susie's light touch on my hand, and I could only describe it as *intoxicating*.

That afternoon, I went home, most definitely in a good mood. I sang to myself as I did the laundry, and then I spent some time trying on the few things I owned to see what fit the best. Unlike a lot of guys in my class, I didn't own a car, and Mom said I wasn't allowed to drive her old beater, even going so far as to hide the keys from me. Worse, I didn't even own a bike made for someone my size. I was almost eighteen and still had a thirteen-year-old's bike. In an attempt to balance travel time with appearing cool, I decided to ride my bike most of the way there and then ditch it and walk the last couple of blocks to her front door.

After hosing down my bike to make sure it wouldn't get dirt all over my clothes later, I went inside and cleaned myself up. I brushed my teeth twice, then combed my longish hair in several different directions. I settled on straight back with a few loose bangs. As I stared in the mirror, I thought about cutting my hair for about two seconds and then I sighed. My haircutting ability seldom rose to passable and the one I sported now was one of my best… just butchered instead of massacred. Knowing barber work was well outside of my skill set, I decided to pass.

I still had a few minutes to kill, so I did some jumping jacks and other exercises to burn off some of my nervous energy, and then I went to my mom's room to share the good news with her. She was passed out again, so I shook her a few times, but that just caused her to go into a volley of snoring. It appeared I wouldn't get to tell her anything. I prayed to Jesus instead and thanked him for my newfound luck, but surprisingly, all I got was a vague sense of unease. I just chalked it up to being nervous.

Susie's house was several miles away, and it took me about half an hour to get there. As I rode, I thought about what I'd say once I arrived there while trying to ignore my growing sense of anxiety. As I got close to her house, a little voice in my head— my voice—said, *"Just park your bike here and walk between the houses."* That seemed reasonable because I noticed a small copse of trees that would perfectly camouflage my ride. Stopping, I wiped the sweat from my brow and stowed the bike. Then I slowly walked between two beautiful houses, mansions really, to give me a chance to cool down before I knocked on her door.

As I neared Susie's home from behind, I came to the edge of her parent's property, and I saw three guys standing on the back porch. Tommy—Susie's muscle-bound boyfriend—was swinging around a baseball bat while his two best friends, Bruce and Gavin, egged him on.

"I'll hold Matthew down so you can bash him," Bruce said.

"Bash the freak in the head! Bash him good!" Gavin yelled out in excitement and then laughed.

"Shut up!" Tommy said, hissing out the words. "The freak has ears, and you're going to tip him off if you don't zip it."

"Sorry," Gavin said in a somewhat quieter voice that still wasn't all that quiet. "It's just… It's just that this is going to be so good. I can't wait to see the look on that know-it-all smart aleck's face when you cave his brains in."

I felt stunned… and then hurt. Standing there on the damp grass, frowning with my hands in my front pockets, I realized I should've known it was all too good to be true… that Susie would never let my comment about her and Tommy pass. *Thank God I listened to that little voice in my head. If I had gone to the front door like I'd initially planned, I would've left in an ambulance… or worse.*

As I started backing away from Susie's house, a blind rage hit me. *Don't they know who they're messing with? I've taken down bigger bullies than these stupid toadies.* A devious but brilliant plan came to my mind that ultimately left me bashing their heads in and then walking off with Susie like a trophy. Not that she wouldn't get hers too. She'd pay big later—when I was done playing with her, of course.

But I stopped myself mid-thought, horrified at the plan I'd come up with. Sure, what they were doing was wrong, but that didn't make my plan okay. I could feel a stronger, darker black rage building inside me, but I resisted it, and it backed off. A moment later, though, the tsunami in me started rising again, and I prayed to God, and it collapsed once more.

I know I used to dwell on evil things sometimes, but I hadn't since I'd gotten saved. *Are the demons back?* I wondered. *No… they couldn't be.* I recalled reading that the demons had to leave once someone was saved. And I knew I was saved, but what did that mean exactly? *I am saved, aren't I?*

I realized the present moment wasn't the time to debate my eternal salvation and decided to duck out before someone saw me. Slipping back through the trees, I found my bike and rode home.

The following Monday, during a break between classes, I came up behind Susie as she opened her locker in the hallway. I lightly tapped her on the shoulder, and she turned with an amazing smile on her face, but when she saw me, her lips twisted into a frown.

"What do you want?" she said as she dismissively waved her hand at me. She turned back to her locker and ignored me. Several seconds later, she glanced back again. "Why are you still standing there? Did you come to apologize to me or something?"

"I did, actually."

"Well, it's too late now," she replied as she turned and poked me in the chest. "That's the last time I'll ever invite you to a party."

I sighed. "Yeah, I know all about Tommy and your party, but that's not what I wanted to talk to you about."

Her blue eyes flashed with irritation. "Did I give you the impression that I wanted to talk to you?"

I looked down at my feet. "Um, not so much, but I need to talk to you anyway. The thing I said to you that day about Tommy's hand… I was wrong to say that. I've seen you around, and you're smart, funny, likable—and you seem like a great person. I know my comment was mean, and it cheapened your relationship with Tommy. It was wrong, and I'd take it back if I could, which we both know I can't. But if I can ever do anything to make it up to you—legal, of course—please let me know. Oh… and there is one more thing I can do for you too. You know that necklace you've been looking all over for? The one you got for your sixteenth birthday?"

Her eyes narrowed and she backed up a tiny bit, saying, "Uh… yeah?"

"It fell off your neck when you were raking leaves. You'll find it over by the big oak tree in your backyard… next to the large gray boulder."

Her eyes went from suspicious to a mix of anger and fear. "How can you possibly know that?!"

I shrugged. "No idea. Sometimes I just know things."

Susie stared at me and then she seemed to relax a little. "So you really think that's where I lost it?" she asked, her voice tinged with hope.

I nodded. "It's there. And remember, if you ever need a favor, just ask."

It felt good that I had patched things up with Susie. I had no delusions about the two of us becoming best friends or anything else, but hopefully, we could be friendly when we passed in the hallway. I hoped to do the same with others that I'd offended.

That night I fell asleep on my bed feeling good about my day, but later on, I woke from a deep sleep courtesy of a gnawing unease in the pit of my stomach. The sensation caused me to sit straight up in bed. It took me a few seconds to focus on my surroundings, but a strange sight greeted me when I finally did. Several trees had grown straight up out of my bedroom floor and died. They seemed utterly dry and lifeless, and nothing living moved in or around them as they just stood there, like silent witnesses to death.

After staring at them for several minutes, I pulled my covers over my head and went back to sleep. When I woke up to use the bathroom a few hours later, the trees were gone.

CHAPTER 55

ADAM MATTHEW

THE NEXT EVENING, I sat at the kitchen table doing my home-work. After a while, my mind started flagging, so I snagged a Red Bull out of the fridge and chugged it. Within minutes, liquid energy flowed through me, and then the cogs in my brain started turning again. With renewed vigor, I attacked the work at hand, and in short order, I finished. I went through my assignments one more time to check for errors, and then I put my books away for the night.

About half an hour of daylight remained, so I decided to go for a run to burn off my excess energy. I opened the front door, ready to charge outside, but found myself blocked by a blond-headed man wearing a charcoal suit. He was looking down as he kicked at a raven pecking at his shiny black patent shoes.

"Stupid bird," he muttered. Then he looked up at me and smiled. He stretched out his hand toward me and said, "Sulli-van Boone, executive producer for the TV show *The Final Say*, and you must be the illustrious Adam Matthew."

I chuckled. "Illustrious? Sure, why not. Can I help you with something?"

"Well, Adam, I was hoping to come in for a few minutes and speak to you concerning a business proposal."

I shook my head. "Don't waste your time. My mom has turned down numerous offers already. Her preoccupations have nothing to do with money."

"So I've heard. But this proposal is for you if you're willing to hear me out."

I opened the door a little wider and waved him in. "Sure. So how can I help you, Mr. Boone?"

I gestured for him to sit in the living room, and after we both took a seat on the couch, he said, "As you surely know, we've been the number one talk show for five years running. The secret to our success is tracking down and bringing on interesting guests, and you certainly fit that bill. You're turning eighteen in two weeks, and you'll be a free agent. Would you be willing to come on our show and talk about your experience at the Basilica of the Holy Heart?"

I thought about how to proceed for about a second and then replied, "No, thank you. I don't care to ever relive it, ever."

He shook his head. "Adam, I think you're looking at this the wrong way. You don't get over bad things by burying them; you get over them by talking about them. And to add a little sugar to the deal, I've been authorized to pay you ten thousand dollars for your participation… on top of all your travel expenses, of course. So now what do you say?"

"You know, Mr. Boone, getting it off my chest and giving an interview in front of a million people are two different things. I think—"

"Well," he cut in, "we'll have to agree to disagree. Talking is talking, and talking is freeing. But what if I could get you, say, twenty thousand for the interview?"

"Look—yes, the money is attractive to me, but the whole affair is very personal, and if I talk, people could get hurt worse than they've already been. Bringing all this up again would be devastating to my mother, and it could open her up to criminal investigation. Words that came from my lips back then broke her, and I will not put her in an early grave over twenty thousand dollars."

"Whoa, whoa! Hold on there, buddy. That's not what *The Final Say* is all about. We're not trying to cause trouble for your mom—or you. Look, son, a great many people are interested in you and your story, and they would like to hear it from your own lips. If you don't want to talk about your mom, then don't talk about her. What you talk about is up to you."

I pursed my lips and gazed at the floor. "Um, I don't know." I looked at Boone again. "The money is tempting, and I'll think about it, but I wouldn't get your hopes up on me."

He puffed his chest out, then sucked on his lips. "All right, kid, I can see you're tough. You should consider becoming a negotiator one day. Before I head out, I'm going to leave you with my best offer. It won't get any better than this, and it's not going to stick around forever, so don't wait too long. For one shoot—one show—I've been authorized to pay you fifty thousand dollars. Most people don't make that in an entire year, and all that money can be yours for a few hours of your time."

That number really hit me hard. *This is tougher than I thought it'd be. We really could use the money.* But at the same time, my gut seemed to tell me it was a bad idea.

I hid my inner turmoil from him. Instead, I said, "Thanks. I'll think about it."

Then I rushed him out the door, and in a parting shot, he

said, "Don't be dumb, kid. Play this right, and fame and fortune can be yours."

I thought and thought about the offer after Mr. Boone left, and it intrigued me. Fifty thousand dollars for a few hours of my time—*and* I could talk about anything I wanted. *How sweet is that!* I didn't want to admit it to myself, but I got pretty excited about the possibilities it could open up for me. *And think of all the good I could do with that much money.* It seemed like a win-win situation. *So why did I feel so queasy in my stomach about the whole thing?*

I glanced out the window and saw it was too dark to go running now, so I went to my room and laid down. When I woke up a short time later, my mind snapped right back to Mr. Boone's offer. I really needed my mom's advice on this, and even though I knew I probably wouldn't get it, I decided to try anyway.

I got up and headed to her room, then knocked on her door and called out, "Mom!"

After waiting several seconds for an answer that didn't come, I pushed open her door and stepped into the darkened room. The first thing I noted was the horrific smell. It was fetid and rank, making me pinch my nose closed. I reached for the light switch and flipped it, but nothing happened. I opened the door wider to let the hallway light in, and the second thing I noticed made my heart stop beating.

Mom was semi-naked and lying on her back atop her bed, her body so emaciated she looked like a victim from one of Hitler's concentration camps. And crouched over her devastated body was a vision straight from Hell.

I stood no more than eight feet away from the demon, and I

looked straight into its yellowish eyes—eyes buried in a human-esque face with red, leathery skin. When I looked into those eyes, the sight surprised me. They radiated immense intelligence, and I could tell the thing would have put Albert Einstein to shame. The look on its face was sane, wise, and knowing. Somehow, though, that same face also appeared utterly bat-flipping mad. The famous photo depicting Jack Nicholson's insane expression in *The Shining* looked like the epitome of rationality and sainthood compared to the thing before me. The seemingly opposite looks existed on its countenance as if the very essence of its being hung on a thread—like it flitted back and forth across the razor-sharp edge of sanity and the criminally insane.

It trembled and jerked with desire to do evil against my mother's supine form. It flashed an unholy smile at me and then thrust a clawed hand into her chest.

Mom's chest rose as she took in a sharp, painful breath, and then her body started spasming.

It looked at me again with those two contradictory expressions, then hissed, "Mine!"

I picked up mom's purse off the floor and threw it at the thing. It passed straight through the demon and hit the wall. Then I yelled at it to go away, but it just grinned wickedly at me. Not knowing what else to do, I left the room sick to my stomach as I couldn't bear to see what it was doing to her.

I was so shaken by my experience that I couldn't bring myself to go to school the next day. It seemed so unfair that the demon could savage my mom, but I couldn't lay a finger on it. It never even dawned on me before this that mom could've been possessed by something too. I'd never understood why she went so far off the deep end, but I was beginning to. She tried to help me once, and I knew I needed to help her now. But could I do so without bringing down ruin upon us?

These thoughts remained ever-present in my mind as I flipped through the family Bible, looking for a way to fight the thing. After two hours of frustration, I flung the Bible away from me. Then I rose and started pacing the floor, trying to dispel the darkness within me. After I lost interest in that, I went to check the mail. As usual, I found two identical envelopes containing food stamps, so I left one on the kitchen table and I pocketed the other one. At least I knew I'd eat well today.

As I walked to the grocery store a bit later, I decided to take a detour and head to the local library first, as it seemed like the most logical place to research and hopefully solve my demon problem. Just because the Bible contained nothing about getting rid of demons didn't mean that no book would. Certainly, someone had experienced the same problem before and written about it.

I climbed several concrete steps and then entered through the double glass door into an old but well-kept lobby. No one appeared to be working behind the blond-maple information desk, nor did I notice anybody among the stacks. I walked across the brown-and-tan checkered carpet to the desk with the library catalog computers, which sat about waist-high so users could stand.

As I filled in the required fields, the women's bathroom door opened, and a pretty lady in her late teens or early twenties walked out, her dark hair pulled into a bun with a pencil sticking through it. Her name tag had *Tina* printed on it.

She flashed me a big smile, then said, "I thought I heard the door open. Is there anything I can help you find?"

"Um... well, I..." My face reddened in embarrassment,

and I found I didn't want to tell her my research subject, so I just gave her a sheepish smile.

But Tina was undeterred. She came right up to me and looked at the screen. She stood so close that loose wisps of her brown hair brushed up against my face. Lightly touching my shoulder with her hand as she read the screen, she jumped as if startled, then quickly moved away from me.

"Wait? Are you a Satan worshiper?" she asked, her light gray eyes bigger than before.

I waved my hands in front of me. "No, not even close. I'm trying to figure out how to get rid of demons."

"Uh-huh. Gee, have you tried an exorcism?" she asked with a half-smile, half-smirk.

I gave a polite chuckle, knowing that she couldn't possibly understand how close to home her question had hit. *Been there, done that,* I thought, and there was no way I was going down that road again. Instead, I said, "I was hoping for something less dramatic."

She rocked back on her heels. "Well, my mom always says that if you turn your back on Satan, he'll flee from you, and that's certainly less dramatic. Have you tried that?"

I shrugged and sighed, "If only it were that easy."

As she stood there looking at me, her mouth dropped open and her hand flew up to cover it. "Wait a second!… I know you, don't I? You're that kid, aren't you? The kid from the basilica? Didn't they already do an exorcism on you?"

I nodded. "Yeah, that's me. But it didn't work. And this isn't for me anyhow. I'm trying to help someone else."

A morbid curiosity seemed to grip her as she bit her lower lip and tapped her cheek with a pen. "Wait? So you still have the demons in you? Are they here now?"

I shrugged. "I think so."

Tina's eyes gleamed. "Do they make you want to do bad things? Like to me?"

"Sometimes," I said. "But mostly, they make me want to do bad things to me."

"You mean like kill yourself?"

I don't know why I opened up to her, but I did. Maybe because she seemed so earnest. Or perhaps because she wanted to talk to me. Most didn't. People at school still avoided me as a general rule, so actual conversations were rare for me. "Sometimes," I replied, feeling a little light-headed from my decision. "But I'm also their home, so they need me to be alive. These things like limiting my choices, and they like to isolate me. They like to suck the life right out of me, and they're big on despair. If you could see inside of me, you'd find blackness. I'm just so dark on the inside, and I'm full of death. Nothing brings me happiness. I have no interests. No relationships. Nothing. I'm as dead on the inside as if I were already in the grave. I try to fight them, but nothing seems to work. They always find a way around it—including hurting those around me. So I'm desperate, and that's why I'm here today.... I need answers."

Tina frowned. "I'm sorry. That's so sad. Have you tried praying to God?"

I nodded. "Some. I found God several months back, and things seemed to be getting better for me for a while, but now it's all coming back again. But the weird thing is, now that I have Jesus, I have hope even though I'm filled with despair. Somehow, I know there's a way to fight these demons if I can just figure it out."

Tina touched my shoulder again but seemed to think better of it and withdrew her hand. "I wish I could help you, but I know nothing about that kind of stuff."

"That's okay." I smiled weakly. "But maybe you could help me by taking me to the section with the supernatural books."

She nodded, and we walked together to the back of the library. It turned out that their entire collection consisted of seven books, and only one of them focused on demonology. Unfortunately, it seemed more concerned with attracting their attention and summoning them than getting rid of them. I closed the book with a sense of disappointment, then headed off to the grocery store.

I returned home with a bag of groceries, and I held it in one arm as I dug in my pocket for my key using my free hand. As I did, that same pesky raven that had been hanging around lately landed right by me and started pecking at my shoe. I kicked at it with my foot, and it started cawing at me—along with three other ravens sitting in a nearby tree. I ignored their scolding, pushed the door open, and blinked as I stood frozen in place. *What the heck?* I could've sworn I saw something that looked like a stunted troll—but only for a second, so I couldn't be sure. I entered cautiously and looked around, but I noticed nothing out of the ordinary.

Setting the bag of groceries down on the kitchen table, I looked around for intruders. *Nothing.* Mom was absent, so I figured she must've taken her brand-new food stamps on an alcohol run. I went back to the kitchen and made myself a peanut butter and jelly sandwich with some of the supplies I'd bought, and then I put away the other groceries. After that, I pulled out a chessboard to burn some time, and I started playing against myself. At some point, I realized it was getting late, and I began worrying about mom. Typically, she was in her room and passed out in an alcohol-induced coma by this time in the evening. About an hour later, I received a call from the police station. Mom had been busted for a second DUI, and they set her bail at ten thousand dollars. From my point of view, that amount was as unreachable as a million bucks.

I gathered my hair up in my fists and screamed.

———

Late that night, I finally fell asleep but it was an uneasy slumber. I found myself walking in a dark place when I was surprised by a reddish glow emanating from the knothole of a large, dead oak tree.

A deep, male voice, sounding like a proclamation from a god, said, "Will you serve me?"

The voice, I realized, had come from the tree itself. I squinted into the ruddiness but could see nothing more.

I shrugged and replied, "Okay, I'm game. What will you give me?"

Ten silver coins fell out of the sky and landed, scattered all about me.

"What about gold?" I asked.

A single gold coin fell out of the sky and landed an inch from my foot.

As I contemplated the meaning of the coins, ghostly fingers wrapped around my person and gently pulled me toward the unholy light. As soon as it touched me, I knew it was demonic. *But what? Lucifer? Satan? Creepy keening creature? Did a crowd of demons follow me back from the Deadlands?... Well, whatever.*

I'd had enough of this nightmare. I resisted the pull and backed away from the demonic entity. "No, I will not serve you."

The glow coming from the knothole intensified until everything around it was painted a deep ruby red. I lifted a hand to my face, and it looked blood-soaked.

"Will you serve me for your mother's release?"

I grabbed my head in my hands and yelled, "No, no, no, no, no!"

My eyes snapped open, and I found myself in bed with fear gripping my soul. My heart jackhammered, and my breaths came in short, shallow gasps. I could've sworn I'd just had a bad dream, but it escaped me already. I could only wonder, *What does my body know that I don't?*

When I'd gone to bed earlier, I didn't want to see anything supernatural, so I turned off all the lights, shut my curtains, and closed my bedroom door. Sitting in my bed after awaking from something demonic—*I think*—I looked into the pitch-black around me with useless eyes. But then I saw something in my room—something so black that I could make it out even in the absence of light… so black that it seemed like an absence of existence… like a hole. The more I stared at it, the more it looked like a man-shaped hole, about six feet tall and wearing a hat. Other than that, it had no defining features.

Gazing at the dark hole, it hit me that this had been the thing squatting in the tree outside our living room window. Given its position in my bedroom, I think it was leaning against my door, facing my outer wall and not me. I looked at it for another five seconds, then pulled my covers over my head and prayed. I didn't come out from underneath them until I knew it was light outside.

At 7:15 a.m., with the sun shining, I climbed out of bed knowing that I had to get my mom back.

I went out to the kitchen and dialed the number I'd kept in my wallet. When a familiar voice answered on the other end, I said, "Mr. Boone? This is Adam Matthew. I'll do the interview as long as I can get an advance of ten thousand dollars."

CHAPTER 56

ADAM MATTHEW

Two weeks later, I found myself sitting on the set of *The Final Say* as stage assistants fussed over my hair and makeup and the lighting overhead and around me. Sullivan Boone, the executive producer, prepped me with last-minute suggestions.

After the makeup artist and hair stylist left, Boone said, "Oh, Adam, we brought in a special guest to help Jamerson conduct your interview today, so—"

"Wait… what kind of special guest?" I interrupted.

He smiled and clapped me on the back. "Don't you worry about that. He's knowledgeable about these sorts of things, so just follow his lead and answer his questions to the best of your ability."

"Thirty seconds to air," boomed a voice over a loudspeaker.

"Okay," Boone said, "that's my cue to leave the set. Break a leg."

He made his exit, and twenty seconds later, the theme music started and a familiar face stepped onto the stage—a face belonging to a well-dressed man in his early forties, sporting wavy brown hair, piercing blue eyes, and a deep-blue Armani suit. He came to a stop near the chair opposite me and stood there in front of the camera in expensive-looking black Italian loafers that probably cost more than my entire wardrobe.

"Good evening, ladies and gentlemen," he said, now taking a seat to my right. "My name is James Jamerson, and this is *The Final Say*. Tonight, we have a special guest." He looked over at me and nodded, then faced the camera again. "Adam Matthew is joining us on his eighteenth birthday to discuss the failed exorcism attempt he endured.... Adam, welcome," he said while giving me a warm smile full of perfect teeth.

"Thanks," I said as a herd of angry butterflies rampaged through my stomach.

"As you know," Jamerson continued, his face pointed toward the camera, "this is a case that has gained international attention and brought renewed light on the role of exorcism in the modern world and the dangers it represents to a civilized society. Because of the uniqueness of this case, we've brought in another special guest tonight to probe Adam's claims. Please welcome famed skeptic and debunker of all things paranormal and pseudoscientific... Dr. Grant Jennings."

Applause arose in the air even though I didn't see a live audience. A man walked onto the stage with the air and dress of a college professor and shook Jamerson's hand in a confident, affable manner. Then he strode over to me and shook mine as he stared intensely at me. As he pulled back, he flashed a smile of barely constrained excitement—*I think*—and then sat down on the other side of the host.

"Thank you for coming, Dr. Jennings," Jamerson said, then turned toward me. "So, Adam, from what I've read, the Catholic Church—in conjunction with one Dr. Charlotte

Brown—determined that you were possessed and in need of an exorcism, and they set about to do just that. Do you know why they thought that?"

"Yes," I replied, "but I'd like to clarify that it wasn't the Catholic Church itself, so I'm not throwing all Catholics under the bus. Rather, one local Catholic priest, along with his bishop and another priest, pushed for the ritual to take place."

"Understood," Jamerson said. "Now, could you enlighten us on the matter of why they pushed for the exorcism?"

I shrugged. "I guess it's because... well, I'm possessed."

Jamerson eyed me, looking like he was waiting for me to say something more. When I didn't, he asked, "Is this what you believe, or is this what you were told?"

"Mmm... both."

Jamerson nodded, then turned to his right. "Dr. Jennings, do you care to comment on this statement?"

"Thank you, James," Jennings said, then turned toward the camera with a thoughtful, knowledgeable look. "This is a textbook case of Stockholm syndrome. It occurs when a victim bonds with their captors and comes to see them in a positive light."

"Oh my, Dr. Jennings," Jamerson said with concern, "that sounds serious. But Adam here seems reasonable and intelligent, especially for a young man his age. Why would such a person fall for something so obviously untrue?"

"A good question," Jennings replied, then steepled his fingers together and rested his chin on top of them. "It's actually a physiological response to extreme stress, and it functions to insulate and protect the individual's mind. As several high-profile cases have shown us, it's tough to deprogram a person inflicted with this condition."

Jamerson looked at me and smiled in a caring, almost

fatherly way. "Does this help explain things for you, Adam?" he asked. "Do you find it comforting to know that your delusions form the basis of a protective mechanism?"

I paused only a moment before answering, "It might help… if it were true."

"Mmm, interesting," Jamerson said, "but as you just heard Dr. Jennings say—"

"Save your breath, James," Jennings cut in. "Research has shown that he'll need to undergo extensive therapy before he's set free from this condition."

Jamerson waved a hand toward Jennings in acknowledgment and said, "Okay then, Doctor. Since this is only a one-hour program, we'll be moving right along." Turning toward me again, Jamerson asked, "Can you tell the audience your story, Adam?"

Audience?… I looked around again and still didn't see anybody anywhere.

"Sure," I said. "That's why I'm here."

Jamerson announced they needed to cut to a commercial break and that we'd be right back. In reality, though—because it was not live—we just kept rolling, with Jamerson cueing us up by saying, "Welcome back. We've been talking with Adam Matthew, survivor of the horrific Basilica exorcism attempt. Most of us have heard one side of the story, but now Adam will share his side of things."

From beginning to end, I told my abbreviated story with only two more commercial interruptions. Both men appeared mesmerized by the tale. Each asked questions or clarifications here and there, but they mostly let me speak.

After I finished, Jamerson said, "That is quite a story, young man. Are you sure you didn't embellish it for the camera?"

I had to laugh. "No, if anything, I under-embellished it."

Jamerson smiled at me, then looked to his right. "So, Dr. Jennings, what is your take on this rather fascinating story?"

Jennings did that *concealed-excitement* smile thing again. "Do you have a few days, James?"

Jamerson laughed that buttery-smooth laugh of his and said, "Well, perhaps the CliffsNotes version, then."

"Of course," Jennings said. "Adam's psychosis goes deep. He has woven a complex story that insulates his psyche from years of emotional trauma and abuse. Without a complete workup, I cannot say for certain, but it appears there is also an element of schizophrenia that acts as the mortar around the bricks of his life. His is a sad story that many will find attractive, and it gives his own humdrum life some meaning."

Jamerson clasped his hands together and looked at me with deep concern. "Is this true, Adam? Are you crying out to the world for attention?"

I shook my head. "There are many things I could cry out about, but a humdrum life is not one of them. Sure, I find life exceedingly boring sometimes, but it is more than offset by times of intense experiences... like now."

Jamerson lifted an eyebrow. "Is that so?" he said. "So, do you feel that right here, right now, this is offsetting your humdrum life?"

"You know what I think, Mr. Jamerson... I think that if I actually had a humdrum life," I said, eyeing Jennings, "I wouldn't be a guest on this television show tonight."

Jamerson turned away from me and said, "He has a point, Dr. Jennings. What would you say to that?"

"What he *believes* is irrelevant. That is the point of a psychosis. Don't let him pull you into his shadowy world of dragons and fairy princesses. For me, my determinations are method-based and factual. While you ask me if his point is relevant, I ask what is the point? That is the true question here, and I have discerned the answer: This boy has mommy issues."

I could feel the hair on my neck rise. "Wait a second, *James*," I said indignantly. "Your executive producer promised me that discussing my mother was off the table."

Jamerson held up his hand to shush me and said, "You know, Dr. Jennings, you may be right. I think you've touched a sore spot. But that's where we'll have to leave it for now because we need to take a quick commercial break."

As before, the camera kept rolling, and over the canned applause, Jamerson continued on. "And we're back with the last segment of *The Final Say*. We've heard from Adam Matthew and Dr. Grant Jennings. Before we went to commercial break, the good doctor proposed that Adam has what he termed 'mommy issues,' with Adam perhaps not really wanting to hear that and myself noting that Dr. Jennings may have indeed touched a sore spot." He looked at Jennings and said, "Continue, please, Doctor."

Jennings gave me a smug smile, then said to Jamerson, "Of course I've touched on a sore subject. My methods never let me down. Although in this case, it's glaringly obvious. He clearly blames his mother for the death of his father. He as much said so during the exorcism when he revealed her unsavory affair to the participants. I've heard the takedown was so brutal, she tried to commit suicide. She survived it, as we all know, but she never really recovered after that. Only an extremely bitter young man would do that to his own mother."

I could feel my face redden in fury, but I held it in check. It unnerved me that I could also feel Abaddon marking Jennings for death. Apparently, demons disliked the guy too.

Instead of getting emotional in my reply, though, I looked him straight in the eyes and said, "It must be amazing to be you, Dr. Jennings. All you have to do is think about something, and all truth becomes known to you. Maybe you can use your methods to give me a foolproof heads-up on the weather tomorrow. But know this: I love my mother, and that wasn't me who took her down."

Jennings raised his eyebrows. "Really? So you expect us to believe that Abaddon—the demonic destroyer from ancient Hebrew texts—rose from the bottomless pit to accuse your mother of adultery so he could ruin her day? Please, Mr. Matthew... this may work with your little friends, but adults are in the room now."

I shrugged. "Well, the way you frame it makes it sound petty and stupid, but that's just you creating your own fantasy straw-man scenario. But I have to say, after dealing with both of you, it's becoming clear to me that you and Abaddon are a lot alike. Abaddon, the destroyer... schemes and destroys. Grant Jennings, the critic... criticizes and destroys. Different methods, same process. And neither one of you can help yourself. Both of you destroy everything you touch, and in both cases, my mom just got in the way. Anyway, that's the way I see it."

Jamerson looked both startled and amused.

Jennings just looked ticked off. But then he inclined his head and smiled. "Just because you believe something doesn't make it true, Mr. Matthew. That's basic Logic 101."

"I'd agree with that," I said. "But by using your same logic, not believing in something doesn't make it false either. And that's basic Logic 102, in case you're wondering." With that, I tilted my head and smiled right back at him.

I could tell that irritated him even more.... *Good.*

With a hard stare, he said, "Which, Mr. Matthew, is why, unlike you, I don't believe or disbelieve anything."

"Unlike me? Really?" I said as I widened my eyes in fake

surprise. "I've never met a man with a bigger ax to grind. You've made a career out of unbelief, and it pays you handsomely."

Jennings brought his well-manicured hand up to his mouth and coughed. "Spare me your sanctimonious preaching, young man. I apply the strictest of scientific methods to all of my endeavors, and they lead to where they lead."

"Oh yeah?" I hurled back at him. "So can your methods write a best-selling love song, create a new favorite flavor, or bring joy to a child?"

Jennings rolled his eyes at me. "Of course not. Your uneducated attempt to conflate the subjective and the objective have no bearings on my methods."

As I nodded, I noted that Jamerson now sat quietly between us, his eyes going my way or toward Jennings depending on who was replying—like some tennis fan watching a tantalizing match.

"Well, Dr. Jennings," I said, "I can make a similar argument. Your educated attempt to conflate the subjective and the objective have no bearing on human limitations. After all, can you put God under a microscope? Can you put the joy of a child under a microscope? Can you even imagine anything more than yourself and what you can conceive? Can a gnat, with all its methods intact, correctly envision the workings of a nuclear power plant even when it's sitting on top of one? Face it, Dr. Jennings, gnats like us don't know what we don't know, and we never will… scientific method and all."

Jennings pulled the spectacles off his face, and with an expression that was apparently his wise look, said, "What an ignoramus you've turned out to be, Mr. Matthew. I don't know why I even bother with the likes of you."

I laughed. "Indeed. I've already admitted to being ignorant, so why are you still trying to argue the point with me? The question is, are you ready to admit that you're an ignoramus too? After all, anything less than perfect knowledge is ignorance, and you can't possibly claim to be omniscient."

His eyes narrowed as he said, "Well, whatever I am, I'm certainly head and shoulders above you."

"Gentlemen," Jamerson butted in with his buttery-smooth voice. "This has certainly been a fascinating exchange, but sadly, we are at the end of our program, and I want to thank the two of you for a spirited debate."

Jamerson talked for another thirty seconds, said goodbye to the viewing audience, and then the camera lights went out, the stage dimmed, and an assistant came and whisked Jamerson off the set... and Jennings followed. I realized that neither had even bothered to come by and introduce themselves to me personally.

Sullivan Boone headed my way as soon as Jamerson left the stage. As I rose from my seat, Boone shook my hand enthusiastically.

"Great interview, young man," he said. "You handled yourself fairly well against our expert. If you keep this up, you may have a future in television."

I laughed a bitter laugh. "A future in television? I don't think so. Why did you lie to me? You told me I could just talk and tell my story. You never bothered mentioning the inquisition part."

Boone gave me a sheepish smile. "Welcome to the talk show racket, kid. We're not looking for prepared speeches. We want authentic responses."

"Well, I won't let you do that to me again, Mr. Boone."

"Don't be so quick to judge, kid," he said as he shook his head and waved a finger at me. "How many eighteen-year-olds pull-down fifty G's for an hour of conversation? Consider yourself lucky that your life is interesting enough to talk about. Most people's life stories aren't worth ten cents."

"I guess," I said, thoroughly annoyed. "By the way, you still owe me forty thousand dollars."

"Forty thousand minus estimated taxes, Mr. Matthew. And don't leave yet. I'll have one of my assistants track down your check."

While I waited, I walked around the set, taking everything in and discovering that it was all smoke and mirrors. What looked real on TV was nothing more than a series of props and facades. I brushed my fingers against a wall as I walked by it, and out of the blue, my special senses kicked in. Like ghosts of Christmas past, scenes of betrayal, lies, half-truths, schemes, and other insipid dealings flickered in my mind's eye. I jerked my hand away from the wall as if I'd touched a live wire. It was clear to me that truth had never found a home here.

As I continued wandering about, I saw Dr. Jennings heading for me. I mused that maybe he wanted to reinforce just how foolish he thought I was.

Instead, he walked up and surprised me by saying, "Good job, kid." He clapped me on the back and continued, "Most adults I argue with don't handle themselves nearly as well as you did."

My mouth dropped open. "Wait… you're kidding, right? You just called me an ignoramus on national TV."

"Yeah, I sure did," he said, then chuckled. "Get over it. Truth be told, you made some rookie mistakes, but you made some good points too. You have a good face for TV and a quick mind. I think you'd make a worthy opponent with a little training and practice, and Lord knows I could use one."

I closed my eyes and pushed down my confusion. Everything here seemed upside down. A few seconds later, I opened my eyes and asked, "And why would you want a worthy opponent?"

"Don't you know? You already brought it up during the interview: for the money. It's how I make my living. Nobody pays big bucks to watch a man with a glass jaw in a boxing match. Two worthy opponents can become legends in the ring. Oh, and by the way, never attack a man for the living he makes. It's poor sportsmanship."

"Okay, if you say so, Dr. Jennings."

"By the way, kid, is it really your birthday today?"

I nodded. "It is."

"Consider this my birthday present to you, then: I went easy on you tonight. The next time we spar, I won't let you off so lightly."

That was light? I thought. But instead, I said, "Thanks. And just out of curiosity, why did you go *easy* on me out there?"

He smiled. "Because nobody likes a bully. Especially when the victim is a sincere, young, good-looking kid. Just ask Charlotte Brown if you don't believe me. Well, anyhow, I'd love to talk to you all night, but I have other business to attend to." He patted me on the arm and said, "Happy birthday, and don't spend all of your hard-earned cash tonight. You have to learn to pace yourself in this business." With that, Jennings turned and walked away.

Once he'd disappeared from sight, I continued my trek and finished checking out the stage and the surrounding areas. As I thought about our conversation, I found it even more shocking than the fakeness of this stage. *Is everything smoke and mirrors on TV? Doesn't anyone care about the truth anymore?* Unfortunately, I figured I already had the answer to my questions.

Later that night, after eating a fantastic dinner courtesy of *The Final Say*, I returned to my swanky hotel room and fell into a sound sleep. Something smacked me hard across the face as I lay there, waking me. The sting and heat of it were immediate. I touched my face, and it felt raw. I jumped up and ran to the bathroom mirror, showing three angry red welts rising on my cheek. Wetting a hand towel with cold water and pressing it against my assaulted flesh gave me some relief, and then I searched the room with the lights on, during which time no ghosts or goblins appeared to haul me off to the netherworld. I saw nothing odd in the room, but I did find a Gideon's Bible in the nightstand next to the bed. Laying the Bible across my chest like an impregnable shield, I tried to get back to sleep. I succeeded, but as always, when the supernatural presented itself to me, I didn't sleep nearly as well after that.

CHAPTER 57

ADAM MATTHEW

AFTER RETURNING HOME from my TV gig, a supernaturally uneventful month went by and I was super okay with that. I kept my fingers crossed that all the craziness was behind me. Along with the absence of spooky, I also had some money now, and I tried to follow Dr. Jennings' advice, but I couldn't. I bought a TV, a stereo, a computer, an old car, and some better clothes.

During that time, I made decent headway on reading the Bible and in making progress with several authoritative books I'd found on the demonic. I still harbored a longing hope in my chest that I could free my mom from whatever tormented her. Something more sinister occupied my chest too... a void. A hole in my soul that stole and fed on my essence. It was maddening as my energy and emotions seeped into it and dissipated. But there was nothing I could do about it, so I did my best to ignore it.

On the other end of the spectrum, something great but

equally maddening was working its way through my life: a book deal. My interview on *The Final Say* had been a big hit when it aired, and people had become more interested in my story than ever. Those who believed in little red men with pitchforks thought I ate Jennings for lunch, while the true "unbelievers" thought Jennings had smacked me down and wiped his feet on me.

Media types couldn't have cared less either way. All they dreamed about were mountains of cash, and offers from them came pouring in. After a bit of a bidding war, I'd accepted a book offer that would pay me an even million on the date the book was published and fifty percent in royalties on the back end. My agent even secured provisions for movie rights contingent upon the book becoming a bestseller. Then the publishing company set me up with a well-respected ghostwriter to help ensure the book went number one.

On top of everything else, I had one other tantalizing change in my life… and it was perhaps the most maddening of all. I discovered girls were really turned on by celebrities… even minor ones. Classmates who had never given me the time of day started clamoring for my attention, including Susie and her friends. The beautiful girl who'd been offended by me began going out of her way to get my attention. Of course, that got her boyfriend Tommy's attention too, but that would be a problem for another day.

It seemed I was finally catching some good breaks in life, and it thrilled me. I gave thanks to God for it and regretted that I hadn't found him years earlier. I regretted mom hadn't found God either. She'd gone to church all those years, and somehow she still missed it. And now, no matter how many times I asked her, she wouldn't even consider stepping inside a church. I even tried to read her my *One Ticket to Heaven* pamphlet, but it made her angry, and she slapped it out of my hand, so I didn't try it again. But I prayed for her a lot after that. When she saw how great my life was going, I figured she'd realize how good God was and accept him.

About a month after we started working together, the ghost-writer and I met up to go over the manuscript, and we got into a bit of an argument. He wanted to add some details to the book that weren't factual. He said it would make the story more exciting. I felt the story was compelling enough, and I wanted to stay true to events. He seemed determined not to take no for an answer, and he didn't appear to be any more interested in the truth than *The Final Say* had been—the only difference being that he wanted to embellish it instead of discount it. It seemed that everyone wanted to put their own spin on my story.

As I stood there arguing with him, my new cell phone rang—bought with the rapidly dwindling funds from my interview.

I put the phone to my ear and said, "Hello."

A tinny male voice said, "Is this Adam Matthew?"

"Yes. How can I help you?"

"Are you Deirdre Matthew's son?"

"Yes."

"My name is Police Sergeant Curtis Andrews, and your mother has been involved in a bad car accident. You need to come to Saint Peter's hospital right now."

I felt my knees go weak, and I choked out, "Is she okay?"

"Look, son, I'm not a doctor, so I can't answer that. Just get to the emergency room as quick as you can. Do you need a ride?"

"No, I'm good."

"Okay then. We'll meet you there."

Twenty minutes later, I rushed into a sterile looking hospital lobby, and not a single blue uniform greeted my sight. The front desk nurse told me she'd seen no police and suggested I try the emergency room lobby at the far end of the building. After signing in, I received a stick-on name tag and got directions to the other lobby and to my mom's room.

I skipped the ER lobby and the police and ran straight for mom's location. Entering the ER, I looked around at its occupants and saw people in various states of disrepair. Most seemed unhappy, and those that weren't appeared unconscious. As I picked my way through the area, I accidentally brushed up against somebody's cast leg and that earned me a scowl and a few harsh words. Off to the side, I saw a series of rooms that ran along a single wall and among them I found my moms. But before I could enter it, a hand grabbed my arm and stopped me.

Looking at my name tag, a frazzled-looking nurse said, "Please wait for the doctor, Adam."

My eyes stared without focus, vaguely aware of her gray hospital scrubs and white lab coat.

"The doctor will be here in a few minutes to talk with you," she droned on, "so if you can wait in the—"

Oh, no! I pushed past the nurse and into the room, finding myself staring at a human-shaped lump covered by a white bedsheet. I rushed over and pulled on it, and as it slipped away, I could see my mother's broken form lying there... like she was dead. Then I grasped her cold hand and held on tight.

As the tears tumbled from my eyes, I searched her form for any signs of life. She didn't appear to be breathing, so I shook her and pleaded with her to wake up. As I begged, it seeped into my thick head that none of the machines by her bed were beeping. *She can't be dead! She just can't!* I draped myself over her unmoving form and wouldn't let go, even when a male nurse tried to pry me from her. It seemed fate just couldn't leave me alone. It must have seen all the good things coming my way and decided that it was time to hit me with the worst possible thing that could happen to me. My dad, sister, and grandparents were gone—and now Mom had joined them too. I had no aunts, uncles, nieces, or nephews. I was the last person in my family line, and I was completely and utterly alone.

The doctor entered the room and started talking to me, though I gave him no indication that I was listening to him. He explained Mom had been driving and hit a tree. It wasn't clear if she committed suicide, but it could have been as simple as falling asleep because her blood alcohol level should have killed her anyway. I knew the doctor meant well, but his words landed crushing blows on my psyche, and he managed to accomplish what the nurse hadn't: I released my mother's prone form and left the room.

An athletic looking man approached me as I walked down the hall. He looked like everything I hoped to be when I grew up.

He extended a hand and said, "Hi, Adam, my name is Ben Brennan, and I'm hoping to talk to you for a moment."

I glanced at him through the darkness of my soul and didn't even slow down.

I heard his footsteps behind me, and then he grabbed my shoulder, saying, "Adam?"

Something inside me snapped. *Argh, leave me alone!* I turned and took a swing at him.

Somehow his body flowed around my fist, allowing my knuckles to brush his shirt and nothing more.

"Whoa, I'm not here to cause trouble!" the Brennan fellow said. "I pulled your mom out of her car after the accident. She and I talked, and I wanted to share her last words with you, but it's okay if you don't want to talk now. Just call me when you're ready."

He pulled out a card and put it in my hand, but it slipped through my fingers and hit the floor. *Did he just say something?* In no mood to talk, I started walking again and didn't stop until I'd made it home.

After shutting the front door behind me, I pulled all the shades shut throughout the apartment, and then I sat on the floor in the dark of the living room. It struck me that no one would ever come home again other than me, and I could do anything I wanted… or nothing. I envisioned I stood at a crossroads and could go in one of four directions. I knew that each would lead to a completely different life with a completely different outcome. The ramifications hurt my head, so I closed my eyes and lay down on the floor.

Once asleep, instead of standing at a crossroads, I found myself walking along a beautiful river at twilight. The surrounding area looked heavily wooded—and green. As I continued on, the foliage took on the colors of autumn and then the ravishments of winter. Dead brown leaves lay heavy on the ground, soon giving way to nothing but dust. As I looked around me, the trees seemed like they belonged to the Deadlands themselves.

A hunched-over form covered in black sat next to a foul river up in the distance. The sound of inconsolable crying drifted to my ears and as I drew close, I saw my mother sitting on a dead stump with her face buried in her hands. I spoke with gentle words, but she took no notice of me. I stretched out my hand to touch her hair, but a tapping sound brought me out of my sleep before I connected.

Rubbing my eyes in confusion, I realized I was still lying on the living room floor. As I moved to a sitting position, the infernal tapping sound continued and it made the hair on my arms stand on end. Driven by morbid curiosity, I approached the picture window and as I touched the drape, the tapping stopped. I pulled back the curtain and locked eyes with a huge black raven. It stood on the window's ledge regarding me with a cold stare that would have made a pit viper proud and then it cocked its head to the side as if taking my measure. When its eyes had gotten their fill, it bent over and picked up an acorn in its beak, and it started hitting the picture window with it... tapping... accusing... condemning. As the feathered harbinger of doom banged its gavel and pronounced my fate, a wave of anger welled up inside of me. *Leave me alone!* I thought, then waved my hands at the stupid thing and yelled, "Go! Leave!" But it paid me no attention. The creepy bird didn't seem fazed by me, so I shut the drapes tight.

I went back to the living room floor and tried to fall asleep, hoping to find my grieving mother again.

CHAPTER 58

ADAM MATTHEW

THE FOLLOWING TWO weeks were the hardest I'd ever faced, and that was saying something considering the life I'd already lived. More times than I would've liked to admit, my mind lingered upon the sweet release promised by suicide, but I came back to myself and life by slow degrees. I obsessed over the crossroads I stood on, but in the end, I decided to continue in the same direction that I'd been walking.

Before my mother's death, I'd been working with a talented ghostwriter to get my story out to the masses, and it seemed like a good place to rebuild my life. Granted, I was often moody, sullen, and a general pain in the butt, yet the book progressed nicely. About two weeks before we came to our extended due date for the manuscript, Casper White, the ghostwriter—yeah, go figure—said it was time I got out more and met people and he talked me into hanging out with him one evening. Casper said the fact that I wasn't legal was no big deal and underaged people hung out in the bars all the time. Even though mom hadn't been much of a conversationalist, I had to admit I'd been lonelier since her passing, so I gave in, though I knew I'd never touch a drink as long as I lived.

After getting off the highway two towns over, I drove through an upscale residential area and then made my way to Main Street. I spotted my destination and pulled my old red Mustang into the parking lot. I got out and walked between the cars in the crowded lot to the blackened glass door, pulling it open and taking in the view. Besides the seedy strip club that Charlotte Brown had inadvertently taken me to, I'd never been in a bar before and didn't know what to expect. It turned out to be a nice place, done up to look like an ancient Buddhist temple. I saw statues of Buddhas, elephants, and other fantastical creatures along one wall. Even the dreaded Shiva stood there among them. The walls and floors were richly ornate with tiles, carvings, and fabrics. Large wooden tables sat close to the floor while partygoers sat around them on padded floor mats. The mood seemed festive, and people ate and drank while animatedly talking to one another in small groups.

After glancing back and forth a few times, I saw a hand waving out of the corner of my eye. I turned and saw Casper signaling for me to come over to the bar where he stood. He was slightly better-looking than the average joe but otherwise of average weight and height. His foppish light-brown hair and dark-rimmed glasses heightened his bookishness, which was the essence of his personality.

As I came up to him, he high-fived me and said, "Hey, bro, what's up?"

It caught me off guard because that didn't sound like the Casper I knew. "Uh, 'what's up?'" I replied. "I'd say you're what's up. What's the deal with the 'bro' stuff?"

"Shhhhh!" he hissed into my ear. Then he whispered, "If

we play this right tonight, we could leave with a woman. I mean, we would each have our own woman—not that we would share one."

I laughed. "Well, I'm glad you cleared that up for me."

His chest puffed up, then he poked me in mine with his finger. "Hey, don't mock me. It beats leaving with me or leaving alone... don't you think?"

"Sure." I shrugged. "So, what's your master plan? Did you bring honey for the trap?"

He slapped my stomach, then said, "I sure did, buddy boy!" Then he chuckled. "Check out this move." He turned away from me to the crowded room. "Hey, Shannon," he said as he waved over an attractive woman with black hair wearing lots of jewelry and a tight blouse and miniskirt. "I'd like you to meet one of my good friends."

Shannon looked at him with a frown, and then she looked at me. Her frown mysteriously disappeared. Instead, a shy smile found its way to her face.

Casper said, "Shannon, this is Adam Matthew.... Adam Matthew, I'd like you to meet Shannon."

She looked me over with big amber eyes and said, "Nice to meet you, Adam." Then she blushed and looked down.

"Shannon," Casper said, "this is Adam Matthew."

Shannon gave a tiny laugh as she looked up. "Thanks, Casper. I think I got it the first time."

Casper leaned in toward her. "You don't understand. This is *ADAM MATTHEW.*"

Shannon shook her head and stared at Casper as if he were nuts, but then I saw a look of recognition flash in her eyes.

"Oh my God!" she shrieked. "You're him... the guy from TV."

I nodded my head and smiled.

"Oh, you poor thing!" she said. "I can't believe someone would do that to you. I was so… so mad when I saw that. Are you okay now?"

I gave a little shrug and said, "I think—"

"Sheila, Jackie!" she yelled out, cutting me off.

Within a minute, a large group of girls and guys surrounded the three of us. Casper proudly went on about me while I wanted to crawl into a hole. I stood there in utter silence while he talked, and after a few minutes, I excused myself to use the restroom. I stepped inside the bathroom, then turned and watched through a crack in the door. With everyone's attention focused on Casper, I slipped out of the restroom and right out the front door.

I made it about a third of the way to my car when I heard Casper's disgusted voice call out from behind me: "What the hell's wrong with you?"

Turning around, I saw his face glaring harshly at me, like an angry headlight. "I could ask you the same, Casper. I came here to meet a friend, and instead, you're pimping me out to get yourself laid."

"Yeah… so?"

"Well, it's not cool, and I don't like it."

"Do you want to know what I don't like?"

I shook my head. "Not really, Casper."

He rolled his eyes. "Of course not. People like you never do, but I'm going to tell you anyway. You have no idea what it's like to be me."

"That's true… and I can live with that."

His face seemed to contort with agitation. "You know, I was born with an amazing superpower. I can write as well as the great masters, but I wasn't born with much of an imagination. I can write the most elegant prose as long as someone else tells me what to write."

"Yeah, that has to suck," I said deadpan.

Casper stepped closer and yelled, "Shut up, Matthew!"

Spittle hit my face so I took a step back and wiped it off with a sleeve.

"You know what Matthew? I'm sick of clueless people like you that moan and groan yet have no appreciation for how lucky they are. I'd give my left leg to have your life. Your superpower allows you to see and experience things most people can't.

It was my turn to contort my face... and I chose incredulous. "That's the conclusion you've come to after listening to my story? That you want to be me? Hey, just so you know, it *sucks* to be me.... I have nobody."

"Oh, please! You have the whole world at your feet. My book will make you a millionaire in a few weeks while I earn a living off of it. You'll make movies and become famous while I continue to write in obscurity about other people's lives."

I shook my head. "Look, I'm sorry you feel that way, but you're not listening to me: I have nobody... at all."

"Really?" He said with trembling lips. "You really want to go there? Fine. Did you see how Shannon looked at me tonight? Did you see how she looked at you? Did you see how they all looked at you? Nobody looks at me, but you come strutting in with your *lost puppy dog* vibe and good looks, and all the girls go gaga over you. And you don't even care! You could go home with a different girl every night if you wanted to, but all you want to do is complain about how alone you are. Well, boo-hoo! If you don't want them, then the least you can do is send them my way. And so what if I used you a little? I'm making you flipping famous, so it's the least you can do for me."

"Wow, Casper, I don't even know what to say... other than to pray for it. Maybe God will let demons stalk and destroy your life, too, if you ask nice." *But whatever,* I thought, *I'm done arguing with this guy.* I turned away from him and stomped off to my car.

After I got home that night, I paced around for what seemed like forever. Casper reminded me of certain people who envied the possessions of the successful while conveniently forgetting about the sacrifice, hard work, and sleepless nights the person had to put in to achieve their goals. Casper was focused on women and money, but neither would make up for the loss of my family or my lost childhood. No amount of fame would make up for being possessed by a devil, fleeing for your life before a nameless hunger, or watching your only living relative self-destruct before your eyes.

As I continued to think and pace, a gray indifference settled in upon me, and I finally calmed down enough to sit and decompress. I sat on the couch staring out of the picture window into the dark night, and I let the numbness flow over me and take me. I was ready to go home—all the way home—and I thought that if I tried hard enough, maybe I would just fade away from this dark world and find myself in heavenly glory.

As I sat and thought about absolutely nothing, a faint sobbing caught my attention. At first, it seemed like nothing more than a tickle in my ear, but it increased to where I could no longer ignore it as my imagination. I stood, and then I followed the sound—to my bedroom. I pressed my ear to the closed door I knew I hadn't shut and listened. An obviously grief-laden female wept inconsolably. It sounded like a woman I knew, and hope blossomed in my chest… though, deep down, I knew better.

I opened the bedroom door with desperate hope and flipped on the light switch, but I remained in darkness. I flipped it up and down, to no avail.

"Mom?" I whispered.

In the low light filtering in from the hallway, I could make out a dark outline huddled and sitting on the edge of my bed. As I took slow steps toward the figure, nausea rose in my throat. An inner sense told me to leave—no, not *told* me, it *screamed* at me to go. But I couldn't do it. I needed to know—*had* to know. I'm not stupid now and I wasn't that night either: I knew she had passed… but I could only think, *What if she's reaching out to me from beyond the veil?* Tremendous guilt filled me for what I'd done to her, and I knew I couldn't live with myself if Mom needed my help and I let my fear damn her.

When I reached her, I stopped and stood right over her. I could see her darkly. "Mom?" I said again, just above a whisper.

She lifted her head from her hands, and I stared down into her beautiful face… a face glowing ethereally. Not the alcohol-ravaged face she'd taken with her unto death, but her previous face, from when she was young and fresh.

Mom smiled radiantly at me, with tears shining in her blue-green eyes as she said, "I've missed you, son. Come home with me."

My heart soared even as the taste of vomit filled my mouth. I looked into those deep, fathomless eyes and said, "How?"

She looked down at her feet, and my eyes followed her line of sight. I could see something lying on the floor, but I couldn't make it out in the faint light. I bent over and picked up the object, realizing that I now held on to a sharp butcher knife.

Looking back at her upturned face, motherly love shone from its surface. I slowly brought the knife to my left wrist and held it there. My deepest desire was to leave this world… to be reunited with my family. Yet there seemed to be one overriding thought that kept dancing around the edge of my mind: *RUN!* I was so close to getting what I wanted.… *Just one little slash.... No, RUN!... One little nip.... No, RUN!* I stood there in complete silence as a battle raged in my mind.

Mom smiled a smile that reminded me of birthdays and goodnight kisses and holidays past as she said, "Come to me, my son. Be with me forever."

I stood there, feeling myself being torn apart inside. In my mind, I asked, *"What should I do, God?"* A small, still voice in my head said, *"Run."*

The knife slipped from my fingertips as I backed away from her.

A crack started running down my mother's beautiful, ephemeral face, separating it into left and right halves. Another crack appeared, and her lovely cheek fell off and hit the floor with a tinkle. Her face shattered like a delicate porcelain mask, and as it did, beautiful pieces of skin that glowed with love fell off and hit the floor in a crystal symphony. Moments later, something hideous with about a quarter of its previous mask still stuck to its face stared back at me through unholy black eyes—a face that still resembled my mother's somehow, but full of pale, corrupted flesh, ashen bones, and worms.

The hideous face before me twisted and hissed, "Your evil mouth did this to me! Your words damned and destroyed me. You were my end, but it should have been you who died. It was always you who should have died."

Deep guilt infused me and I felt my shoulders slump.

She lunged upward and grabbed my wrist with a bony hand. My entire arm felt like ice—an ice so cold that it burned like fire.

"Pick up the knife now!" she commanded.

As she held on to my arm, my mind filled with understanding, and I saw that the world would have been a much better place if I'd died that night in the Deadlands when I was thirteen years old. I'd foolishly considered myself a good guy, but now I knew better. People connected to me died, disappeared, got maimed, or went to jail. Misery followed me around like a harbinger, and I destroyed everything I touched. I could clearly see that it was right for me to die, that it was time to cast my black soul into Hell.

As I bent over to retrieve the knife, I saw myself in yet another light… another point of view. I saw myself as a victim of forces bigger than myself. I saw myself as a child of God… a child who was loved. Someone who had done wrong but was forgiven. I chose to latch onto this vision of myself, and as I did, whatever hold this mom-thing had on me weakened.

She shrieked as I tore myself away from her. I ran right out of my bedroom and continued out the front door. As I went down the apartment stairs outside, I stopped dead in my tracks because of another creepy sight. Taking in my surroundings, I saw hundreds of silent, shiny little eyes watching me. It felt almost as scary as the thing in my bedroom, so I hurried down the steps to get as far away from this place as possible.

As I neared the bottom, angry squawking shattered the silence, and I saw ravens all around me, swirling up in mass and then dive-bombing me. I started swinging my arms around like I was batting at an angry swarm of bees, and as I did, a dark shadow approached me.

I turned and tried to go back up the stairs, but my feet tangled beneath me, and I tripped and fell, feeling myself descend into darkness.

CHAPTER 59

BEN BRENNAN

SOMETHING TOLD ME that the young man from the hospital was in great danger, and the pressure on my soul to find him was unrelenting. It would have been much quicker if I soul-traveled to him, but I sensed the importance of taking my body along, which required a car. Besides, I could always ditch my physical self if needed, but I sensed I had a little time before my presence became critical. The time of night aided me too since I encountered very few cars on the road. In fits and starts, the area I drove through became poorer as I neared my destination. It reminded me of a time in my past when I'd been down and out.

Within the last one hundred feet of my trip, it felt like everything right in the world had fled... like I was drowning in a deep darkness. *Good.* I'd arrived in time. My senses fully engaged with my physical self, and I felt a thrum as a golden light rushed through me. Exiting the car, I caught sight of a young man running down some apartment steps. He looked around frantically, and I saw a flicker of Adam's face. His eyes were wide and his facial muscles were taut with fear. He waved his arms around him as a smoky-black mist danced among his fingertips and around his arms, appearing to congeal around him.

I stepped out of the shadows, but when Adam saw me coming toward him, he turned away and started back up the stairs. He tripped and came down hard on his head, knocking himself out.

"Demon, leave the boy alone!" I commanded.

The black smoke turned a large blood-red eye toward me and hissed, "What have I to do with you, blessed one?"

A holy zeal burned inside of me. "You harass God's child. Now, answer me, demon: What is your name?"

"My name is Arato, the reaper, but what is that to you?" The semi-solid black mist started expanding and contracting like a heartbeat as it chuckled.

My eyebrows raised in surprise. "And what is your purpose here, Arato?"

"Suicide."

A demon of suicide? I frowned. All of the Devil's own I'd encountered till now were secretive to the extreme. And in the supernatural world, names held real power. Questions posed to demons always resulted in half-truths, lies, and word games. And these were followed up with threats, demands, and deals.

"Why are you so careless with your name tonight, foul creature?"

Though its evil eye never wavered from me, the mist around it started spinning, and a weird gurgling sound emanated from it, which I took as laughter. "Begone, lowly servant," the black mist commanded, "for that is what you are. My master is here, and we are 'The Storm'."

As I unfolded both pairs of legs from my back, Arato fled into the boy and then a black mass formed around him and rose to a height of forty feet. It solidified into a serpent shape with massive wings, though it seemed to have a man's face and the mane of a lion—easily the largest demon I'd ever seen on the physical plane. It surprised me that such a being was here. As I considered that fact, the demon lunged its massive bulk at me with such speed that I barely dodged the thing—and that's saying something, given my ability to move many times faster than the fastest humans.

As its head flashed past me, I swung downward with my upper leg and smashed it against its neck with a force that would have decapitated a marble statue. The demon hissed in rage. But its displeasure lay in its pride, for its scales were like armor and I don't think I'd even scratched it. It reared back up, and as it did, its mouth opened impossibly wide and its head became snake-like. I realized the demon was preparing to eat me like a bug—which, ironically, was kind of appropriate. But I had no intention of being dinner tonight, so I pulled out my Vorpal blade, a powerful spiritual weapon, and Abaddon's softball-sized black eyes widened in recognition. In response, the demon tensed up and coiled its lower body in a tight knot around the boy, causing his human body to convulse.

A ruse. It has other plans for Adam. "Demon," I yelled, "if you destroy your home, where will you go? Will you latch onto me?"

The thing hissed in response and released its grip on Adam. Then its body swung around in a sinusoidal roll as its cow-sized head rushed at me like a freight train. I brought the Vorpal blade upfront and center, and its head froze within inches of it. As I locked gazes with the foul creature, impending doom approached my backside, and I ducked just as its tail swept over my previous position. Taking advantage of its failed sucker punch, I leaped and grabbed its caudal end and drove the tip of my blade deep into its being. The demon shuddered along its entire length and flung its tail hard. My body violently disengaged from my perch and whistled as it flew through the air. The parked car that intersected my trajectory exploded as it absorbed my newly acquired velocity.

I'd just picked my way out of the wreckage when its massive head struck… again and again and again. I twisted and turned, and it took everything I had to avoid its strike. Then its tail whipped into my back and my body hurtled into a large SUV, causing an eruption of glass and metal parts. As I extricated myself from the vehicle that had wrapped itself around me like a baseball glove, its snake-like face drew in close and I stared into baleful eyes that radiated hatred and death.

It hissed, "Blessed of God," then it spat like the words had dirtied its mouth. "Any last words? Childish expressions of pleasure and pain… truths and lies… platitudes and beggings. Speak, gnat! I grant you the working of your tongue before your slaughter—before your miserable soul descends into the netherworld in defeat."

Definitely a demon prince and the lead trouble maker here. Big, bad, and talks too much. I cleared the wreckage and walked to within feet of its obviously pleased face.

"Abaddon the destroyer, you like listening to yourself talk, don't you?"

"Yesssss!" it hissed. "Words are my plaything."

Indeed. I drew in even closer, within inches of its face, nose to nose. "You speak truth. Words strung together can soothe the soul or ensure its demise. Words spoken outwardly rearrange the very reality around us. Master your tongue, and you will master life. Foul worm, words will be your downfall today."

Its lithe form strummed like a guitar string the instant understanding hit it—that it had walked into a trap. The thing was fast but did better over distances. Mere inches didn't give it the space it needed to achieve its impressive speed. I thrust upward with the Vorpal blade, knowing the demon wouldn't strike me for fear of being impaled on it. As predicted, it pulled back. Despite my speed, I only managed to clip its snout. It rose high in the air and shook its massive head back and forth in pain as a black ichor leaked from the wound.

I cupped my hand over my mouth and yelled, "Words you want, words you'll get! I command you, Abaddon, in the name of Jesus Christ of Nazareth to begone!"

Its black form seethed with rage even as the smell of burning spirit filled the air. It gave a mighty shudder, and then it dissipated. The feelings of doom and death also evaporated and I knew the demons were gone.

I mused the demon might come back… maybe. But I could always contend with it again once Adam was safe. I ran to his unmoving form, picked him up, and carried him back to his apartment.

CHAPTER 60

ADAM MATTHEW

As I CAME to, my head pounded like the devil. I'd just had a bad dream. *So lifelike.* Then came the knowledge of lying on something soft, maybe a sofa. *My sofa?*

I opened my eyes and drew back in surprise. I had company. Through my foggy, pain-tinged eyes, I saw a handsome man with chiseled features, blue-gray eyes, and blondish-brown hair. He looked like he'd been out for a jog, or maybe a movie shoot, and his body was ripped. Oh yeah, the guy from the hospital—Berman, something or other. He sat across from me in my living room, staring at me.

I shook my head, trying to clear it. "What… What happened?" I asked groggily, sitting up in slow motion.

He leaned forward and said, "You, my friend, were under a spiritual attack."

I gingerly touched the knot that had formed on my throbbing forehead and winced. "So it wasn't a dream?"

He shook his head. "No. Everything you just experienced was demonic."

I shrugged. "Well, maybe in my bedroom, but the raven attack outside seemed real enough."

"I know, but trust me: That was demonically inspired. It's how the thing chose to manifest itself to you."

"Thank you for that, Mr. Berman," I said as I looked down at my feet and then back up. "Maybe I'm weird, but I find that strangely comforting."

He grinned. "The name's Ben Brennan and I have to admit I've never heard 'comforting' used to describe a demon attack."

The back of my neck was super tight, so I rubbed it to relieve the tension. I hoped it was just stress and not damage from my fall outside. I made a few rolling circles with my head, then continued, "What can I say?… I've had plenty of time to wrap my head around the existence of demons, but killer birds? Not so much. Pardon my bluntness, but why are you here?"

"I'm here for you, Adam—to talk to you and teach you."

Huh. I tilted my head. "Come again?"

"It turns out we're kindred spirits, you and I. When I was a young man like you, the supernatural world made my life miserable too, and I was desperate for help but never got it. So I'm here to give you the help I wanted but didn't receive."

That wasn't what I expected to hear, but… *Help?… For me?* I mouthed a silent *"Thank you, God,"* and Mr. Brennan smiled. I eyed him, wondering how he could've picked up on that.

"Okay," I said, "so tell me, why am I like this?"

His countenance became serious as he looked me in the eye. "We'll get to that in time, Adam, but we need to discuss other things first." With a frown, he said, "I'm the one who pulled your mom out of the car crash before she—"

"Wait! What? You were… You were there?" I stammered as

my heart started pounding in my chest. "Right… at the hospital, you said something about that, didn't you? Tell me what happened… please."

He nodded. "I saw your mom swerve hard to the left and hit a tree dead-on. According to several eyewitnesses, it looked like she tried to avoid hitting something, but no one saw anything in her path. The police report speculated that her intoxication caused her to hallucinate."

I eyed him. "Is that true? Do you think she hallucinated?"

"No," he said as he shook his head. "I saw a black mist materialize in front of her car. I don't know how it manifested itself to her, but she was murdered."

My face fell and then scrunched up as if I'd just tasted something horrible. "Why are you telling me this?"

"Because you need to know it. And in case you haven't already figured it out, you're next."

I pushed my fingers through my hair and sighed in frustration. "But why me? I'm nobody."

He shrugged. "I'm divided on that. It could be as simple as: Why not you? Destruction is destruction, and you're as good a target as the next person. Maybe you were just in the wrong place at the wrong time. But it's probably not that simple. It's much more likely that you're a threat in some way. You're blessed with the ability to see into the world behind our world, and you're a child of God. With a little training and purpose, you could be a potent threat to the enemy."

"Was my mom a potential threat to the enemy too?" I said, feeling my chest tighten. "Is that why she had to die?"

"There's no easy way to say this, Adam, and I'm not going to lie to you. I believe she just got in the way. Getting rid of her weakens you. And speaking of your mom, I have a message for you. She told me you don't think she's noticed, but she has, and she's proud of the man you're becoming. She told me she loves you and asks for your forgiveness."

His response sat in my stomach like lead, and the vague platitudes angered me.... There was no way my mom had uttered those words. I closed my eyes and replayed the fragments of that incident in my mind. *Today is a special day, you little minx... pierced his heart every single day... damned his soul... an eternity in Hell.*

Finally, I said, "My forgiveness? My own words killed her."

He shook his head. "No, Adam, they didn't. You and the demon are not one. It wants you to think you are, but you are two separate consciousnesses with two separate wills and two separate destinies. You are Heaven-bound, and it is Hell-bound. You are a child of God, while the demon is beholden to Satan. The two of you couldn't be more different, and don't you ever forget that."

I pushed down my warring emotions. "I guess, maybe, but I need to know something. Deep in my soul, I know I'm going to Heaven. During the exorcism, the demon said my dad was in Hell, and he said my mom was going there too. I tried to tell my mom about God, but she wouldn't listen to me. Will I ever see them again?" A small shudder went through me. I desperately wanted to be reunited with my family, and the thought of an eternity in Heaven for me while they spent an eternity in torment was overwhelming me.

He shrugged. "I honestly don't know. The veil between life and death guards its secrets well. Like you, I witnessed to your mother, but she rejected what I had to say too. She said she'd done too many bad things in her life and felt she wasn't worthy of Heaven. I didn't have enough time to dissuade her of that notion before she died. I'm sorry, I really am. But I think you should pray on it."

Listening to him was giving me a headache.

"Really?" I said sourly. "She's already dead. How is praying going to change anything now?"

"God says that all things are possible through him, so who knows... and it certainly can't hurt. Besides, I've seen impossible things that would blow your mind, so don't be too quick to judge what God can or can't do based on your limited experiences."

This Brennan fellow was touching on a huge sore spot for me and I didn't even know the guy. *Time to redirect the conversation...* "Speaking of mind-blowing, I have something else to tell you. I saw something in my bedroom that might have been my mom. I don't think it was her, but I'm not a hundred percent sure."

"Yeah, I've already checked it out. It was demonic."

This guy is too much. "Really? You went wandering around my place after I knocked myself out."

"No, you were awake," Ben said, and smiled.

My eyes narrowed. "How is that possible? You haven't left the room."

"It's a trade secret.... Can't tell you."

I shook my head. "You know, you're a little spooky."

"You have no idea."

"Well, that's not exactly reassuring. Should you be leaving now?"

"Only if you want to die prematurely."

His statement caused my adrenaline to spike, and I became hyperaware. "Are you threatening me?"

"Relax, Adam, I'm here to help you. Aren't you frustrated that demons can wreck your life while you watch helplessly?"

"Yes, but I don't want any more people to die or go to jail over me."

"And why would that happen to me?"

"Oh… I don't know. Maybe because it happens to everyone else? Horrible things seem to happen to anyone who gets too involved with me."

"So it seems. But what if I told you how to gain control over—Hold on, my cell phone—"

I watched him as he said to the caller, "Yeah…. Yeah…. You sure? Okay. I'll be right there."

"Everything okay?" I asked as I cocked my head.

"Sorry, Adam, but I have another emergency right now. I'll find you tomorrow, and I'll teach you how to go on the offense."

I looked at him incredulously. "Wait… you're leaving now? You dangle hope, then walk away? Can't you give me a couple of pointers before you leave just in case they come back?"

"Once again, I'm sorry, but this takes precedence. Just stay inside, try to get some sleep, and I'm sure you'll be alright.

I had hoped to get something useful out of him, but he left my apartment so fast it was startling. One second, he was there, and then he wasn't. *Jeez, he looks like a movie star and moves like Superman. Some people get all the luck.* I walked over to the door that he'd left open, shut it, and then engaged both locks. After that, I turned on every light in the place. If it glowed, I turned it on, even the oven light. Next, I grabbed a butcher knife from the kitchen and sat on the couch while channel surfing. I settled on *Friends* and then a *Seinfeld* episode after that.

My eyelids started getting heavy, and I fought it since I'd heard you shouldn't sleep after getting a concussion, which I assumed I had. Instead, I stood and checked again to make sure nothing bad had snuck in, then I grabbed my Bible off the shelf and settled back down on the couch. I laid the book across my chest like a shield as I'd done in the hotel room, and then I continued channel surfing.

Sometime later, while sound asleep, a sense of dread seized me. It snapped me out of my slumber and my eyes flew open. I rubbed them, and then I rubbed them again. Either all my apartment lights had gone out, or I'd been struck blind. I thought something like this might happen, so I'd prepared myself. I pulled a penlight out of my blue jeans and pushed the tip.… Nothing happened.

As I smacked it against my palm, trying to get it to light up, my already nonexistent sight became blocked by something much darker than the black room—like an absence of light or existence. (Those who have seen it understand what I'm talking about. For those who haven't seen such a thing, it's a blackness that makes a completely dark room look dark gray in comparison.) Other than its outline, I couldn't see the thing directly… or maybe more accurately, I saw the less dark room around it. Whatever the case, the hat-wearing, humanoid-shaped black hole was back again. Unfortunately for me, this absence of light was converging on me. It reached out and placed an ice-cold hand hard against my chest, and a crushing pain pushed itself into me. My sense of dread skyrocketed when I figured out I was experiencing a heart attack. My hand shook as I picked up the butcher knife sitting on my lap and slashed wildly at the thing. But I hit nothing—and not because of poor aim. It's just that the blade had no effect on it, passing right through it every time.

I continued swinging, but the blade lost its force as a coldness invaded my body and shut it down. I realized I'd be finding out about my parents' eternal destiny a whole lot sooner than I'd thought. Ironically, I was getting exactly what I'd prayed for. I should have been specific that I wanted knowledge… not firsthand experience. Another rookie mistake, I suppose.

As a dense fog covered my mind, making it difficult to

think, the black thing suddenly flew off me, and then I saw a faint light surrounding it. Staring, I realized that two beings were in the room with me, and the soft glow came from the new one. This new being was also humanoid in shape, but spider-like as well. The dark thing and light being started battling each other, and they moved so fast they became a blur. As I watched, they materialized into place, facing one another.

It might have been my imagination, but the being of light looked a lot like Ben Brennan crossed with a spider. I shook my head to clear my vision, and as I did, the glowing arachnid pulled out a wispy, ethereal sword that flashed black and light—and the blade somehow felt more real to me than anything else in the room. It carried weight and dread, and the black hole of a creature recoiled from it.

The sword flashed out, and the black creature disintegrated into the dark gray of the room. A half a second later, the lights flickered back on, and I was alone.

CHAPTER 61

ADAM MATTHEW

THE FOLLOWING MORNING, Ben Brennan made a brief call to check up on me and tell me he'd be by in a few hours to talk to me. I turned the TV on to burn some time, but being 10:00 a.m., it was all soap operas, talk, and game shows. I turned off the TV and listened to the stereo instead. Anything to escape the surrounding silence. I tuned in to a popular local rock station and listened for a few minutes but soon realized I wasn't into music. I considered that a talk show might be just what I needed after all since it would give me the illusion that I wasn't alone.

Flicking up and down the FM dial, I heard, "My name is Sid Roth, and welcome back to *It's Supernatural*."

It was the *supernatural* part that caught my attention. *Maybe I'll finally learn something useful.*

"So, as I was saying before the commercial break," Sid continued, "you, too, can cast out demons in the name of Jesus Christ."

A snorting laugh escaped from my lips. I'd heard about these crackpots before but had never sat down and listened to one. Normally, I would've been curious, but I wasn't in the mood for it after the previous night. I wanted real solutions, and if it wasn't helpful, I didn't want to listen to it. I continued flipping through the channels… yet, subconsciously, somehow, I came back to it again.

"Yes," Sid said, "as a child of God, you have the power to cast Satan out. God gave his only Son—"

Now don't get me wrong. It's not that I didn't believe in God; I unequivocally believed. But believing in God and listening to some religious whack job were two different things. It upset me that snake oil salesmen like Sid gave God such a bad name, and I started working off my frustration by pacing. It bothered me even more that I'd made a conscious decision to listen to him. Besides, I'd been dealing with demons for years, and I knew how powerful they were. Nothing that easy could ever work with them, and if it did, I felt sure I would have heard about it before now. *Why go through a formal exorcism if you can just command Satan around like a lapdog?… Ridiculous!*

I walked back to the receiver and started flipping through the channels again, and after a minute or so, something in me shrugged, and I thought, *Why not?* I tuned the radio back to Sid Roth for the third time.

His voice enthusiastically emanated through the speakers. "You sit at the right hand of the Father in the name of his Son, and through him, you have authority over powers and principalities in his name. Don't wait any longer. Take authority over Satan and get your life back. Tell the adversary to begone."

Hmm, well, guess it couldn't hurt. I'd fallen for worse in my life.

I raised my hand high in the air and said in a loud, clear

voice, "Satan, I command you in the name of Jesus Christ to begone."

And then I projectile-vomited right into the stereo system.

A great heat flushed through my body as I thought, *Oh my God!… Oh my God!* over and over.

Shaking hard, I raised my hand in the air and shouted, "Satan, begone in the name of Jesus Christ!"

Every hair on my body stood up, from the tips of my toes to the top of my head. A roaring sound assaulted my ears, and I caught myself before I fainted and hit the floor. As I stood there trying to steady myself, my entire body was enveloped in flames. I could feel the intense heat, but the fire didn't burn me somehow.

I raised my hand a third time and said, "I told you, Satan, to begone in the name of Jesus Christ." Every sweat gland in my body let loose, and in the space of a second, I went from being dry to sopping wet. Drops of sweat were falling off me as if I'd been standing in the rain.

Feeling utterly drained, I collapsed to the floor, then sat down. Somehow, I sensed the demons that had plagued me for so long were gone, and a pang of fiery guilt blossomed in my head. Sid Roth had it right, and my narrowmindedness almost cost me my freedom. *How could I not have known this? Why didn't the priests know about this?* I felt strangely elated and depressed at the same time. I was glad I'd finally figured it out after so long, but my mom might still be alive if I'd done so sooner. Heck, if anyone had known to do this years earlier, so much pain could have been spared for so many people.

As I sat there thinking, my elation and sadness drained away, leaving me feeling empty on the inside, and it was weird. I'd grown used to hearing faint, mysterious voices and urgings in my head, to where it had become normal for me. All my aloneness had been on the outside… all around me. But now, the voices were gone, and I felt alone on the inside too, and I didn't know what to make of it.

A nasty, vomity smell snapped me out of my retrospection. If I didn't get it cleaned up soon, it would soak in and I'd have to live with the smell for months. I pulled the front door wide open to air the place out, and I grabbed a roll of paper towels to start the arduous task of cleaning vomit off the stereo, floor, and walls. I couldn't believe so much had come out of me since I hadn't eaten for over twelve hours.

As I finished up, a familiar face appeared at my door and Ben Brennan let himself in.

He raised an eyebrow and said, "Upset stomach?"

"Sure. I had a bad case of the demons." I opened my mouth to speak again, but his intense stare shut me down.

"You look different now, Adam. What happened to the dark energies you carried with you?"

I folded my arms across my chest in apprehension. "Well, if you mean demons by 'dark energies,' I cast them out. They're gone."

Ben eyed the kitchen. "That statement is true, though overstated. You've cast them from your person, but one of them is sulking next to your refrigerator right now."

My head whipped around of its own accord, but I saw nothing. I turned back toward Ben and said, "If you say so."

"I do, and I see you've discovered the power of Jesus's name in the supernatural realm."

"Aren't you happy for me?"

"Of course… although I'd hoped to talk to you about it first."

"Well, nothing was stopping you," I muttered. "You were the one who rushed off last night."

"Yeah, pressing business."

"I saw, and… thank you." I scratched my head and said, "Ben, who and what are you?"

"Sorry. Like I said, trade secret."

"Ok, fine. So why didn't you just use Jesus's name against it?"

Ben stood there rubbing his chin for several seconds before he answered. "It's complicated. First off, it only works on entities from the heavenly realm. For example, you can't use his name to get rid of me or any other human, living or deceased. On the other hand, devils and demons, fallen angels, and their offspring must obey when you use his name. The shadow person you encountered is called the 'Hat Man,' and it is extremely dangerous. No one I've met knows what it is. It could be an alien, an interdimensional, a Nephilim, or something else. It kind of responded to the name of Jesus, so I'm not sure what to tell you concerning it. But the response may not have been enough to save you since it was in full attack mode. I just don't know. But it was trying to kill you."

I looked away from him and stared down at the floor. "But why would it kill me? I'm no threat to it."

Ben shook his head. "In truth, you are a big threat to a supernatural world that thrives in the dark. You went on national TV and talked about it. Then you wrote a book that further exposes this realm. By the way, it's a great book; I enjoyed reading it. But the point is, you are a threat, and you need to be careful."

I pinched my lower lip. "So… help me then. I've got the demons down, so how do I deal with the other stuff?"

"Actually, Adam, you don't have the demon part under control either. They are sentient beings, not automatons, and that's why I didn't tell you about using the name of Jesus."

My mind started racing. *How could it not be beneficial?*

"I don't get it," I said. "Isn't it a good thing that demons have to obey?"

Ben tilted a hand back and forth. "Yes and no. You need to understand that the demonic world is very legalistic and big on legal rights. You can command them to leave, but they can come back if they have a legal right to you."

"Well, what if I don't give them any legal rights to me?"

"That would be a good thing because they derive their rights from your sins. You can cast them away from you, but unrepented sin gives them a way back. Ultimately, your protection doesn't come from commanding demons, but by staying in God's word."

That's fine by me. I thought. Just thinking about them makes my skin crawl. But it didn't jibe with what I knew. "But how can that be?" I asked. "I'm a Christian now. I read somewhere that Christians can't be possessed."

Ben blinked and looked down at me. "Well, Adam, that gets us into the finer points of possession. What you read is correct in that demons cannot possess you in the classical sense, but that doesn't stop them from *oppressing* you."

I scratched my head. "I'm not getting it. What's the difference?"

"In a possession, demons dwell in your inner man, and their influence is intimate, internal, and direct. The victim rarely knows where the demon ends and they begin. The two seem more like one. In oppression, the demons are on the outside pushing inward, but they're never in your inner man. Demons will still try to push you in certain directions, but they don't have true control over you."

"So it makes that much difference whether they're inside or surrounding you? You're telling me it's all about geography?"

Ben nodded. "Let's look at it another way. Think of

possession as a brain infection and oppression as a skin infection. Both can be caused by the same microorganisms, both can make you miserable, and both can kill you. But the brain infection directly influences thought processes and can make you hallucinate and act in bizarre ways. The skin infection can make you itchy and break out in open sores, but it doesn't change your mental faculties. The skin infection can push you to act in certain ways, but you retain control of your mind."

My eyes widened, and I sucked in a quick breath. "Wow, I wish someone had explained this to me years ago."

"Indeed. In the Bible, God states, *'My people are destroyed for lack of knowledge.'* And that, Adam, is why supernatural beings like to stay in the dark. Most people only believe in what they can see and touch. Such people are ill-equipped to deal with supernatural attacks, making them easy targets. But, honestly, the demonic side of the equation is the less important part. Tell me about your walk with God."

I shrugged. "Well, it's pretty simple. At the lowest point in my life, I found a salvation tract, and I chose to believe it. See? Simple."

Ben cocked his head. "Hmm, I doubt it was as simple as that, but how do you know you're saved?"

"I don't know… I just do." I sucked my cheeks in, then puffed them back out. And I was being truthful; I knew that I knew, but I couldn't say how.

"Okay, Adam, tell me about your inner state. What is it like inside of you?"

"I dunno… black, I guess."

"Do you ever feel like a whitewashed tomb that looks good on the outside, but on the inside is full of dead men's bones? Is the darkness inside of you a deep darkness? Does the darkness steal your zest for life?"

My mouth fell open. "Yeah, but how do you know that? Am I that obvious?"

"Actually, I was describing me—or at least me as I used to be. And this condition is more common than you would ever believe. It's caused by sin, and what you're feeling is called many things, but its most accurate description is *separation from God.*"

"But, Ben, I know I have Jesus, so how can I be separated from God?"

"If you truly have Jesus Christ, then your eternal salvation is safe, but sin can still interfere with your relationship with him here. I want you to confess and repent of all the sins you can think of, and then I want you to ask God for his forgiveness and fullness. Can you do that?"

My face turned red with embarrassment. "Do I need to say it out loud?"

Ben issued a warm smile. "No, it's between you and God, but I'll pray for you while you do."

I started out on my knees but found I prayed much better while standing. I confessed all my sins while pacing furiously, and then I asked God to send me his fullness.

The following morning, I tuned back in to Sid Roth's radio program, and while listening, a warm glow blossomed in my chest, light entered my darkness, and joy seeped into my soul. A wonderful, indescribable peace descended upon me, and I knew I was standing in the presence of God.

CHAPTER 62

FOUR YEARS LATER
ADAM MATTHEW

MY LIFE CHANGED in dramatic ways after my encounters with Ben Brennan and God—so much so that the same me felt like two different people with two polar opposite lives. While my previous demons made their presence known from time to time, I sensed that they remained at a distance now. My walk with God became palpable, and my luck and blessings grew exponentially. My empathy and discernment also grew by leaps and bounds, and my success skyrocketed.

Before my encounter with God, even the good things that happened to me had a way of turning to sorrow. After my encounter with God, even the bad things that happened to me had a way of turning out to my advantage. Soon afterward, my book and then a second book became overnight sensations, leading to numerous television and radio show appearances. They made my first book into a movie, in which I played the part of myself, and it was a box office hit. (In addition, I'm in talks for a second movie now. Then there are the paid speaking engagements and royalties from my merchandise. I have more money than my father could have earned in several lifetimes.)

Life was breezing along nicely, and then something happened that changed everything. Even though I had moved to New York City, I still liked to keep in touch with my roots, and I did that through a subscription to my old home's most prominent local newspaper. I was flipping through the daily paper two weeks earlier when I came across a news story about a missing boy. My stomach dropped when I got to the part that mentioned his age. It couldn't be a mere coincidence that he was thirteen years old. I kept checking the paper each day to see if the boy would turn up, but deep down inside, I knew he wouldn't. In addition, I had the growing sense that this problem was being laid at my feet and that God expected me to deal with it. I tried reasoning with God that I'd be much more useful spreading the word about the supernatural through books and movies. Still, the sense of urgency to return to my hometown and confront the problem only intensified. It reached the point that I knew that I knew what God wanted, and to walk away from it would be direct disobedience.

In the end, I owed God everything, so I didn't see how I could say no. However, in my defense, I sensed this wouldn't be a two-way trip. The feeling was so strong I drafted my last will and testament with my bewildered lawyer. I apportioned part of my wealth to anyone I'd ever wronged. Another portion went to those who'd shown me kindness when I'd so desperately needed it. Since I had no living relatives, the remainder of my wealth and my future royalties were to be divided among several religious organizations that did admirable work with orphans.

After calling and discreetly saying goodbye to several

friends and business associates, I found myself driving down the interstate in my beautifully restored, vintage candy-apple-red Porsche 911 Carrera—my most prized possession. The top was down, and it was exhilarating to feel the speed and the wind blowing through my hair. Before I arrived, though, I had to put up the top, not wanting my presence to cause car accidents. Being a celebrity had its perks, but it could also be a pain in the butt.

When I returned, the first place I visited was the only real home I'd ever known—our old house in the Brook Spring neighborhood when I still had two living parents. It struck me that it seemed so much smaller than I recalled. Except for the shutters being painted pink, the house looked pretty much like I remembered it.

Next, I went to the local cemetery and placed flowers on my parent's graves.

After that, I visited the old train bridge where I'd found God. The bridge was so old it amazed me that my younger self had found enough courage to walk onto it in the first place—and I felt even more amazed that I'd made it off of the death trap with my life intact. I was confident that God had a hand in that.

Finally, I visited the local library to do internet research on creepy creatures. I walked up the concrete steps and stepped through the double glass doors into the old but well-kept lobby. It struck me as weird that years had gone by since I'd come here and talked with Tina… mostly because everything looked the same, right down to the worn brown-and-tan carpeting. I walked over to the aging bank of computers and began my internet search. Twenty minutes in, I found some valuable information on my nemesis. It turns out a ghoul is both vampire and zombie, yet neither. It is a demon-like creature that eats human flesh and is most often found in graveyards. In some cultures, it's also referred to as a *Djinn*. I searched my memories and recalled seeing a few graves in Mr. Crab's basement. Apparently, that had been good enough for the ghoul. Some accounts stated they're shapeshifters, and that notion matched my experience with the thing in Crab's basement. I read on and discovered that they reputedly have extraordinary regenerative powers, so killing them involved inflicting massive damage, like cutting off their head. Anything less, and they'd just shrug it off.

I logged off and got ready to head out to the local gun shop when I heard someone call out, "Adam?... Adam Matthew, is that you?"

I turned and saw a pregnant, but very attractive woman heading my way. She wore a blue muumuu and had a small gold cross hanging from her neck. I glanced at her name tag and read the name printed on it.

I looked into her eyes and stared as I said, "Susie, as in Susie Clark?... Like, Tommy's Susie?"

She swept her hands outward. "Guilty as charged."

I smiled and nodded down toward her belly bump. "It looks like congratulations are in order."

Susie scrunched up her pretty face. "I suppose, well... I mean, don't get me wrong, I wanted kids, just not so soon. I was hoping to get a college degree under my belt and travel first, but... life gets in the way sometimes, I suppose."

"So, I assume Tommy's the father? How's he doing anyway?"

"You know, I prefer not to talk about me right now. It makes me sad." She shrugged, then put on a smile. "But how are you doing, superstar?! I saw your movie; it was awesome. And I have to say it scared the heck out of me. I even had to sleep with the lights on for several nights, which is what everybody I know says. It's all we talked about around here for weeks." She touched my arm and said, "Oh, and I have to say you really are an incredible actor. But then… I always knew you'd do amazing things. The first time I saw you, I said to myself, 'That boy is going to make something of himself someday.'"

That came as news to me, and I doubted she'd thought that at all, but I kept it to myself. Instead, I said, "Thanks, Susie."

She gave me a mischievous smile and playfully slugged my shoulder. "So, what brings you back home? Got bored in the Big Apple?"

I shook my head. "No, actually… I'm here to tie up a loose end. Something has been stalking and killing teenage boys around here for many years, and it needs to stop."

Her blue eyes grew large. "You figured it out? Can you tell me more?"

Why not? I thought. *Seems one person should know the story before I'm gone.*

I opened up and told her about the dark secret I'd carried around inside of me for years. I told her about Mr. Crab and the ghoul he kept in the basement. Then I shared the story of how it had hunted me down multiple times and almost killed me. As I talked, I watched her eyes for any signs of doubt or unbelief, but I didn't see any. It felt like someone had lifted a weight from me when I finished.

"Wow… just wow," she said, an intrigued look on her face. "You certainly are an interesting one, Adam Matthew. Quirky and cute." Then she flashed me one of her dazzling smiles. "I think you should make a movie out of that story too. I bet it would be even scarier than the last one."

And I might if tomorrow doesn't find me digesting in a ghoul's belly.

A weak smile formed on my lips. "Thanks. I'll keep it under advisement."

Looking a little unsure of herself, Susie said, "Can I ask you for that little favor now?"

I bunched my brows together. "What favor?"

"Do you remember when you apologized to me?" she said as she twirled a strand of blonde hair around her finger. "When you told me where to look for my lost necklace?"

I thought back to that day, a day that felt like it belonged to a different me, another life. "I do," I said.

She held her breath for a few seconds, then let it out. "Well, you also told me I could ask you for a favor… any favor I wanted, as long as it was legal.

"I remember… sure."

She locked eyes with me. "Kiss me."

I felt my knees go weak, and my heart started hammering in my chest. *The most popular girl in my high school wants a kiss from me?*

I tried speaking but found I'd been struck inarticulate. Not that it mattered. Susie leaned in with slightly parted lips and kissed me. It felt sweet, yet passionate, and sad somehow, too. Nothing overly long… but a kiss, nonetheless. She pulled back and smiled while my heart continued to pound. Susie looked genuinely happy for a moment, but then she covered her face with her hands.

"You know," she said with a trembling chin, "when we were in high school, I thought I had it all… thought I had it all figured out. My life was supposed to be fabulous like yours, but there you are, and here I am." Moisture started rimming her pretty blue eyes as she went on. "Life has shown me that I picked all the wrong people and made all the wrong choices. I'm going to be a single mom pretty soon and I look like a fat cow. I'm still living at home with my parents, and I'm not really sure how I ended up here." Her tears started flowing freely as she swiped at them with her hands. "Then there's you. Somehow, you got all the important things right. There's something about you that I can't put my finger on, but I want what you have."

The library was empty of people, so we walked over and sat at a wood reading table while I told her my life story. Not the "made for Hollywood" version, but my true story. The inner story. The one in which I was less of a hero and more fearful and confused all the time. I told her about the loss of my entire family and my ensuing struggles and grief. Then, I discussed my battles—both victories and defeats. I explained how I'd found myself alone and defeated, standing on a rickety old bridge where I ended up finding salvation instead of death. We talked about God and all he'd done for me. I didn't tell her I'd named her in my will or that it felt right that I had done so. Hopefully, the money would help her—and her coming child—get to a better place in life.

I pulled out my *One Ticket to Heaven* tract, read through it with her, and then led her into the arms of Jesus Christ.

CHAPTER 63

ADAM MATTHEW

AFTER SUSIE AND I exchanged numbers and said our goodbyes, I headed out to the local gun and surplus store, and then I headed for William Crab's mansion as dusk arrived. First, I drove through the friendly looking neighborhood with its cozy-looking homes. But as I drew closer to my destination, the houses started getting larger and more spectacular looking… but simultaneously, they looked less inviting. Dark brick and stone, cast iron, ivy, gargoyles, and humongous trees seemed common accoutrements of the rich, at least the rich from the late 1800s. Learned behavior dies hard, and it compelled me to stare at Dr. Polonsky's home as I passed it. The good doctor had taken the blame for the disappearances of numerous children over the years—children who got dragged into his house screaming, only to be chopped up and hidden in the walls. It turned out those stories were false, at least concerning the perpetrator. The actual monster lived a few doors down in a mansion I'd called home for several months in my youth.

I could feel my heart rise in my throat as I pulled up to the most massive estate of them all. Even after all the time that had passed, the place still had a visceral effect on me. The colossal stone and brick mansion sat perched atop the large hill like a dark, brooding evil waiting to ensnare victims that came too close. Its gothic features combined to give it a ghoulish look. Coming home to it had been the worst part of my day when I was a kid. And as before, I couldn't shake the feeling that it was indeed a living, hulking predator waiting to devour me.

Once I'd made it to the door, I said a silent prayer and felt my sense of dread lessen somewhat as if something had dampened it down for me. Before entering the mansion, I peeked into several side windows, but I didn't see anybody. I knew I could pick the front door lock, but on a whim, I walked over to a large black granite rock and a grin broke out on my face. I couldn't believe the spare key was still there after all these years.

Removing it from its hiding spot underneath the rock, I carefully unlocked the door. Quietly stepping onto the brownstone entryway, I looked around, and all appeared as I remembered it. And I remembered it well. Fear will do that for you. The mansion seemed as silent as a tomb, and I didn't see William Crab or his so-called fiancée about. I had only ever seen Old Man Crab in the kitchen, so it was time to see if his son William shared his father's predilections.

As I neared the kitchen, I heard a loud slurping sound. I rounded the corner, ready to pounce on William Crab, but instead, I drew back in surprise. A man sat on a stool at the end of the long gray-slate countertop, slurping soup out of a huge, ancient-looking stone bowl, but it wasn't William Crab. Yet it looked like him… like a young William Crab—or a really young Old Man Crab. Whatever the case, he couldn't have been much older than me.

I stared at him and asked, "Where is William Crab?"

The guy turned and smirked at me. "So... the prodigal son returns. And what manners! You break into my house and make demands of me? What a scalawag you've turned out to be."

Scalawag? Is this guy for real?

"Let me guess... you're William Crab's son?"

"Sure... why not," he replied.

The guy certainly looked like him and had the same mannerisms, and I could see he was arrogant like William Crab. They had to be related to each other. I opened my mouth to speak but was cut short by a vague smell of honey... and rot. *Such an unusual smell.* I sniffed the air and realized the odor was coming from the soup. The mansion always held a certain amount of tension and fear for me, so I guess I'd been too preoccupied with other things as a boy to notice the particulars, but I looked at it now. It looked... well... disgusting. It had the consistency of thin, lumpy oatmeal, with a greenish blackness running through it... almost like uncooked rotting flesh.

He watched me staring at the soup, then put another big spoonful in his mouth, smacking his chops together as a small amount of the soup oozed out of the corners of his lips and ran down his face.

"Ah, sweet meat for the lips," he crooned.

Watching him made me want to retch. "How can you eat that?" I said as I placed a hand on my queasy stomach.

"I don't know... you tell me, kid." With a smug look on his face, he said, "I didn't see you complaining any the last time you chowed down on it."

The thought of eating that slop made my stomach twist, and my hand involuntarily raised to my throat. "What... What are you talking about?"

"Don't remember, kid? Oh, that's right... I guess you were

in a coma at the time." Then he cackled out, "Well, let me fill in the blanks for you, stupid. Master brought your sagging, bedridden body by for a stroll, along with a tasty morsel for my pet downstairs. It was good fun. A deal was struck. Soup was given, and you awoke from your coma, all revitalized. Fresh as a baby's rear end."

As a series of memories flashed in my head, I had to put my hand on the slate countertop to steady myself. I'd heard the stories of me going from a bedridden, sore-covered mess to looking like a poster child for health magazines in the span of one night. I also remembered how Hunter Campbell—one of the boys who'd accompanied me to the crypt—had disappeared just before I came out of my coma and they'd never found him. Was my recovery bought with his life? Did that disgusting soup actually represent the fountain of youth… or at least one version of it?

I reached behind me and yanked out the Glock I'd tucked into the waistband of my pants, bringing it to bear on the grinning young man.

"You work with that ghoul in the basement?" I hissed. "You feed children to it? Why?"

He quivered with excitement, then yelled out, "Come on, pea brain!… Just one more push. Crank it hard… you can do it!"

Then I got it. My eyes widened as understanding hit me. "You're Old Man Crab!" I shouted. "You're William Crab. It was always you. You've exchanged the lives of children for youth. You work hand in hand with that thing."

With a grin so big it looked like it would split his face, he said, "We're going to have so much fun playing together!"

As I stared at him in disbelief, he dropped behind the island and out of my line of sight. I rushed behind the counter with both hands on the semi-automatic, but I didn't see him there. Stalking around the kitchen, he was nowhere to be found. I didn't know how he'd gotten away, but I had a good idea where to find him. He'd probably run straight to the ghoul, which meant I had little time.

I removed the backpack from my shoulders and filled my pockets with some of the table salt it contained. After that, I drew out a sharp ancient sword I'd bought just for the occasion and swung it around me. Finally, I took out the battery-powered lantern I'd brought, then walked up to the heavy wood door that led into the basement… and pushed it open.

The old wooden plank stairs that I remembered so well dwindled into the darkness as they descended downward. I took a few moments to say a silent prayer to God, then I held my lantern out toward the basement and started going down. When I reached the bottom step, I pulled on the light string dangling in front of me, but the weak, anemic light produced by its bulb paled in comparison to the lantern light. The enormous laundry room had the same damp, stinky smell as before, and I still saw spiderwebs everywhere. The walls remained unpainted; thick roots from the outdoor trees had worked their way through the basement wall in even more places, crawling about and looking for new areas to invade. Other than the bank of washers and dryers against one wall, the rest of the room still appeared to be stacked high with worthless junk. Apparently, the young Crab was no cleaner than his older self. Last, my eyes settled on the bricked archway that led to the rest of the vast basement under the house. It yawned open like the mouth of death, and it looked like it wanted to swallow me whole… which was fine with me. That's why I was here.

Normally, it would have taken me hours to explore through all the junk, rooms, and twisting passageways in the massive basement, but I caught a break. The air down here was stagnant with rot and still as a tomb. Without moving air, nothing disturbed the markings on the floor and most of the scuffed and disturbed dust led in the same general direction. As I walked, I was taken aback by the unnatural, eerie quietness surrounding me—a silence so deep it turned my heartbeat and breaths into loud exclamations. Then, as before, the feeling of death and the seductive urge to give in to it tried to overwhelm me. I could feel its frustration as I pushed through it.

I continued tracking the trail of disturbed dust and debris through a series of underground rooms and passageways, and as I progressed, the smell of rot increased. Several minutes later, another smell appeared—the scent of lime and water—so I knew I had to be close to my final destination. Without warning, the manufactured walls gave way to a tunnel that consisted of carved-out bedrock, as evidenced by the numerous pick marks. Eventually, the marks disappeared and were replaced by smooth limestone walls created by water erosion. I ran my fingertips along the damp wall of the cave as I continued, but my special sense didn't provide me with anything useful.

Taking a side tunnel, I stood in a large natural chamber, and I let my lantern light play across the skeletal remains strewn about—human remains. My memory wasn't perfect, so I couldn't be sure, but it seemed more bones laid about since the last time I'd been here. I shook my head at the sight before me, and then I ducked under a low archway. Once again, I found myself standing in a small graveyard—a desecrated cemetery... likely because of the ghoul, but I couldn't say for sure.

I cautiously walked about the disturbed and broken coffins, but nothing jumped out at me. I ran my fingertips over tombstones, coffins, and the cavern itself, but nothing came to me. In fact, it appeared I had reached a dead end. I stopped and rubbed the back of my neck in frustration while trying not to cut myself with the blade. I'd been so certain I'd find the ghoul down here that I'd never even considered the alternative. Now I'd have to wander about and hope I didn't become complacent or tired if the search became drawn out.

I drew in a sharp breath and then let out an impatient snort. The ghoul had always tracked me down in the past, so it stunk that I had to go looking for the thing. *Well, buddy, thinking about it isn't getting the job done.* I turned to retrace my steps when my eyes settled upon a small, deep shadow marring one wall. I cautiously approached with the lantern and sword held firmly before me, realizing it wasn't a shadow but a tunnel. When I put my head inside it, a sense of corruption overwhelmed me, and I knew I had found the entrance to the ghoul's den.

Before entering, I put the sword and lantern into my backpack and removed a small penlight, which I then held in place with my mouth. Getting down on my hands and knees, I crawled into the dusty, rocky tunnel and started moving in a downward-sloping direction. I knew I'd be in serious trouble if the ghoul attacked me here. But I couldn't do anything about it as I continued on. The tunnel curved, and when I'd cleared it, I rose and stood in awe... and apprehension.

I stood in a massive subterranean cavern so large that my penlight didn't carry to the far end of it—or maybe its size had nothing to do with this optical curiosity. Somehow, the darkness resisted the light in the distance, and if I concentrated, I could almost swear that it contained dark twisting tendrils along with something that looked wispy white. *Fog?* It seemed as if the very air danced for me. Desperate for more sight and protection, I dug into my bag, retrieving my lantern, then my sword... and accidentally dropped both. Unseen eyes bored into me while a burning fear erupted in my stomach, and I knew I had to hurry. I spit the penlight out of my mouth, quickly scooped up the dropped items off the cave floor, and turned on the lantern.

Contrary to what my seething gut told me, there wasn't a ghoul in sight. I took several deep breaths to calm myself, then held the lantern high. While it carried farther than the penlight, it still didn't illuminate as well as it should have, and it seemed a fifty-foot semi-circle of light was all I was going to get. And maybe that was a good thing as the semi-circle revealed an ancient-looking graveyard, and I felt all the hairs on my body stand on end. My lantern illuminated a rolling ceiling that looked like an inverse landscape varying in height from about eight to forty feet. I walked over to one of the low points, stood on a small boulder, then reached up and ran my hand over the rough surface above me.

My special gift finally kicked in, and ghostly images surrounded me. As I watched and listened to the echoes of past events, it became clear this place had been a subterranean graveyard for the entire region. Its location chosen to thwart grave robbers that were oh so common back then... That is, until a wealthy but mad individual—at least as far as the local inhabitants were concerned—bought it and had the entrance bricked over. Many years later, an equally rich descendant built a mansion on top of the long-forgotten graveyard and then moved in. Now I understood why the mansion sat on the only hill in the neighborhood. In reality, the estate sat atop a massive geological anomaly... one containing an ancient graveyard. It also seemed clear that this space was the ghoul's actual residence. The whole thing seemed crazy, but it made a strange kind of sense given what I knew.

It seemed likely that Old Man Crab had befriended or

trapped the ghoul and needed a place to keep it. Somehow, Crab learned that as long as he fed the ghoul a steady diet of young victims, it would bestow long life and youth upon him. He must have created the whole graveyard/mansion thing as a permanent solution to hide a ghoul and cover up his own very long unnatural lifespan. I had to admit it was pretty clever too. Who would've ever thought that the eighty-year-old man was now a fifty- or twenty-year-old guy? It would've been easy to buy into the narrative he gave people: "I'm Old Man Crab's son" or "I'm his grandson." Even I'd fallen for it, and I had lived with him for a short time. Then, of course, whenever he aged normally, from young to old, he didn't have to change his identity at all. No wonder God wanted me to intervene. Crab and the ghoul might have been responsible for hundreds or even thousands of deaths.

A flash of white out of the corner of my eye caught my attention, but only the graveyard met my sight when I turned and looked. I walked over to a small tombstone in the shape of a cross, and I saw a date of *1503-1516* on it and realized that the graveyard had to be ancient. It wasn't lost on me either that this grave belonged to a thirteen-year-old. I brushed my hand against its cold stone, and for a mere moment, I could feel the occupant's fear and pain as if they'd buried it along with the child.

A disturbing thought occurred to me, so I looked at a few dozen headstones in the general area, and as suspected, a disproportionate number of them belonged to children of the same age. I brushed the back of my hand up against several other tombstones and realized some were only markers for the deceased children because their bodies were never found. Then another thought occurred to me I had no answer for: How had

I escaped this foul creature when so many others had fallen to it? Providence… or luck?

Was I born for this day?

I started walking up a dusty incline to get to some of the larger gravestones and crypts when a tingly feeling caused the hairs on my body to stand on end. I turned around in a giant loop but saw nothing. Spying out what looked to be an old gray stone table or altar, I headed toward it, then put the sword, lantern, and backpack on its surface so I could switch to the Glock. The handgun was loaded with steel-tipped ammo, and it would allow me a greater range when fighting this thing. As I felt around in my backpack, a whisper of wind touched my back, causing me to withdraw my hands and reach into my side pockets. Each grabbed a handful of salt and flung it directly over my head and behind me. A hideous screech that made my toes curl up greeted my gift of salt, but nothing was there when I turned.

I snatched up the Glock and the ancient iron sword lying near me—and looked up just in time to see a pale-white streak heading toward my face. I ducked and shot the thing in the gut, and it screeched again. It bought me just enough time to put about twenty feet between us. I stepped behind one of the larger tombstones and peeked around its right edge to get a better look at the ghoul. The thing was just as menacing-looking as I'd remembered it, and its skin still looked rotten—like a dead, waterlogged fish or whale. It smiled at me with an impossible shark-like mouth, full of razor-sharp teeth, as its long pink tongue slithered in and out of its mouth as if tasting the air, and then it started making its way toward me.

Typically, the Glock would've been more than enough for violent encounters. Unfortunately, the thing healed so fast that the gun was nearly useless against it. With that realization, I tucked it back into my waistband and brandished the sword with both hands.

"Come and get me, you jerk," I hollered.

It gracefully flowed in my direction in complete silence, and then it extended its left hand toward me. With a flick of my sword, its hand separated from its wrist.

It held the now blackened and smoking stump up to its face and hissed in displeasure, so I took the opportunity and slashed at its face too. I didn't connect, but needless to say, the ghoul didn't seem to appreciate that gesture either. Expecting it to follow up on its attack, I brought my sword up and pointed it at its chest. Instead, it backed up and ducked behind a large limestone crypt. I followed it but found nothing when I looked around. The ghoul had become more subtle in its attacks than in the past. Making sure I stayed within the dim circle of light provided by the lantern, I prowled around several more ancient dusty tombstones, but the ghoul wasn't showing itself.

As I drew close to the boundary separating the lantern light from the unusual darkness, I came upon a steepled building that looked as if it might have been a church at one time, but a small one as its base appeared to be no more than a ten-foot square. I stuck my head under the arched doorway and looked around. If anything of importance had been housed in it, it was long gone. As I pulled back out, I placed my hand on the cold stone structure to steady myself, and the surrounding darkness resolved into fine detail. It turned out the air wasn't moving at all. Instead, its many inhabitants were in motion.

Well-camouflaged demons hiding among dilapidated gravestones flitted about while gaunt, shadowy children with sorrowful, staring eyes hid amongst those same graves trying to avoid their tormentors. With a start, I knew I'd seen this scene once before: charcoaled in great detail on my bedroom wall before it mysteriously disappeared. In fact, it was accurate in all details, save one. Only the ghoul itself was missing from this scene. *A trap!* I threw myself to the ground hard and just missed being impaled by my nemesis. Instead, it slashed empty air as it exploded out of the small building. It screeched in apparent frustration and disappeared once again.

That was close.

With my heart pounding in my ears, I steadied my breath again. Twenty seconds later, I started moving and heard a single scrape behind a large crypt. I reached into a pocket and took out another handful of salt, and then I came flying around its left edge. I flung the salt into... to my surprise, not the ghoul, but Crab's youthful face, and he shrieked as he tried rubbing it out of his eyes.

Disgust filled my frame as I watched him, and my lips twisted into a sneer. "I know what you did to all those boys, Crab, and I'm putting a stop to it!... Your immortality ends today."

He approached me with a subservient posture and a pleading look. "But, kid, you don't understand," he said with a wavering fear in his voice. "Don't... Don't be mad at me.... I had to do it.... It made me."

As I looked into his imploring eyes, his lips curled up at the edges like the Grinch that stole Christmas and then his eyes flicked to the left and behind me. I threw the remaining salt in my hand over my shoulder in anticipation of an ambush, and when I turned to look behind me, a searing, white-hot pain erupted in my belly. My head snapped forward, and I saw a bloody hand with ghastly white fingers sticking into my gut. I followed the rotten pale flesh of its arm all the way up to its shark-like mouth. As I watched in horror, it tilted its head upward, and its mouth opened wide enough to bite off one of my shoulders, which I'm pretty sure was its intention. A small voice in the back of my mind told me to swing at the head while it was occupied, so I pulled back with my sword arm and swung with all my remaining strength. It connected with the ghoul's neck, and its noggin went flying and thumped against the ground.

Still standing upright, the headless body jerked violently as Old Man Crab yelled, "Noooooooo!"

Crab's face twisted in pure rage, and his hands curled into claws. As he rushed me, I dropped the sword and retrieved my pistol. I shot him in the left thigh, and as he stumbled, he came into direct contact with the decapitated ghoul. The ghoul's body continued to spasm, and its remaining clawed hand caught Crab in the midsection and eviscerated him. Crab let out a high-pitched squeal, and then he collapsed. His wounds were so severe he died in less than thirty seconds. Shortly after that, the ghoul's body collapsed and along with the head, disintegrated into a pile of chalk-colored dust. Then the entire cavern seemed to breathe out, and I was alone. No more Crab. No more ghoul. Even the ghostly apparitions were gone. In fact, my lantern light stretched much farther now, and the cavern and graveyard were far larger than I'd imagined.

Any relief I might have felt by my victory was dampened when I looked down at my profusely bleeding belly and realized the ghoul had severely wounded me. Much to my chagrin, I knew nobody would ever find me if I died down here. I'd spent so much of my life by myself that I had really hoped not to die alone. I'd even prayed on it. And being lost forever was the thought that spurred me on. At first, the return journey wasn't too bad. But by the time I reached the upstairs and then the front door, I was down to strength of will alone.

I fumbled with the doorknob several times before my

blood-soaked hands got it open, and once I did, I stumbled to the front porch and collapsed. As I fell into unconsciousness, I consoled myself with the thought that surely someone would find me now.

CHAPTER 64

THE DAILY BEE

THIS MORNING, LOCAL authorities were stunned when Adam Matthew—age twenty-three, best-selling author, screenplay writer, and actor—was found dead. His body was discovered at approximately 6:30 a.m. by local resident Dr. Samuel Polonsky during his morning walk. Upon initial examination, Adam's body had sustained several stab wounds to the abdomen, and police speculated that severe blood loss caused his death.

Despite his impressive accomplishments, Adam is best known for his role in the failed exorcism attempt on his person. In a case that caught the attention of the world and inflamed passions on both sides of the aisle, Adam went from insignificance to celebrity overnight. His case brought to the forefront the shadowy world of exorcism and the church's role in this questionable practice.

We reached out to Dr. Grant Jennings, famed paranormal debunker and friend of the deceased, for comment, and he said, "My heart goes out to this young man. From the day this detestable practice marked him, his scarred psyche used writings and works to exorcise itself from the cruel trauma inflicted upon it by misguided authority figures. In the end, it was a sad but predictable outcome."

Agnes Kurtz, a parishioner who attended Adam's church and knew him personally, said, "If you go chasing the devil, you'll get the devil. And it seems to me that boy done found exactly what he was looking for."

We also reached out to the participants in Adam's failed exorcism attempt, but we have received no comments.

Adam leaves no surviving relatives.

EPILOG 1

DR. CHARLOTTE BROWN

IT WAS HOT and humid, but laundry detail beat sitting in a tiny jail cell all day long… but not by much. I've always hated heat and humidity, and as soon as something better opened up, I planned on getting out of this God-forsaken job. Hopefully, my Ph.D. would get me into something clerical, but who knew? The prison operated on rules that seemed to defy common sense, so I might be stuck in laundry for the rest of my flipping life, or the remaining twenty years or so of my sentence… whichever came first.

I opened another humongous washing machine and put the damp prisoner uniforms into the waiting basket cart, and after I finished, I pushed it on bare feet to the next washing machine. I heard my name as I continued my laundry run and cringed. It was that busybody Mable, and I could see she was on an intercept course with me. It galled me that someone with a tenth of my education kept trying to lecture me.

I waved her away from me and said, "Leave me alone, Mabel. I've already told you I'm not buying what you're selling."

Mabel grinned and looked thoroughly amused. "Come on, girl. You know I've made you my mission, and I'll never give up on you."

My face fell in disbelief as I brushed my damp, stringy brown hair away from my face. Deep anger bubbled up inside me, and I exploded. "What part of 'Leave me alone' don't you get?! I'm not buying your voodoo, and you can stuff it where the sun doesn't shine!"

Mable just smiled. "Girl, don't be like that. Jesus just wants a relationship with you, is all. I was angry like you too, but Jesus did me wonders, and he can do you wonders too."

I put my hands on my hips. "Mable, I'm not buying your Kool-Aid, so don't even go there. And for your information, it's a good thing he doesn't exist because if he did, I'd spit in his face."

"Now, why would you go do that?" Mabel said with a frown. "Jesus never did you no harm."

I could feel my face reddening. "Never did me no harm? What? Seriously?" I sputtered. "You know, I went to church every single week, and I did all the sacraments required of me. I gave money to the church, and I tried to live a good life. So how does your so-called God repay me for all my good deeds? I'm locked up for twenty-five years for trying to do God's work, Mable, so I don't want to hear any of your self-righteous responses."

"Really?… So God came down and told you to break the law? He told you to falsify a medical report? He told you to exorcise that boy, and if it didn't work, to strangle him? Well, if he did, girl, you ain't listening to the right god."

"SHUT UP!" I yelled as I trembled in rage. "I tried to help

them! I tried to do what was right! You weren't there, so don't you dare stand there and judge me! I tried to help that boy and his mother. I really did. But what does the kid do? First, he gets rich and famous climbing over my back, and then he goes and gets himself stabbed and murdered. And his mother was no better. She drank herself into an early grave. All that work I did was for nothing... less than nothing."

Mable offered up a sad smile. "Charlotte, I'm sorry things didn't work out so good for the boy and his momma, but don't you go giving up on you, and don't you go giving up on God. It's not too late for you. He'll help you."

"Help me?" I said incredulously. "Fairy tales don't help anybody, Mabel. I'll kill myself before I accept that malarkey again. I believed in the church once, and it cost me my career, husband, home, freedom, and dignity. It cost me everything I had and loved, and I'll never make that mistake again as long as I live. No God worth serving would ever let that happen to someone, and it made me realize that this crappy life is the only one I have, and when I get the courage up, it will all be over for me." *Just one little slice against my neck or wrist, and then sweet release, and nothingness.*

"Well, that's your problem right there, Charlotte. You was believing in church attendance, good deeds and whatnot, and not in Jesus Christ. You'd gone and put your trust in the wrong place, is all."

A red haze settled over my vision. I'd had enough of Mabel's mouth, and this conversation was over. I stormed out of the laundry room, and I didn't even care if it landed me in hot water with Administration. Soon, very soon, it would all be over for me.

Epilog 2

Adam Matthew

I lay there on the front porch of Mr. Crab's mansion for I don't know how long. I couldn't believe I had missed the fact that all the different Crabs I'd known were actually one and the same… or that Old Man Crab had been in league with the ghoul. It all seemed so clear to me now. If only I had realized it sooner…

Oh well, I thought. *At least it all worked out in the end.*

I felt my strength returning to me, so I figured I better get some medical attention before I expired. I stood and examined myself, and to my surprise, I seemed perfectly fine as far as I could tell. In fact, I was more than fine. My belly wound, along with all my aches and pains, were gone.

I looked up, and a glorious sight greeted me. The most beautiful light I've ever seen glowed on the front lawn in every color I had ever seen and then some. It radiated peace, and I could feel it calling to me. As I walked to it, my heart soared, and I knew it was where I was meant to be. I looked behind me, and in the deep darkness, I saw a body crumpled on the front porch. I had the distinct impression that it was me—*But I'm standing here, so... go figure.* I walked into the light, and then I saw a brilliant flash all around me that didn't hurt my eyes at all. A moment later, I found myself standing in a white fog.

As the heavenly mist gently swirled around me, I saw a lone figure in a white linen robe and a beautiful gold sash approaching me, and I could feel incredible love and peace coming from him.

He came up to me, placed his hand against my heart, then embraced me. He pulled back, smiling radiantly, and said, "Well done, my child."

His presence made me want to dance with joy, but his words made my heart heavy because I didn't think I'd done well at all, and I said so: "But, Jesus, I let myself get tricked, and I made so many bad decisions, and so many people were hurt because of me. Apparently, even I died. I don't see how I did well at all."

He gently touched my shoulder. "Indeed, from an earthly perspective, the whole thing is a mess, and your story is a great tragedy to many. But Heaven sees the true state of things. The people who died around you were not yours to save. That responsibility belonged to others. However, those who were yours have been saved."

I bit my lip and drew my eyebrows together. "But who did I save, Jesus?"

"All the creature's future victims. Hundreds who would have fallen to its hunger will now live because of your self-less act."

Wincing in guilt, I said, "But what about the people who were hurt trying to help me? People went to jail because of me."

"No, people suffered because your world is fallen and they foolishly entered into territory that would give angels pause.

They had free will, but they didn't use it wisely. When they prayed, I told them it was not their task and not to proceed, but their ears remained closed. Even so, know that those who allow me to save them will be saved, and those who don't will perish."

I shook my head. "But why let them perish at all?"

"Because love demands it. You cannot have love without free will, and you cannot have free will without the ability to choose."

Grief as sharp as a knife cut through me. "So my family had to die and go to Hell because of free will?"

A pained expression came over his face as he sighed. "You are correct in that Hell is a choice. But it is not my desire that any should perish, and I go to great lengths to save each and every one of you. I hung on a cross for you, so how could it be otherwise? Even so, in the end, the choice is yours. But tell me, why do you say your family is in Hell?"

"Well, uh, I… I guess…" I stammered, in deep pain. "The demon said my dad was already there, and he said my mom was going there too. I assumed my sister was there because… well… she's a demon…. Well, maybe…. I don't know for sure."

He looked into my eyes with a piercing gaze. "Demons deceive, and you should have cast it away from you immediately. Your father accepted my salvation as a young man, and the demon was guessing at the ultimate destination of your mother. She almost succumbed to death in her grief and sorrow, but I reached out to her one last time, and she accepted me with her last dying breath. As for your sister, you've never met her. She's been here since she passed, and she is a delight. Truly, you should have heeded the warnings and avoided the deceiving spirit altogether."

"But… But, Jesus," I said. "It was… It's more than that. I think it was me that brought it into the world."

His eyes burned with righteousness. "You played Ouija on a threshold—a doorway in your world to dark places... a doorway to Hell and its many iterations. Abaddon, the destroyer, answered your call into the void and attached himself to you. Through you, he breached the barrier between his existence and yours. Once he gained access to your world, he pretended to be your sister to gain your trust. Once you granted him access to you, he set in motion devious plans that will in time bring human civilization to its knees."

My face and body started twitching from my internal mortification. In shame, I covered my face with my hands. "I'm so sorry, Jesus," I said, "please forgive me. I never meant to cause any harm."

"What is done is done," he said with iron in his voice. "But you were merely the tool that Abaddon used. His coming has been preordained from the beginning for the time of great testing. With or without you, he would have found a way."

I peeked through my fingers, and relief descended upon me in waves as Jesus's face radiated great love toward me.

I looked into his amazing eyes and said, "So you're not sending me to Hell?"

He smiled and cupped my face in his hands. "My dear child, I paid a heavy price for you because I love you so much. Why would I discard you now?"

My heart rejoiced with his words, and a great weight lifted from me. Me and my family were in Heaven! It was the best possible news I could have asked for—more than I could have asked for. It brought me great joy to know they were here with me, and I should have been satisfied.

However... an unanswered prayer still ate away at my soul, so I asked my last burning question: "Jesus, please don't think I'm complaining because I'm not. But why did I have to die alone? I feared going back into that basement by myself, and I prayed that I wouldn't be isolated and unaided if I died there."

"My dear child!" he exclaimed, then laughed with great warmth. "Your prayer was answered in abundance. Not only was I there with you, but also all the heavenly host. And a goodly number of the rulers of Hell watched too. The countless multitudes of Heaven prayed for your strength to hold, and they cheered mightily when you prevailed. Few on Earth have accomplished as much as you have today."

"Okay, but how come—"

Jesus held up a hand. "Adam, I desire to answer another of your prayers first and answer your remaining questions later. Many wondrous things await you here in Heaven, and now, I want to take you to one of your great rewards—the fulfillment of one of your greatest desires."

Jesus waved his arms, and the surrounding fog dissipated to reveal a beautiful field containing a magnificent city that defied any explanation I could possibly put to it. Suffice it to say, it was marvelous. But that wasn't even the best part. As I looked on, my breath caught in my throat. I saw three figures heading toward me, holding hands and shining like the sun. A short distance behind them stood a multitude of people that I somehow knew were related to me, family, and they all longed to fellowship with me.

I ran toward them with a face beaming with joy and embraced my dad, mom, and sister, and I knew that after a long, dangerous journey, I was finally home.

THE END

AUTHOR'S NOTE

When reading nonfiction books concerning the supernatural, there tends to be a strong connection between the subject matter and religion. On the other hand, in most thriller/horror/suspense supernatural fiction books I've read, the relationship between the supernatural and religion is tenuous. Even though God, religion, and the supernatural seem to be tightly intertwined in real-life accounts, most fiction stories either ignore these relationships altogether or relegate them to a minor third-seat role—a role that is convenient, incidental, or even harmful to the protagonist.

With this in mind, the more I read about real-life experiences people had with God, the supernatural, the demonic, and similar nonfiction accounts over the years, the more I wanted to write a novel that explored the relationship between the religious and the supernatural more deeply, and certainly, more accurately.

When I first told my family and friends that I wanted to write a supernatural thriller from a Christian perspective, their response was always something to the effect of, "Why? They don't have anything to do with each other." I reminded them that the Bible is the most epic horror story ever written. The Bible and Jesus Christ, himself, discuss Heaven and Hell, angels and demons, along with humanity's blessings and curses, trials and tribulations, hope and despair, and how the diametrically opposed forces of light and dark relate to one another. While the Bible is known for its uplifting stories, wisdom, songs, and poems, it also explores the common and uncommon evils that plague humanity and contains stories about devils and demons, war, famine, disease, as well as people's betrayals, failures, and inhumanity to one another. The Bible delves even deeper into our shortcomings and attributes them to the unseen supernatural realm. "For we wrestle not against flesh and blood, but against principalities, against powers, against the rulers of the darkness of this world, against spiritual wickedness in high places." The Bible also reminds us to "Be sober, be vigilant; because your adversary the devil, as a roaring lion, walketh about, seeking whom he may devour." While some liberal theologians will claim that biblical writers used these words allegorically, I believe its authors, and Jesus Christ, himself, could have made their points without creating imaginary fiends and places. Because the Bible treats the supernatural as real, I treat it as real in this novel.

Lastly, this story was primarily written from the protagonist Adam Matthew's point-of-view, along with the occasional points-of-views of the other characters involved. Since it is mainly written from a first-person perspective, the reader only knows what the collective characters know and nothing more. I wrote it in this manner to allow the reader to experience Adam's life more intimately, as he takes a dangerous journey into the dark, and then escapes into the light.